DECEIT AND DARKFIRE

DECEIT AND DARKFIRE

Empire of Cinders Book II

M.A. LIGUORI

Hydra Publications

ISBN: 978-1-948374-33-0

Hydra Publications

Goshen, Kentucky 40026

www.hydrapublications.com

To family, friends, and fellow readers of fantasy fiction

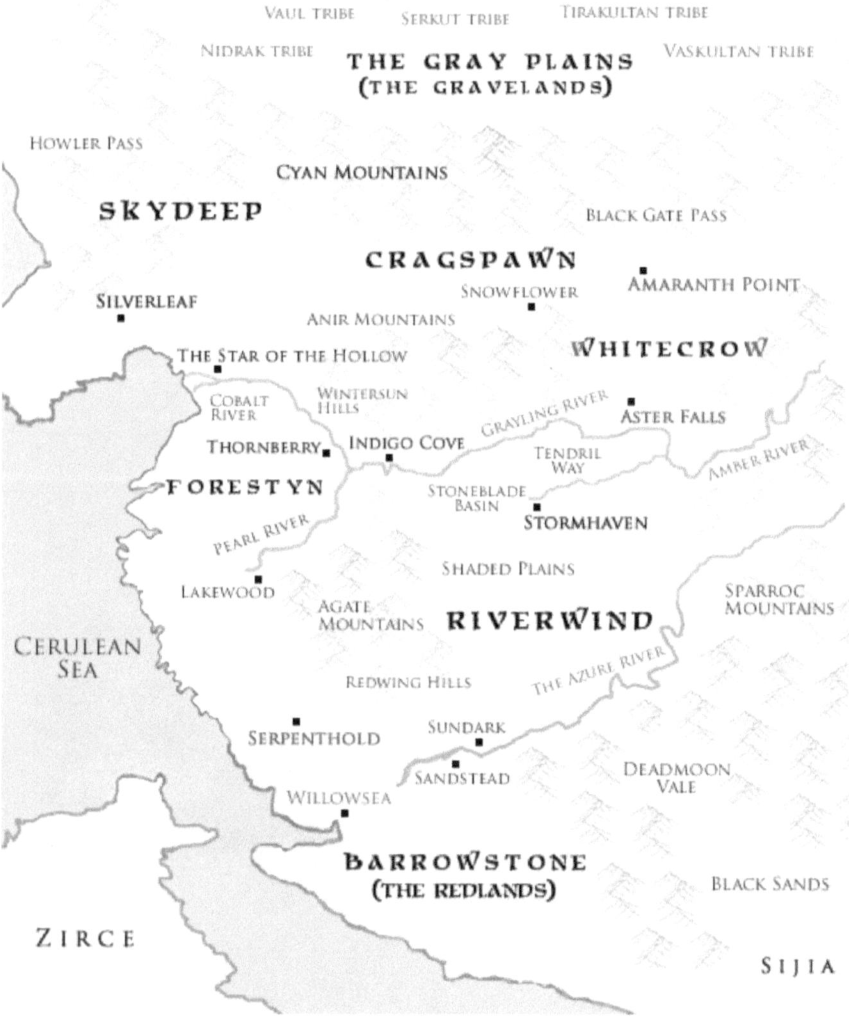

VAUL TRIBE SERKUT TRIBE TIRAKULTAN TRIBE

NIDRAK TRIBE **THE GRAY PLAINS** VASKULTAN TRIBE
(THE GRAVELANDS)

HOWLER PASS

CYAN MOUNTAINS

SKYDEEP BLACK GATE PASS

CRAGSPAWN

SNOWFLOWER AMARANTH POINT

SILVERLEAF ANIR MOUNTAINS

THE STAR OF THE HOLLOW **WHITECROW**

COBALT WINTERSUN
RIVER HILLS GRAYLING RIVER ASTER FALLS

THORNBERRY INDIGO COVE TENDRIL AMBER RIVER
WAY

FORESTYN STONEBLADE
BASIN STORMHAVEN

PEARL RIVER

SHADED PLAINS

LAKEWOOD SPARROC
AGATE MOUNTAINS
MOUNTAINS **RIVERWIND**

**CERULEAN
SEA** REDWING HILLS THE AZURE RIVER

SUNDARK
SERPENTHOLD DEADMOON
VALE
SANDSTEAD

WILLOWSEA

BARROWSTONE BLACK SANDS
(THE REDLANDS)

ZIRCE

SIJIA

PROLOGUE

The great double doors of the Hall of Obsidian Light closed behind her, and the cheers of the crowd were swallowed by the wretched emptiness of the corridor.

Everything is ruined, Miriana Athera thought. *Everything is ruined and only I am to blame.*

She moved in a distraught shamble, her long ceremonial outer skirt threatening to tangle and trip her every step. *You were supposed to be strong, Mir. You were supposed to do what had to be done. But now it's too late, and now your husband has been inaugurated as emperor of the Anir. Oh, how those fools cheer for him! You should've killed him when the opportunity was ripe. Why didn't you?*

Imperial Guard Captain Cyrille Vileron strode beside her with his usual clink and clang of blackened steel armor. She observed his elongated shadow in the flickering sconce light, dark outlines of jutting spaulders and wispy cloak serrations and ragged forearm wraps. *My loyal protector and friend*, she thought. *Perhaps the only friend I have left.*

A rugged pair of sentries were posted outside of her private chamber, fresh faces both, one pale and bearded, the other paler and beardless. Both wore the standard gray-black cloaks of the empire, clasped at the neck by a silvered Sadralen brooch. To greet their empress they straightened their posture and bowed their heads, but Miriana kept walking. Her destination was farther down the hall, at the end of the far wing, where a steep stairwell took her down into the lower laboratories.

The main workroom was usually a dull, vacant place, but lately it had been brimming with noise and bustling with activity. Pistons pumping, chain drives clanking, various mechanisms and contraptions whirring and whining. A thick acrid odor encased the air, the odor of botanical and chemical extracts, be it the spicy smoothness of cinnabar or the garlicky aroma of orpiment. Miriana couldn't see very well, but it was obvious that the entire laboratory had recently been overhauled. Cupboards were moved and worktables set beneath heavy fume hoods, while a network of shelves and markers holding vessels and vials and cucurbits lay haphazardly about. Alchemists and their apprentices moved to and fro, each man and woman clad in robes of the deepest maroon.

She found Grand Physician Arden Lorian hunched over an old bookkeeper's desk, idly surveying the room like an overworked and underappreciated warden. His hairless, mottled head turned Miriana's way when her presence was announced by a door sentry. The physician looked older than usual (he was already north of seventy), but he also looked terribly disheartened. He'd been this way since the tragic news of his beloved son, Orbrey, had reached the capital.

The physician motioned politely for her to approach, and, when she did, his wrinkle-buried eyes studied her up and down. "You look lovely today," he said without joy, then paused before adding, "Your Majesty."

Miriana had a servant bring over a low chair, and when she sat down, she immediately removed her heeled leather shoes. She despised the pair for being overly tight and entirely unbreathable, but by the gods did it feel good to rub her achy feet. That done, she reached up to unclasp the celebratory capelet that was fastened at her neck. It was another uncomfortable vestment, warm and itchy and embroidered with a geometric design that was a bit busier than she would've liked. Still, a coronation was a coronation, and she had promised to look her best for her husband. *As if he cares about such finery.* She couldn't wait to discard the garment like a tattered dishrag. "What is the Grand Physician doing in an alchemist's lab?"

Master Lorian exhaled a languid breath. "Do you think my interests lie alone in the ways of the healing arts? No, I am a man of varied avocations."

Her response was a smile. In truth, she missed the old physician. She was so used to having him at her side that it pained her not to see him these last few weeks. *First Vylas, and now you.* Master Arden Lorian had always been an annoying little hound, but now *she* seemed to be the annoyance. "You should've attended," she said.

"What?"

Miriana had to speak up over the noise. "I said you should've attended. The ceremony, my husband's coronation."

"Oh, yes, yes, I probably should have."

Her eyes wandered for a bit. The laboratory was buzzing like a hornet's nest; not a single man or woman moved without a sense of purpose. "What is all this? What have you been doing down here?"

He opened his mouth to answer, but a sudden flash from across the room drew his attention. A small chemical fire caused a minor ruckus, but, once the flames were smothered, the mood of the lab returned to its former edge of urgent instability. "As you are aware, Your Majesty, the realm has no lack of enemies," Master Lorian said.

She waited for him to elaborate, only to frown when he didn't. "And what does that mean?"

"Emperor Zantherei has been funding a specialized team of

alchemists for a clandestine project. I've been given time off from my physician duties to serve as its overseer, handling the day-to-day operations."

She made a point to move her eyes across all the complex—and undoubtedly costly—alchemical apparatuses. "Do we even have the funds in the treasury for such a project? What does the Minister of Finance say about this?"

"I'm afraid I don't know, but you can ask him if you'd like. Your Majesty."

When will you stop giving short shrift to my concerns? She had to say something, to confront him about his attitude. "I'm sorry if my presence offends you."

"Don't be."

"Then I'm sorry about your son. Truly, I am."

His aged face scrunched with displeasure, as if he'd just taken a whiff of a week-old corpse. "Your crooked Imperial Advisor *killed* him. Removed his head and strung him up in the snow like a rabid dog." Anger drew his lips back, making visible his pale-yellow teeth. "My son was *not* guilty of any such offense. Orbrey was an upright, honest man. A bit clingy like his father, but neither deceitful nor dangerous. Why was he killed?"

"I don't know," she said softly. "Seric Dyre has betrayed us all. He's been stripped of his title and declared an enemy of the realm. I wish I could change what happened, Master, but I can't, and I don't know how to ease your pain."

"You can start by leaving me alone." He must've immediately regretted such a sharp retort, because his follow-up was much gentler. "You look tired, Your Majesty. You should return to your chamber and have your attendants prepare a dream tonic."

She shook her head. "I need my wits about me tonight. I'm leaving."

That made him freeze. His head shifted to look directly at her, his old eyes opening just a touch wider than usual. "Leaving? You are Empress Miriana Athera of the Anirian Empire, the Lady of Divine Whispers."

She looked down. *Yes, I am, but ranks and titles are worthless if you're not alive to hold them. Still, to give up everything I've ever wanted, everything I've ever desired . . . the pain may be too great to bear, and yet I must. I've made a grave mistake, and now I must suffer the consequences.* "Yes," she simply said, "but I won't be empress for long."

His eyes flicked briefly to an apprentice who was fussing with a gourd-shaped aludel. The boy was attempting to fit it into the bottom of another vessel, but his hands proved too large and clumsy to make any progress. Lorian whistled over a more experienced alchemist to aid the hopeless lad, and then he gave a pronounced shake of his head, muttering, "I'm a glorified babysitter." He turned back to Miriana and spoke matter-of-factly. "You fear for your life. Not being able to give your husband what he wants."

Miriana swallowed a lump in her throat. "Zantherei distrusts me. I can see it in his face. How much longer do I have before he learns the truth of my actions? I'm under the thumb of his minions. I can feel it. My circle of friends grows ever smaller. I know not whom to trust. Nothing is safe from prying eyes in this gods-forsaken place."

The old man murmured quietly at that. The bustle of machinery seemed to overtake the room, a loud and jarring din of furnace burners and driving pumps along with the occasional accenting clinks of a copper beaker or bronze retort. When Arden Lorian spoke again, his voice was barely audible. "Where will you go?"

"You know I can't tell you that."

"Too many eyes, too many spies, I know. Will you at least be safe?"

She nodded and gestured to the tall armored man standing behind her. "Captain Cyrille Vileron will make sure of that."

"And Vylas?"

The thought of her one-eyed half-brother made her chest cramp. She didn't want to leave without him, but she couldn't take him along . . . not after his awful misdeed that night in her private bedchamber. "Keep a watchful eye on my brother, won't you? He'll be lost without me."

His nod was sincere. "As will we all, Your Majesty."

Her eyes grew warm enough for tears. She loathed these feelings of glumness and gloom, but even when she tried to harden her heart she failed, and her words came out as softly as a child's. "Since this may be the last time we speak, I will ask you again . . . what sort of wicked scheme is my husband hatching?"

Master Arden Lorian didn't answer right away. He simply stared at Miriana, his wrinkly eyes probing her with cautious consideration. At length, he beckoned to one of the working alchemists, a small, dark-skinned fellow with a shrew's sharp face and a yak's mop of dark hair. He was obviously of Sijian descent, but this man wasn't a servant of any kind. No, his robe was of the finest cross-stitched silk, which was embroidered and dyed in hues of grayish-black and orange, not unlike the embers of a dying firepit. In stature he was rather short, but there was a watchfulness about his expression that commanded attention, eyes so brooding and cavernous it was as if they regarded the world with pompous indifference.

"Nanjen is his shortened name," Lorian said. "And he is the mastermind behind all you see."

The little Sijian fellow bowed so daintily it almost passed as a curtsy. "Pleasure to make your acquaintance, Your Majesty." His command of the Anirian tongue was clear and cultured, but his voice was high and reedy, probably one of the shrillest voices a grown man could possess. That made her immediately dislike him, and yet she couldn't keep her eyes off him. Not in a way of attraction, but in the way you couldn't help but observe a wreck about to happen. And then it did happen; he somehow let slip the gourd-shaped vessel in his hand. The object hit the ground and shattered, ceasing all activity in the lab. Nanjen's face scrunched comically, his shoulders shooting up like a child frightened by a peal of thunder.

What a knuckleheaded fool this man is, Miriana thought.

Servants were quick to respond, using boar bristle brooms to sweep up the broken pieces. When it was done, Master Lorian turned back to Miriana and sighed. He seemed to take a moment to collect his thoughts. "As I said earlier, the realm has no lack of enemies. Raas Dragath and his disciplined Redlander army. Seric Dyre and his Zhoulish host and defected Anirian soldiers of Aster Falls. Even our newly enthroned emperor's own brothers are critical threats, especially Alarin, who has absconded like a rat with the Imperial Seal. With the empire so divided, Zantherei has no choice but to quell these false pretenders and their foolish supporters." He extended a mottled hand to the Sijian fellow. "Nanjen has guaranteed us victory."

Nanjen's narrow face beamed with smugness.

"And how can he guarantee that?" Miriana asked.

"A unique admixture," Master Lorian answered. "Ingredients of rare and mystical origins. Of course, I'll lose my head if I reveal the names of those ingredients, but let's just say we have experienced alchemists working through all watches of the night." His old eyes flickered with sudden life. "Do you think the cloudfalls are the only magical herb this realm has ever known? So much has been omitted from the Annals of the Anir, mostly by the fearful emperors of former dynasties. So much lost, and yet you'd be surprised at what—"

"Nothing surprises me," she cut in. "Not anymore."

"Well, I assure you what I'm telling you is—"

"A lot of talk and little substance."

Arden Lorian closed his mouth.

Nanjen cleared his throat. "Your Majesty, may I speak?"

She allowed it.

"I commend you for having a skeptical eye. Many believe it's a sign of true intellect. With that in mind, it occurs to me that a wise woman like yourself requires evidence." His eyes flicked to Master Lorian. "May I?"

When Lorian nodded, Nanjen snapped an order to his alchemists. Moments later, a cauldron that was sitting among a long string of cauldrons was hauled over and placed upon a large stone block that rose a good foot off the floor. It must've been a heavy thing because it required two men to carry it across the room, and, even then, they seemed to have trouble keeping it from dragging across the floor. Still, the pot looked as ordinary as any other: blackened cast-iron base and sides, with a wide mouth, no hanger, and no ornamentation, save a narrow band of scrollwork beneath the rim.

"The entire process requires months," Nanjen said. "Lots of oils in equal and unequal parts, lots of waxes and fats, and twice the volume in aqua vitae. Some burying is involved, a few hours of distillation too, and of course a bit of dried dung to give it some body." He removed the lid, letting a handful of unpleasant smells breathe into the humid underground lab. "And then there's that one final ingredient." He produced a small snuff bottle from a hanging pouch inside his robe. "A little touch of what we call the Sadist's Soul."

He removed the stopper and decanted three of four drops into the cauldron. *WHOOSH.* Flames leaped upward, not the typical red-orange flames, but those of a smooth and sinister black. The rushing odors of brimstone and turpentine and camphor punched Miriana's nose, a pungency so powerful she had to cover her face with a sleeve. She pushed herself out of the chair and staggered a few barefoot steps back, her long outer skirt trying once more to topple her. The hot sting in her eyes made it difficult to do anything but blink, but even when her vision finally cleared, she still couldn't believe what she was looking at. *Black flames . . . black bloody flames. This must be the vilest thing I've ever witnessed.*

Even Nanjen seemed cautious of it. More so when the cauldron itself began to sizzle and melt. Yes, somehow, the metal base of the pot was liquefying, the black flames eating away at the stone block beneath. The fusion of metal on stone produced a faint scream like a shellfish in a pot of boiling water. *I was wrong,* this *is the vilest thing I've ever witnessed.* Nanjen redrew her eye when he raised a hand over the partially melted container, as if displaying a prize of surpassing opulence. His slanted smile was darkly sinister. "This is the key to total conquest," he said. "This is darkfire."

BOOK I: DEPARTURE

CHAPTER ONE

It was a dreadful situation.

Regiment Commander Thayer Dal gazed across the narrow stretch of arid scrub, his eyes inevitably drawn to the red foothills rising to the northwest. He liked nothing about those hills. Not the overhanging ridges nor the uneven slopes. Not the clustered stands of cottonwoods nor the occasional low-branching shrub. *Too many advantages for the enemy, too few for us.* He removed a hand from the reins of his horse to tighten his double-wrap sword belt, all the while listening absently to the column of soldiers following behind him. It was a dreadful situation . . . and yet Thayer's heart was filled with glee.

"The march continues, General," Lord Merio said. He was speaking to the dark-eyed and white-clad Yuseth Valate. Both men were armed and armored and seated upon fine battle chargers, but where Merio's was spotted near the peytral and crinet, Yuseth's was as white as an ice field. "How many times must I tell you? You're beginning to sound like my brother. Not the one with the same name—well, only the last part is the same, the *'seth'* part. Not him. I meant my crippled elder brother, Alarin."

"Forgive me," Yuseth replied. "Raas Dragath may be a brute, but his chief strategist Hiriam Thraves is not. His skirmish parties are harassing our frontal flanks from the rifts in these hills. We have to draw our lines away."

Lord Merio balked at that. "You know well that Raas Dragath has departed from Lakewood to Serpenthold, and the lower foothills is the most direct route there. I'm not asking these men to summit the Agate Mountains. I don't care how tired they are, and I don't care how difficult the terrain is. Do you think my daughter had a choice in her own matters?"

Thayer averted his eyes, pretending not to overhear. It was said that Lord Merio hadn't been the same since Cathia's death. Gone was his affable nature and childlike cheerfulness, leaving a lost and embittered man who no longer cared about the cleanliness of his garb or the shininess of his armor. His cloak and personal standards were still the same deep purple hue, but they were as unwashed and ragged as the gray-black banners of the empire. In contrast were the snow-white standards of Yuseth's own sigil, rising skyward like puffs of clouds in a soft blue sky.

"I'm not blind to the reports, General," Lord Merio went on. "But wounds are few and casualties are fewer. It's harassment with a touch of needling, nothing more."

"Or maybe they're testing our defensive shoulder, gauging how easily they can break us."

He twisted in his saddle. "Should I demote Alarin and appoint you as my chief military strategist now? Because I can do that. I'm still the Lord of Stormhaven, you know."

"My lord, I've seen such tactics before. A mere nuisance at first, but under persistent harassment our soldiers will grow discontented. Words will soon spread through the ranks, words that might undermine morale."

"So do something about it. Send detachments to stamp out the harassers, use your words to uplift the spirits of the men. We're not discarding the bouquet because of a few thorns. The main body will continue the march."

"The men need rest. Not nights of full squadrons cramped in tiny six-person tents. A deeper rest found in a home or cottage."

"Look around you, General. There are no settlements to be found."

"Not here, but a day's ride south we'll find plenty of fishing villages along the northernmost spurs of the Azure. These places can serve as temporary barracks. Put the Initiation of Housing Soldiery Law into effect and give your soldiers the reprieve they need."

"It's too far of a deviation. Besides, our men will take advantage of their gracious hosts. Steal their warm beds, drink themselves stupid, and bed their daughters. No, I don't think so."

"You know I won't let that happen."

Lord Merio shook his head. "I'll not divert my course, General."

"My lord—"

"I've said enough. Question my orders again and I'll strip your whites and dress you in the drabbest tatters I can find." He gave the slightest of pauses. "Forgive my harsh words, but I need to crush Raas Dragath and show the world how capable I am. I'm heading back now, General. Keep me informed."

Yuseth opened his mouth—but held his tongue. And with that, Lord Merio pulled the right rein of his charger to turn the beast away, then he cantered back to position in the center ranks.

Thayer maneuvered his horse beside General Yuseth's, but, before he spoke, he paused to hawk an impressive wad of spit. "Some might say Lord Merio is blinded by vengeance, but I believe he has true courage in him. A hero's courage."

Yuseth's dark eyes sized him up, then the corner of his mouth curved up into a half smile. "Sarcastic bastard," he muttered.

"Well, you didn't promote me to regiment commander because of my integrity."

"True, I promoted you because I like having mouthy underlings. Not that I should expect much from a man plucked out of a ragtag group of mercenaries."

It was true. Before his enlistment, Thayer Dal spearheaded an underground shield service for the farms and fiefs of wealthy land-holders, serving mostly the borderland districts where the law was weakest, and the brigands were strongest. It was good money for dangerous work—just as Thayer liked. That might sound strange to some, but Thayer had always lived an erratic lifestyle: good with a blade but unsteady with employment, bored by routine and always looking for the next rush. He considered himself a risk taker and a swashbuckler and a bit of an opportunist, but most of all, he was a void seeker, a man who welcomed death. Fortunately, the realm in its current state provided ample opportunities for his type.

As the demand for his services increased, Thayer eventually roused the attention of Stormhaven's governmental bodies. And so here he was, a self-made regiment officer of only twenty-four springs, in command of a thousand men, yet never having felt the sting of an arms instructor's switch. Best part was, he finagled some of his closest companions to serve as deputy officers. Yurin Gray-heart, Rander the Ripper, and Keven the Unkind. *Crazy bastards, the lot of us. The Jackalmen we were called, and the Jackalmen we'll always be.*

"You still with me?" General Yuseth clinked his mailed fingers in Thayer's direction.

"Yes, what? What is it?"

"I said you must keep that wild tongue of yours in check. An officer without self-restraint is like a city without walls."

"An officer without self-restraint is like . . . what? That's silly. But you're the commanding officer, so I must bow my head and say most graciously: 'Yes, my lord.'"

Yuseth gave a snort, and for a while the rearward clamor of stomping infantrymen and clopping cavalrymen took over. The afternoon grew ever later, and in the dusky light the surrounding formations rose like colossal anthills, their pigmented ridges layered with ruddy shales and siltstones. The lower reaches of the land were pocked with sinkholes, while outcrops of rock gypsum made the hilltops sparkle like mirrored glass. And all through the winding canyons, a thick fumigating fog blew freely, like the acrid breath of a pipe-smoking giant.

Thayer spoke while admiring it all. "I have doubts about Lord Merio's capabilities. Tell me why you chose to serve him over the other lords of the realm."

Yuseth didn't hesitate. "Lord Merio is the unsung hero of House Athera, a cultured man gifted with grace and dignity and ample virtue. He's held firm command of Stormhaven for many long and turbulent years, which is more than anyone can say of the tyrant, the cripple, and the vagabond he calls brothers."

"The folk of the lesser districts despise Lord Merio."

Yuseth gave a halfhearted shrug, then took a moment to readjust his riding posture. He seemed uncomfortable, as if the saddle seat wasn't the right size for him. "You may not believe this, but I was once a lowly squad runt of the Gray Spear Regiment, a quiet, self-effacing soldier living in the shadows of bolder men. For years I watched the lesser-minded rise in status while I remained stagnant. People often assume that a man who talks a lot has a lot of wisdom to share, while a man who speaks little is a man of little importance."

"Not everyone thinks that. Just the mediocrities of the realm."

"Maybe, but they are the majority. Lord Merio is not among them. Where other officers overlooked me, he recognized my talent for arms and my composure under pressure. Without him, I'd not have risen to such an illustrious position."

"A heartwarming tale, but it does nothing to alleviate my doubts. You are indebted to Lord Merio, and so you blindly follow him. But I know you're not blind to what's happening to our men.

They're beleaguered by harassment, weary from forced marches, and weak from days of short rations. Look at them. Look at how defeated and demoralized they are."

When Yuseth didn't look, Thayer decided to turn in his saddle to spare a look himself. Hundreds of drawn faces and sagging shoulders and red-rimmed eyes stared back him. It was not the typical redness of exhaustion either. No, it was a frantic exhaustion, brought on by the constant fear of an ambush. Thayer brought his eyes forward. "To launch a military campaign with anger clouding your judgment is a fool's gambit, but to put your men through terrible hardship is pure idiocy. I don't understand what Lord Merio is thinking?"

"The head of his beloved daughter was brought to him in a sack. How would you react?"

"I don't have a daughter."

Yuseth stiffened him with a glare. "You are young yet, so I'll ignore such a thoughtless remark. Let's try this. If you had a daughter you loved more than anything in the world . . . no, wait. You tell me, who is the one person in your life you love or have loved, more than life itself? Everyone has that person, be it wife or husband, mother or father, son or daughter. Tell me."

"I have no one. No wife, no daughters, no sons." He smiled. "I'm quite certain I never had parents either."

He dismissed that with a snort. "What about your jolly band of ex-mercenaries?"

"The Jackalmen? I suppose I've invested in a certain mutual fellowship with those cud chewers."

"Fine. So these men you care about, these men of camaraderie and companionship, I want you to picture them. Don't just say it but *truly* visualize . . . choose a memory that brings a smile to your heart, a memory that offers a spark of joy to an otherwise joyless campaign."

Thayer recalled an incident in which they swindled a renowned group of thieves by pretending to be crooked constables. Mischief and hijinks abounded that whole evening, and he recalled fondly Yurin's belly-laugh when he confessed the deception. Pure merriment.

"You have it?" Yuseth asked. "Good. Now don't let any distractions get in the way. I want you to watch helplessly as your little band is trussed up against their will, and then I want you to imagine each one being dismembered, one limb at a time, until their profound and deep suffering is finally freed by death. How does that make you feel? To see the dead eyes of their decapitated heads staring up at you, decaying lips asking why you weren't there to save them. Think about it. Don't just nod and give it a passing thought. Truly visualize it. These are your companions, remember, your most cherished friends. How does that make you feel?"

Thayer didn't realize it, but his hands were clenching the reins of his horse, all clammy palms and white knuckles. He relaxed them, flashing a casual smile. "I never liked them much anyway."

"Stop jesting. How does it make you feel?"

"I suppose I feel like stabbing the bastard who killed my companions."

"Now turn around and look. At the soldiers who are enduring this so-called *hardship*."

Thayer did. He looked long and pensively at the serried ranks of the forward army, and, when he turned back, he let out an exhausted breath. "I understand now," he said.

Three days later, three soldiers had died (two from typhoid, the other from an enemy broadhead arrow that pierced his carotid artery), while dozens more suffered minor to moderate wounds and illnesses, including a nasty case of camp itch. Still, there was a glimmer of hope in the air. The harassments from the hills had ceased. Spring's sudden hot spell was loosening. Men, for the first time in weeks, reformed their lines while laughing and clapping each other on the back. Voices carried sparks of enthusiasm and traces of hope. Thayer observed these changes for a while, then his eyes returned to the quiet hills and the backdrop of blue sky. A vision of welcome tranquility. *Our luck is beginning to turn,* he decided. *Perhaps Lord Merio was right to cut through these hills after all.*

An encouraging thought, but one that proved to be dead wrong.

War drums erupted from the western ridges, a pounding so sudden and so fierce that Thayer's horse bucked, and he had to seize the pommel with two hands to keep from tumbling off. *BOOM BOOM BO-BOOOOOM.* Again. *BOOM BOOM BO-BOOOOOM.* Thayer dug in his heels to force control over his mount, and next he knew he was scrambling to form up with his regiment, scrambling and scrambling while the drums pounded in his ears like the stomping of overweight giants. *BOOM BOOM BO-BOOOOOM. BOOM BOOM BO-BOOOOOM.* A mass of shadows rose from the hillside crannies. The sunlight revealed mounted men in red cloaks, armored in shoulder-to-waist cuirasses and armed with long-handled sabers and heavy halberds. This was a full Redlander charge.

It was just as Yuseth said, Thayer realized, a bit too late. *The enemy lulled us into a false sense of security. Why have we not prepared for this?*

Thayer searched for his principal officers but only saw gray-cloaked subordinates. For some reason, he laughed. *Take control, Thayer, it's time to take control.* He shouted commands and thrust signals at the flag bearers, his heart racing with purpose, his mind weaving complex calculations of time and distance. Of the flank he arranged in double rows of spearmen, light of depth but wide of spread to smother the incoming charge. *To defeat a snake, we will surround and strike,* he mused, then cackled like a madman. *Break their cavalry to constrict their—*

Boom. His horse jolted forward and Thayer lurched with it, whiplashed by the thrusting force of his own rankmates. *What the hell? Struck from behind?* Another jolt and suddenly the sky was spinning, and when the ground rose up he slammed into it with a jarring thud, his head bouncing off a block of hard sandstone. Dust leaped into his eyes, big fat flecks of it. *Shit, shit, shit,* he thought—or shouted, not sure which but likely both. His gauntleted hand reached up to feel the dent in his halfhelm—and again he laughed. *My silly brains should be dashed all over the place.* Shadows flitted past him, shadows that touched the open rays of sunlight and became red-cloaked men. *Redlanders . . . where did they come from? A second detachment from the east. A pincer strike.*

"Get up, get up, get up," a voice shouted. Thayer couldn't tell if it was friend or foe, but the moment he rose he was struck back down to the dirt. *Thump.* This time he landed on his back, where he got a clear view of his own battledress: the lacquered lamellae chestplate and doeskin lacing, the segmented cuisses and shin-protecting greaves—and the globs of mud that sullied it. *I should probably get up,* he told himself, planting his hands into the earth, elbows up. *I should probably find and protect Lord Merio.*

There was a flash of crimson cloth as a Redlander foreranker pounced on top of him, and suddenly Thayer was punching and pulling and clawing for his life. His foeman barely had a face, just a dull helmet cusped over the eyes, with strips of quilted fabric covering the sides. The bastard must've been injured or weak or simply tired, because he gave little fight when Thayer powered into a dominant position, then drove the boss of his helmet into the man's head, so hard the man's mouth burst open in a flash of crimson. Thayer snatched up the dagger that the Redlander dropped, then drove it into the man's neck, an upward stab that tore through tissue and ligament and bone. The sound it made was awful, but the sound of the Redlander's gurgled scream was worse. Blood trickled from his neck, only to gush into a red cascade when Thayer dislodged the blade.

That's a lot of blood. It was bright in color too, like a mash of ripened strawberries. In globs it sprayed Thayer's vambraces and breastplate, tiny red blossoms wedged between overlapping scales. It looked stylish. He pushed off the dead man and sprang to his feet, discarding the dagger and unsheathing Bloodless, his white-hilted saber and steadfast companion. Bodies clashed and rolled around him, friends and foemen grunting and growling like rabid beasts. Thayer took it all in, *breathed* it in, the mud and sweat and spit and blood. Never had he felt more alive than at this very moment; it was as if he'd been a walking corpse during his downtime hours. He raised his weapon heavenward, then gave a roar, as though an angry demon were climbing out of his throat, and with that he dove into the sea of battle.

The sounds were like the whirring of dense machinery, the smell was like overheated steel, and the dust was so thick and red it was like the hills were on fire. Showers of sandstone pelted the head and shoulders of the enmeshed formations, while blades hissed and blood answered and death waited behind every man like a patient shroud. There was no order to be found; all Thayer saw was a jumble of bodies jockeying for position in this great nest of violence.

Time slowed as it usually did, and all rational thought fled from Thayer's mind. It was his fighting spirit that enswathed him now, like a garment of velvet that guided every slash and stab of his saber. Techniques came to him masterfully, like a dancer during his most passionate performance. *The Step and the Shadow.* Blood splashed as a Redlander dropped with a shriek. *The Nightwolf's Bite.* Another toppled like a sack of gristle. He pushed the next foeman to the ground and then stabbed his rankmate in the belly.

The Wind in the Darkness. He killed another and another—and he smiled as he did.

Sword-tips came screaming at his face, but Thayer was swift and tireless on his feet. He could feel the breeze of the arcing blades tickle his skin, could sense the hunger in every sweeping cut. *Yes, that was close, too close.* Bloodless responded by killing and maiming and killing some more, and every time he killed, he donned another badge of his dead foe's blood. His gauntleted hands were sticky with it now, his saber slick and wet and thirsty for more. The blood was everywhere. He inhaled it when he breathed, tasted it when he swallowed, watched it fly in shiny ribbons. Blood, blood, endless blood.

He worked his way through the battle, and soon a cool burst of fresh air thrust itself into his lungs. Thayer exhaled like a man escaping the clutches of a quagmire. His eyes drifted skyward, to Merio Athera's purple banners flapping listlessly in the wind. The Lord of Stormhaven's crack unit lay on the ground nearby, most downed and wounded, or sprawled out and dead. General Yuseth Valate was among them. *Oh no, this is bad. This is very bad.* The general was lying there, dead as a sun-cooked snail, his once pristine and winter-white battledress now covered in blood and grime and pinkish silt. *The Lord of Winter . . . by the gods, he was a great swordsman, matched only by few. Who could've done this?*

Thayer's eyes trailed up, following the heap of bodies that led to a single man: Raas Dragath.

Oh no, he's here. The fucking Red Terror is here.

Not only was he here, but he was standing against Lord Merio himself. And while the handsome Lord of Stormhaven looked dead on his feet, the Redlander warlord appeared fresher than a morning breeze. His bulky, gray-bearded frame stood poised like a great armored bear, while Lord Merio's cracked chestplate was leaking lines of red from several joints. Still, if he was in any pain, he didn't show it. The man's eyes were pure fire.

There was a brief exchange of words between the two, but Thayer couldn't hear what was said. Lord Merio couldn't have been more than thirty paces away . . . and yet, it might've been a thousand for all it mattered. He was just too far. *But I have try . . . I have try to save him.* His legs sprang into movement. Thirty paces became twenty-five. *I'm coming, I'm coming.* Twenty paces now.

Lord Merio charged forward, curved sword leaping and turning, an adept string of maneuvers that pressed Raas Dragath on his heels. But the warlord's timing and speed were sharp for such an aged and bulky man, and each thrust was met with a deflection, each slash turned with a counter. Up and down, left and right, Raas Dragath wielded his long-handled spear like a man possessed, but just when the duel turned in his favor, the outstretched arm of a corpse snagged his foot and dropped him to a single knee.

He's beaten, Thayer thought.

But no, like an eager recruit Merio rushed in for the finishing blow, abandoning all defense and sense of restraint. The southern warlord must've read this at once, because he sprang forward and delivered a haft strike that smashed Merio's oncoming chin. The sound was awful, like the vicious crack of thunder, which was probably the sound of Merio's jaw breaking. Momentum drove him forward, tumbling and sliding across the dusty scrub like a broken doll, before he ended up slumped over on his knees, dazed and silent.

No, no, no. Thayer's calves cramped with ache, but he didn't stop. *I'm so close, I'm so close now.* Fifteen yards. Ten. He raised his weapon and . . .

BOOM. Someone had slammed into him, a blindsiding blow that sent Thayer spinning to the ground. He wanted to rise, but first he had to place the sky above him and the ground beneath him. *Clear your head, hurry and clear your head.* He didn't even attempt a look at his assailant, didn't care who it was. His eyes focused only on Lord Merio and the powerful Raas Dragath who loomed over him, meaty hands wrapped around his upraised poleaxe. Thayer shouted at Dragath to *STOP*, but the warlord didn't spare him a glance. He twirled the haft to an overhand grip and plunged the butt spike down Merio's throat. Teeth shattered as his neck gave a sickening jerk. Then the blood came. A terrible rush of blood.

CHAPTER TWO

Elder Brother, I know you've been busy during my unfortunate absence. Don't think I am blind to your transgressions. Run all you like, but you can never escape the bonds of your fraternal duty. I've taken the necessary steps for my assumption of the imperial throne, but an emperor cannot rule without his seal of office. You will return it, and you will offer your full submission. Do this and you will stand once more as my Imperial Advisor. Deny me and you will be considered an enemy of the realm. Of your response do not tarry. - Z

In the principal chamber of the Rosebud Hall, Alarin Athera sat at his writing desk, staring down at his brother's letter. He didn't know how to reply, so he stared and stared until the words stopped being words, until all he saw was a blurry string of characters scrawled on a crinkled sheet of silk. He refocused his eyes and read it again, and then once more, before deciding that he'd seen enough. When he rose from his seat, his missing right leg flared in pain—the usual phantom pain—but he didn't bother to reach down, knowing well that the cold metal braces of his carved wooden leg could not be soothed.

"And in the s-shining of the c-cloud f-falls . . . the First Em-mperor Th-thal-as-tor Siven healed his . . . l-lifelong c-condition." It was a child's voice—Silas. He was seated at a burgundy-black table that was lacquered in mother-of-pearl, his eyes buried in an open tome, legs dangling off the seat of a carved trestle bench. His small voice sounded even smaller in the imposingly spacious hall. "And aw-woken within him was the w-wisdom to forge a new d-dynasty. The land would once again know u-unity and h-h-harmony." He looked up and blinked like a housebroken puppy. "Did I do good?"

"You did well," Chamberlain Rennerin Rothar answered. "Now keep going, turn the page. Go on."

Silas obeyed but not without a frown and a huff under his breath. He had such a plain face, a non-ruler's face, a face no different from any of the urchins you'd see at any market square. Features ordinary and forgettable, lacking any youthful hint of the hard eyes and chiseled jawline of his late father Demien Mordall. "I'm tired of reading," he moaned. "I don't see why reading is necessary."

"You are the emperor now," Rennerin told him, "and an emperor who cannot read is like a soldier who marches to war without a blade. Wisdom and prudence are your weapons, Your Majesty, you must learn how to wield them. It is the responsibility of a ruler to forgo pleasurable activities for the greater good of the realm. So let us continue, shall we?"

Alarin observed the two quietly, fingers scratching at his balding pate. He'd misjudged Chamberlain Rennerin when he'd first arrived in Stormhaven, having gone so far as to express the desire to shove his cane down the man's throat. *What did I call him? Ah yes, a fat, foppish wretch of a steward.* But in truth, Alarin was beginning to understand why Merio had chosen to appoint him. Once you looked past Rennerin's longwinded nature and excess weight and hideously garish outfits, you'd find an upstanding fellow who made decisions based on sound judgment. *Good to know he's not just another toady like the rest of Merio's toadies.*

Beside Rennerin, and towering comfortably over him, was General Szathan Mordall. Even without the bulk of his heavy scale armor, the general still appeared monstrously broad and massively wide. His blockish and rather ugly face gazed upon his nephew Silas with familial compassion. There was no better protector in the realm. Szathan had long proven himself to be among the most loyal of military men, and he coupled that with an innate need to protect the only son of his beloved late brother, Demien.

Rennerin must've seen Alarin gazing in their direction because he excused himself from the lesson and approached. He had an easy gait, a subtle bounce to his step that spoke of self-assurance. Unfortunately, the breezy blue silk robe that trailed behind him was anything but subtle. "Is something amiss, my lord? Shall I call for your attendant?"

Alarin shook his head. "Just lost in my thoughts, as usual." His smile lacked vigor. "Your work with the boy, it pleases me, Chamberlain."

"He's young yet, he learns quickly."

Silas called rather bashfully from across the room. "May I take my leave?"

"No, Your Majesty, keep at it," Rennerin answered.

The boy slumped down in his seat, little fist pressed against his cheek. General Szathan immediately leaned over to place a reassuring hand on his nephew's robed shoulder.

Rennerin turned back to Alarin, his voice sinking to a low murmur. "Forgive the boldness of my tongue, my lord, but I must admit I'm rather surprised that you're still here. Didn't Lord Merio order you to—"

"I know what he said." Alarin's eyes unconsciously wandered

the hall, pausing briefly at the fancy ornate pillars and intricate bas-relief carvings and, of course, the massive Sadralen beast suspended from the tiled ceiling. It was a snake-skinned leonine sculpture, horned and fanged and about the size of an arctic whale. Alarin had never found any joy or comfort in it, the same of all this expensive finery and décor. In his eyes, it did nothing but showcase a man's weakness for extravagance, which in turn did nothing but push the common folk away. How could Merio not see that? Well, perhaps he did. Alarin had almost effected a change in his brother, with Merio even going so far as to have much of it removed, but after Cathia's death, all the sculptures and furnishings returned like a child's spiteful retaliation. By the gods, Merio was stubborn, but that shouldn't surprise anyone. He belonged to House Athera, after all. Brothers Zantherei, Anseth, and even Alarin himself had always been the same.

"What's bothering you?" Rennerin asked.

"My brother."

"Which one?"

Alarin heard himself laugh. "All of them."

"You shouldn't fret, my lord."

"I have to. Zantherei is threatening war, Anseth is becoming a barbarian, and Merio is blind with vengeance." His eyes dropped. "I regret Merio's western campaign. I should've remonstrated with him. I should've at least sent General Szathan with him."

"Lord Merio won't fail with General Yuseth Valate at his side. The Lord of Winter is said to be unbeatable."

"No man is unbeatable." His gaze drifted to little Silas. The boy's eyes flicked across the foxed pages of the open tome, but he wasn't reading. No, he seemed to be engaged in a discussion with Szathan, and though Alarin was out of earshot, he could still discern the reason for their debate. The boy believed Demien was alive, and whenever he brought up the desire to track him down, Szathan would grow tense and irritated, just as he was right now. And yet, for all of Silas's mousy timidity, this was one claim the poor boy seemed adamant about.

Alarin turned back to Rennerin. "I intended to go north, before the shining of the cloudfalls. North of the Amber River. Anseth is there, holding a protective line against Seric Dyre, awaiting my word."

"So go north. Reunite with your brother."

Alarin sighed. "It's been ten years . . ." *Time moves so quickly, yet some memories remain stuck in the heart like mud. I must remember that Anseth is the commander of the barbarian tribes now.* He cracked a thoughtful smile at that. In his mind, Anseth would always be that little rascal of a brother, smart and scrappy but not suited for high command. The change in him must've been significant. "He's rather small, my brother, while the host of barbarians he commands are rather large. An interesting sight to behold, I'm sure."

"He is born and trained in the Athera clan. I've no doubt of his courage, whatever his size."

Alarin placed a free hand on the chamberlain's robed shoulder. "Your silver tongue knows just how to stroke a man's ego. A shame though, I was just beginning to like you."

When Chamberlain Rennerin smiled, his plump cheeks swallowed most of his eyes. "I'm no lickspittle, my lord, but I am honest. Go on. Appoint General Szathan Mordall as your escort. The boy is safe within the palace walls."

"The boy is not my concern."

"What is, then?"

"Pitting brother against brother. I've already drawn Merio to my side, and now it's happening again with Anseth. My struggle with Zantherei should be mine alone."

"Your struggle is for the good of the realm. Your struggle is to protect the *true* emperor." He extended an oversized sleeve toward the boy. "Just as the cloudfalls shined for the First Emperor Thalastor Siven, so too did they shine for the son of Demien Mordall. Heaven and all its gilded shrines have granted the boy a voice, and with that voice comes the burden of restoring a fractured realm under a new dynasty. You are fated to protect him from those who would oppose this union, be it Lord Zantherei, or Seric Dyre, or Raas Dragath, or whomever. If they fail to disregard their own ambitions and acknowledge Silas as the true son of heaven, they must be branded as traitors to the realm."

"I wish it were that simple."

"It is. It can be."

Alarin was about to respond, but a sudden clamor wrenched away his attention.

It came from outside the hall, in the antechamber beyond the open doors. Alarin wasn't sure how long a commotion had been stirring, but it was all he could hear now. Rennerin instructed the hall sentries to investigate, but just as they crossed the entranceway threshold, a host of Stormhaven soldiers rushed inside. A collision nearly ensued, and from the armored throng a small man popped out —a scout by the looks of his lightweight leathers and cloak.

Alarin started toward him, but at that moment his leg chose to flare up like an angry boil, which left him struggling to walk even with the aid of his blackthorn cane. It didn't matter; the scout darted across the hall and dropped to a single knee before his lord. The face that looked up was pale and drawn and weatherworn, and the outer leathers that sheathed his body were smeared with filth and flecked with gobbets of mud. *This isn't good,* Alarin thought. *He didn't even spare a moment to brush the mud from his clothes.*

The scout's head sank into his shoulders. "News from Iron Station, first outpost of the western line, my lord."

"Yes, what did you bring, go on, tell me."

The scout hesitated. It was as if he'd spent all his energy finding Alarin, without having first considered the words that needed to be said. "Forgive me," he croaked at last, eyes plastered to the floor. "It's about Lord Merio . . ."

CHAPTER THREE

"I don't like this," Cyrille Vileron said. "You should have a full escort with you. Fifty picked men, at least."

"Fifty men and one is bound to reveal my whereabouts. I must move in secrecy." Her chin rose slightly. "Besides, I don't need fifty men when I have you."

The big man's vulturine face perked up at the flattering remark, but it wasn't enough to alter his view. "The province isn't safe. Bandits and highwaymen lurk behind every ridge and road, waiting to pounce on unsuspecting travelers. Like us."

She didn't bother answering that. What would she say? Traveling was a risk, sure, but she had no other choice. The safest path was to move along the outskirts of the Starwing Road, using the forest's edge as concealment. It was deep into spring, which meant the land was alive with chitters and croaks and sparrow-song, and these commingled with the nearby groaning of oxcarts, the clopping of pack animal hooves, and the muffled voices of merchants and wayfarers and itinerant monks.

Vileron's tattered gray cloak was clasped tight to hide the blackened plates of steel mail beneath, the hood raised to cover his bald head and partially conceal those nasty facial scars. It wasn't much, but it was enough. Now if only he would remove the frayed leather strips wrapped around the vambraces of his forearms, since these were dead giveaways to an observant eye.

Miriana herself chose ragged and inconspicuous attire: an undyed blouse and men's trousers beneath a homespun gray traveler's cloak. Peasantry clothing was unbecoming of a lady of her status, but she had to remember: she wasn't that lady any longer, not since stepping foot out of the Hollow's gates. *Already I yearn for the days in which I sat comfortably as empress. If I could go back, I'd make the tough decisions, the ones that would keep me on the throne.*

"I don't like this," Vileron said again.

"Then go back," she told him. "Return to the Hollow, fasten your cord and seal, don your imperial blues, and stand at my husband's side. As captain of the imperial toadies."

He sneered at that. "You know I won't leave you."

She did know that, and yet she goaded him all the same. "Why not? Because of a promise of faith from years ago? You don't owe me your loyalty, Cyrille. If you no longer wish to serve as my escort, then go back. I'm strong, I don't need you, I don't need anyone."

He didn't answer, but when she looked up, he was still wearing that same lip-curling sneer. An expression she didn't like at all. "Did I make a jest?" she asked.

"No. I don't think you should abandon your city. You've toiled too long for it. Watch your step. Here, come this way."

There was a pit in the ground, large and rectangular and partially covered by strewn hardwood branches. The sides were mortared blocks of gray stone, stained by salty moisture and eroded by time. Predator pits such as these were constructed near farmsteads to trap wolves for easy killing, but to an incautious human they could be no less treacherous. Miriana might not have avoided the pit were it not for Vileron's warning. Still, she didn't bother to thank him. Instead, when she was led safely around, she said, "I know how hard I've worked. I don't need you to remind me." *I know how hard because it kills me every moment of every day. But I failed to act, and now Zantherei has recovered and claimed the throne for himself.*

"Talk to your husband. He may yet forgive you."

She scoffed. "I knew you'd say that. Are you truly that much of a fool?"

As if to reinforce her point, the big man stumbled on a jutting tree root. It was a brief falter of balance, barely noticeable, but when their eyes met, they shared a quiet laugh together. It felt good. *By the god, how many days has it been since I laughed?*

Vileron cleared his throat. "It's unwise for a lord to turn to hostile lands to escape domestic troubles."

"Fortunately for me, I'm not a lord."

"Lord, lady—you know what I mean. The ruling house has fallen, the empire stands divided. Warlords and self-styled rulers have risen in every province, and the people are suffering for it. Discord and chaos run rampant."

"Yes, and that is what drives my little journey. Someone wiser than you once told me to always look ahead, always to your next advantage. Learn from the past, don't dwell in it. Just as family and friends can become foes in a flash, foes can become allies all the same."

"Raas Dragath will never be a friend."

"Raas Dragath is the only one I can turn to. His promised bride is dead, murdered because of Alarin Athera's deception. He still desires a strong woman to stand beside him. What better candidate than a woman who once ruled the capital city?"

"Do you think he'll welcome you with open arms, just like that?"

"Of course not, but I will make him trust me. I have my ways."

Vileron didn't seem convinced. "I don't want to see you suffer as Lord Merio's daughter has suffered."

"Then go, like I said. You're slowing me down anyway." A gust of wind whipped her hair into her eyes. She brushed it aside, fingertips moist from the sweat on her forehead. "I once thought you a stout-hearted man."

"Stout of heart is not the same as foolhardiness."

She didn't offer a reply to that. A wash of crepuscular light flooded the northwestern sky, a deeply beautiful hue that bathed the numerous oaks and needled pines. Nightfall's cloak soon fell behind it, turning the land darker than a stagnant marsh. Miriana's pace was slowing, but she needed to get farther away from the capital. Even though her disappearance would go unnoticed for days, she still feared being seen by Zantherei's agents. Returning to the capital in fetters would be a shame she couldn't bear.

She wanted to cross the Cobalt River before settling down to rest, but Vileron was drawing heavy breaths and struggling in his heavy armor. "We should stop here," he huffed, indicating a suitable spot that looked no different from the last suitable spot, which was either a half-dugout or overhanging crest or some other hidden cranny. But Miriana spurred him on, despite her own weariness, and Vileron obeyed for a while, but then his heavy footfalls ceased and did not make another sound.

Miriana was running out of patience. "What are you doing?" She could barely see him in the semidarkness, just a tall shroud wrapped in a tattered cloak.

"I need to rest." His voice was a winded rasp.

"The river's just ahead, we'll rest once we've forded it. Come along."

He didn't budge. "I said I need to rest."

Miriana gave her most exasperated sigh. "Fine, do what you want. I'm not stopping. Not until I cross the river." With that, she turned and walked off.

Miriana's boots crunched across the litter of the forest floor, her nose tingling with the smell of pine needles and earthy soil. She expected to hear Vileron's footfalls behind her, but when she didn't, the fear of isolation swiftly crept into her heart. *He'll follow, he won't leave me alone like this.* Along the outskirts of the wood, thicket rose like sharpened tines. And looking deeper, she saw nothing but twisted claw-like branches and curling shadows, like a static vision of giant shambling demons. Miriana steeled herself and moved on, and soon the dark monstrous shapes wilted away into a low floodplain.

Moonlight cascaded down from a sky of coruscating stars, its glistening glow bouncing off the many deltas and tributaries of the Cobalt River. The waters were calmer here, which meant it shouldn't be difficult to find a place to cross. Her eyes wandered to a stretch of crags that rose beyond the river. *And once I do cross, it won't be difficult to find a suitable place to rest for the night, above the ground and away from nasty insects.* She had to hurry. Nightfall's inevitable chill was deepening. She looked back, but Vileron was nowhere to be seen. Nothing but dark thicket and twisted shadows of bare trees. *You didn't leave me.* She kept looking, but there was nothing. *No, you didn't leave me.* She paused, then whispered to herself, "Did you leave me?"

"Did I what?"

Miriana's heart leaped from her chest. *That wasn't Vileron's voice.* To her right, a few paces outside the wooded periphery, a lean man was squatting beneath a stone outcropping. His trousers were down about his ankles, his legs hairy and bare in the moonlight. She knew it wasn't Vileron, and yet she whispered his name anyway.

"Sorry, friend." His voice was polite but razor sharp. "Just an asshole shitting in the woods."

A lump rose in Miriana's throat, a lump she couldn't seem to swallow. Her eyes drifted past the man, to the dark wall of thicket, waiting and waiting for Vileron to emerge and rescue her. *Any moment now,* she told herself. *Any moment.* But when he didn't come, her throat became even tighter, so tight she could barely take in any air. *I . . . I can't believe you abandoned me.*

To her left something crunched underfoot, and for a moment Miriana's heart fluttered with relief . . . but no, it wasn't Vileron. It was a second man, as lean as the first, but half a head taller and twice as ragged. "Who's this, a peeper?" he grunted.

The first man shrugged. He was standing now, tying the cord of his trousers, one hand fitted with a large, fingerless glove of hard leather. "Don't think so. Our friend here's a woman."

Miriana's mouth opened, but nothing came out. *Oh Cyrille, where are—*

The man moved so fast she didn't have time to react. One hand seized the back of her neck, while the other reached up to yank down her hood. "Oh, look at that. A woman indeed. And she is *stunning.*" His voice was terrifyingly calm.

"Let me see," the second figure blurted, moving for a closer look. Miriana looked up at a dirt-slathered face with two giant fish eyes and a single bushy brow. "By the gods," he said. "She *is* stunning. And look at how tall she is. Truly a gift from the gods."

"Are you alone?" the first man asked her. He was an ugly bastard, face small and snouted—like a mole's face perhaps, or maybe she just thought that because he had a large black mole in the center of his left cheek. *Am I making any sense?* It was face you'd expect of a brigand: shifty, sleazy, utterly repulsive. He smiled wickedly before continuing. "Because a beauty like you shouldn't be out in the wilds alone."

She wanted to tell them she wasn't alone, that the powerful Cyrille Vileron was nearby . . . but the words wouldn't come. It was as if she'd forgotten how to speak. Apparently, she'd also forgotten how to move. Her body just didn't respond. Legs, hands, nothing. She had never been so afraid in her life.

"Never mind what you're carrying," the mole-cheeked brigand

said. He tightened his grip on her neck and pressed his lower body against hers. Firmly, lecherously, so that his groin rubbed against her hip. His mouth was inches away. The muggy spring air made the stink of his breath much worse. It was almost as bad as the stink of his body. "I just want you."

"I want her first," said the fish-eyed brigand. "She's too pretty for your ugly puss."

Molecheek laughed at that. "Too pretty, yes. Maybe you're right. How's this?"

He punched her.

Miriana heard her face *crack*, and suddenly her world was spinning and undulating and rotating in waves. *He hit me. The bastard hit me.* Warm blood trickled into her mouth, thick and clotty and hard to swallow.

Molecheek was laughing at her. *Laughing.* "Look at that," he said. "I just broke her fucking nose."

Miriana spat a wad of blood. *Do something. They're going to rape you, and they're going to kill you. Do something, damn it.* She remembered the traveling dirk sheathed at her hip, and so she brought it out and brandished it in Molecheek's face. He didn't seem too concerned, probably because her hand was shaking like a sunflower in a snowstorm. "Stay away," she told him. "I once cut off a man's hand with a blade like this."

Molecheek tossed her a dubious grin. "Shut up," he said, then reached out to seize her.

She thrust the blade at him with all her strength, but somehow the man knocked it aside, a move so quick she barely saw it. He caught her wrist, his grip terribly strong, and with that stupid, sleazy smile of his, he drew back his free hand and balled it into a fist. Miriana winced.

"*Don't* hit her."

She looked up just as Cyrille Vileron emerged from the brush, a towering baldheaded titan wrapped in a ragged black cloak. One gauntleted hand clutched a serrated and ringed saber; the other was free and beckoning to Miriana. She rushed to his side at once.

The two bandits took a wary step back. They no longer looked so frightening to Miriana. *They are barely men. I bet I've seen more winters than these two.* Miriana wiped a streak of blood from her numb face and straightened her posture as best she could. "You were right," she told them. "I'm not alone."

"Obviously, you stupid bitch," Molecheek shouted.

Fisheyes pulled a rusted blade and pointed it at Vileron. "It's two against one, you big brute. Better run, odds aren't good for you."

Of course, Vileron didn't run, but strangely enough, that was exactly what the brigand decided to do. He just turned and bolted, *zoom*, right into the woods. Molecheek was left with a stupid look on his stupid face, as if expecting his friend to return in a bout of mocking laughter. But he never did return, and now Molecheek had a decision to make. In the end, he decided to follow his friend's footsteps, and run.

Too late. Vileron had already closed the distance. He shouldered Molecheek to the ground and chopped at the lower legs like a tree, delivering two or three good hacks before the man's foot began to split grotesquely from the calf tendon. Molecheek howled so loud the entire forest and all its nocturnal symphonies seemed to shut down. He tried to get away, but when his half-dismembered foot wouldn't let him, he resigned himself to clutching at the gash and moaning in pain. Blood fountained freely; it was dark in the night, visible only when it touched the bars of moonlight.

"Please," the brigand cried. Over and over. "Please. *Please.*" His teeth were gnashed in agony. Vileron walked over and removed the glove from the man's hand. "Please," the brigand bawled once more.

Vileron dropped the glove at Miriana's feet. Closer, she saw the details of the oily leather, the thickness of a hidden metal plate, and the row of small spikes spread along the knuckles. "A cestus, it's like an iron glove," he explained. "Not military-issued, this was probably stitched and tailored for the sport-fighting cities of the far south. This bandit scumbag must've robbed someone for it."

Oh gods, this is what I was struck with? Her hand rose to touch her face. Everything felt numb, but when she withdrew her fingers, they were slick with blood. "How bad is it? Tell me, how bad?"

"It'll heal."

"What if it doesn't? Dragath will reject me. Do you understand what that means? Goddamn it, Cyrille, what the hell took you so long?"

"You told me to leave, you said you didn't need—"

"*SHUT UP.*" She wiped her nose with a hand that came back bloody. "I didn't think you would actually *leave.*"

Vileron tightened his thin gray lips, then his eyes drifted over to Molecheek. The brigand was attempting to crawl his way to freedom, and to his credit he'd made decent progress, although that trail of glistening blood wasn't helping him any. "What about him?"

"He shattered my nose. What do you think?"

Vileron nodded and went off.

Miriana collapsed against the rocky outcropping. She felt exhausted and sick and vulnerable. "Just get it over with," she shouted. *I'm in too much pain to care about revenge.* With her free hand, she unslung her rucksack and began rifling through it. *Where the hell—ah, here it is.* She grabbed the look mirror, leaned into the moonlight, and held it up.

Her face was a mess—much worse than she had thought. A spattering of blood painted her cheeks, bright specks mixed with thicker, darker globs. The flesh around her eyes was beginning to swell and empurple, and her nose . . . well, looked like a piece of red pulp. The only consolation was that her teeth were still intact. Somehow. *All this from one punch?* She raised a hand and gingerly touched the wounds, poking and prodding before recoiling from the pain. It was a red-hot sting that spread from the bottom of her brow to the top of her mouth.

For a moment she thought about returning to the Hollow. Yes, she could sneak back into the city, make her way into the palace district, and return to her private bedchamber. She'd summon Master Lorian to tend her wounds and plead illness to escape a fortnight of duties. Zantherei would never know. He was too busy with his newfound power and prestige anyhow. Yes, she could go back. She could go back and have her attendant prepare a bath. A nice hot bath, and Miriana would shed these filthy tatters and let the water wash away all the nightmarish memories of this ordeal. Yes, she *should* go back. It wasn't too far, she should go—

No. Returning to the Hollow was a coward's way out. Miriana was better than that. She was *stronger* than that.

Still, she couldn't remember the last time she felt so miserable. And her journey had only just begun.

CHAPTER FOUR

It had been two weeks since the news of Lord Merio's death reached Stormhaven, and the palatial district remained deeply drenched in mourning. With the body unreturned, the funeral wasn't the customary chamber burial inside a tomb, but a ceremony centered around an elaborate cairn. Alarin attended the service, but only briefly, choosing to observe from the low slope of a distant mound. The rows of well-dressed mourners and their fancy robes and furbelows displeased him. How could one bear such concern for one's attire during a time of grief? Such were Merio's people, he supposed. Still, Merio deserved better than this. *He deserves a true Anirian funeral, like father had.* But without the body, there could be none.

Alarin listened to the posthumous titles that were bestowed upon his brother, then he watched as the bronze vessels were brought out for the ritual sacrifices of goat and lamb. After that, he turned and hobbled back to the central hall, where he sat down (with a painful grimace) and stared once more at Zantherei's letter.

After an hour of fidgeting in his seat, he'd managed to remove the brushpen from its holder and dip it in the inkwell. But he made no further progress. The blank sheet beneath the letter remained blank, and eventually Alarin placed the brushpen back onto its holding rack, and then he sighed. It bothered him that the common folk were not so saddened by Merio's death. Still, it was understandably so, since Merio had always catered to the city's aristocratic blood. And yet, despite Alarin's own pit of grief, there was a part of him—a small, shameful part—that began to ponder an undeniable truth: Merio's death might serve to benefit Alarin's position. It was true, and yet he felt guilty all the same.

A knock on the chamber door arrested Alarin's attention. He gestured to an ungainly guardsman who began the long hike across the chamber, armored footfalls thumping against the tiled floor like steel pistons. Alarin's eyes returned to his writing desk, glancing again at Zantherei's letter, but when the door groaned open, he looked up to see Regiment Commander Thayer Dal standing in the entranceway.

He was a gangly grasshopper of a man, narrow of features and nimble of gait, with a mismatched pair of stormy blue-green eyes that gazed vacantly beneath a dark shock of scraggly hair. His soldiers and friends called him the Wild Goose, a fitting style, as he was strange and unpredictable with his movements, and rather nutty with his words. But as a commander he was loyal and he was capable, and he was also one of the few who made it out of the ambush alive.

Alarin urged the officer inside, and Thayer crossed the chamber like a skulking wolf, taking small, cautious, overly observant steps. When he reached the center brazier, he paused to run a few fingers through the flames, then with a gratified smile he moved to Alarin's desk, dropping to his knees like a marionette with strings cut. "My defeat at Redwing Hills is an inexcusable offense, and only death can repay this transgression." He seemed almost *glad* to say those words, and when he slapped down his seal of military command on the floor before him, it gave a resounding *clang*.

Alarin considered the officer, one hand rising to rub his balding pate. "The campaign has placed a heavy burden on our treasury, and we can't even petition the Hollow for aid. The dead are many, the wounded are many more, and our roster of competent physicians grows ever short." He shook his head gravely. "And since Raas Dragath has absconded with my brother's body, we couldn't have him properly interred in the burial tombs."

Thayer spoke after a somber pause. "The ambush was well executed. The camouflaged trenches along the embankments went unnoticed by our scouts."

"A clever tactic. Draw your eyes to the east and strike from the west. Only an experienced strategist could've have countered that move. The Redlanders are a force under the direction of Hiriam Thraves. The man's in the prime of his talents."

Thayer nodded. "General Yuseth was cautious of Hiriam. But Lord Merio, he was . . ."

"Stubborn." Alarin raised a hand, motioning. "Up, Commander. The fault lies not with you. Merio knew the risks—he knew the dangers of marching against Raas Dragath. He was my brother and I loved him, but he was a fool for allowing emotion to overtake good judgment."

Thayer rose. He pushed pale fingers through his dark crop of unctuous hair. He wasn't a handsome man, but there wasn't anything particularly unhandsome about him either, although at the moment he looked more disheveled than anything. "What will become of Stormhaven?"

Alarin didn't have an answer prepared. Not that he hadn't thought about it—in fact he'd been mulling over little else since the news had touched his ears. But for right now, he had to respond with whatever words came to him. "I suppose until Emperor Silas Mordall is of age to rule, the seal of the city and its surrounding districts will pass unto me. That means I will see to all important matters at court before they are presented to His Majesty. And if you choose to serve me as faithfully as you did my brother, then you shall have generalship over our entire military garrison."

Thayer's expression softened, then hardened, then turned listless, then restless, then finally it softened to a look of understated delight. He nodded a good six times before replying. "My honor, my strength, my spirit, my life—everything I have is yours to command."

Alarin leaned back, satisfied. "With you and Szathan Mordall at my side, I have all the strength I need to return this city to its former glory."

Later, when the pinkish light of dusk had settled, Alarin suffered the pain in his missing leg to visit the alcove of cloudfalls. For a time, he studied their soft puffy whiteness as they swayed gently upon the stone tiers. *This was Merio's greatest project,* he thought. *This is his legacy. And now he's gone to the next life without having witnessed the fruit of his ambitions.* He thought about how their beautiful petals opened and shined their brilliant light, restoring young Silas Mordall's voice. He didn't care to call it magic, but there was no doubt the boy had a supernatural connection with these flowers. Perhaps Alarin had been caught up in the moment when he placed the Imperial Seal around the boy's neck, but it was a decision he didn't regret. Silas Mordall *should* stand as the emperor of the realm, just as the First Emperor Thalastor Siven had.

When he returned to the main hall, Chamberlain Rennerin was seated at a table and sipping from a goblet that was carved as an open lotus. He was still dressed in his mourning whites and would be until the next lunar month. An honorable gesture, but Alarin didn't care for the richly embroidered sleeves and fancy silk fringes. *Is he grieving or showing off his latest ensemble?* Still, it was obvious how deeply Merio's death had affected him. The man's once plump and jovial face looked wan and withered, his once zestful air now slow and tired. And apparently, he was the type of griever who didn't eat, because a dish of roasted chicken and parboiled rice remained untouched on the raffia placemat before him.

Near the center brazier, General Szathan sat on a low stool unfastening the many straps of his blackened steel armor. Aiding him was young Silas, and it was a strange juxtaposition with the boy dressed in his high imperial silks, all white and blue flowing vestments, yet acting as a meager squire to a field officer. And of course, the boy was terribly timid and obviously inexperienced, but the big general never once snapped at the lad, nor did he ridicule or intimidate him like so many hard-boiled men are wont to do. Alarin couldn't help but admire what he saw. General Szathan Mordall may not have been known for his intellect, but such a display of patience was certainly a sign of it.

"You made a wise move," Rennerin said to Alarin. "Elevating the general's rank. Thayer Dal is a man of unsurpassed courage, a man whose past exploits are filled with derring-do."

"Some say he's a madman," Alarin admitted. "But as a commander he's loyal and capable. To throw a man like that away would be foolish."

To Alarin's left, Szathan grunted softly as he removed the unstrapped chestplate from his body. He handed it to little Silas, whose unprepared hands struggled with the weight.

"So you'll stay in the city then," Rennerin said to Alarin.

"You sound disappointed."

"No, of course not. Having you here is a boon for our city. But what about your brother Anseth?"

"He must hold the river until we uncover Seric Dyre's next move. I plan to send a rider north." His gaze drifted to Szathan.

The general ceased fiddling with his armor and fixed Alarin with a confused stare. "My lord, I'm needed at His Majesty's side."

"I can't send a nameless rider to my brother. I need a worthy name to go in my stead, someone I trust. I'd like it to be you."

Szathan's giant brow-ridge rose. "I know nothing of the northern barbarians. Not their language, not their customs, nothing."

"Anseth's the chieftain, you'll be speaking to him. He's the same man who fought at Black Gate Pass. He'll welcome you with all the respect you deserve. Trust me. I'll apprise you of the details later."

Szathan nodded, then his fingers went back to working his armor straps. Silas didn't seem happy about this, but the boy was clearly too shy to speak up. All he did was stare at his uncle with big frightened eyes, and Szathan responded to that with words of reassurance.

"A risky move," Rennerin said. "Raas Dragath may choose to build on his momentum and storm our city. Our armies are weakened, our people frightened."

"I am aware."

"Then what do you intend to do?"

"I intend to win the affections of this city."

"And how do you intend to do that?"

"By doing right by the people."

Rennerin looked dumbstruck. "And that means . . .?"

"Lowering taxes and impositions, rectifying improper laws, reducing fines and labor service, providing fairness in market pricing, raising pay, promoting prosperity in agriculture and sericulture and rural development. Basically, I plan to eliminate the separation between the wealthy and the common." He looked Rennerin in the eye. "The human factor is key. Approval, not dismissal. Motivation, not discouragement. Praise, not punishment. Hope, not despair."

Rennerin's incredulous expression twisted into a doubtful smirk. "We can't finance such an enterprise."

Alarin took a long, pointed look around the hall. "Lord Rennerin, how much do you suppose all these fancy statues are worth? If say, we took them down and sold them to overseas traders?" He kept looking, eyes moving up along the gilded brackets and molding. "And for all this gold and silver . . . we could contract a few master smiths to melt it into coin. Yes, I think it'd be worth quite a sum." He turned to face the chamberlain directly. "More than enough to offset the losses sustained by Merio's failed campaign."

Rennerin looked absolutely dumbstruck. "My Lord . . . that's not proper. The palace grounds serve as home and hearth to all civil officials. Such lavishness is needed to show the greatness of those who reside here."

"It's vulgar and ostentatious, and it does nothing except fatten noble egos while embittering the common folk. Any sensible lord of the Anir would have the excess removed."

Rennerin was tapping the tips of his plump fingers together. "Yes, well, you're right, my lord, but the dynasty of the Anir is no more. Emperor Thavian Siven is dead. We live in a new age. Under Emperor Silas Mordall, the true claimant of the throne. What he deems fitting is—"

"Stop grasping at dust, Rennerin. A wise and noble lord does not decorate himself in gold and jade and pearls, nor does he dress himself in snobbish silks and ridiculous ruffles. A wise and noble lord reduces his desires and restricts his will."

Rennerin's fingertips kept tapping. He seemed determined to counter Alarin's words, no matter the odds. "Even if you succeed in your philanthropic endeavor, it may not be enough. To stand against the Redlander army we may need the support of the capital. You should be working toward a common alliance against the man who slew your brother."

Alarin's gaze drifted down to the letter sitting patiently on his desk. "I'm aware of what I must do, Lord Chamberlain. But Zantherei hasn't thought highly of me since I had two legs. He'll blame me for Merio's death."

Rennerin didn't seem to be listening. Or if he had, it didn't register. "Zantherei is Lord Merio's brother, his blood, as he is yours. The realm knows how strong the bonds of House Athera are. I am sure he will cast aside all differences and agree to this union. Lord Zantherei's suffered a terrible hardship and an irreparable loss. His outlook will be different now."

Alarin scoffed at that. "My brother's suffered hardship and loss throughout his entire life. It only makes him colder." *If that's possible at all.* He looked down once more at the letter. "This proves my point."

"*This,*" the Lord Chamberlain said, slapping his palm flat on the desk, "was before Merio was cut down in the field. *This* was before that scoundrel Raas Dragath crushed our forces."

Alarin didn't respond. Perhaps Rennerin was right. Perhaps he should request an alliance with his brother. Forget about the Imperial Seal and forget about all the squabbling over royal entitlements —none of that was important now. The youngest son of the great Lasarin Athera had been slain in cold blood. The family he left behind will grieve, no matter where they stand. Alarin couldn't help but think of Nyvia. *The poor woman, she will be devastated.*

Without another word, Alarin sat down, lifted the brushpen from the rack, dipped it in the inkwell, and yet . . . he still couldn't bring himself to write.

CHAPTER FIVE

The thieves were a score at most, but when they forded the shallow tributary and vanished inside a stand of broad-leaved oaks, Ansetheral Athera halted the pursuit.

Horse hooves churned the spring grasses as the company of two hundred Vaskultan riders maneuvered back into formation. A fierce folk they were, each man outfitted in a fleece-lined longcoat as dark as the boiled leather armor worn beneath. Horn bows were slung across the chest, brass-buttoned quivers were strapped on the back, and single-edged backswords were sheathed at the hip. Their adornments were scant: a necklace of finger bones on one, a wristband of stretched black horn on another—in truth, they didn't need such accoutrements to appear fierce; their faces were already as hard as sun-beaten leather, their expressions as cold as midwinter frost. Anseth may not have shared their savage blood, but he commanded these men all the same. The Earthstone around his neck was proof of that, a proof he'd obtained by beating the former chieftain's son to death.

Severak Bonesplitter approached astride a shaggy mare, his hawkish face so twisted by puzzlement it was almost comical to look at. The veteran war general wore his customary longcoat trimmed in black wolf fur, which matched the lining of his baggy trousers and felt boots. And savage though he appeared, the man was as even-tempered as they come.

Unfortunately, the fiery war maiden at his side was another matter. Her name was Ikara, and she was as broad-shouldered and hardhearted as any Vaskultan male, with a face like a pottery bowl that was dropped too many times. Still, there was a certain hint of attractiveness to her features, an undeniable symmetry once you looked past the scars and dents and puffy ears. Her stature was also quite impressive; she easily towered over Anseth when not on horseback. "Why call it off?" she asked in Vaskulti, a tongue as harsh and unrefined as the northern tribes themselves. "We outnumber them ten to one."

Others agreed, which made Anseth gnaw on his lower lip. *Did I make the wrong decision? No, don't doubt yourself. A strong leader never wallows in indecision.* "I don't trust the terrain. Looks like a lure to an ensnarement."

Severak clicked his tongue at that. "A rabble like that? Doubtful. They have no order, no organization . . . how could they manage such a tactic?"

"The same way they managed to steal from our encampment without our noticing."

"But we did notice."

"Only after the third effort."

"You're too cautious," Jakken cut in. The battalion subcommander wasn't tall for a Vaskultan, but just because Anseth didn't have to crane his neck to meet his eyes didn't mean he had to like him. In truth, Anseth had only promoted Jakken because of the endorsement of his many admirers, including Severak, who had proclaimed again and again Jakken's skill as a marksman. The man was talented, no question about that. Anseth had seen him pierce the breast of an ouzel bird moving along a rocky streambed some fifty paces away and against a jagged northern wind. But as skillful as he was, the man was also moody and unsociable—poor qualities for any leader. Still, for some reason the men took to him, probably because he was loud and boastful and opinionated.

Severak gave Jakken a proud clap on the back. The two men were close comrades, but that wasn't surprising considering how adaptable Severak was. The general could find common ground with anyone—hell, even Dariok had liked him, and Dariok hated everyone.

But Dariok's dead now, dead by my hand, and every day I praise the Skybringer for that. Anseth looked ahead to the wooded cleft. White oaks and shagbark hickories skirted a stony ridge that narrowed to a lower dell. It looked darkly suspicious, a place where a forward advance might get trapped. "We stand down for now. At nightfall we'll take a closer look. A small reconnaissance party, on foot, no more than twenty. Jakken, you want the lead on this?"

"Never thought you'd ask."

Anseth took the subcommander aside to relay instructions on where to disperse his men along the stone pathways, and how to move the advance. Jakken nodded absently as he listened, his gaze fixed on the lower clefts and jagged pillars that rose like great stony limbs. The mustached man always looked one click away from anger, what with those unblinking eyes and ghoulish frown. He had a deeply receding hairline, but no regard to the shaggy nest that remained on his head. Knots and loose braids tumbling in every direction, as though he were perpetually caught in a powerful gale. "Of course, of course," he kept muttering. "Of course, understood, of course." Strange, every time Jakken spoke he also inched his mare forward. A little more. A little more and then he stopped, looked back, and with a devious little twinkle in his eye, he whipped his mare into a run.

What the hell are you doing? Anseth shouted at him to stop, but of course he didn't stop, and when Jakken raised his backsword and unleashed a furious war cry, the forward company of Vaskultan riders hoisted up their yak-tailed banners and fell in line with their rallying commander. And just like that, two hundred northern barbarians galloped off toward the lower clefts of the Stoneblade Basin, and there was nothing Anseth could do about it.

Not true, I can stop it. I must *stop it.* Anseth laid the whip to his mare and raced after them. Gusts of hot wind screamed in his ears, throwing hanks of hair into his eyes. *Bastard's defying his chieftain's command. Defying MY command.* His free hand wrenched the Earthstone talisman from his tunic, and, thrusting it skyward, he shouted at the men to stop, stop, *STOP* . . . but he might as well have been holding a rotten piece of fruit for all it mattered. The warband simply didn't hear him, and already they were deep in the cleft, bottlenecking themselves between earth and outcrop, horse hooves pitching wads of black muck behind them. Anseth laid the whip harder, rushing faster down the declension. *Damn them,* he thought. *Damn them, they're charging right into a—*

The view opened, revealing a spread of downward paths that moved around a lake and halted at a great headwall. The thieves had been corralled there, backs against the rock. Trapped. Nowhere to go. Their stolen blades were bared, and their faces were fiercely desperate—but against a fifty-yard Vaskultan fusillade they were helpless. Bows twanged and arrows screamed across the sky. It was so quick—one moment the thieves were ready for a fight, the next they were scattered about the valley, punctured and bloody and begging for quarter.

Jakken was at the fore, perched in the saddle of his black mare, that ugly ghoulish frown emblazoned on his face. "Reconnoitering complete," he said. The Vaskultans at his side contributed to that with a bit of vocal fanfare.

Anseth rode up, curved backsword in hand, pommel extended. *Crack.* The blow to the jaw sent Jakken tumbling off his horse. The onlooking Vaskultans exchanged stares; for a moment they looked ready to band together against Anseth, but then Jakken lifted himself out of the moist earth, spat a piece of a tooth, and started laughing. Laughing and snorting and laughing, with shards of mud dripping from his unkempt hair. "I deserved that," he said, then laughed some more.

Anseth dismounted from his roan. The Vaskultans moved aside as he approached the subcommander. "You're done. Stripped. You know that, yes?"

That only emboldened the man's laughter.

Anseth pointed the tip of his backsword at the man's face, right between his big stupid eyes. By the gods, if he had any less self-control he would've cut the bastard down right then and there. A clean beheading if his strike were true; a messy, partially severed one if not. *I should do it. I should. The bastard deserves it for defying me.* But Anseth wasn't a reckless man, and besides, Jakken had stopped laughing. Not only that, but the puzzled expressions plastered on all the Vaskultan faces further discouraged him. *They don't understand, they think Jakken was just following orders. Can't have them rebel over a misunderstanding.* With that, Anseth sighed and sheathed his weapon.

When Jakken finally spoke, his voice had become grave. "He claims to be the chieftain of the north, yet he has no plans to leave the south. I don't wish to follow a chieftain like that."

"But you will," Anseth said, and walked off. *No one would've done that to Lord Volduk. Not even Dariok.* He returned to Severak and Ikara and shot a glare at both. "I want Jakken clapped in a cangue. Until the full moon turns, and not a single day less."

Severak gave a halfhearted nod. He made a gesture at something. "What about them?"

Anseth turned. The few surviving thieves were sprawled out in the muck or pressed against the rock wall. One man lay in a supine position with trembling hands raised in surrender. "Leave them," Anseth said. "Or chop off their hands as punishment, I don't care.

Just bring our stolen equipment and livestock back." Anseth didn't mean to be so cruel, but he wasn't about to show any measure of clemency, not after suffering the insubordination of one of his own subcommanders. *Fear, dissent, despair, they all grow like weeds,* Lord Volduk had once told him. *From the root they must be plucked.*

The other Vaskultans would soon come to understand what had happened. Having your command blatantly disrespected was a deft blow no matter how quickly it was dealt with. Being a chieftain of the tribe was a continuous struggle for power and authority— Jakken's little offense made that quite clear. Unfortunately, Anseth still had something to prove to these barbarians . . . but prove it he would. *I am the rightful chieftain,* he thought. *Vaskultan blood or not, I am the rightful chieftain.*

Kirik Half-Ear was waiting at the perimeter of the encampment. Anseth's personal bondsman had a strangely elongated face, almost reptilian in appearance, yet still somehow pleasing to look at. He was dressed in the typical Vaskultan longcoat and baggy trousers, with braids of linen in his long hair and a bit of black tar smeared around his eyes. He may have been a thrall from a conquered tribe, but he was still one of Anseth's closest friends. Kirik was whip smart, calm under pressure, and mentally tougher than a badger. He wasn't the boastful sort either; just a no-nonsense, nothing-to-prove sort of fellow, with a surprisingly frisky sense of humor.

Right now, however, he was all seriousness. "I heard about Jakken. I should've been there."

"Your mother's ill," Anseth said, dismounting from his roan. "It's fine. Jakken will be punished."

The two men began their hike through the encampment, passing the livestock pens and horse paddocks and weaving stations and rows of fur-and-felt yurts. It was deep into dusk, so most of the activity was quiet, but the smoke billowing from the soldier yurts was thick and heavy. It was spring and it was warm—nothing like the cold of the Gray Plains. "I'm told Urryk just returned from the north. I need good news right now."

The man shook his head. "Don't have any. With Lord Volduk's death the Nidraks are pushing back, and now the Serkuts are once more whispering words of insurrection. General Kaigon requests the return of the main force."

"Does he request *my* return, or just my forces?"

Kirik cocked his head. "Someone piss in your shoes this morning, lord?"

Anseth swallowed, a bad taste in his mouth. "I've served Lord Volduk for ten years, I've lived among these people for ten years. And yet, ten years or a hundred years, to some it matters not. In their eyes, I will never be anything more than an Anirian."

"Not true. You've proven your worth ten times over, lord."

Anseth didn't reply to that. *It's all coming undone. This is Lord Volduk's fault. He made me believe in myself. What am I doing here? Am I truly stupid enough to think I could hold the tribes together? If anything, I've only made things worse.* "I need to see the Dyre boy. We'll talk again later."

With a reluctant nod, the bondsman turned and left.

The bone yurt was just ahead. A handful of burly sentinels parted to reveal young Veldries Dyre sitting alone on a fur mat just outside the entrance flap. He was draped in an oversized Vaskultan longcoat that was trimmed in fox fur. At close to twenty years his olive-toned face was becoming slim and handsome, his green eyes maturing into a sharp gaze like that of his father. In truth, he looked very much like Seric, save perhaps the fullness of his cheeks, which reminded Anseth more of his sister, Nyvia. Anseth sat down with his back against the yurt, bone-cords rattling and ratty furs wavering.

"Did you get them?" the young man murmured in the Anirian tongue. "Your livestock thieves."

Anseth nodded. "Idiots, stealing from Vaskultans." A warm rush of wind burst through the encampment, howling with a god's wrath and tugging at the edgings of the yurt. After it died, another gust swiftly followed, this one so forceful it caused a nearby sentinel to plant a hand on his head to keep his knitted cap from blowing off. Anseth's gaze drifted back to the boy. "Are you hungry? Thirsty?"

"I'd rather drink mud than that rancid stuff you call blackmilk."

Anseth smiled, but a moment later he looked down and gave a sigh. It was a regretful sigh, one that he didn't mean to express. "I'm sorry to detain you like this, but we must wait until your father's intentions are made plain."

"I know, Uncle, and I don't feel as though I'm being held against my will. You've been too kind to me. Is something wrong? I thought the thieves were dealt with."

Anseth didn't know how to answer that, but he did his best. "I ran into a snag today. A subcommander of mine used trickery to undermine my authority."

Veldries leaned back and scratched his neck, thinking. "My father once told me that a wise leader recognizes the early signs of betrayal and acts swiftly to defend himself. Did you fail to do that?"

"I . . . I suppose so." Anseth reached up to finger a loose cord dangling from the yurt. He twirled it mindlessly. "This incident is but a sliver of a greater issue. The tribes of the Gray Plains are beginning to falter. Dissent and infighting are growing unchecked. My general petitions me to mobilize the main force to the north, yet I am reluctant to leave."

"Why, Uncle?"

"My elder brother's welfare may depend on my protection."

"I understand. You can't hold the north if you don't leave the south."

"You're a shrewd young man. Your father has already taught you much."

That made Veldries laugh, a sharp squeal of a sound surely inherited from Seric. "Not so much, I reckon. I believe my father is an overrated strategist. You've already outwitted him at Amber River, drowning his men and his confidence in the flood."

"One victory doesn't make me the superior man."

Veldries shrugged. "Sure seems like it. Perhaps your barbarian gods favor you."

"I serve the Anirian gods, same as you."

The boy's youthful eyes flicked up and down. "Are you sure?"

Anseth's eyes trailed down to his Vaskultan attire. Calf-length longcoat, boots of rough doeskin, leggings of thin oxhide, plates of hard brown leather. The boy was right; he looked every bit a barbarian—and he made no attempt to hide it.

"Go north then," Veldries said, "but allow me to return to my father. I'll express in earnest how humanely you've treated me, to ensure he doesn't seek retaliation."

"I can't do that." Anseth straightened his shoulders a bit. "I can't go north, and I can't let you go. What I must do is stay and protect my elder brother. But I'm aware that once Seric Dyre finds out where you are, he will move mountains to reach you, and crush anyone in his path." He gave a defiant snort. "And I will be ready."

CHAPTER SIX

Over the passing days Miriana's face had transformed from swollen and throbbing to deflated and tender, while the color of her skin shifted from red and purple to ochre and black. Today it looked puffy and pinkish, like a child's face after an adverse reaction to a bug bite. The nose itself had grown painfully raw, and even the slightest breeze was enough to give her a sharp sting. Drawing in simple breaths became a grueling task, and she often found herself swallowing globs of spit, which occasionally carried an aftertaste of blood. It was hard to focus on anything but the pain, and, of course, the ugliness. *Oh, how ugly I've become.*

Vileron had done his best to treat her wounds, but the landscape provided little in the way of vulnerary herbs, or maybe he was just an inadequate healer. Probably the latter, since the gels of comfrey leaf did little to relieve the pain, while the anti-inflammatory herbs she ingested only seemed to worsen her countenance. She knew this because the look mirror was never far from her hand. Sometimes she gripped it so hard she could feel the tortoiseshell grooves digging into her palm. Her face was like a session of grisly torture;

no matter how heinous it was, she couldn't look away. *Damn it, why can't I stop?*

Earlier this morning, she'd stuffed the look mirror into her rucksack. That worked—but only until midday, when it found her hand again. She stuffed it deeper down, but again it returned to her hand. *This is ridiculous. Am I that undisciplined?* With a scowl and a grunt, she threw it to the ground and smashed it under the heel of her boot. She also spat on it, cursed at it—did everything except crouch down and piss on it. And when it lay shattered on the hard-packed earth, she gave a grand sigh of relief. It was over. No more gazing at her hideous face.

Through it all, Vileron hadn't said a word, but she knew what the big boor was thinking. She could all but see his stupid lips mouthing the words, *I warned you.* Yes, he did warn her, but if he hadn't abandoned her, her face would never have become such a mangled mess. She resented him for that. Perhaps even hated him. *You were supposed to protect me. Why the hell didn't you protect me?*

The broad-leaved trees crackled and whined under the relentless winds, each gust more forceful than the last. The humidity had become something of a sentient being—a living, breathing beast intent on sapping her strength by way of head pains and joint aches. And when the rain came, it never seemed to cease. *If the gods are trying to thwart my journey . . . well, they are doing a fine job.* Mud piled itself in the dikes of the untrodden bypaths, a thick heavy sludge that threatened to swallow a careless foot. Misery was at its highest now, despair at its deepest. The very thought of her private bedchamber was enough to bring Miriana to tears. Still, she refused to give up. *Can't go back, Mir. You have to keep moving south . . . and you have to stay strong.* But it was hard to stay strong when she was filthy and hungry and soaked to the bone.

"Look," Vileron said, pointing.

A plume of smoke rose skyward in the distance, melting into the gloom of cloud cover. It was a faint wisp, and yet it was the first sign of human activity they'd encountered in days. "Maybe a wine shop or roadside inn?" Miriana questioned.

"Don't think so. Too far from the road. Stay here."

"Cyrille—" She reached for his arm, but the tall man was already moving ahead.

Miriana remained there for a time, fighting an unwinnable fight against the squall. It howled at her, it threw sharp rain at her, but most of all it devoured her patience. *It's too damn wet to wait, and besides, I don't trust him wandering off without me.* Maybe she was overreacting, and if so, the downpour was to blame for that.

His tracks were easy to follow in the muck. Large prints, long strides. They led her up a narrow incline and through a stand of green-coated hickories, and there she was greeted by a solitary longhouse perched atop a rounded embankment. Such dwellings were governmentally funded and used to house displaced citizens affected by some sort of natural catastrophe. Mostly flooding, sometimes quakes. Miriana knew this because she'd signed plenty of forms for their construction. Still, this particular one seemed a bit too far from the main road, and it appeared private in ownership.

Surrounding the house was a short wall, no more than ten feet high and constructed from a variety of hardwoods in a variety of lengths and thicknesses. Vileron halted at the gate, motioning her to stay back. She approached anyway. Something had forced the gate open; iron braces were bent, wooden boards were shifted and broken. Vileron ran a finger across the splintered wood, careful not to cut himself. Then his eyes trailed down, to the mash of prints on the ground. They looked fresh. "We should leave."

"Leave? We've nowhere to go. I'm tired, I'm hungry, and I could use a bath, preferably with heated water."

"Don't you see what happened here? This is a forced entry. Bandits, most likely. Remember last time?" He pointed at his nose. "There's nothing good to be found here."

Miriana unslung her rucksack and pulled out the cestus glove. She slipped it on her hand, then pulled tight the double straps. Her fingers moved easily in it, the weight and size surprisingly comfortable.

Vileron's eyes drifted sneeringly to the weapon. "And what are you going to do with that?"

"Defend myself, if necessary."

He seemed amused. "You have to actually know how to punch to use that."

She brushed off the comment and stood on her toes to peer inside the gate. "Maybe the invaders are gone."

"Unlikely."

"I'm not afraid. These are untrained men, are they not? Three, four, five at most. No threat to someone like you."

He shot her a look of disbelief so rarely seen from the stoic man. "Who do you think I am?"

"You are the Captain of the Imperial Guard, the sworn protector of the emp—"

"I *was* the Captain of the Imperial Guard. Now I'm a defector and a deserter, a criminal to the highest degree."

"No vassal should be punished for his devotion and loyalty to his lady."

Vileron paused to sigh, then again to rub his sickle-shaped eyes. "It's unwise to go inside."

"Did you leave your guts at the Hollow? You once boasted that you could outclass the great Demien Mordall in combat. The man who slew seven traitors to save the emperor's life. You do remember your claim, yes?"

"I remember."

She scoffed. "I saw you, the day you two squared off in the emperor's chamber, right after his consort was hauled out. I saw your eyes. They looked the same as they do now. *Afraid.*"

His jaw clenched. "Don't goad me, woman. I'm the only protection you have."

Miriana was shocked at how carelessly he called her 'woman'. "You must've forgotten how I enlisted and ennobled you, how I groomed you to become the Captain of the Imperial Guard. Without me, you'd still be a smalltime ruffian breaking bones for rich moneylenders. Am I wrong? Am I, Cyrille?"

His wormy gray lips parted, but no words came out. He simply stared at her. She could tell he was focusing on her busted nose, and probably her blackened eyes. The urge to hide her face crept up on her. She also thought about checking her likeness in the look mirror, but then she remembered breaking the thing yesterday. *Was it only yesterday? It feels like a month ago.* Uncomfortable and frustrated, she pushed past him. "I suggest you follow this time."

He hissed at her to wait, but she ignored that and slipped inside the broken gate, her feet pushing through sludge and slop as she advanced toward the main entranceway. The structure itself looked old and tumbledown, the roof a sunken semi-arch that dearly needed re-thatching. The timber walls were poorly reinforced by a patchwork of heavy cloth and animal skins, which the rain battered mercilessly.

Vileron urged her to turn around. He reached out to grasp her arm, but paused before he could get hold of her, his nose raised in a scrunch. "Do you smell that?"

Miriana said no; she couldn't smell anything because her nose was busted, but Vileron didn't seem to realize that. "Smells of overcooked meat," he said.

Miriana's gaze drifted up to the haze of smoke, so faint in the heavy rain. "Around back." She turned away from the longhouse and moved along a winding cobbled footpath, skirting the rectangular garden plots of warm season melons and gourds and amaranths and green grams. Gardening tools and grafting equipment lay carelessly about, weeders and tillers and trowels half-buried in the muck, as if discarded with unexpected urgency. Beyond that stood a large circular well of mortared brickwork, ceramic-coated and ringed in a glaze of frost. Rising over the well was a vertical pole with a Y-notched pivot, a contraption to suspend a reed basket for drawing water, though the bottom pit looked all but empty.

Nearby was a shallow ditch, and inside this ditch lay the source of the smoke. Miriana moved closer. Even she could smell the char now, a pungent punch that made her frown despite the rain and her broken nose. She didn't want to look—and yet she forced her booted feet another step closer. Closer and closer . . . until finally she saw it. A smoldering heap of blackened bodies, four adults and two children and one tiny babe, all thrown together in what appeared to be an act of extreme cruelty. It was an awful sight, a horrendous sight—empty black sockets staring lifelessly up at the sky. Sockets that once held eyes, and eyes that once held dreams and opinions and purposes and loves. Now all those things were gone, gone like the smoke in the heavy rain. *Be strong, Mir, strong as silk. Strong as—*

Nausea twisted her insides and vomit rose in her throat. She gagged and covered her mouth, only to spew the morning's meal onto her hand. It wasn't much: a few chunks of squirrel meat and a few boiled pinecones—all brown and sticky between her fingers.

Vileron looked disappointed. "My lady . . ."

"I'm fine," Miriana said brusquely, though moments later she had to fight another urge to vomit. She didn't know why she was reacting this way. She'd seen worse—she was strong, and she'd seen worse. *Get a hold of yourself, Mir.* Vileron tried to usher her back, but Miriana wrenched herself away from his grip. She heard a strange sound. A woman crying, or maybe a girl. It was hard to tell, since it wasn't a loud whine or an urgent wail, just a low, mournful sobbing.

She continued past the ditch and moved toward the longhouse.

The structure itself was built on stout wooden posts, so she had to climb a rickety stairway to reach the rear entrance. The door was neither barred nor locked, just a rough-joined slab of wood swinging idly in the wind. Her body tensed when she pulled it open, but it made no sound in the driving rain. Inside, a long corridor stretched over a ground floor where chickens and other livestock lived between the wooden posts. To her left were the separate, private rooms. The first looked like a place where domestic work was done. The second was a kitchen area. The third room was where she heard the sobbing.

Miriana nudged aside the door curtain for a peek. In the center of the room, a thin waif of a girl lay curled up on the hard floor-boards, half-clothed in muddy tatters. Poor thing looked no older than sixteen, not far from Miriana's age when she'd first entered the life of a courtesan. And like Miriana she was quite handsome too, although right now she looked sadder and more frightened than anything else. A longhaired man stood over her, filthy hands working to remove his own muddy clothes, a slow and clumsy showing.

Anger rose in her heart. *Bastard is keeping her alive for pleasure.* She nudged Vileron forward with her cestus glove. The stoic man resisted, but that only made her nudge harder. "Help her," she mouthed. *Help that poor girl.*

Vileron's thin eyes weren't focused on the girl or even the man; they were darting around the room, making sure there were no others around. Once satisfied, his huge hand dropped to the hilt of his sheathed dagger, and with that he moved inside.

It was so easy. The clattering rain allowed Vileron to move swiftly and quietly, his booted feet trailing the tiniest splotches of mud on the floorboards. He stopped directly behind the longhaired man, loomed over him while the oblivious wretch continued to undress himself. Vileron's hands rose slowly . . . ever so slowly. The bandit, now bare-chested, stepped out of his trousers and moved to his smallclothes. After peeling them off, he spent a moment teetering naked and off-balance, and just when he righted himself, a heel slipped and he stumbled back—right into the brick wall that was Cyrille Vileron.

One gauntleted hand seized the nude man's hair; the other drove the dagger into the back of the skull. A quick in-out motion, silky smooth, like sticking your finger in a bowl of junket. The man never knew what happened. One moment he was disrobing and humming, the next he was dropped to the floor like a sack of old meat. With his bare legs awkwardly splayed, Miriana paused at the sight of his manhood, the way it twitched mindlessly for a few moments, before shrinking like a sausage in the sun.

The girl remained lying on her side, still making that low sobbing sound. Miriana grabbed the dead man's discarded cloak and placed it over her, gently, like a mother swaddling a newborn. *Poor little thing, I'm sure you were once so full of life, but now look at you, so sad and damaged.* Miriana leaned close and whispered in the girl's ear, whispered that it would be all right, that nothing bad would happen to her. The girl eventually stopped sobbing and looked up—but not because of Miriana's consoling words. No, it was a panicked look, brought on by the muffle of voices outside the room. Drunken slurs and vulgar belches followed by bouts of laughter. Vileron immediately sidled up beside the door curtain, bloodied dagger in hand.

The girl began to tremble. Miriana was growing impatient. "If you want to live through this," she whispered, "tell me how many more there are. I can't help you unless you tell me."

The little girl's hand twitched. Two fingers. Miriana flashed the number to Vileron. He nodded.

One bandit's voice grew louder. "Hey idiot, you almost finished? I want a piece of her before this wine wears off." He started to laugh, but when no reply came, the laughter abruptly stopped. "Oi, did you hear me?"

Vileron stared sidelong at Miriana, frozen like a statue. The bandit's drunken footfalls grew louder and louder before they stopped just outside the door. Miriana saw his bare feet beneath the curtain, big toe scratching the top of his other foot. "Idiot must've passed out," he grumbled. Then, louder: "I'm coming in."

The door curtain rose with a low *whoosh*. The shirtless bandit stood in the threshold, one hand scratching his hairy potbelly. He stopped scratching when he saw Miriana. "Who the fuck are you?"

Vileron drove the point of the dagger into the man's breast. The bandit stumbled back, arms flailing, but when he righted himself, he gazed down at the wound, eyes staring dumbly at the slit in his flesh. A moment later his mouth opened, but before he could speak or scream or do whatever the hell he was about to do, Vileron's second slash tore a chunk out of his neck. The body collapsed with a squelching *thump*, blood from the gashes pooling near the girl's feet.

Vileron spat. Blood painted his scarred face in dots and streaks, with more speckling his cloak and chestplate. Miriana was speechless. She couldn't even warn him when a second figure came bounding inside. This bandit was larger than expected—and surprisingly quick, too. When Vileron grabbed him, the man drove his shoulder forward to break the hold and drop Vileron hard on his rump. Miriana must've screamed, because the huge bastard turned his head and fixed her with a cold gaze. "Stay there," he growled, then turned and fell upon Vileron.

Thunderous fists followed, *boom, boom, boom,* each pounding against Vileron's upraised vambraces. Miriana watched in horror. *Help him, Mir, you have to help him.* A few blows were getting through; she could hear the thump of Vileron's head against the floorboards. She made a fist of the cestus and took a few steps forward. *Hit him, hurry up and HIT HIM.* She raised the fist, but the bandit shoved her back with a single hand. "I told you to fucking *stay*," he hissed. For a moment she did stay, but then she realized

that she was Miriana Athera, not some trifling whore to be intimidated by some lowlife scum. She marched forward and punched
him with her cestus glove, *bang,* right in the side of the head. But
the man didn't even seem to notice, so she threw her arms over the
bandit's shoulders and gave a hard yank.

Next she knew, the floorboards were beneath her and he was on
top of her, pinning her down with powerful hands. The warmth of
his breath touched her face, but she didn't smell a thing. She could
hear him though, could hear him grunting and muttering curses.
One hand wrapped itself around Miriana's throat, while the other
pushed down on her face, forcing it sideways. *I can't breathe.* Her
lungs seemed ready to burst, her teeth ready to crack. She reached
up in desperation, clawing and punching at his face. It was no use.
The bandit postured up to protect his eyes, so Miriana shoved two
fingers inside the bastard's mouth, hooking the inside cheek. She
pulled and pulled, and the man's skin stretched and stretched, but
the bastard *still* wouldn't let go of the choke. Her strength began to
fade, and as her hand dropped to the floor she stared helplessly
across the room, at the little girl who still wasn't moving. *Help me .
. . help me, you little brat. Why won't you help me?*

Darkness crept upon her like evening fog. *I don't want to die
like this,* she thought. *I don't want to die like this.* Her hand slapped
the floorboards, a desperate attempt to find something, anything . . .
but there was nothing. All she kept thinking about was her stupid
decision to enter this place. Vileron was right. *We should've stayed
away . . . we should've stayed away. But we didn't, and now we're
going to—*

The bandit's hands vanished from her neck. Air rushed into her
lungs, cold, precious air. For a long moment she lay there, breathing
in and out, in and out, while beads of red dripped down her nose.
The wound . . . it must've reopened. She pawed away the blood and
turned to look at the bandit, and to her surprise she saw that Vileron
was perched atop him. He'd put his dagger through the bandit's eye

socket, so deep the crossguard caved the man's orbital bone, while the blade-tip emerged from the back of the head to jam itself like a nail into the floorboards. Blood was leaking out, along with that strange clear fluid of the eye.

Vileron rolled off the man, taking huge breaths. His gaze drifted from the dead bandit to Miriana, and when their eyes met his bruised face offered a nod that seemed to say, *I hope the girl is worth it.* With that, he braced himself on his elbows to rise, but paused when something caught his eye. "Where's she going?"

Miriana turned. The little girl was on her feet and limping toward the exit. "Don't leave," Miriana called. "*Wait.*"

The girl ignored her and continued on, bare feet pattering down the corridor. Miriana pulled herself up and went after her. "Wait, wait . . . *please.*" Her voice sounded terribly hoarse. She swung the door open and stumbled out into the rain, holding her achy head with her free hand. A knee buckled; she grabbed the stairway's wooden railing for support, then shrugged off the pain and moved toward the smoky ditch. The girl was there, on her knees, over-looking the blackened bodies, her sobbing resumed and more sorrowful than ever.

Miriana bent down and put a gentle hand across the girl's shoulders. "I'm sorry about your family. But you're safe now. No one will hurt you."

The girl didn't answer. She remained on her knees, unmoving except for the slight vibrations of her body as she wept over the blackened corpses. Miriana tried once more to console her, but the girl didn't seem to hear her. Without warning she rose and was off again, this time in a full run. Miriana shouted at her. "*Wait. WAIT. Where are you—*"

The girl dove headfirst into the well. She didn't scream as she fell, but there were plenty of sounds to be heard. A low scuff, an awful thump, and a final, sickening *crack,* which must've been her little body finally meeting the bottom.

CHAPTER SEVEN

Seric Dyre was bored of this city.

Aster Falls, the great eastern port of the Anir, he thought with scorn. It wasn't so grand—in fact it was little more than a seaside stinkhole filled with greedy fishmongers, cutthroat traders, and sweaty seamen.

He often thought that he'd find some measure of contentment once he settled in. Perhaps he'd grow to appreciate the way the waterfront twinkled at twilight, or the way the district gates, building terraces, jetty walls, garden pergolas, and rooftops all glowed under the stretches of lantern light. It was like a great bright swath cutting across a giant shadow, a brilliant illumination of gold and crimson that gave life to the palace halls and towers and endless tilework.

But no, he never grew to appreciate it. Nor did he enjoy the public displays of devotion that the civil and military officials showed the former lord, Emeron Mathius. Months later and *still* they grieved for him. Seric didn't need a constant reminder of an old, dead friend. *Or his menagerie of stupid songbirds.* In fact, he planned to authorize an order to execute any man who was found publicly mourning—and he would've, were it not for General Wyath's reproval. *He's a man of good conscience,* Seric thought.

The two were walking along the promenade of the palatial district, both clad in light cotton cloaks that were clasped over burnished plates of case-hardened steel. It'd been weeks since Seric had worn armor, and it felt heavier and tighter than expected, especially around the midsection where the black cords bit into him. He'd rather have thought that his squire did a poor job of girding it on, but in truth, he'd probably gained a bit of weight over the past month or so. Inactivity usually did that to a person.

General Wyath Silth looked as trim as ever. The man had just reached his thirtieth year, and his slender, upright frame rose to a narrow face that looked dignified and sensible. A traditionalist of the Anir, Wyath was a simple man, humble and loyal and direct. A sharp contrast to Seric's often showy disposition, and yet they meshed like brothers all the same. And the people here, as mournful as they were about Lord Emeron's death, were quick to accept Lord Wyath as their new lord and protector, just as Seric knew they would.

"At this meeting," Seric said. "Whatever happens . . . I'll not forget how loyal you've been to me."

"Don't be so dramatic. I'm not abandoning you, or this city."

"Consider your future. A wise man always looks toward his greatest gain."

"That sounds like an ambitious man. I'd reckon that a wise man never forsakes his lord and master without just cause."

That little show of faith made Seric clap him on the back. They reached the end of the promenade, then crossed an arched footbridge and moved into the heart of the palatial district. Above, flags and banners flapped carelessly from tall pine spars. Lower, sentries bowed their heads and stood aside, each clad in feathered cloaks that had the quills painstakingly removed. Seric brushed past them without a word, then weaved around a porter carrying a large sack with the aid of a trumpline, all while ignoring the persistent beckoning of a young bootblack.

The meeting hall was a three-storied structure with a projected roof and gray-glazed tiles. It had an elegance to it that the other halls lacked, a feathery and floral façade fronted by a colonnade of stone and soft turquoise. The main entrance was barred by two giant slabs of lacquered wood, so Seric chose to move through a much smaller and less obvious wicket door. Inside, the avian theme continued, as beautifully etched pillars rose from a floor of spiraling travertine tiles that made him dizzy if he stared too long. Milling about the main area was a company of about fifty Anirian soldiers, hard and rowdy men strapped in blackened mail and serrated gray cloaks.

Seric looked around. "Where is he? I don't see—"

"There," Wyath said, pointing.

The envoy stood at the far end of the room, a small figure who stood not in the typical flat-footed stance of a man, but in a smoother, less linear style of a woman. *A female envoy?* Seric moved closer, pushing through the haze of steel armor and gray cloaks. As he approached, the figure turned—and Seric halted. It wasn't just any woman, but a woman he knew well. "Nyvia?"

An awkward moment of silence followed. Seric averted his eyes, unsure of how to greet her. *Should I embrace her, should I rebuke her, or should I just politely bow?* He couldn't come to a decision, so in the end he simply asked, "You're the envoy?"

She ignored the inane question. "My son—is there word of my son?"

So that's why you've come. Seric gave a soft shake of his head. *Of course, a mother's love is boundless.* He decided not to answer that question just yet. "Sit with me. On the dais, away from the noise. Come. Are you going to sit?"

She gave a hesitant nod before following him up the small steps to a lacquered long table. The surface was dusty and due for a good soaping, just as the floor was in need of a good sweeping. Seric's eyes wandered to other issues in need of attention . . . but then he realized all he was doing was avoiding Nyvia's gaze. *She was once your wife. Look at her.* He didn't know why he had such a tough time doing so, but when he finally did meet her eyes, he was surprised by what he saw.

Her usually plump face had thinned a bit, but whether it was a natural thinning—or perhaps caused by grief or stress—he couldn't say. Still, the new teardrop shape allowed her large eyes to command more attention, and her ashy eyeshadow enhanced that with a touch of desirability. Her outfit was a long outer jacket worn over an imperial blue blouse with an inverted pleat in the center. Leggings were slim and black, shoes were flat-soled and made of cattle hide, and a fashionable silvered circlet pulled back the curls of her dark hair. She looked a bit more self-assured, like she did during the early days of their marriage.

Maybe he was overselling her appearance. He'd been alone for quite a while now. Not to say he hadn't spent time in the brothels of the upper districts but bedding a lowborn whore had quickly grown humdrum. No matter how beautiful or buxom or bold in bed, they all paled in comparison to Lady Miriana. *How could they not?* Miriana was an empress . . . a beautiful empress at that, and Seric had shared his pillow with her on multiple occasions. Still, those moments of pleasure had become a hazy memory, as if they never happened at all.

But Nyvia was his first love, the esteemed daughter of the former regent Lasarin Athera. Since then he'd always favored women of nobility. Perilia Valayne was one of those women, the minxish governess of Silverleaf. Seric thought about her often. Too bad she remained halfway across the realm, stuck with that sickly old slob she called her husband. Seric had sent a missive to her when he'd first arrived in Aster Falls but had yet to receive a reply.

Nyvia cleared her throat. "Don't mistake this for a personal visit. I come to you strictly as Emperor Zantherei Athera's imperial envoy."

Seric wasn't used to her direct and diplomatic manner. For so long she had been timid and soft spoken, and he had to catch himself from scoffing outright. "Nyvia, this is silly. An envoy? What do you know of military affairs?"

"Will I be heard or not?"

Seric leveled his gaze at her. "Fine. So, what does the His Majesty's imperial envoy wish to speak to me about?"

"He seeks to unite the upper provinces under a single banner of the Anir."

"Of course he does. *His* banner, the tyrannical—"

"He seeks an alliance, Seric."

"An alliance . . . with me?" Seric wasn't expecting that. "Lady Miriana has agreed to this?"

"Lady Miriana no longer serves the Anir."

A chill crawled up Seric's spine, quick and uncomfortable like a centipede. "What's happened to her? Where is she?" *Zantherei, you cruel bastard, if you've harmed one lock of her pretty hair I swear I'll kill you and everyone you love. Including your little envoy of a sister here.*

Nyvia raised her gaze slightly, extending her chin, as if to take note of his reaction.

Seric didn't care if he looked like a worrisome wretch. He needed to know the truth. "Tell me what happened, Nyvia. You have to tell me. Did something happen to her? Did something happen to—"

"She's gone, Seric. On the day of my brother's coronation she fled the capital. There's a reward for either her capture or any lead on her whereabouts, but nothing tangible has stirred yet."

It took him a long moment to digest that. *She fled because she fears for her life, and rightly so. She should've killed her husband when I told her to.* He pictured the poor woman alone in the wilds, drained and hungry and desperate for aid. *Sweet Miriana, where have you gone?* For a moment, the briefest of moments, he wondered if she would seek sanctuary here at Aster Falls. *It's possible . . . yes, perhaps she realized there's decency in me after all. My past actions may have been falsehearted, but my love for her has always been true.*

His expression must've evinced too much emotion, because Nyvia frowned at him. "She used you, Seric. You were only a means to her."

The words hurt, spiteful though they were. Seric's mouth opened, but it took some time for the reply to come out. "It matters not."

A large and slope-shouldered attendant appeared to offer a serving of wine. Nyvia declined with courteous grace, while Seric gave a curt flick of his hand. When the man was gone, Nyvia continued. "You must acknowledge my brother as the true emperor of the Anir. Before him you will kneel, but against the false lords and pretenders of the realm you will stand. Do you comply with His Majesty's wishes?"

"Do *you?*" he shot back. "You know your brother is a false lord just as much as Raas Dragath and the little Mordall boy are. So I have to ask, how do you feel about that? Your own brother claiming something that's not his by right."

She crossed her arms. "It's not my place to *feel* anything. You're speaking of sentiment, Seric. I am here on the principle of duty."

She's too prepared, most likely coached. "And what happens if I do accept this offer of alliance?"

"You will mobilize your forces and march upon the city of Stormhaven, and once there you will crush the enemy, subdue the populace, and bring Alarin and the Mordall boy in fetters back to the capital."

"So, he wants me to bloody my hands while his stay clean."

"No one's hands will be clean."

Seric tapped his cleft chin with the tip of a finger, then his hand moved down to touch his plain black neckerchief. He wore it to cover the scar given to him by Raas Dragath's assassin. It was different from the silk filigreed cloth Nyvia had given him, and she gestured to it, noticing. "I see you've already discarded my gift."

"It was lost at the battle of Amber River." He added that he was sorry, and after a thoughtful pause he said, "As much as I'd like to set my revenge against Alarin for slandering my name, I don't wish to aid Zantherei by doing so. Even if I did—and again I don't—it'd be a bit difficult given my current circumstances. You see, there's a horde of barbarians poised between my city and Stormhaven. A horde commanded by yet *another* brother of yours, the crafty little Ansetheral."

She was looking at him with those round eyes of hers. It reminded him of the way she used to look at him, that long-ago time in which they'd laughed and shared secrets and bedded one another. Before Veldries was born, and before he treated her so poorly. "I'm sure you're aware of my defeat at Amber River," he said. "Does it surprise you to learn who orchestrated such a maneuver? The Athera clansmen are like leeches. Latching on and sucking the life out of everything good. And like leeches, they're a pain to get rid of."

Those round eyes of hers dropped, a sudden and dejected motion. "Not all of them. Merio is dead."

The news stunned him. *What does it mean for the province, and the realm?* Obviously, it was a terrible blow for the city of Stormhaven, but at the same time, it placed Alarin in a position to take command of the city, an opportunity he'd not likely pass up. Still, Seric didn't know how to reply to the news. *Should I console her? Should I act aloof?* In the end, all he managed was, "How?"

"Cut down in battle by Raas Dragath's own hand." Nyvia's voice was shaky. She loved Merio, just as she loved all her brothers. Seric saw the anguish in her eyes, and oddly enough he took a small bit of pleasure in it, even though he knew it was wrong. *Yes, there's the fragile woman I remember.* "So that's what spurned Zantherei's little crusade to conquer the south. A justified vengeance."

Her expression didn't change, but her voice became firm. "You still didn't answer me. Will you agree to this alliance and march against Stormhaven or not?"

"Look . . . to accomplish such a task requires more resources than I have. War is nasty work, and it's also expensive."

"You'll receive funds to cover a portion of your provisions and wages."

"I'll also need more hands in the field."

"You already have plenty. Seven full regiments, that's seven thousand Anirian soldiers. And that's not counting your Zhoulish auxiliaries."

Seric leaned back to coolly regard her. "I see Lord Zantherei has primed you well for this meeting." He rubbed the scar beneath his neckerchief. "It's still not enough."

"A so-called master strategist like yourself doesn't need to outnumber his enemies. He only needs to outfox them."

Another line straight out of Zantherei's mouth. By the gods I hate him. "True, but to do so I need brave and worthy generals at my command. I'm told Aldebron Pentagath has returned to the capital. Is that true?"

She nodded. "General Pentagath has been appointed vanguard commander of the campaign against Raas Dragath."

Seric tried to hide his disappointment. "A worthy man fighting for a worthy cause. Raas Dragath is a warmongering traitor who deserves to die."

"I agree."

Seric's eyes drifted to the crowd of gray cloaks. A large veteran with a few missing teeth was drunk and growing rowdy, so much so that an officer from Aster Falls had to intervene. Fortunately, the situation de-escalated before Seric also needed to get involved.

"Zantherei will conquer the Redlands," Nyvia went on, "while you will conquer Riverwind. And once you succeed in taking Stormhaven, you will be welcomed back to the capital, where you shall receive a full pardon for your past transgressions."

"And?"

She smiled at that, as if to acknowledge Seric's predictability. "Saving your own skin isn't enough for you. Always need some sort of private gain."

He nodded briefly. "You're not wrong."

"Well, you won't be reinstated as the realm's Imperial Advisor, if that's what you seek."

"So what will I receive?"

"A tactician's position, which is more than you deserve.'

"Better than working an abacus for your cousin. Why is Zantherei in such a forgiving mood?"

"In these uncertain times he needs talented and capable men at his side. You are one of these men. And oh, he would like his saber back. You know, Sunburst?"

Seric feigned a sheepish smile. "Why my dear former wife, I know nothing of this weapon you speak of."

"Don't play games, Seric, I know you far too well. Now about the proposal. Do you agree or not?"

Seric thought about it. To return to the Hollow and be cleared of all transgressions was tempting, but to serve the rest of his career as a middling military official was not. Betrayal or not, he certainly deserved more. He already ruled over Aster Falls; it was all his now. The coin, the power, the lordship over other high ministers. He couldn't give that up to return to a life of groveling to that prick Zantherei Athera.

He rose, an abrupt movement. "I appreciate your time, Lady Nyvia, but I must decline your brother's offer."

She looked stunned, confounded, shocked as though Seric had

just kicked her in the shin. "What do you mean, 'no'? This isn't a negotiation. You must submit to my brother's demands."

"Or what?

She glared at him but offered no further words, then her eyes dropped to the floor, as if looking for an answer there. When she finally spoke, her voice was much quieter. "So . . . you're declining?"

"Don't look so surprised, my dear."

She didn't seem to hear that. Her big doe eyes were still cast down. "I thought you were a smarter man than this, Seric. I thought more of you."

"Insult me all you want, but my answer is still no. And Zantherei can stick his prick in a viper hole for all I care. Wait— what are you doing?"

She'd risen from her seat. "I'm leaving. The matter is closed, and there's nothing left to discuss."

"You're leaving now? You've only just arrived."

She'd already turned away, and now she was organizing her men to depart. For some reason, Seric didn't want her to leave. Not yet. "I never told you about Veldries. Do you wish to know what happened to our son?"

The mention of his name gave Nyvia pause. She spun on him, her teardrop face twisted into a scowl. "I already know what happened, Seric. You lost him at the river. Tell me, did you recover his body?"

Seric looked down. "No, I . . ."

She stomped forward to stand directly in front of him. For a second Seric thought she would slap him, but she didn't. All she said was, "Goodbye," before turning back around and walking off.

"Nyvia, wait. Don't go. Zirian, stop her."

The massive bareheaded Zhoul moved in front of the lady, olive-skinned hands clutching a giant, crescent-bladed axe. Nyvia had no choice but to stop; even her largest guardsmen seemed to shrink away from the Mad Wolf. Without turning she spoke. "Let me leave, Seric."

"You can leave if you wish . . ." Seric began. He moved around the table to stand at her side. "But I implore you to stay. A week, a fortnight. Stay and enjoy the beauty of spring." He took her arm, gently, but not in a way that would be mistaken as tender or affectionate. "My spies and scouts are combing every inch of the river. Word of our son is expected any day now. Trust me, Nyvia. I will find out what happened to him."

Nyvia's features were lost in the shadow of the towering Zhoul. When she turned her head to meet Seric's eyes, the darkness retreated to reveal a face etched in indignation. "Fine, I'll stay."

"Good, thank you. Now you can witness my rise as king of Whitecrow."

BOOK II: RETALIATION

CHAPTER EIGHT

The arrival of summer was swift and urgent in the northern heartland. The plenteous spring rains had dwindled to an insignificant footnote, and the long stretches of sunshine scorched the land with the spitefulness of a god. It was an insistent and unbearable heat, one that cracked the topsoil and starved the root systems of the outlying forestland. Only three weeks in and already the sweeping stands of hickories and oaks were browning with thirst, while the once lush and verdant meadows were left to wither like untended gardens. The dearth of moisture had grown so critical that rumors of wildfires were not uncommon.

Szathan Mordall wished he hadn't worn his heavy battledress— or better yet, he wished he hadn't agreed to embark on this little expedition at all. He sat astride a barded snowflake stallion, the beast's neck and withers lathered in sweat, its breathing growing more rapid and unsteady by the quarter-hour. When Szathan dismounted to check its gums, he saw the usual healthy pink color, but the beast's unsteady gait persuaded him to stay off the saddle for a time. A nagging headache persuaded Szathan to remove his winged halfhelm, and not long after he removed his chestplate, too.

His under-silks were drenched in sweat. *I must look like a hairless bugbear after a bath.* A humorous sight, no doubt, but Szathan didn't have the energy to feel embarrassment. He was big and he was ugly, and there was no avoiding that.

The weather brought back memories of his younger days, those carefree summer mornings in which he and his brother Demien would practice arms beneath the oak tree near the family farmstead. Monster and Huntsman was their favorite game, a combative take on the pursuit-evasion type. Funny thing was, Szathan hadn't always been cast as the monster. That thought made him smile. *You were always considerate of me, Brother, even when others were not. Without your support, I wouldn't be where I am today. I wouldn't be who I am today.* A heavy sigh left his body, and with it came a pang of grief. *The world isn't the same without Demien Mordall.*

Just after noontide, outriders cycled back with the location of the Vaskultan encampment, but it wasn't until the hour before dusk that Szathan himself had arrived. Rows and rows of rounded, felt-covered tents greeted him from the lee of a stony hillside, like a cluster of undisturbed anthills. *What a strange way to live,* Szathan thought, *to have a home and hearth that travels with you like a giant rucksack.* A nomad's life seemed an impractical one, but even he knew better than to underestimate these barbarians. Rumors told of their resilience and durability, but it was their unpredictable and hot-blooded nature that made Szathan uneasy. And though Alarin had assured him that he would be received without any trouble, Szathan donned his chestplate and urged his company of riders to remain alert.

But alert or not, it made no difference at all.

Shadows rose from unseen dugouts in the ground, shadows that swiftly became leather-clad warriors. Twenty, maybe thirty in all, each with bow drawn and arrow knocked. Szathan halted and proffered the kidskin pouch in his hand—slowly, gingerly, without any sudden movements. The barbarian who snatched it was tall and robust and clad in black wolf-hide with black trimmings. His hard and hawkish face studied the pouch's horned Sadralen mark and outer lines of filigree, and then his eyes flicked up to give Szathan the same measure of consideration.

"From Alarin Athera," Szathan said, but he wasn't sure if the words were understood. Yet after a few grunts and a few quick motions, the leader in black turned around and led Szathan's company into the barbarian encampment . . . and what an encampment it was.

What looked like a ragtag cluster of yurts was actually a carefully structured arrangement to deflect the elements and defend against enemies. The rounded, conical walls were wrapped in a light patchwork of linen and felt, and each framed level was tightly secured by horsehair ropes. Tent flaps were open and bottommost layers were raised to provide ventilation in this muggy air, while peaked roofs allowed cookfire smoke to escape. As uniform as the yurts appeared, not all were built the same. Some were cruder and smaller in style (perhaps for thralls or squires), some had extra padding of fur and felt (perhaps for the sickly and moribund), and some were larger and framed in yak or water buffalo bones (perhaps for those of higher rank).

Vaskultan warriors stared from behind various barricades and blockades, eyes cold and brooding like those of prowling wolves. Even the women looked bone-hard and belligerent, quite the opposite of the generally docile ladies of the Anir. Still, most barely spared Szathan more than passing glance, which was odd considering how unusual the general must've appeared to them. *A giant pale-skinned man in a taloned battledress receives so little attention. Unexpected . . . but not unappreciated.* Deeper within the encampment, Szathan saw a sizeable number of busy-bee workers, from felt makers to wool beaters to canvas layers and sledge pullers. Livestock herders tended the pens of goats, sheep, swine, and a rather colorful assortment of fowl, while butchers and smiths and fletchers worked their trades beneath the open sky. The master bowyers seemed especially respected, and it wasn't hard to understand why. Vaskultan bows were not some crude tools of war; no, these were meticulous carvings of horn and wood, strung expertly with gut to give a precise pull and tension. Years of innovation matched with years of experience—a truly formidable combination.

The chieftain's yurt was in the heart of the encampment, a huge structure, four or five times the size of an average dwelling. Similarly large yurts stood around it, and although Szathan wasn't the smartest of men, he could tell this was done to keep the exact whereabouts of the chieftain concealed. When the Vaskultan escort stopped, a narrow-necked groom approached to take the reins from Szathan's hands, and with that, the big general headed toward the indicated yurt.

Unlike the entrance flaps of other yurts, this particular structure had a door, and this door was a large slab of corded bones with a second cloth door behind it. There were no nails or hinges but hard dowels that fit into holes in the framework, and hanging beside these dowels were leather bags full of a sharp-smelling liquid. Before moving inside, the Vaskultan commander grabbed one and swished it around a bit, probably a ritual churning of that nasty fermented drink the barbarians enjoyed. Blackmilk, they called it.

Inside the yurt was rather cool compared to the outer swelter, but it was also so dark Szathan could barely make out the silhouettes of the waiting trio of Vaskultan guardsmen. They were huge men, not so tall as Szathan (although one came impressively close), and when they stood aside, the room opened into three openwork chambers. Furnishings were spare: a blade rack, a saddle stand, some earthenware crockery, dingy shag furs on the floor, and a few sundry items. At the rear of the center chamber, Szathan saw two figures standing in the semidarkness. One was a lean and muscular fellow with a sharp chin and an abnormally elongated jaw. He appeared to be guarding the second man, who was rather diminutive in build, although Szathan could tell he was a man of respect. *Are you the one I'm looking for?* It was difficult to see past his long black hair and dirt-stained complexion, but moving closer, yes, Szathan could see now, the man's face was pale. He was an Anirian, without question. *You must be Ansetheral Athera.*

Szathan lowered his head in a deep and solemn bow.

————

He's huge, Anseth thought. Not only was he huge, but it was an unnatural size, with proportions that were ugly and ungainly and downright peculiar. Small facial features with a great block-like head; small wrists with great bearpaws for hands. His armor made him look even more colossal, especially the bulky chestplate, segmented cuisses, and those sharp, talon-edged spaulders. The man was so tall he could barely stand without grazing the roof poles. Even Anseth's personal guardsmen—giants in their own right— couldn't match his height.

"Should I make him kneel?" Kirik's reptilian face was peeking out from behind the giant man's arm, a rather amusing sight—and rare to see the bondsman so dwarfed. *I can only imagine how I must appear,* Anseth mused. *Like a child, no doubt.*

"Let him stand. The pouch, please."

Kirik handed it over. Anseth used a single finger to rub at the texture of the goat leather, tracing the grooves of the Sadralen sigil and the markings of filigree. At length, he took in a deep breath, then he removed the letter and read:

. . .

I wanted to come to you personally but pressing issues have prevented our overdue reunion. With great sadness I must inform you that our brother Merio was slain in battle against Raas Dragath. His campaign to subjugate the Redlands has ended in failure, and it is with a heavy heart that I ask you, as a brother and as an ally, to decamp and join me at Stormhaven. Together we will chart a course of vengeance and victory for the true emperor of the realm. With bated breath I await your reply. – Alarin.

Anguish struck the back of Anseth's knees like a mallet. *Merio . . . are you truly gone?* His eyes fell from the letter. It wasn't supposed to happen like this. No, upon Anseth's return the clan was supposed to unite in grand and glorious fashion. Friends and family members all laughing and embracing and raising their flagons of wine, a celebration in a joyous hall with lively music and great black Sadralen banners. *But no . . . I wasn't there to protect him, and now he's gone, and there are only three brothers left.* It wasn't supposed to happen like this. *Merio wasn't supposed to die, neither was my father, or even Emeron Mathius. How can I remain with my northern tribe when my homeland is embroiled in conflict?*

And yet, Anseth had waited so long to become the Vaskultan chieftain. He couldn't just abandon his position now. *Nearly a decade of toil and turmoil, from captive to commander to chieftain. I am the Supreme Lord now, through and through.* And as such, there was only one move he *should* make. But he was torn.

Anseth snapped free of his thoughts. He was suddenly aware that his guardsmen were teasing the big general in the Vaskultan tongue. With a curt command he put a stop to that nonsense.

Kirik leaned forward and spoke quietly. "Something wrong, lord?"

Anseth answered that with the shake of his head. He folded the letter and fixed his gaze on the giant. "You must be General Szathan

Mordall," he said in the Anirian tongue. "Your name has long been known to me."

The general's head tilted back, his eyes rising from the floor. Small blackberry eyes. "As has yours, my lord." His voice was a titan's rumble. "I've sworn an oath to serve your elder brother until the end of my days."

Anseth had a horn of blackmilk in hand; he decided to offer it to the general. Szathan graciously declined, so Anseth downed the contents in a single swallow. The fermented drink was too warm to satisfy his already overheated body. The summer air was stifling; even General Szathan looked uncomfortably sweaty in those heavy plates of armor.

"My northmen are ill-prepared for this blistering heat," Anseth said. "It's quite unnatural, even for summer." He walked toward the nearest tent wall, rubbing a finger against the fabric. "Felt is water-resistant and an excellent insulator, and that serves well in the Gray Plains. But here, south of the Cyan Mountains and during this unusually hot season, it's not so serviceable. You see, felt is dark, and it's also heavy. And as you can probably tell—" A hand shot out and snatched something fluttering in the air. "It attracts moths." He opened his palm. The squashed bug twitched a dead leg.

The huge man gave a pointed nod. "Wildfires are breaking out across the land. The talk is of ill omens."

Anseth didn't know what to make of that, so he decided not to comment on it. He extended a hand. "Sit, General. Please, sit with me."

The general did as he was asked, and the two men got comfortable on yak-skin cushions before a center cook pit. Anseth ladled out another horn of blackmilk, and once more he offered the general a taste. This time the general accepted, and after taking a gulp he wiped his lips with a giant paw of a hand and examined the horn as if it were a witch's strange brew. "Not so bad. A bit like charred meat mixed with spoiled milk."

"Most first timers spit it out straight away," Anseth said as he took back the horn. He swished the liquid around in the vessel, thinking about what he ultimately had to tell this giant emissary. *Abandon the north and reunite with my brother, or abandon my brother and unite the north?* There was no suitable outcome to satisfy both parties, and that was painful to Anseth's heart. "General, I know you have no desire to be here, surrounded by these strange northmen. So I'll make this quick. I'm riding to Stormhaven with you. We leave tomorrow at dawn. Until then, a guest yurt will be arranged for you, and a meal will be delivered. I hope goat's head suits your palate. You don't have to eat the brains; we will not take offense. As for your accommodations . . . if you look past the furs and the filth, I think you'll find a certain countryside charm."

"I'm sure I will, my lord."

Anseth turned and switched to the Vaskultan tongue to issue a few orders, and then he watched as the big general was escorted out of the yurt. Kirik remained there, scratching his half-torn ear while waiting for an explanation. Severak approached too, Ikara beside him. The tall and brawny woman wore a look of suspicious concern. "Assemble a company," Anseth told them. "Five hundred picked riders. Kirik and Ikara are coming with me, the Dyre boy as well. Severak, you will hold the encampment until I return."

Severak's hard, hawkish face dipped into a frown. "Why? Where are you off to?"

"I can't leave the south without seeing my elder brother."

CHAPTER NINE

"Smash it, break it, tear it all down," Alarin Athera said. "Fill the carts and barrows and haul it to the foundry."

The head mason was a gloomy-eyed man whose face drooped noticeably to the left, as if it were perpetually tugged on by some tiny invisible creature. After handing Alarin a dour nod, he turned and went off to instruct his team of laborers.

Alarin was left to gaze at the inner wall of the palace district, and he couldn't help but shake his head at what he saw. Behind the masonry equipment and double-row scaffolding was a band of bas relief sculptures, each depicting nude or seminude women engaged in lewd acts with men and boys and even beasts. So many different angles, so many different positions, each more indecent than the last. *How long did it take to carve all these? How many hours of planning, designing, detailing?* It was disgraceful to see such obvious talent wasted on vulgarity. The naked centaur's engorged horse member had to be the most repulsive sight of all, and the mere sight of it made Alarin's stomach turn. *My dear brother, you tactless idiot, what the hell were you thinking?*

Merio had always been a strange sort of man, affable and

outgoing in public, eccentric and pleasure-seeking in private. He'd veiled his vices well while growing up, but once given the seat of Stormhaven, his immoralities knew no bounds. When word of these strange goings-on reached the Hollow, it didn't take a thought-reader to know that his father was displeased. Lasarin Athera had planned to make a personal visit, but his death put an end to that. Soon after, the realm had fallen into turmoil, and Merio went unobserved and forgotten until Alarin had arrived last spring. Of the inner district he'd immediately hated what he saw, and now, he was glad to finally be rid of it.

Alarin turned away but must've twisted his hip the wrong way, because a streak of pain shot up a leg that was no longer there. He groaned and leaned on his blackthorn cane for support, then used a free hand to motion back a trio of attendants who rushed to his aid. "I'm fine," Alarin grunted, a little more aggressively than he would've liked. The same free hand reached under his robe to readjust the socketed brace of his carved wooden leg, and with that, he began the long limp away.

Chamberlain Rennerin Rothar scuttled to his side, his flowing overrobe the color of the plainest gray rock one might find in a volcanic wasteland. His plump cheeks were flushed, and his normally lively voice sounded thick with distress. "My lord, I beg you to reconsider these arrangements."

Alarin grimaced while he hobbled. "Why would I?"

"Well, as obscene as it appears to some, this wall is an acclaimed masterwork. Over a hundred artists contributed to its design and implementation, including some of the most distinguished names in their respective fields."

"Over a hundred is it? Thank you for sharing that little tidbit."

"My lord, this is serious. Completion of those wall sculptures required an enormous amount of time, labor, and coin. By tearing it down we offend all those who contributed to its creation."

"Well, I don't wish to offend anyone," Alarin told him, "but the carvings are disgusting and demeaning. They have no place in an Anirian palace—or anywhere, for that matter."

Rennerin was scratching at the tuft of white hair near his temple, the way he always did when he wanted to speak but wasn't sure if he should. "I understand your point," he said after much deliberation, "but you already removed all the statues and vases and idols from the inner palaces, and you also removed all the fine raiment worn by the high ministers. Don't you think you've gone too far?"

Alarin halted. Pain coiled up his phantom leg, but he grimaced it away. "It's a difficult transition, I know. For years you've frolicked in a palace run by an eccentric aristocrat with a taste for the saucy and the strange. But you have to understand, all this finery . . . this isn't the way of the Anir. It's just ribbons, accoutrements, a gilded brooch tacked on a beggar's tunic. It may look pretty enough, but ultimately it's useless. You must imagine yourself above the city, an eagle's view. Only then will you see that the buildings are the bones, the streets are the veins, and the people are the blood. Do you understand—the people are what matters."

"Of course, but—" The chamberlain stopped, finger scratching once more at his temple.

"Out with it."

"The ministers of the White Fang Council . . . they've not been so receptive about the changes. They demand an audience to discuss the matter."

That made Alarin sigh. *Demand? They are growing bolder by the day.* "Sure, I'll meet with them. Right now."

Rennerin's jowls drooped when his eyes widened. "Well, I mean, the council can be arranged at your convenience, of course."

"Now is convenient."

Alarin's stump was on fire by the time he crossed the threshold of the lesser White Fang Hall. Coincidentally, the high ministers were also filing inside, which meant he had to endure awkward greetings and stiff unfriendly bows as he made his way to the dais. The foot traffic was a bit thick, but thankfully the hall was spacious, as the fancy statues and gilded urns and window ornaments had all been removed, melted down, and sold to finance the treasury. What was left was a tiled floor of a mottled mudminnow color, which was broken up by six fluted pillars whose grooves resembled the look of grated cheese. Alarin thought it an improvement over the gleaming gaudiness of before, but others didn't seem to agree.

As councilmembers found their seats, the hall fell into a steady rhythm of movement, conversation, and the occasional echoing cough. Alarin was among the last to reach the dais, Thayer Dal moving behind him in a clangor of armor. The Wild Goose seemed impatient to adjust to his limping lord's sluggish pace, which of course made Alarin miss the tolerance of Szathan Mordall. *When will you return, Lord General? I feel vulnerable without you.* Still, there was no need to fret here. For all its faults, Stormhaven wasn't the den of wolves that was the Star of the Hollow. No, Alarin was the only wolf here, crippled or not.

He stepped onto the dais and halted before a crescent table whose lacquered surface was nicked and peeling like overtanned leather in the sun. Seated around it were the high ministers of the White Fang Council, a foppish group of fogies who took pride in titling themselves as fanglords. All were frowning; there were so many frowns that Alarin almost laughed. And each frown was deeper than the last, as if they'd held private seminars to learn how to perfect the art. Amusement aside, Alarin didn't like the look of these frowns, but he wasn't at all worried. *Sorry that you are all so displeased, but this was never your city.*

Chamberlain Rennerin rose and began wending his way through the initial greetings and formalities, but Alarin decided to cut the pomp and get to the heart of the matter. "I am told your ministers have some grievances with the way this city is being managed, is that correct?"

Rennerin blinked at him, then, after an awkward moment of silence, he held out an inviting hand, plain gray sleeve dipping low. "Ah, won't you sit, my lord? Sit, so we can speak freely."

"I've too much to do to today. Best make this quick."

Rennerin's hand withdrew, then shifted up to rub at a thinning temple. The tufts of white between his bean-bald head looked messy today, more so than usual. He cleared his throat and spoke. "As servants of the Anir and high ministers of the city of Stormhaven, we would like to pay our respects to the Lord of Thun—"

"Enough with the fancy talk," Alarin said. "Just get on with it."

"You turned this place into a shithole," one of the high ministers said.

Alarin turned his gaze upon the speaker. He was probably the youngest of the council, a stringy man of fortyish years with a patchy beard, protruding eyes, and puckered nose. His name was Byort, but many called him Bugmaster Byort, as he not only was a self-proclaimed expert on insect identification and behavior, but also a man who shared the bug-eyed face of one. "The division between us and them, it's not the same," he explained.

"By 'us and them' do you mean the filthy rich and the extremely poor?" Alarin asked.

"I mean the civil officials and the populace. Don't put words on my tongue."

Alarin fixed the minister with a glare. *Watch yourself, my bug-loving friend. I may be a cripple, but you're as threatening to me as a roach.* At length he widened his gaze to capture all the frowning faces. Some he recognized, others he didn't. The fanglord to his immediate left looked like an elder version of Byort, although he still had some hair. *You are the father, Dobbin.* Next to Dobbin was a small, camel-headed fellow with a long beard cradled in a silk pouch. *You're Fallon, or Fusspot Fallon, as some like to call you.* Beside him was a slender woman who dressed like a girl of sixteen, though her age was probably thrice that. *Your name is Elisa, and you wear far too many bangles.* The remainder of the council wasn't important or influential enough to be bothered with names, just a handful of gasbags and pettifoggers and shysters.

Alarin's gaze eventually settled on Fanglord Dobbin. "As our city's illustrious Chief of Finance, surely you see how our treasury has tripled since we've initiated these changes. Would you care to share your reports with the others?"

"We've seen the reports," Byort cut in. He may have looked frail and toothless, but the man had more bark than all the other ministers combined. Still, that didn't mean much. "We're talking about the ruination of a once grand city. The removal of the blue-blooded lines that separate us. It's like the allegorical tale of the Ants and the Aphids. Once the aphids lived fabulous lives under the protection of the worker ants, while in return they allowed the milking of their sweet secretion of honeydew. It was what you would call a symbiotic relationship. But then an evil dronelord came along and sucked every bit of honeydew from the aphids, and so the ants abandoned them. Do you see the lesson here?"

"Are you suggesting that I'm an evil dronelord?"

Byort grunted. "Let me give you another example, a simpler one, that you might better understand. My father was in the market the other day, haggling over the cost of some lambswool, when a disgruntled hawker kicked mud on his attire. The offender was accosted and hauled away at once, only to reappear back at the same stall the very next day. Why was he released? Such insolence would not have been forgiven by Lord Merio."

Alarin nodded to show he was familiar with the incident. "The man was questioned by the district magistrate. It was a mistake, he didn't recognize the minister. He paid a fine and kept his head intact."

"Oh, I see. So he didn't recognize the minister . . . surely because of these tatters we are FORCED TO WEAR."

"They're not tatt—"

"It's an AFFRONT to the high nobility."

Dobbin agreed with his son, and suddenly the other fanglords were chiming in. A moment later it was too loud to even think. Alarin tried to calm the table, but he was losing control, and the tide of discontent was turning against him. His eyes drifted to Thayer. The fiery Wild Goose stepped forward and slammed a gauntleted fist on the tabletop, BANG, cracking wood and shaking the structure to the very core. The officials reacted at once: some recoiled in fright, others blanched in shock. Cowards, these men were, rich, sniveling cowards. Thayer's singsong voice broke the quiet of the hall like a rasp of scraped steel. "Lord Alarin Athera commands this council. Let him speak."

Alarin cleared his throat. "Now, Minister Byort, I apologize if your son's pride was hurt, but you will need to learn that when the division between 'us and them' shrinks to its natural state, you may find your ego tested. This is normal and should not be feared. In time, you will understand that we serve the people—we are the civil officials."

"Yes, but you seem to forget," Byort said. "That when you stripped the city of all its gilt and glitter, you also stripped the officials of their dignity." Others agreed with that, which only bolstered Byort's resolve. "All we ask is to have a piece of that dignity back. Give us some measure of redemption. Allow us a bit of flare, that touch of luxury we treasure so much. We are Anirians—we'll still be Anirians, heart and liver and soul. Why force us to be unostentatious about our wealth and station?"

Alarin sighed. "Because it's not the Anirian way, and we must duly consider the people."

Byort's bug-like eyes twitched. "We should be discussing this matter with His Majesty. Why is Emperor Silas not present?"

"Because I am by all measures the acting regent until His Majesty is of age to rule. I have the emperor's mandate, as well as the Imperial Seal, to prove it."

Byort leaned back, scoffing venomously under his breath. "Your ways are too antiquated, your laws too draconian." The bug-eyed man shook his head before deciding he had more to say. "It's unwise to make your high ministers so unhappy."

I'm going to ignore that little threat, Alarin mused. "You must understand, it's a temporary thing, your unhappiness. I don't know if you've noticed, but the city itself has made a sharp turn for the better. The people are enjoying lighter taxes, greater encouragement, and fewer punishments. They are happier than ever, and in turn, they are producing more. The city is thriving. And when the city thrives, the government thrives. *We* thrive."

"*You* thrive. Not us—you. The people . . . they sing your name and shower you with praise. Only you."

"Do you truly question why that is?" Alarin's voice rose in volume. "*I GAVE* them what they needed. I gave them what you had denied them, for years and years." His mouth closed, and he curtailed his anger as best he could. When he spoke again, his voice was calmer, more even-tempered. "In time, when things return to an ideal state, you will see the correctness of my ways. Now, is there anything else?"

Now it was Byort's turn to slam a fist on the table. A valiant effort, but it had a fraction of the intensity of General Thayer's blow. Still, he plowed on. "That's it? Council's adjourned, just like that? Nothing was mended, nothing changed." He shot to his feet and thrust out the silk piece of paper that was in his hand. Alarin hadn't seen it until now. "We have demands. Demands that must be met, or we will be forced to take action."

Alarin wanted to smack the man with his cane, hard, right in the jaw. "Meaning what?"

"We'll resign from our positions, all of us. Stormhaven will be without the White Fang Council." He straightened his back, like a gander posturing up against a threat. "Then you'll see how well this city runs without us."

Alarin's gaze passed across the other councilmembers. No other expression held the same level of conviction as Byort's; they all looked unsure, anxious. *It's a bluff*, Alarin thought. *It's a bluff and I'm not falling for it.*

"Resign then," Alarin said. "I don't need you. Any of you. Chamberlain Rennerin alone is more capable than the lot of you. You're all toothless old rats, scared because the cheese wedge you've been nibbling on for years is suddenly being removed." He didn't mean to belittle them, but he couldn't help himself. *They need to accept the truth, all of them.* His voice became softer, more assuasive. "Listen to me. Your old life . . . that life of idle luxury and endless riches . . . it's over now. You have to earn your place again. How, you ask? It's simple. Diligence and decency will be rewarded, greed and laziness will not." He raised two fingers, middle and fore, and passed them across the councilmembers. "For too long you've abused your positions of power. The life Lord Merio gave you . . . it's over now. I'm sorry." With a quick motion to Thayer, he turned to depart. Limping, limping, cane thumping with every step. It was a long walk, but he was too irritated to concern himself with either the pain or the embarrassment of being a cripple.

When at last the lacquered doors of the hall closed behind him, Alarin stopped and let out a deep breath of relief. Thayer was standing beside him, shaking pointedly his helmeted head.

"I know," Alarin said. "I could've handled that better." He gave a soft chuckle.

"The bug-eyed one threatened you. Byort."

"I know."

"Are you just going to ignore it?"

Alarin paused to think about that. He started to walk, and only when they were out of earshot of the door sentries did he reply. "Who said I'm ignoring it?"

"You didn't address it. Some may interpret that as weakness."

Alarin sighed. "For ten years those idiots lived like kings. Surrounded by servants and sycophants who gave them anything and everything they wanted. Admiration, affection, praise, power— they had it all." He shook his head. "A cloud that high . . . it's difficult to come down from, sometimes even impossible." His gaze drifted to the long corridor stretched out before him. With all the fancy furnishings gone, the space looked homely and gray and perfectly Anirian. "I expect they will despise me for a time, but I must endure. Trust me, if I gave an inch to their demands, I'll never regain that ground. An authoritarian fist is required to effect change in all matters."

Thayer gave his usual quick-fire nod, but when he responded, it seemed more like a murmur to himself. "I can see why he spoke so highly of you."

"Who?"

"Lord Yuseth Valate. He always spoke so highly of you."

"Well, don't get attached. I tend to disappoint people, especially those closest to me. Have you forgotten about my failed marriage ruse? The murder of Merio's daughter will forever stain my hands." He shook his head to free himself of that foul memory. "I'm just a . . ." His voice trailed off.

"Just a what?"

Alarin shook his head and started down the corridor. *Just a stubborn old cripple who should've died years ago.*

———

The hour was late when Thayer finished supping at the barracks hall with his usual cohorts. The call of the void was strong tonight, an infectious force like a liquid darkness filling up inside him, flooding his lungs and stealing his breath until he was clawing like a demon for release. And this release only came by listening to the call and obeying its wishes.

Yurin Grayheart was engaged in a friendly game of throwing knives, but he was so drunk he couldn't score a single stick in a triple spin from fifteen paces away. The target was a rectangular slab of timber balks, overlaid with a thin wooden slab painted as a nude woman in a suggestive pose. After the next shot pinwheeled wide, Thayer stood in front of the target and emulated the woman's stance, then began coaxing the bearded man into throwing. Yurin laughed, but he wouldn't bite. "I'm too damn drunk not to be sure I won't kill you," he said, half in burped speech. "The hell's wrong with you?"

"Do you really have to ask that," Rander the Ripper put in while noshing on a pork rib.

"So much is wrong," Keven the Unkind added. "Goose's missing that love o' life."

Thayer laughed and left them there, and next he knew he was wandering the upper reaches of the outer wall, making his way to the wallwalks of the upper turrets. He walked along the top ledge of the battlements for a while, up a merlon, and down a crenel space, up and down again and again, balancing on a ledge no more than half a foot thick. He could feel the breezy summer air whistle in his ears, could feel its gentle hands attempt to shove him off. And most of all, he could feel the void sweet-talking him from below. One slip-up, one minor misstep, and down he would go, a fifty-foot drop to a broken-boned end. That was what the void wanted, what it demanded. So fragile, the human body. So soft and careless, the mind. The shadow inside him wanted to fall, dearly wanted to, but his body wasn't ready. Not yet. Up a merlon and down a crenel space, up and down and up again, so close to the edge, so close to the end.

He did this for the remaining hour of the fourth watch, and then he went to bed.

CHAPTER TEN

I t was like a sequence of notes that played unremittingly in her head. A low *scuff*, an awful *thump*, and then a final, heartrending *crack*. They were the sounds of that poor girl falling down the well.

Miriana Athera carried them around like a tangible item. *Scuff, thump, crack. Scuff, thump, crack.* They haunted her most at night, when she would lie awake before the smoldering fire, the forest around her alive with the trill of raccoons and the buzz of insects. *Scuff, thump, crack. Scuff, thump, crack.* The sounds wouldn't stop. She covered her ears, but they just wouldn't stop.

Her struggle was constant, her emotions battling freely with her spirit. Yesterday she was sad for the girl; today she was angry with her for giving up so easily. *How could you just off yourself like that? How could you place no value on your youth and health? You were in pain, but such is life. I've been through worse, much worse, and I'm still strong. Strong as silk. Am I not?*

In truth, it was growing more difficult to endure the ravages of the wilds. Exhaustion and malnourishment were the seedlings of despair, and despair was a pitfall in the face of survival. The mere thought of such hardships made Miriana want to break down and weep. And this happened *all* the time. Every second of every day—all she wanted to do was breakdown and weep. But she wouldn't give the gods the satisfaction. Or Vileron. *The man's right. I'm not ready for a journey such as this.* He had tried to warn her, but Miriana didn't listen. *He knows I had no choice. He has to know that, doesn't he?* Still, one patronizing word out of his mouth and she'd give him a verbal lashing; her tongue was cocked and ready for it.

The girl should've valued her life. She should've found the strength to overcome her torments. Miriana would've taken her in, and after settling in the south, she would've raised the girl as her own. Loyalty was all but certain when plucking a man or woman from an unfortunate situation. But the girl never afforded herself the opportunity. She'd simply gotten up and walked outside . . . and then she . . .

Stupid girl, why did you jump? We saved you. How could you do that after we saved you?

The accusations eventually turned inward. Why didn't you stop her? *I tried.* Why didn't you try harder? *I couldn't—I was slow and in pain. I yelled for her, but she didn't listen.* You should've yelled louder. *I did . . . but she still didn't listen.* You should've called out her name. *I didn't know it. Oh gods, why didn't I ask her name when I had the chance? If I had established some sort of personal connection, maybe she wouldn't have ended her life.*

Miriana knew, deep in her heart, that these were some dark paths to tread. Her sense of self was drifting away now, as if dragged by an unseen hook. How many moments of rational thought had she lost to those sounds? *Scuff, thump, crack. Scuff, thump, crack.* All she did was follow Vileron through the wilderness. Mindlessly, aimlessly. Her eyes observed the same trees, the same bushes and brooks and bird chirps and animal chitters. Everything was the same and yet nothing put her at ease.

Where are we anyway? She didn't even remember leaving the longhouse, but here she was, moving along the rocky byroads, unfocused, exhausted, and terribly malnourished. Cyrille Vileron moved a length or two ahead of her. She couldn't bring herself to talk to him. If she did, he would probably wag a calloused finger at her, as if to say, *I told you so*. When he finally did speak it was later that night, when they were alone and huddled beneath the beetling bank of a hill, and while Miriana felt lightheaded after the third evening without a substantial meal. She couldn't even remember exactly what he said, but nevertheless it made a swell of anger burst from her chest. "*Just shut up,*" she snarled at him. "*SHUT UP.*"

The big man tried to calm her, but when that didn't work, he did as she commanded and shut his mouth. But her wrath was uncaged now, and she wasn't finished scolding him yet. "So what if you were right, so what if this was a bad idea? I had *no choice.* Do you understand that? If I had remained at the Hollow my husband would've executed me. What choice did I have? You tell me, *what choice did I have?*"

His voice was a stern rasp. "Not south. Not Raas Dragath."

"Then where? East, to Seric Dyre, the most despicable traitor in the realm?" Her grunt was a nasally sound, like a sow in heat. "That's the first place Zantherei's agents will search for me. And once he learns of Seric's past complicit behavior, he'll take his head just the same. So no, I won't find sanctuary there. Where, then, should I go?"

"Thornberry, Indigo Cove, Snowflower—hell, even Lakewood. Any modest city where you can lie low for a time."

"I won't hide in some filthy hovel and live out the rest of my days as a common slug. I won't do it."

"Hubris," was all he said.

"You don't understand. I've worked myself to the bone for what I've accomplished. I've spent years in the brothels and pleasure houses, forcing a smile on the outside while weeping on the inside.

You have no idea what it's like to be beaten, raped, and abused by cruel drunkards and wicked panders. But I didn't give up; I was strong. I was strong and I clawed my way out of the muck. It took years, long, hard years, but I won the hand of the Lord Regent of the Anir, and later I became the empress. I am Lady Miriana Ath—"

"Be *quiet*."

"What? How dare—"

He hissed at her. "I said *be quiet*." His lofty frame was positioned in a strange, half-turned crouch, his sickle-shaped eyes peering through a stand of thicket.

Miriana dropped down beside him, looking, looking, and then asking what he saw.

He didn't answer right away. "Riders."

"From the capital?" Her heart began to pound.

"I don't kn—"

A horse whinnied from somewhere nearby, so close Miriana gave a start. She feared they'd been discovered, but the mounted rider galloped past in a hurry, horse hooves pounding across the hard earth. More horsemen followed, a score at least. There was shouting too, urgent and frightful sounds. Miriana clutched Vileron's leather-wrapped forearm. "What's happening? *Tell me.*"

His bald head shifted back, his scarred face twitched, and his eyes seemed to stare at nothing in particular. "They're not after us."

She gave a forceful tug on the forearm. "Then what, Cyrille—what is it?"

"Do you smell that?"

She wanted to cuff him on the ear. *My nose is busted, you idiot. I can barely smell anything.* "No, what is it?"

He spoke the word quietly under his breath. "Fire."

"Fire . . . as in hearth fire?"

"No, as in wildfire."

"Wildfire? It's not dry enough, nor is it even the season for such a thing."

"And yet we're downwind of it, and it's moving quickly. We need to avoid its path. Stay close to me."

"Wait. If the wind is blowing toward us, aren't we supposed to run *against* it?"

He didn't seem sure. "I reckon we should run in whichever direction avoids the fire's course." He was up and moving then. Miriana did her best to stay in stride, but the big man's movements were erratic and awkward: a forward zigzag here, a sloping backpedal there, an occasional about-face, and a frequent pause to gauge and re-gauge the wind. He guided her around deadfall and undergrowth and across vacant bypaths and winding trails, but no matter where they went, or how quickly they moved, they couldn't escape the growing heat and the enclosing fingers of dark smoke.

Vileron cursed, spun, and darted in a different direction, then spun back, and now Miriana could barely keep up, her legs stiffening with exhaustion, her eyes blurrily clinging to the frayed ends of Vileron's traveling cloak. She asked him if they were almost out (she had to yell), but he didn't answer, or maybe he did, and she just didn't hear it.

They continued like this for a while longer, without a steady course or direction, moving and weaving and sidling like two frantic mice across a snake-infested field. And then, suddenly, Vileron stopped—it was so abrupt that Miriana had to swerve to avoid crashing into him. She wanted to scold him for his carelessness, but a glance over his shoulder revealed a fiery glow in the distant trees, like the whirring of giant orange scythes. The image grew larger and larger until it was screaming toward her like the onrush of cavalrymen. *It's so fast, it's moving so fast.* Above, tree canopies burst into flame with awful whooshing sounds, one after another, *whoosh, whoosh, whoosh,* like a series of synchronized blasts from an arbalest.

"*Run,*" Vileron said, not loud, not urgent, but with a plaintive calmness that was no less frightening. When she didn't obey, he said it again, this time louder, and then a third time, which was louder still: "*RUN!*"

Miriana started off—but Vileron caught her wrist and bolted ahead, pulling her along. Gusts of heat assaulted her body. Sweat latched onto her face like an invisible mask. *Are we running the right way? It feels like the wrong way.* She wanted to ask him, but she knew he wouldn't respond. The fear in his steps was palpable, a deep lacerating fear rarely seen in him. She allowed herself to be jerked along, moving this way and that, until at last Vileron rounded a stand of pines and darted beneath an earthen embankment. For a moment she thought it was safe . . . but then a tide of flames leaped out at them, giant fiery tentacles hungry for flesh. Miriana's hands rose to shield her face. The flames came just shy of reaching her, but the heat was so intense it almost felt *cold*, and the air that filled her lungs was so thick it almost felt solid.

Vileron had gone stock still. Firelight highlighted every feature of his hardened face, down to the jagged detail of those crisscrossed scars. The glistening reflection in his eyes was among the most haunting sights Miriana had ever seen. *He doesn't know what to do. He's afraid and he doesn't know what to do. Gods be damned, I'm not going to die here—not like this.* She shoved him, ordered him to take her away from here. But he didn't obey, so this time she snatched *his* forearm and yanked *him* along, except he was so heavy it was like a wounded dog dragging a sledge.

With her free hand she clawed through the smoke, but whatever fumes she inhaled rushed down her airway like hot bile. She stopped and coughed and spat the taste from her mouth, then she reached over to make sure Vileron was all right. The big man stood on wobbly feet. A layer of ashes ran across his shoulders like a gray mantle, while tiny embers blew past his head like sparks. It was as if the wind had turned into a living beast, and its howls were igniting the bushes and the bramble around them. Moments later, a second wave of smoke rolled in, thicker than the first, so thick

Miriana could barely see Vileron standing in front of her. Coincidentally, that was when he shoved her to the ground, *hard*. She landed face-down in a ditch, her knees and hands scraping against rocks and pebbled earth. Her mouth swung open to complain but her voice broke as he pressed his weight on top of her. She could feel her body sinking into the soft ground. The world became dark, and it took Miriana a moment to realize that Vileron had pulled his cloak over her. He hissed at her to be still, even though she hadn't dared move a single inch.

Flames roared over them. It was so loud . . . like the collapse of a mountain, or the charge of an army of hellhounds. Miriana was screaming now, screaming a terrified scream that was swallowed like a whisper in a driving blaze. *Please gods, I don't want to die like this,* she thought. *I don't want to burn, and I don't want to die. PLEASE.*

She was still screaming when the fire passed. Her voice . . . she could hear her own voice now, how hoarse and desperate it sounded. When she finally stopped an odd tinge of embarrassment swept over her. Vileron didn't say a word about it. The world had become eerily quiet, the only sounds being the faint hum of smoldering earth and a wind that ran off with the blaze like a reckless child. Miriana blew the ashes from her mouth and spoke in a whisper. "You saved me . . . once again."

Vileron's response was an awful-sounding cough, and that soon turned into a string of louder coughs that made his body shudder. Miriana crawled out from underneath him. The man flopped to the ground, still coughing. She didn't know how to help him, so all she said was, "Stop coughing, you big idiot." And when he didn't stop, she hissed at him to shut up. "You're too loud, *please* stop."

But he still didn't stop, and suddenly he was retching and spitting, and it was so bad that Miriana's concern shifted into panic. For a moment she thought about getting away, just up and leaving before his ruckus drew unwanted eyes, but then the large man's breath caught in his throat, and with a final unpleasant burp, his coughing finally ceased. *Thank the gods,* she thought.

Vileron lifted himself up. His traveling cloak was a burnt scrap of cloth and the blackened steel armor beneath was covered in ash. His leggings were in tatters, his greave-straps burned so bad the protective plates were left dangling from his shins. When he spoke, his voice was a scratchy whisper, as if he'd swallowed a handful of broken glass. "I'm fine."

But he wasn't fine, and Miriana knew it, yet she could do nothing to help him. *Caught in a wildfire . . . is this some sort of cruel joke?* Her eyes rose to the sky, attempting to gaze beyond the great gray canvas. *Which one of you foolish gods did this—was it you, Mersis? Or Elysa, perhaps? Why do you choose not to protect me, Azrael?* Her gaze dropped to the ground. *This journey was supposed to be a simple and uneventful affair. Why do these awful things keep happening to me?* A small brushfire popped nearby, as if to mock her. That almost made her angry, but she was too damn tired for such an emotion. *You're still strong, Mir . . . strong as silk . . . strong you ever were.*

Did she even believe that self-motivational tripe anymore? Her shoulders sagged as she gave a pitiful sigh. She wanted to weep, but her eyes were just too dry.

CHAPTER ELEVEN

"Another promise of faith . . . broken," Nyvia said. "I should've expected this from you."

Seric rested his arms on the sill of the unlatched window, his gaze roaming the seaside district below. It was a beautiful summer day, hotter than usual, perhaps even blistering to some. The promenade that skirted the outer wharf was filled with bright faces and bustling bodies, and each seemed to move with either blasé nonchalance or pressing urgency. Beyond, seamen and deckhands whistled and caroled from the distant dry docks, many tending the hull of a merchant craft ported for repairs. Above, striated clouds swept across the sky like great white bristles, and lower, a gentle breeze nudged the peach trees of the palatial orchard. It was all quite picturesque, if one found beauty in such simple things.

Seric had other concerns. "I need more time."

"You've had enough time," Nyvia countered, with a fearlessness that Seric wasn't used to. "Summer is come, and still my son's body remains missing. Why have you not found him?"

Seric wished he knew. His latest company of divers had pulled out yet another handful of waterlogged corpses from the Amber

River, but Veldries wasn't among them. Seric knew this because he'd personally gone to the river to examine each bloated, leech-covered body. The boy was undoubtedly dead, but until the body was found Nyvia would not be appeased.

Her coldness toward him was unfamiliar and unappreciated. Seric preferred the meek and timid woman she used to be, not the bold and pushy one who now asserted herself as Zantherei's envoy. Maybe it was her grief that drove her, maybe it some other motive, but in any matter, Seric was beginning to think that keeping her here in Aster Falls was a mistake.

She turned to speak with the captain of her guardsmen, a sturdy man who looked to be nudging forty years, yet his brown ducktail beard lacked a single strand of gray. Seric remembered this wretch from the Hollow. His name was Bergane, and the way he was touching Nyvia's hand as he spoke was irritating. *Gods, are you two more than just vassal and lady?* The thought filled Seric with resentment, even a bit of jealousy. Nyvia was once his wife, and many years ago they had produced a son together. And because of that son, Seric now felt obligated to keep her here until their son's body could be properly eulogized and interred.

She turned back to face her former husband. "I can't wait any longer. I'm leaving tomorrow at dawn, and I'm taking Sunburst with me. If you have a change of heart about your planned kingship, you'd best inform me quickly. Otherwise Zantherei may not be so kind when next you two meet."

Seric laughed at the threat. "I don't fear that ox. He may be strong, but he's as stubborn and witless as they come."

"You *should* fear him," she shot back, although she turned her head away at once, as though regretting the words.

Seric was intrigued. "Oh, and why is that?"

"After he defeats Raas Dragath and subjugates the southern Redlands, he will set his eyes to the east."

Seric found that amusing. "Overweening fool, his conceit will be his downfall."

She didn't answer. The only response she gave was a strange, almost sympathetic sigh, and with that, she left the room.

Later that evening, Seric thoughtlessly overdrank his wine and fell asleep in the council chamber, and the following day he didn't leave until the early afternoon. His boots tapped relentlessly against the flat stones of the circular stairwell, a sound that matched the pounding between his ears. Sentries acknowledged him with courteous bows or friendly salutes, but Seric barely spared them a glance. Zirian was walking at his side, but when the Mad Wolf tried to engage in small talk, Seric shrugged it off. All he could focus on was his own groggy thoughts, and how they continued to pile up like bricks on the brain.

The empire is broken, and the divided provinces are pushing against one another, much like the events of the second dynasty. He decided it would be best to brush up on his reading later, when he was feeling better. The lessons of history must be kept fresh in the mind, to see all the possible angles of the present. *To claim the whole of this land, I must heed the action—or inaction—of past conquerors. Let the strong battle the strong, and when they both become weak, spring forth to devour them.* It was an uncomplicated strategy, but one that required a level of discipline that few ambitious warlords possessed.

He reached the bottom of the stairs, then made his way across the large courtyard that led to his private apartments. He stopped midway, then decided on a different route. *I need to clear my head. Only a woman can help with that.* He headed around the southern veranda and into the private bathhouse, where he was immediately accosted by the fragrant mix of citrusy bath salts and lavender incense. The bathmaster was seated on an openwork bench in the antechamber, an old man whose attention was focused solely on a young female attendant. She was long-limbed and busty, but her narrow face and noticeable overbite left much to be desired.

Seric wasn't in the mood for civility. He banged his knuckles on the wooden counter. The old man turned at once, his irritation fizzling when he saw who it was. Behind him, several cages of startled songbirds began to flutter and chirp.

"Prepare a private bath," Seric said over the noise. "And I thought I asked you to remove those damn cages."

The master motioned to the female attendant. Then, wearing a smile that reeked of feigned politeness, he began to apologize for the disturbance, but Seric cut him off. "Don't apologize, just do as I say."

"Of course, my lord. Will you be enjoying some company today?"

"Fetch the tall, dark-haired bawd from the pleasure house. Ravia." *The one who looks like Miriana.* He almost said that last part aloud, but thankfully he caught himself. "I'd like to see her again."

The bathmaster bowed and went off. He nearly bumped into the mighty Zirian on his way out, which left him apologizing profusely before darting past. Seric ordered the Zhoulish general to guard the beaded door of the bath chamber, then he moved behind a screen and removed his clothes and neckerchief, allowing the attendant girl to apply a dry brush treatment to exfoliate his bare skin. After that he entered the bath. It was a wide semicircular basin constructed of heavy marble inlaid with dark filigree. Vermeil sconces clung to the chamber's east and west walls, while a row of ornamental pillars rose across the front ledge like a palisade fence. The steamy water was heated from below by a furnace piped through tile flues, so it was pleasingly hot. Seric could feel the tension exude from his body. It didn't take long before his eyes closed—and yet they reopened a moment later, when he heard Ravia enter.

The courtesan was draped in a semi-sheer robe that was decorated in wispy black wings, as if Seric wasn't already tired of birds.
"I do believe this is our third meeting this week," she said,
removing the robe to provide an immodest view of her naked figure.
"You must be growing fond of me."

"Just get over here," Seric said. "You talk too much."

With a giggle she did as she was told. At first glance she
appeared tall and pale like Miriana, but up close, the truth was a
different tale. Where Miriana's breasts had been firm and perky,
Ravia's were soft and slightly disproportionate, and where Miriana's legs had been slender and strong, Ravia's were thick and
marred by stretch marks. In short, Ravia was blessed with only a
fraction of Miriana's beauty. Still, under a dim ambient lighting they
looked similar enough, and that was all Seric needed.

She sashayed herself into the bath, the fragrant waters rising just
above her navel, leaving the ends of her long dark hair to curl daintily upon the surface. A hand rose to caress Seric's face, a soft and
loving caress, which then moved lower to trace the jagged scar on
his neck. He brushed her off. "Leave it," he said. *Why does
everyone want to touch it? It feels just like a scar, I assure you.*

She placed her arms on his shoulders, caressing the back of his
head with her fingertips. They kissed briefly, then she pulled back
and asked, "So . . . *are* you growing fond of me, my lord?"

"Sure."

Her face scrunched at his thoughtless response, and after
feigning a pout her hand rose to bop him playfully on the head.
"Well, you should. I have many admirers, you know. But none will
enjoy my company so long as I'm with you."

"I'm sure you are quick to make that little fact known, yes?
Whores love attention."

Her bubbly expression remained, even though the jab clearly
bothered her. "Men from every district whisper about Ravia Ravenhair." She had the sultry yet authoritative voice of a sexually

repressed priestess. "They wonder what I've done to draw the eye of the most powerful man in the city." After a moment of silence, she bopped him again and asked, "Well?"

"What? Oh, you want me to answer that?"

"Yes, silly. What have I done to deserve your attention?"

Seric looked elsewhere. "You remind me of someone."

"Did this someone make you happy?"

"Once, she did."

She lifted his dimpled chin with a finger. "Well, then, maybe I can make you happy as well."

"Only if you stop talking."

Her mouth closed and she seemed offended by that, but a moment later her expression softened, and she continued to play her game. He could tell she was trying her best to please him, using the skills acquired through her years of experience. But Seric wasn't interested in idle talk or cheap foreplay. He had a hunger that needed to be filled, and he just wanted to bend her over and get on with it. But before he could do that, a silhouette appeared between the front pillars of the bath. Fear clutched at Seric's heart for a moment, but then he saw who it was and sighed. "I was in a sensual mood, General, but your bony mug just ruined it."

"Good, I was hoping to do just that," Wyath said.

Seric exited the bath and motioned to the female attendant. The girl toweled him dry and handed over his trousers and boots and feather-embroidered tunic. Zirian Revil was standing at the threshold of the beaded doorway, peering in with soft-lidded eyes. Seric gave him a quick look before turning back to address Wyath. "You're not the type to invade my personal space, so I'm guessing the matter is of some urgency.'

"Scouts returned bearing a gift for you. A northern barbarian."

"A Vaskultan?"

He nodded. "And a commander by the looks of it. Appears to have escaped detainment from his own tribe."

"Smells of trickery. Do we have a translator here?"

"Not in civil operations, but I do know of an officer who briefly commanded a border patrol unit after the battle of Black Gate Pass. He'd picked up the tongue through years of bartering with the northmen and has since been redeployed as a corps commander of your forward army."

Seric nodded. "Bring them both to the Hall of Sparrows. Zirian and I will head there now."

Wyath nodded and was gone. Seric was left to sort through this new pile of thoughts, which sat precariously on top of his previously pile. *A Vaskultan captive may be of great benefit . . . unless of course it's a ruse. Time to go see what's what.* Only when he was halfway down the palace corridor did he realize he'd forgotten to say goodbye to Ravia. Poor woman was still in the bath, naked and alone and probably feeling quite rejected. Seric didn't mean to abandon her so callously; he'd just forgotten she was there.

The Hall of Sparrows was not a grand place; some might say it was too small and cramped to be called a hall. There were no tables, no benches, and no dais—only a small incense table and a handful of sedge mats arranged in a checkered row. A frieze of stone vines ran across the base and capital of the four wall pilasters, then moved down to frame the gloomy nightscape mural at the far end. Lord Emeron Mathius had once used this hall to meditate on critical decisions, but Seric thought it worked equally well as an interrogation room.

Wyath brought the two men inside. The Anirian officer was a comely man of middling height, and—

"Madderin Ruk," the officer announced, perhaps with a bit too much poise, as though his name was worth remembering.

Seric gave him a nod. "I need you to ask our barbarian friend a few questions. Can you do that?"

He squinted. "I have to admit my memory of the tongue is a little hazy. But shiny stuff usually jogs it right quick. What are you offering?"

Seric couldn't help but smile. *Smooth talking, fearless, and not an ounce of dignity. I must admit I like him.* "Fifteen ounces of gold. How does that sound?"

"Like beauty in a bottle. What else?"

"What else do you want?"

"Rank. A corps commander is noble in its own right, but I've always wanted the station of a general. You have a regiment in need of one."

Seric waited for Wyath's nod before answering. "Fine. I'll grant you a provisionary rank. Disappoint me, however, and you'll regret it." He gestured toward the Vaskultan. "Ask his name."

Madderin spoke in the jarring barbarian tongue. It barely sounded like words, just a short string of staccato grunts. The Vaskultan replied with a few grunts of his own, and then Madderin turned back to Seric. "Claims to be a former subcommander of the Black Cloud, a Vaskultan war division. Name's Jakken."

"Does he know who I am?"

More guttural words. The translator hesitated before revealing the Vaskultan's answer. "He said you're the fool who let a bunch of fools drown in the river."

Seric's face tightened at the insult. He took a moment to give the Vaskultan a good once-over. The man wore the typical barbarian longcoat, though it was of a thinner material for summer breathability. His hair was long and curled and knotted on the sides but receding terribly on top. Of his stature he was rather short, which was rather strange considering most Vaskultans were generally much larger in build. Still, he certainly did not look unfit or lacking in self-assurance.

Seric turned back to the translator. "That word—he keeps using the same word. *Berz-gek.* What is that, an insult?"

"Borzkek," Madderin corrected. "There's no true translation, but it's akin to calling someone an earth-eater, or one who offends his god by defiling the sacred land."

Seric examined the barbarian closer, hand reaching out to touch the ragged nest of retreating hair. "Look at you, all savage and unclean. I can't tell if you're brave or bold or just incredibly stupid."

"Do you want me to translate that?" Madderin asked.

Seric shook his head. "Find out why he was imprisoned by his own kind."

The translator grunted and the Vaskultan began speaking quickly in reply, and soon the translator had trouble following along. Seric kept asking what was being said.

"Something about the south, he wanted to leave . . . but the chieftain . . . something about an ambush and livestock thieves. He was stuck in a cangue but escaped. He's talking too fast now . . . he keeps saying a specific word, I don't understand what it means."

Jakken locked eyes with Seric, and the Vaskultan's mouth split into a ghoulish grin. "Veel . . . drees."

Seric pointed a finger at the captive. "What did he just say? What the hell did he just say?"

The Vaskultan repeated it. "Veel-drees."

"That's my son's name. How does he know my son's name?" He pushed the translator aside and grabbed the Vaskultan by the neckline of his longcoat. "Where is he? Where is *MY SON!?*"

The man flinched, but his eyes remained bone-hard.

"He's goading you," Wyath said.

"I don't care." He spun on Madderin. "I want an answer."

A few more grunts were exchanged. "He said the boy is alive."

"Where is he? *Where?*"

While the translator spoke, Seric paced the hall a bit, running a clammy hand across the projecting wall pilasters. *He's alive. By the gods . . . my son is alive.*

"He wants a fast horse and a week's supply of dried meat. Beef, pork, mutton . . . enough to get him beyond the northern mountains."

"He'll have it. Tell him. Go on."

As Madderin spoke, Jakken looked down, nodding. Seric couldn't stop clenching and unclenching his fists. The Vaskultan captive eventually responded with a few quiet yet guttural words, which were promptly translated. "He will give you the location of the barbarian encampment. He says the boy's there, under the Anirian chieftain's care."

Seric returned to his pacing but stopped just as quickly. "Anseth, you clever little bastard. I should've known."

Wyath spoke. "I don't trust him. The barbarian could be a lure."

Seric nodded. "Or he could be telling the truth. If there's a chance my son is alive . . . I can't let my suspicions overcome my faith. But I'll not give this defector what he wants. Not just yet. For now, he will enjoy the not-so luxurious accommodations of the lower cells. If it turns out he is playing me false . . ." Seric looked pointedly at the Vaskultan, put his fingers to his eyes, and simulated plucking them out. "An eternity of suffering for you, my friend."

The Vaskultan subcommander understood the message before it was translated. For the first time, his bone-hard features gave way to a soft under-shell of fear. Seric would've enjoyed it more had he not remembered something. "Nyvia," he blurted, turning to Wyath. "I need you to summon Nyvia."

"She's gone, Seric. She left at dawn, her company's at least twenty miles off."

"So bring her *back*. Her son is alive, and I'm going to rescue him. A full southern campaign. All forces, main, auxiliary, and conscript." His gaze settled coldly on the Vaskultan ex-subcommander, though his words were spoken to Wyath. "The stratagems I've employed in the past were mere hints of my true talent. Now you'll see what Seric Dyre can do."

CHAPTER TWELVE

Alarin hadn't slept a wink since receiving word of his brother's coming. *Ansetheral Athera is en route to Stormhaven, at last.* Nearly a decade had passed since the Anirian army suffered a crushing defeat at Black Gate Pass, and nearly a decade had passed since the northern Serkut tribe had unhorsed and captured his little brother. It was a harrowing battle and a devastating loss—and not only did Alarin lose his brother during the campaign, he also lost his leg.

Alarin hadn't slept a wink and yet he'd never felt more alive than when he saw the Anirian honor guard approach from the north. At the head was Szathan Mordall, a huge man in huge plates of armor who sat astride a huge snowflake stallion. Around him flourished the horned Sadralen standards of the Anirian soldier company, and farther to the rear were the yak-tailed banners of the Vaskultan warband. These grizzled and rough-looking northmen were mounted on short-shouldered mares and draped in lightweight jackets of treated cotton over boiled leather armor. There weren't many, but if Alarin's pale little brother was among them, he certainly couldn't tell.

Szathan dismounted and stood before Alarin, lowering his head in a deep bow.

"My heart is glad to see you again," Alarin told him. "I've been feeling rather like an exposed nerve as of late."

"Glad to be home." The general's smile was a gap-toothed thing that made his oversized head look even weirder.

"You brought some stragglers, I see." Alarin leaned leftward to look past Szathan, at the rows of frowning barbarian faces.

The big general shifted to open the sightline of a center figure who was saddled on a frosty gray mare. At first, he appeared as any other Vaskultan rider, but given a closer look . . . yes, past the knotted hair and grease-covered face . . . it was easy to see that this man was none other than Ansetheral Athera.

Alarin held out a hospitable hand and put on his best brotherly smile. "Welcome, welcome. I pray General Szathan has treated you and your host with the utmost honor and humility."

Anseth didn't answer. He simply nudged his mare closer, slowly and cautiously, and when he decided it was close enough, he gazed down upon Alarin with a cold and somewhat curious eye. It saddened Alarin to see that his features were noticeably thinner, noticeably harder, and somewhat unrecognizable. Anseth's nose was crooked from a bad break, his cheekbones and brow ridge dented from years of combat. Even his hair, once so shiny and straight, was now a matted mess of uneven tangles and knots. Of course, Alarin didn't expect to see the face of the scrappy brother of old, but beneath all that wool and grease and dirty hair, he'd hoped to find *some* semblance of the man he once knew. *Gone is the spirited little son of the great Lasarin Athera. All that remains is a stone-faced northman who stares at me with mistrustful eyes.*

"I'm old now, I know," was all Alarin could think to say. He raised his blackthorn cane in a displaying manner. "But this makes me appear even older. Come down so we can talk, won't you?"

An Anirian groom appeared to take the mare, but Anseth didn't oblige the youth. Instead he shot the same cold gaze he'd given to Alarin a moment earlier, one that clearly marked his suspicion for any non-northman. The groom had no choice but to step back, and caught in the awkward moment, he began fidgeting idly in place, toying with the tether in his hands. *This isn't going as well as I'd hoped,* Alarin mused, *but I must remain patient. Anseth has lived among the northern tribespeople for nearly a decade. It's foolish to expect a warm smile and tearful embrace.*

Anseth turned to his fellow Vaskultans and uttered a few commands in their barbaric tongue. So fierce and guttural these words were—and quite unnerving to hear his once spirited young brother speak them. A moment later Anseth dismounted and handed the reins to a tall warrior woman with a gourd-shaped face. Then, alone, Anseth approached, ever so slowly and ever so warily, while his big, muscle-bound minions looked on protectively. Alarin couldn't help but think back to his joyful reunion with Merio, which was a noticeable contrast to the gloomy reunion of today. "I've no plans to harm you, Little Brother," he said. "There's no need for caution here."

"There's always a need," Anseth replied. Despite the disagreeable tone, it was nice to hear him speak the Anirian tongue. It made him sound a little more like the plucky brother of old. "The last Anirian lord to invite me inside his walls attempted to murder me."

Alarin tried his best to not take umbrage at that. "Yes, and I was the one who warned you of such treachery. Anseth, look at me. I'm your elder brother."

"Yes, you are."

Alarin was sinking here; perhaps offering a little reassurance would work. "The Sadralen pouch . . . do you not remember the letters we've exchanged throughout the years?"

"I remember."

Another uncomfortable moment followed. Alarin's phantom limb was beginning to throb. He needed to remove the artificial leg, perhaps apply a soothing balm or liniment on the stump. "Come inside, won't you? I've arranged a banquet to honor your arrival."

"My wife and child, are they within?"

Guilt draped itself like a cloth around Alarin's heart. Such a firm and forthright question—and one that Alarin wasn't prepared to answer. Not here, not before they've wound down with a few measures of grape or lychee wine. "You had a long journey, and nightfall is nearly upon us. Come inside."

"Where are they?"

Alarin sighed. *I can't withhold the truth any longer.* His mouth worked, his mind struggling to find the right words. "They're dead, my brother. Been so for almost eight years now. When you were presumed slain, your grief-stricken wife killed her child and then herself. It happened unexpectedly—if I had any knowledge of her declining state, I would've intervened, I would've . . . ."

Anseth's eyes remained bone-hard—not even the slightest touch of softness there. "You did what I asked of you."

"Yes, perhaps . . . but I should've told you." His fingers rose to scratch his balding pate. "A selfish decision, I admit, but it was just after your darkest days with the Serkuts . . . the slave camps, the thirst punishments. I thought the news might break your spirit in a way that could not be mended. And as the years went on, the truth became more difficult to disclose."

Anseth didn't offer any response to that, which made it difficult to know if he begrudged Alarin's decision. In truth, it was difficult to know if he was affected by the revelation *at all.* "We'll talk more inside," Alarin said. "Come, let us fill our bellies with fine cuisine, and let us loosen our tongues with wine. Our master chief has prepared a number of your favorite dishes. When was the last time you feasted on spit-roasted pork chops and whole salted herring, with sides of whitebait fritters and fresh watercress? I promise you, it will all taste just as it did back at the Hollow."

Anseth didn't look tempted, but his dark eyes did eventually wander to the grand walls of the city, a long and steady gaze. At first Alarin thought he might reject his offer, but in the end, Anseth gave a nod. "We've not eaten today," he said. "Lead the way."

The chefs, servers, assistants, and masters of the interior were all moving in a hustle-bustle as the feast went underway. Nearly five hundred Vaskultans crammed themselves into the Rosebud Hall, a rowdy horde that ignored the comfortable seating of the trestle benches for the dirty furs they laid across the tiled mosaic floor. In groups of five or six they sat cross-legged like jolly tentmates around a cook fire, and when they ate it was with their fingers like sloppy, ill-bred children. Slurping the soup from their earthenware bowls, ripping the meat apart with their fingers and teeth, and sucking noisily the pink marrow from the bones. They lacked both manners and etiquette, and not once did they show any measure of courtesy. Instead of sampling each particular dish as it was presented, they pigged out on everything at once. And when they were done, they picked at each other's trenchers like starving vultures. Even Anseth partook in these nasty habits, although he did stop and looked around on occasion, as if to make sure no one was eyeballing him.

Alarin observed the spectacle from his silk-cushioned seat on the dais. To his left, generals Szathan Mordall and Thayer Dal seemed unperturbed by the racket, but to his right, Chamberlain Rennerin Rothar wore an expression of horror so grand it was almost comical to look at. The poor, plump man sat with mouth agape, eyes as wide as lily pads, utensil in hand but frozen in midair. When a series of barbarian burps and belches cut across the room, the servers and scullery staff frowned and gasped, but Alarin was quick to address the incivility. "Don't take offense. The sounds you hear are gestures of approval to the northern tribes and should be taken as such."

The staff seemed to relax at that, and after another few moments of raucous feasting, Alarin rose and limped over to his brother's circle and sat down to join them. Well, he *attempted* to join them, but no one budged, so he had to sit outside the circle. His presence quickly drew suspicious glances from the nearby Vaskultan diners. One particular fellow to Anseth's right was especially watchful. He wasn't overly large for a northman, but he looked as fierce as any man could look, especially with that elongated jaw, half-torn ear, and a dead-eyed, almost lizard-like stare. He seemed comfortable at Anseth's side, a personal bodyguard perhaps. Alarin did his best to ignore his gaze, an admittedly difficult action.

"How does it feel, brother, to return home after all these years?"

Anseth spared a long moment to nibble on a pork bone. "My home is to the north. I've come only to pay my respects, and to honor our long-standing union."

"Say what you will, but the Anir will always be your home, and I will always be your brother."

Anseth stopped eating and looked up, his gaze shifting left and right to study the grand hall—or the emptiness of it, rather. Where once Merio's assortment of sculptures and treasures used to stand and hang, now only old scuff marks and dust spots remained. Even the bas-relief wall carvings had been covered by long gray-black banners. Anseth made no comment about what he observed, but after a long moment his sharp eyes placed themselves back on Alarin. "I have many brothers now," he said. "You see these men around me? They are *all* my brothers." He spoke something in that glottal barbarian tongue, probably the selfsame statement, since it made the men around him grunt and nod.

"Your letters spoke differently, Little Brother. A yearning to come home. What changed your heart?"

Anseth seemed to ponder that question for a while. "My wife and child are dead, and my father has also passed. My youngest brother was recently slain, my eldest is disabled, and the second-born is a tyrant who seized the imperial throne. Home, you say? This place is nothing like the home I once knew."

Alarin's gaze lowered to the floor. No one spoke, and the two brothers were left with yet another awkward silence. Well, not entirely true. Anseth didn't seem to mind. He sucked the pork grease from his fingertips and said, "You have a guestroom prepared, I presume? I'd like to retire for the evening."

———————

That night, sleep wouldn't come. Anseth tried, by the gods he tried . . . but it just wouldn't come.

What is bothering me? It wasn't his dead wife and child, and it wasn't the fall of the empire and the breaking of the realm. It wasn't his behavior toward Alarin, cold and distant though it regrettably was, nor was it even the very sight of the lamed and withered man. No, it wasn't any of that. *What is truly bothering me?* Perhaps it was this bedchamber. Yes, everything about this place offered promises of coziness and warmth and tranquility, and yet Anseth found none of that. The featherbed was large and soft and yet Anseth couldn't stop turning and kicking beneath the silk sheets. The bowls of incense gave off a sweet fragrance that did little except sting Anseth's eyes and make his head ache. *What else?* Oh yes, it was these damn walls. He felt enclosed by them, like a rat stuffed in a keg. As a Vaskultan he'd grown accustomed to sleeping beneath the stars, on a lofty plateau overlooking the open plains. This, in contrast, was a prison, a four-walled cell, musty and dark and full of discomfort and disquiet. In truth, Anseth needed to get out.

He pulled down the silk covers, then sat up and swung his legs off the bed. He had to piss, but he wanted to piss on a tree or the good earth, not down some foul-smelling privy hole. *What is truly bothering me?* It was the room, but it wasn't *just* the room. What truly bothered him was that he didn't belong here. This wasn't the Hollow, sure, but the luxuries and the food and the people were the same.

The disappointment he felt now was something he never could've imagined, not after all those years of capture and then self-exile in the north. Nearly a decade of yearning, of longing, of dreaming and wishing . . . and for what? Only when he finally got what he wanted did he realize how little he actually wanted it.

This city wasn't his home; this land wasn't either. He didn't belong here. Not anymore. The Vaskultans were his people, and he'd fought hard to become their chieftain. Wisps of memories from the cage of bones seeped into his thoughts. He'd killed Dariok that day, killed him in brutal fashion, and in doing so he'd officially asserted his position as the Supreme Lord of the Gray Plains. The old Anseth would've never accomplished such a feat. The old Anseth was soft, pliable, easily overpowered, and physically unre-markable. Why would he want to go back to that life as that person? He wouldn't. No one would.

He didn't belong here.

Outside the room, Anseth moved down an unfurnished corridor that led him to a recessed staircase. The staircase took him down to a dark landing, then down a second corridor, and finally to a central courtyard. He found his fellow Vaskultans stretched out beneath a star-spattered sky, resting on furs of muskox and reindeer and patchy combinations of other arctic land creatures. The evening was warm, but it wasn't the uncomfortably humid heat that had recently plagued the heartland.

Anseth chose a spot and unrolled his fur, then he lay down, slid two hands behind his head, and stared up at the night sky. Yes, this was better. Much better. His lungs took a deep pull of the fresh air. So quiet, so peaceful. The moon was a glowing crescent, like a workman's sickle-blade dipped in liquid ivory.

It wasn't long before Kirik joined him. The bondsman had a silvery herring in each hand, and when he placed the heads sideways so the fish eyes replaced his own, the result was a rather amusing sight. Still, Anseth couldn't gather the energy to puff out a laugh. Not even a little one. "You didn't have to follow me," he muttered.

"I can't sleep in a cage either," the bondsman said, sitting down nearby. He took a bite out of a salted herring, then spent some time chewing it. "We don't belong here."

"I know."

"Your brother . . . how does he lead when he can't even run?"

"For the people of the Anir, strength comes not from the body but the mind, and also from the standing of one's house."

Kirik didn't seem to understand. "He looks weak."

"Never judge a man based on his appearance," Anseth said. "Alarin Athera was once among the greatest heroes of the realm. In his prime he was unbeatable in combat and unsurpassable in strategy. The Thunder of the North, they called him."

Kirik seemed more confused than impressed. "Thunder is loud, sure, but it has no bite. No true strength."

"Deception is the way of the Anir. An outsider like you would be wise to remember that."

Kirik went back to his herring then, dangling the food vertically as he took a generous bite. After chewing and swallowing, he wiped a hand on his light longcoat, and spoke in a grave voice. "Have you decided yet?"

"Decided what?" Anseth asked, even though he knew what Kirik was asking. At length he said, "This isn't my home, I belong in the north."

Kirik's demeanor relaxed a bit, and he started gobbling down the second herring. When finished, he belched and tongued his teeth, then he began to speak about small matters, which eventually shifted into their plans of moving north. Anseth did a lot of agreeing, a lot of nodding from his reclined position, but his attention was suddenly diverted when something caught his eye from above. It was a shadow skulking across the eaves of the tower's tiled roof. There one moment, gone the next. *Am I seeing things? Probably just the trickery of moonlight and cloud cover.*

Kirik was still talking. "General Kaigon's lancer subdivision is stationed at Bladed Pass. If we arrange a rendezvous at the primary checkpoint, we can unify our forces and—"

Anseth sat up. *There it is again, that same shadow.* It moved swiftly and gracefully across the roof, halting somewhere above the high balcony of the palace tower. *That's not cloud cover.* It remained still for a long moment, then like an overripe fruit it dropped soundlessly upon the terrace of Alarin's personal chamber.

"Kirik, look there," Anseth interrupted. "Higher, beside the archway of that tower. What do you see?"

The bondsman's sharp eyes squinted. "It . . . it looks like a man."

"What sort of man?"

"I don't know, he's wearing a mask . . . wait, he's holding something . . . hard to tell, it's concealed against his body. Something metallic, I think. Is that a knife? Who is—?"

Anseth didn't hear the rest. He was already up and running.

Kirik called after him but Anseth didn't stop. He wished his legs were longer, or that his strides could've covered more ground, but he did his best to race through the open gateway of the palace. Two sleepy-eyed sentries bucked to attention as Anseth bolted past. A quick right turn and now his booted feet were stomping across the tiled corridor, sconce-light throwing shadows at his feet. He reached the tower stairs and vaulted three at a time, spiraling up and up and up, his lungs wheezing, his breath burning from exertion and brimming with panic. He reached the top and dashed for Alarin's room —but suddenly his sense of direction was gone, and around him rose a row of wooden doors, the first no different from the last. *Shit, shit—which one, which one?*

The sound of the sentries' booted footfalls rose up behind him. Voices commanded him to halt. Anseth did halt—and then he spun on the two men. "My brother's chamber, *WHERE IS IT?*"

The taller one told him to calm down, but the shorter one gestured to the second door on the right. Anseth ran to it, pounded it open, and threw himself inside.

The shadowy figure was standing across the room and beside the center bed, head turned at the sound of the open door. A slender man, neither tall nor imposing, but faceless in that black-painted mask of distorted clay. A curved dagger glinted in his hand. On the bed, Alarin began to stir. "Brother, that you?" he called.

The masked assassin turned back to the bed. His hand came up and down, fast, in repeated stabs that tore through fabric and flesh like rice paper. Alarin made a string of odd *oomph* sounds, and Anseth heard himself utter a cry before his legs burst into motion. The world shrank to a narrow funnel hole; time seemed to stop altogether. The distance from the door to the bed was no more than twenty paces, but it seemed an eternity before Anseth was close enough to leap at the assassin.

Flesh and fabric collided in a great deadened thud. Anseth latched onto the man and pulled him down to the floor—only to end up on the bottom himself, and now he was struggling to wrest away the bloody dagger. There was little distance between them, so the assassin's blade could only poke and nick, but even still, Anseth's forearms were already seeping blood through the sleeves.

He raised a hand and yanked the assassin's mask down; the face beneath was round and youthful and rather unmemorable. Anseth balled a fist and slammed it into the man's chin; two, three, four blows before the assassin caught Anseth's wrist and dug deep gouges into the skin. "You ruined it," the man said in a voice that was almost weepy. "You ruined everything."

"Ruined *what?*" Anseth growled. "*Why* are you doing this?"

"I don't want to. Please, I don't want to."

"Then *STOP* fighting me."

"I am, I am." But the assassin didn't stop, and when he lifted Anseth's arm and bit down hard, Anseth in turn grabbed his stringy hair and jammed a thumbnail into his left eye socket. The *squish* sound was nasty, the liquid oozing out was nastier still—but the man's shrill scream was most horrific of all. After that the man was gone, tackled by the sentries who had followed inside. Anseth lay there, pulling heavy breaths as he listened to the two armored men subdue the assassin, which consisted of a lot of beating and holding and more beating. But no, somehow, the assassin broke free of the sentries' grasp, and then he threw himself out of the unlatched window, his scream fading horrifically as he plunged several stories to the ground.

No, no—we needed him alive. How did you two lose your grip of him?! Anseth tried to say those words aloud, but his throat was full of phlegm and dust. Something wet kept splashing on his head, a constant *drip-drip* down his knotted hair and eyelids. Was it rain? *No, silly, you're inside.* When he touched it, his fingertips came back slick and red. It was blood—Alarin's blood, leaking down the bedside. *Oh no, oh no.* Anseth turned and climbed to his feet.

His elder brother was lying in a twisted sprawl, half inside the silk covers, half out. Dark blood pooled like rainwater in the creases of the bedding, ruining it and also the silk nightshirt he wore. Anseth began tearing strips of his own cloth to staunch the flow, but there was so much blood, so many wounds, and he couldn't tell which needed his attention most. Confused, despairing, he threw his head back and gave an urgent cry for a physician or anyone else who could help. And when he looked back down at Alarin's face, he saw an expression that wasn't full of fear or panic. In truth, Alarin seemed more disappointed, wearing a simple frown, wan though it was. "Don't let me die," he croaked. "Don't let me die."

CHAPTER THIRTEEN

In rapid marches they had cut twenty days of travel down to
twelve.

From the predawn dampness to the darkening trails of
dusk, the Whitecrow army moved in a collective chug and clangor,
with booted feet and horse hooves and wagon wheels all chewing
up and spitting out the earth. Still, as grueling as their pace was, it
proved an effective strategy. By the time the Vaskultan army blasted
the horns of alarm, Seric Dyre's main force had positioned itself
two hundred yards from their encampment, nestled between a ring
of forested hills and a protective river. And with the evening light
encasing the area in a shadowy mantle, it became an ominous little
spectacle, to be sure.

Still, it was impressive to see how quickly and efficiently the
barbarians reacted to the threat. In minutes the lower flatlands were
lined with serrated rows of Vaskultan horsemen. These were big,
swarthy men strapped in pieces of boiled leather armor, hands
clutching spears and pikes and those single-bladed backswords. In
the rear, mounted archers clutched horn and birch bows, with arrow
shafts rising from behind clothed shoulders. So methodical in

formation, so systematic in purpose; they waited across the battle lines now, fierce and deadly and worst of all—patient.

Seric didn't attempt to communicate with the barbarians. He'd already learned that Anseth wasn't with them, so the notion of delivering terms was pointless. Instead he spent the early evening in the rear commander's tent, ignoring Ravia's affections while mulling over his final preparations. Terrain maps and paper markers were carefully positioned on a low table, their plots and paths detailed by hours of sharp-eyed diligence. He was exhausted, but rest would come later. First, he had to hold a meeting to address each of his high-ranking military officers.

At the onset of midevening, two dozen battle-hardened bodies made their way inside, men who held esteemed titles that ranged from wing commander to corps commander to signal leader and regiment captain. There were no lesser men here; the lowest-ranking officer still had command of about one hundred men. Zirian and Wyath were the principal generals, along with a third, the recently promoted Madderin Ruk. The handsome man had a swagger about himself since attaining his newfound rank, a confidence that stretched above his already overblown confidence. Seric wasn't too sure if he still liked him, but the soldiers seemed to regard him with respect, probably because he was charismatic and of good stature. Long locks of honey-blond hair trailed down his delicate face, parted at the middle and tied loosely back to frame those brooding eyes and a jaw chiseled from pale stone.

"I know this may seem heavy on the managing of details," Seric told them. "But this is a matter of crucial import. As your lord and commander, I need to make sure you've all heard me. Now forgive me for circumventing the usual policy of passing orders down the ranks, but I must stress once more, if my instructions are not fully heeded, if there is the slightest deviation in plans, the whole operation will go awry. And if that happens, it is *you* who are to blame." Seric paused to clear his throat. "Two drumbeats to set the initial ambush. One, two. Precisely when the Vaskultans turn. Understood?"

The signal leader nodded.

"Fail me in this, and the signal drummer will be executed, his squadron will be executed, and his commanding officer—that means you—will be executed. Got it? The same goes for the flag bearers outside the forest. This is an unorthodox move, so we need to make sure the Vaskultans don't read or intercept our orders. Flag left to move right, flag right to move left. Any deviation is punishable by death. Understood?"

The officer nodded.

"And for the final charge . . . again, two drumbeats to initiate. One, two. As soon as the Vaskultan front emerges from the edge of the wood, my detachment will hit them head on, cut off their retreat, and crush them to a man. Also understood?"

The officer nodded.

"Now those are my orders, and they must be obeyed. Any man who moves too early, moves too late, or falters from the formation —will be put to death. This goes for *any* man, including my top generals and even myself. We are all at risk here. *All* of us."

His assembly of military officers nodded and bowed obediently, though some clearly didn't like the given orders. *Too bad,* Seric thought. *I didn't spend all that time organizing a complex stratagem just to see some inattentive numbskull foul it up.* His strictness would guarantee obedience. "Our success depends on the cohesion of the units," Seric went on. "I've pored over the tiniest of details and I've gazed down every channel of intent. If we strike with strength and swiftness, we will be victorious. If we remain sharp and untouched by their cunning, we will be victorious. If we band together and move as one, we will be victorious. Obey my commands and . . .?"

"We will be victorious," the officers answered in unison, though it was a rather halfhearted effort.

Seric gave an approving nod all the same. "The great Vaskultan horde will prove no match for the forces of Whitecrow." His gaze turned to the moonlit land. "The operation begins at fifth watch. Good? Good. Looks like you're dismissed, gentlemen."

As the officials shuffled out Seric thought he heard a few mutters of discontent, but he made no mention of it. His three regiment generals remained, none looking pleased at the situation: Zirian, with his huge Zhoulish arms crossed; Wyath, with his sharp eyes lowered; and Madderin, with his chin raised in proud defiance. It was Wyath who spoke first. "It is the very nature of man to make mistakes."

"There can be no mistakes, not this time, not against the Vaskultans. I don't need to remind you of our loss at Amber River, do I?"

General Madderin replied to that. "That was your mistake, not ours."

Seric shot him a dark look. *Hmm . . . what do we have here? Yes, look at you, already growing too big for your boots.* "Yes, and I intend to correct it, but to do that I need the full support of my officers. Do I have your support, General?"

"Of course," Madderin said.

Wyath's blackened plates of armor creaked when he reached up to scratch his chin. His expression said he was attempting to understand Seric's perspective, but the doubt in him was tangible. "No man is infallible. Not even you. You shouldn't have included yourself in the orders."

"If I hadn't," Seric told him, "these men wouldn't have listened. A worthy leader is one who doesn't allow himself extra privileges because of his rank." He paused to rub the scar beneath his neckerchief. "I'm not worried. You and Zirian are my most esteemed generals; I know you won't disappoint me. And you, Madderin Ruk, now is the time to prove yourself. I am loathe to punish any officer who spoils my plans, either intentionally or not, but if it must be done, then it must be done."

Wyath seemed content with that. Seric turned and switched to the Zhoulish tongue to address the Mad Wolf. "Don't forget, after the initial clash, when the Vaskultan line falls back, do not give chase. If you do, the Vaskultans will reform and crush you before my detachment can provide support. Remember, wait for the signal before you engage."

Zirian nodded, his half-lidded eye gazing expressionlessly.

"What you're planning here . . ." Wyath began in that stoically calm voice of his. "It's unusual. Arbitrary even. I won't lie and say that you don't have doubters."

Madderin agreed. "Some might think your ego is surpassing your abilities."

That made Seric frown. "And what do you believe?"

"I don't know. This stratagem is very . . . unusual."

"It's unwise to disappoint me so early in your career, General."

"I'm being honest."

"And that is why I won't punish you. Listen, there will always be one rotten apple in the bushel. Doubtful men, shortsighted men . . . lurking and hiding in nondescript places, infecting others with their discontent. Even officers like you are not immune. That said, if you feel your mind has become contaminated, General, I suggest you tell me now, so I can reduce your rank."

"Of course not, my lord. My heart bears no doubts."

"Then as I said earlier, mistakes cannot happen. Now I need you three in top form tomorrow. So go on, get out of here. Get some rest."

The three generals made their way out, with Ravia was standing near the tent flap, offering a courteous farewell to each. Before exiting, Wyath turned to her and quietly told her to make sure Lord Seric gets adequate rest himself. Then he added, "His Lordship looks like he needs it."

Seric pretended to ignore that, and once the generals were gone, he remained hunched over the small roughhewn table for a while, eyes plastered on the maps and markers, mind going over every nuance of his plan, again and again, until fatigue sapped his focus. He leaned back in his stool and rubbed his eyes. *You've done all you can do. Don't overthink this. Don't create errors or holes where none exist. You've got everything covered. Now you just need to sleep.*

He'd forgotten about Ravia until she touched him gently on the shoulder. When he tensed, she purred softly in his ear and said, "So tightly wound." A hand rose to stroke the back of his hair. "Why don't you lie down, let my hands work you over with my oils."

"Not tonight."

"You need it. It'll help you unwind. Perhaps I'll slip into that lacy black camisole that makes your eyes light up . . ."

He removed her hand from his head. "I said *not* tonight."

A brief moment of silence. "Do you even enjoy my company?" Her voice had turned from sultry to stiff.

Shit on the gods, now I've offended her. He rose from the stool and turned to face her. The smoldering brazier light threw itself onto her low-cut robe, highlighting the sleeveless fringes, tight-fitting hem, and soft mushroom color. Tresses of lovely dark hair tumbled past her shoulders—the same length and volume as Miriana's—but the face curtained by those tresses was long and hook-nosed, and no amount of wine or wishful thinking would change that. And for that reason, Ravia vexed him, almost as if she were to blame for her imperfections.

"If I'm to be ignored," she said, "why even invite me along?"

Seric gave a pointedly irritated sigh. "It's the eve before a decisive conflict. Are we really going to do this now?"

"I don't know, are we?"

"Do you know what is at stake for me here? Do you have any idea what sort of challenge I'm facing?"

"Yes, I'm not a straw-headed strumpet. But why did you ask me to come?"

"I don't know," he said at last. "I thought I could use the company. Clearly it was an error in judgment."

She huffed at that. "Listen, this is a time for battle. I understand that. But pleasure can still be beneficial for the time being. If you let me, I will show you just how right I am. Let me ease you."

"I said no. I don't want to right now."

She recoiled from that. "Your words are like daggers to my flesh."

Seric's fingers slipped beneath the neckerchief to touch the scar. "Stupid woman, you have no idea what that truly feels like."

"Maybe not, but I know the feel of a man's cruelty well enough."

That made him laugh. "You think me cruel? I'll show you cruelty. How about this? I don't care about you, I don't want you around, and I certainly don't love you. You're immature, spoiled, stupid, and you're certainly not as pretty as you think." His hand gestured to his face, mocking the size of her nose.

Her mouth opened wide; her eyes too. "You bastard. I am starting to see why you are alone."

He shoved an imaginary dagger into his heart. "Oh, such a hurtful retort."

She bent down and swept her hand across the table, knocking the maps and markers to the floor. Seric's anger surged, white-hot. *Oh no, you didn't just do that.* She was tall, almost Miriana's height, but when Seric rose over her, fists clenched, she shrank in fear. "A lesser man would strike you for that," he growled. "A man with far less control over his impulses." His fist opened and a single finger pointed to the exit. "Get out."

It took a moment before she realized that she wouldn't be harmed, and when that happened, her expression twisted into one of defiance. "Fine, maybe I'll spend the night in the company of another man, perhaps one of your officers. I see the way the long-haired one looks at me. Madderin is his name, no? Quite the handsome fellow. I'm sure he'll treat me as a lady should be treated."

"Good, and when his face is buried between your legs, please ask him how my cock tastes, won't you?"

She scowled at that, then turned and stormed out of the tent.

Have fun, whore, Seric wanted to say aloud, but she was already gone. The interior immediately returned to silence; only the faint hum of a lone brazier was heard. Seric turned to examine the mess. The maps and markers were all scattered on the floor. Just a great jumble of nonsense now. He thought about picking them up, even knelt and started to, but after a few moments he stopped and snorted to himself. *How am I so talented in military affairs, yet so incompetent with women? A conundrum only the gods could decipher.*

He dismissed such purposeless thoughts from his mind. *My only concern is the ambush against the barbarian army. And the retrieval of my son.* His postured straightened, his heart pulsing with fiery determination. *I'm coming for you, Veldries. I'm coming to save you.*

CHAPTER FOURTEEN

Alarin Athera wanted to see the face behind the assassination attempt. He wanted to feel the coldness of the plotter's heart and the hatred in the plotter's thoughts. He wanted his visions to show it all to him, but when his unconscious mind asked of it, nothing happened. He begged the gods to show him, just as they'd done before (the fall of the dynasty, Anseth's betrayal at Amaranth Point, and the southland advisor Ravathyr's untimely end), but again, nothing happened. Only a black shadow rose before him, like a cloak thrown over a cityscape, or a gravesite at the devil's hour.

But no, after a long moment Alarin realized it wasn't a black shadow at all—it was fire. Not a natural fire as one would expect, but a blaze much darker and more sinister in hue. The smell was rancid, like being stuffed in a tiny storeroom with a week-old corpse. Alarin felt the fear rise in his body. He fought against it but couldn't take control. He could only watch as the fire swept across the land like a horde of locusts, blotting out the light and scorching anything it touched. Villages, suburbs—even entire cities, all reduced to cinders. Alarin could offer no help. All he could do was watch the land around him burn and burn and burn. The fire was pervasive . . . the fire was inexorable . . . the fire was coming.

————————

"He's awake."

Ansetheral Athera stood beside the sickbed and observed his elder brother's eyes flicker behind closed lids. Over and over again, they flickered and flickered until at last they opened, slowly, as if pulled apart by a metal retractor. Alarin's chapped lips parted soon after, but no words came out. Or rather, none that could be heard.

Anseth leaned in closer. "What is it? What are you trying to say?"

Alarin gave no answer. It was hard to see him this way. His face, once so defined and strong, was now but a shrunken mask, while his bare upper body was pale and drawn and marred by purple welts and bruises. Eight anterior stab wounds in all, from the left shoulder to both sides of the torso and down to the right forearm. His left lung was punctured, his gallbladder torn, his sternum fractured. But through it all, Alarin remained alive.

He tried once more to speak, but again it was too low to be heard, so Anseth moved even closer, his ear to Alarin's mouth as he asked him to repeat it. His elder brother's respirations came in disjointed, desiccated rasps, like the sound of an old tomcat choking up a hairball. But after a deep, shuddering swallow, he managed to utter a single word: "Fire."

Anseth leaned back. "What does that mean? Elder Brother?"

A pair of hands ushered Anseth back. It was the city's master physician, Penry, a stout and owlish man who moved with the waddling speed of a very slow tortoise. On one side, it was good to see him not give in to pressure and panic, and yet, Anseth wished he had a bit more urgency in his step. But there was an undeniable confidence in his movements, and whenever he gave an order, his attendants were quick to comply, so Anseth thought it wise to give him space.

Blood coated the physician's forearms, and when he moved a few droplets splashed onto the tiled floor. He explained that he'd just finished snuffing out the bad spirits, and now he was suturing the surface wounds with strings of catgut. When Anseth unthinkingly moved a step too close, the physician diligently urged him back. "You did everything you could, now let me work." His voice had a strange, muffled tone to it, as though his vocal chords were perpetually swollen by sickness.

Anseth wanted to speak but didn't know what to say, so he asked the only question he could think of, which was as straightforward as it was basic: "Will he live?"

The physician seemed slightly irritated by that, but his answer came with polite professionalism. "His right distal pulse is agitated; the median pulse is faint. I need to improve respiration, fortify the blood flow, and apply a lenitive gel to the surface area."

"Yes, but will he live?"

"I will do what I can, but only the gods are omniscient. Now please, my lord, you're in the way."

Anseth stepped back. "Make sure he lives," he said, and with that, he took a final look at his elder brother, before turning about to face the small gathering of eyes. Among them were the two Anirian tower sentries, Kirik and his Vaskultan guardsmen, and of course the titanic Szathan Mordall, who approached like an eager hound waiting for its master's command. Near to him stood Thayer Dal, the Wild Goose general; and farther left was Alarin's personal steward and palatial chamberlain, Rennerin Rothar, who was a bald, overweight man dressed in plain silk robes.

Szathan was the first to speak. "What did he say? What did Lord Alarin say?"

Anseth didn't bother craning his neck to meet the general's eyes. He simply spoke to his chest. "No name. Just a word. *Fire*."

Szathan had no response to that, but after a moment his monstrous hands began to twitch. "The assailant . . . where is he?"

"Dead. He broke free of the tower sentries and jumped out of the window."

That sparked a flame in Szathan. The giant man strode forward, tiny blackberry eyes flashing with fury, meaty hands upraised as though ready to choke the life out of the two sentries at once. Anseth tried to hold him back, but Szathan was far too big and far too strong. He shrugged Anseth off like a gnat, which caused Kirik and his Vaskultans to spring into action. Madness followed. Men grunted and shoved at one another. Anseth tried to quash it, but a stray forearm slammed into his mouth, staggering him back a few steps. His bottom row of teeth sparked with pain, and his tongue tasted blood.

"Who's behind this?" Szathan kept shouting, at anyone and everyone. "*WHO* is behind this?!"

The physician spun; there was a stern professionalism to his voice, like that of a father scolding his child in front of guests. "That's *enough*. I need you to leave. All of you. I cannot administer aid unless my focus is placed entirely on Lord Alarin. Please leave."

Anseth touched his swollen lip. "I'll not abandon my brother."

The physician opened his mouth to reply, but he must've seen the resolve in Anseth's eyes, because he simply said, "Then wait in the adjoining chamber. Please, the longer I talk the less time we have. I beg you. *All* of you."

Anseth looked down. Shame filled him, shame for allowing disorder to take over while his elder brother lay so close to death. He beckoned for the others as he moved to the waiting area at the opposite end of the room. It was a quiet place, empty save a handful of wooden benches and slender floral sconces, a pair of which framed a large painting of an after-dark cityscape. His eyes clung to that painting for a moment, and with preoccupied interest he observed the tiny smudges that represented the handful of people moving through an otherwise vacant market square.

Szathan was pacing back and forth, taking huge angry steps, *boom-boom-boom*, while growling and grumbling to himself. "I must do something," he said to no one in particular, which made it even more unsettling. "But I don't know what to do . . . what do I do?" He slammed a boot heel on the tiled floor, turned, and went back to his pacing. Anseth watched him, one hand held out to stay his Vaskultan guardsmen. He was angry, too, but it wasn't sensible for a lord and chieftain to show his emotions so transparently. *I must remain calm, and I must put all my efforts into finding the perpetrator of this evil plot.*

Chamberlain Rennerin was the last to join them, and to do so he had to weave around a handful of large barbarians who stood in the way. As he did, he put a plump hand to his chest and said, "Oh, heavens . . . you northmen are dour fellows, aren't you?"

This man is as flowery as they come, Anseth thought. *I don't think I could find a greater contrast to myself.*

Rennerin halted before Anseth and gave a bow that was a hair away from being disingenuous. "My sincere condolences for what has transpired," he said. "The people here loved your brother. As did his ministers and civil officials and courtiers, most of whom are outside weeping in the courtyard. Truly, truly sad—but I'm told that you foiled the assassin's attempt, and for that, we all thank you."

Anseth nodded. He studied the chamberlain's face carefully before speaking. "This dead assassin, do we know anything about him?"

"Likely a hired outsider. Might as well have been faceless; no one will identify him. Of that I am sure."

Anseth nodded. *How, then, do we find the bastard who arranged to have my elder brother murdered?* "I need your help, Lord Chamberlain. I need to know the names of any man or woman with a gripe or grievance against Lord Alarin. Anyone from the most snobbish patricians down to the lowliest of street curs."

The chamberlain's gaze dropped to the floor, but only for a moment. "I promise to report any developments as they come to me."

Anseth shook his head. "Don't play the fool with me. I know you're the eyes and ears of this city. Nothing gets by without your knowing, so give me something . . . *anything.*"

"I assume this was done by an outside hand. Likely for a great wealth of coin, perhaps. Or a promise of power."

"I don't think so," Thayer Dal cut in. His unusual singsong voice matched well with his lanky build. "I reckon this treason was arranged in hearth and home."

Rennerin objected to that at once. "The civil officials are not capable of such violence. Unless you are suggesting this is a military matter." He wilted a bit after saying that, an unsurprising action considering he was standing among some mean-looking military men in full battledress.

"You're wrong," Thayer said. "Lord Alarin lowered civilian taxes and increased soldier pay, and the people loved him for it." He turned his attention to Anseth. "But to raise the coin to fill the treasury, he melted down and sold all of Lord Merio's luxuries to foreign dealers. The elite members of the White Fang Council . . . they didn't like that at all." He turned back to Rennerin. "Isn't that right, Lord Chamberlain?"

A bead of sweat dripped down Rennerin's wrinkled forehead, but he made no move to wipe it. "Initially, yes. Many, myself included, were displeased to return to the more homely Anirian lifestyle. But over time we began to understand Alarin's vision, and we were happy to give up our own finery to create a more harmonious relationship. He gave this city direction and purpose, something sorely needed after Lord Merio's death."

Anseth brushed a strand of knotted hair from his face. "I see. But surely not all of your officials have come to accept this new lifestyle?"

"Well, that is true . . . not all were fully turned."

"I'll have their names."

When Rennerin hesitated, Thayer Dal spoke up. "The bug-eyed son of the Chief of Finance. Byort, they call him. He threatened Lord Alarin during a recent meeting with the White Fang Council. A threat as clear as a chrysalis."

Anseth turned to General Szathan, who had finally stopped pacing. "I would like to speak to him personally."

"My lord," Rennerin interrupted timidly, stammering each word. "Minister Byort is outside the city's jurisdiction on imperial tax-collecting duty. He isn't expected back until the evening of the new moon."

Anseth shook his head at that. *How convenient.*

"Perhaps I may speak to him upon his return," Rennerin added. "Quietly, outside the—"

"Fetch his deployment papers," Szathan boomed. "I want his routes, his feudal tickets—I want every scrap of information you have." His tiny blackberry eyes flicked to Anseth. "I'll have him back before the week is through."

Rennerin nodded, but the look he gave Anseth was full of doubt. "Is it prudent to accuse this man without substantial evidence? All we have is General Thayer Dal's suspicions, as telling as they may be."

Anseth regarded the chamberlain quietly. "You believe he is innocent?"

The plump man scratched at his temple, a nervous tic of some kind. "Byort is like a son to me. I've known his father Dobbin since we were children. Through marital bonds our clans have long been intertwined."

"Lord Chamberlain, if you place friendship over the whole of the realm, then you don't deserve the seal of office you wear around your neck."

Rennerin again scratched at his graying temple. "Perhaps we should consult with the young emperor. His Majesty may be able to shed some light on this dark situation."

"Emperor Silas is but a boy," Anseth shot back. "And a boy cannot make the hard decisions needed to unearth the truth. Feel free to apprise him of the situation, but my word is final." Anseth turned to Szathan. "Take a small company, no more than a dozen. And take Thayer Dal with you." Szathan immediately gave protest to that last point, but Anseth was quick to silence him. "He will be joining the expedition, General. Your judgment is clouded by anger, and I fear you might harm the accused on sight."

Szathan grumbled a few words to himself. Beside him, Thayer spoke. "And who will remain to protect Lord Alarin?"

Anseth raised his hands, palms open, to show off the dry blood that encrusted them. "Am I not enough? I did foil the assassin's plot."

Thayer made a shameful hiss at himself. "Forgive a fool's tongue, I only meant—"

"I know what you meant. Now please remember, both of you, Byort is under suspicion, not deemed guilty. So don't kill him, and don't make a mess." His eyes returned to the Lord Chamberlain. "Do we have an expert torturer in this city?"

Rennerin's nod was hesitant. "We do."

"Good. Send him a summons of preparation." Anseth cast a long look across the room at his bedridden brother. "The truth will come out soon enough."

CHAPTER FIFTEEN

Cyrille Vileron wouldn't stop coughing. Every hour of every day, he would expel the most awful and forceful of sounds, like a man desperate to exorcise a demon. At first Miriana found it irritating, but after a week her irritation shifted to concern, and that concern doubled when Vileron's coughs morphed into shrill, unbearable wheezes, as if he were ready to puke out an organ or two.

The late summer heat worsened matters. Miriana's mouth was dry as salt, her lower back and under arms all gluey with sweat. Evidence of wildfire seemed to follow them around like a bad memory. Fortunately, Raas Dragath's stronghold was only several days away now, a south-southeast cut through a split of low-backed hills. When she ordered Vileron to move with greater haste, his response was a ragged cough. She disliked the sound of that cough, but she disliked more the look of his vulturine face. How could a complexion so healthy and pink quickly become so strained and ashen? His distinctive crisscross of pink scars had faded to a ghostly ivory color, his once sharp eyes looked tired and unfocused, and his bald head was ringed in sweat, as though he'd donned a crown of tears. Even below the neck he looked noticeably weaker, and it wasn't a stretch to say that he was in some degree of pain, but the man was too stoic for his own good.

You have to make it, Cyrille. I can't do this alone. When she tried to tell him that, he brushed her off and said that he was fine, and then he coughed and gurgled up another mouthful of mucus. "I'm tired and suffering from a headache, that's all." His voice was terribly hoarse, as though someone had shredded his larynx with a pocket blade. "I must rest. I'll be fine after I rest."

Miriana had no choice but to consent, and so she spent the remainder of the daylight hours building a crude framed shelter (as best she could under his instruction), and, at the onset of twilight, she cast nets of twine and torn cloth into the nearby lake. The gods of the hunt must've guided her hand, because the nets returned with a handful of minnows, a small speckled trout, and a hearty trio of crayfish. Not only that, but while returning to their campsite she'd happened upon another treat: an abandoned merchant cart. Broken and looted at first glance, but a careful search revealed a leather flask of toddy stuffed in a hidden compartment in the sideboards. So that night, while they feasted, they drank and laughed and allowed the liquor to loosen their tongues and free their worries. Even Vileron showed a measure of improvement, both in body and spirit.

"Here, Your Majesty. Take another," he said, offering a prime cut of their prize kippered trout.

The flaky meat was tender and tasteful in her mouth. She savored it a bit, then swallowed, and finally she said, "I haven't heard that title in a while. 'Your Majesty'. Sounds rather ridiculous out here."

"Well, you are still an empress in my eyes. And I reckon you'll be hearing it again quite soon, once we are welcomed inside Serpenthold."

She was pleasantly surprised by that. "I thank you for the assurance. I know how much you despise Raas Dragath."

"I do. He is a tyrant and a traitor and a thug, but any man who can carve a kingdom out of dust must have some degree of shrewdness. But I won't put my trust in him, and I won't enjoy witnessing an old man lust after you." He coughed a throaty cough.

"Cyrille, are you concerned for my safety, or are you jealous of my future suitor?"

He smiled a tiny smile, the most he ever mustered. "There's a certain bond between a protector and his lady. Not a lovers' bond but a different sort, yet no less strong." Another cough.

"If only others shared your mindset. Vylas, for one."

The scar-faced man swallowed a cooked minnow, then wiped his gray lips with the back of his hand. "I've often wondered why your brother hasn't accompanied us. Did something happen—a disagreement or fallout perhaps?"

Her nod was hesitant, as if unseen hands had moved her head for her. "It happened a few nights before my husband's wakening . . ." The memory was unpleasant, yet for some reason she almost laughed about it now. Perhaps because the offense seemed so trivial in the vastness of the unforgiving wilds. "Vylas . . . tried to have his way with me."

Vileron stared at her, the flask of toddy slowly lowering from his gray lips. "He did *what?*"

"He was drunk, but he . . . he wouldn't stop."

"What did you do?"

She thought about that for a moment, and this time she did laugh. "I booted the scrawny bastard out of my chambers." She paused to shake her head, as if that would somehow remove the memory of that dreadful evening. "He's avoided me ever since."

A shadow obscured Vileron's face. "You should've told me. I would've strangled the bastard."

"That's exactly why I *didn't* tell you."

"But you tell me now. Why?"

"I don't know. The life we had in the Hollow . . . it seems so far away now. And Vylas—it's almost as if I never knew him at all."

"That doesn't mean he should be forgiven. Half-blooded or not, a brother's duty is to protect his sister." He was scowling, though it might've been from the pain. "What he did was heinous, though I won't say it surprises me."

She leaned back, a reflexive action. "Why do you say that?"

"I've never met a man who didn't desire you, either in secret or in plain sight. Your beauty is a rare form, an intoxication so powerful it can sway even the most faithful of men. If Zantherei Athera fell victim to it, why would Raas Dragath or Vylas Voren fare any differently? It's a kind of beauty no verse of poetry could describe, no god could emulate, and no red-blooded man could resist. It is a beauty that is coupled with intellect—a combination deadlier than the wealth or standing of any aristocrat. Truly, it is you who holds the realm in the palm of your hand. I've always known that, and that's why I've always followed you." He coughed a few times. "But make no mistake, I'm your sworn protector, nothing more."

Miriana looked down. She was shocked to hear him speak with such articulacy. Vileron had always been a man whose emotions seemed no deeper than a puddle. Even after all their time together, enduring and overcoming every obstacle in the wilds . . . he'd never offered more than a passing shred of compassion. But now, to see this side of him—well, it was as unusual as it was unexpected.

He offered her another measure of toddy, and Miriana took a generous swig. The hoots and chitters of summer's nocturnal residents filled in the conversational gaps. A tawny owl's tremulous call; a coyote's long and mournful howl. For some reason, the thought of the jumping girl returned to her thoughts. After a long moment she said, "I was fifteen when I was first employed as a courtesan. They say the first year is the hardest; if you can survive that, then you'll survive the trade. My beauty was a curse then—

every man wanted to overuse and abuse me. I had nightmares . . . I was so weak. By some great fortune I befriended a fellow courtesan, and this woman lied for me, covered for me, took turns with some of the nastier clients, so that I could have that tiny sliver of peace I so desperately needed. Were it not for her, I probably would've offed myself."

Vileron was quiet for a long moment. "What happened to her?"

"She got a little lippy with a few unsavory fellows, and they killed her. Right in the next room from where I worked. I heard it all, and yet I did *nothing* to stop it. They killed her, and then they dragged her outside and strung her naked to a post, and it was winter, so her body took a while to decompose. Every day I had to look at her. Every day I had to feel that same guilt and that same shame. I didn't do anything to stop them. I let her *die*."

"No, you didn't," he said, casually slurping down the remainder of his fish broth. "She died because she disrespected those brutes. It's not fair, but it happened. There was nothing you could do."

"You're right. Forgive me, the stupid mind of a stupid woman."

"You're far from stupid, my lady."

She fought back a few threatening tears, then looked away, listening to the synchronized chirping of field crickets. "Hard to believe that was already ten years past. I'm growing old too soon."

"You're only twenty and five," Vileron said.

"Youth is beauty, and beauty is all a woman has. A man's influence comes from status and strength, a woman's comes from beauty. It's a powerful weapon, maybe even the most powerful, but it's fleeting. Short-lived. When it's gone, she has nothing. She *is* nothing."

"Now you're talking rot."

"It's true. In twenty years I will no longer have the same influence over others. Such is a woman's curse."

"And what of men?"

She had to think about that for a moment. "Men are expendable."

Vileron's laugh was brief but loud, and its abrupt ending was punctuated by a sharp, mucous-filled cough.

"I fear I've lost my beauty," she went on, "when that wretch struck me with his . . . cas-teh—whatever the hell you call that thing."

"Cestus," Vileron corrected, before swallowing. He wiped the grease from his fingers on his cloak, then he reached up to touch gently her chin, holding it still to examine her nose. "It healed well enough. The gods have favored you. A minor imperfection on an otherwise perfect face."

"Too kind." She reached up to remove his hand from her chin, but when their fingers touched, he gave a gentle squeeze, and the two exchanged a warm gaze. Miriana withdrew her hand, her eyes shifting downward. To dispel the awkwardness, she said, "So you do have a gentle heart under that hard exterior. I never knew."

"Well, now you do."

They spoke about minor things for a while, about how the moonlight shadowing the outlying thicket gave the impression of sinister, long-limbed creatures, or about how Vileron in his youth feared the call of a black-banded wolf, whose howl sounded like the scream of a distressed child. His uncle had told him that it *was* the sound of a distressed child, who had been snatched from his family by a forest bugbear. "I used to hide in the barn all night," he confessed, "so afraid to move that I'd end up pissing myself."

They shared a laugh, brief but heartwarming. Vileron's tone had softened when next he spoke. "I was lying about what I said earlier . . . about being your sworn protector and nothing more. Truth is, I'm no different from the others. You shouldn't look so surprised."

"Cyrille, I . . ." she began, but stopped when she knew not how to reply. Vileron was indeed a powerhouse of a man, tall and strong and skilled with a blade, but he was also quite unattractive, with or without those scars. She cringed at the thought of lying naked beside him, giggling and caressing one another as lovers do. She would never see him that way . . . even now, at the height of her loneliness, at a time in which she was so undeniably desperate for another's touch. *How long has it been?* Even when her husband Zantherei had neglected her, which was often, she had her personal attendant Yana to please her and provide the warmth of steady contact. *Oh, gentle Yana, I wish you were here right now.*

Still, a delicate situation such as this required a touch of verbal finesse, as unrequited love was known to make some men crazy. Miriana didn't want to insult Vileron, or outright reject him—but she also didn't want to mislead him or promise him something she knew she wouldn't deliver. No, Miriana had to choose her next words carefully, to be certain not to cause any offe—

"But I'm no fool," he blurted with a cough. "I know I'll never be anything more than your sword and shield. I've accepted it, so let's not waste our breath discussing it."

———

Anseth was trapped in a figurative vise. Before him lay his gravely wounded elder brother, yet across the way stood the impatient eyes of his Vaskultan warriors. Anseth did his best to ignore the latter, but the looks were turning tense, which meant an explanation was sorely needed—and soon. *Why are we still here?* their eyes seemed to ask. *We belong in the north.*

Even Kirik couldn't restrain his displeasure. "Commander Kaigon is waiting, lord. We need to mobilize, the northern horns call for our return."

Anseth didn't reply right away. He returned to the waiting area and sat down on the same couch he'd been sitting on for the past two days. Then he spent the next few moments observing the owlish physician Penry, who was busy tending Alarin. "He's my elder brother, my blood," Anseth said at last. "He needs my protection. I can't leave. Not yet."

"He is protected by his own people. Your *true* brothers need you. The north needs you."

"So return to the encampment, gather the men, and go. I'll return when I can."

"The tribe cannot stand without its chieftain."

His bondsman was probably right, but that only made Anseth release a frustrated sigh. To stay or to depart; no longer was it an easy decision to make. *Once I would've given anything to return to my homeland, but when I finally did I couldn't wait to go back north.* His eyes drifted back to the painting, the one that had been occupying his mind for the past two days. It was strange—at first glance it looked no different from every other cityscape painting, but upon closer inspection there was something darkly mysterious about it.

Looking straight on, the evening market square appeared to be a quiet, routine place, but peering from another angle revealed a different story. The hawker who was sweeping out his stall was actually holding a severed arm. The sacks of grain in the porter's barrow were actually a cluster of human heads. The woman who was dumping swill from an upper story building was actually dumping fresh blood; a second woman standing beneath the plaque of a four-story inn wasn't pretty but monstrously ugly. And the two toughs crouched in the alley weren't chatting idly—no, they were feasting on the entrails of a still-breathing man.

Anseth had never seen a work of art like this. *How was it made?* Penry had called it a 'lenticular' painting, or a marvel of optical illusions arranged to mislead the eye from various perspectives. He also revealed the title: *In the Shadows of Deceit.* Anseth stared at it now, as he had stared at it yesterday, and the day before, for hours on end. Certainly, an odd choice for the waiting area of a private chamber, but Anseth couldn't deny how it drew the eye.

"We need to know, lord," Kirik cut in, "if our chieftain is with us."

Anseth had no answer; he remained torn between his brother and his people. *Years ago, when I was first taken by the northmen, I fought and fought until I found myself in the forefront of the Vaskultan ranks. Everything I did was for a greater purpose. Everything I did was to get where I stand right now.* His eyes drifted once more to his elder brother. *But Alarin needs me. There's no choice to be made.*

Anseth reached inside his Vaskultan longcoat, pulling out the Earthstone talisman and offering it to Kirik. "Take it. Go on. My home is here, with my brother. He is my blood, my *true* blood. Take it, please . . . before I change my mind."

Kirik looked offended, as if Anseth tried to hand him a venomous fish. "Lord Revek . . . I can't take this. I'm just a bondsman."

"And I'm an Anirian. Remember, Vaskultans chose men based on merit, not blood. And I choose you."

He seemed to consider that for a moment, but in the end shook his head adamantly. "I can't accept this."

"You can. Take it and lead the men back to the north. Unite the Gray Plains. Do it in my honor if you must or do it in Lord Volduk's memory. Do it, and when it is done, when all the north is united and all the tribes are as one, then make your choice. Keep it or step down and pass the stone to Volduk's grandson, should he prove worthy enough. Then live out your days surrounded by the beauty of the natural world. This is my final command, and it must be obeyed."

Kirik didn't move. He continued to examine the Earthstone

quietly, cautiously, as though it were a disc of hot iron. "I'm no chieftain. I can't lead the men."

"You must," Anseth admitted, and suddenly a wellspring of unspoken truths came tumbling out of his inner heart. "I can't do it any longer. I'm tired, Kirik. Every day I must fight to keep my position. Every goddamn day. It's a constant struggle; I never know who's looking to challenge my place. I'm tired of proving myself, and I'll be damned if I'm ever forced inside that bone cage again. No, I've fought in bloody battles and I've gotten lost in lightless caves and I've teetered on the precipice of mountains, but nothing is as harrowing as walking into that bone cage. Because once I'm inside, I know there's only two ways it can go: I either kill or I die. No, I don't think I can do that again."

Kirik's long face remained tense as he considered Anseth's words. "I didn't expect this from you, lord. You've never showed such . . . uncertainty."

"No chieftain should, but it's the truth. You may be young, and a bondsman, but you've shown the strength and wisdom required to lead the tribe."

Kirik didn't seem to know what to say, but in the end, he stubbornly shook his head. "Stay with your brother. I will take the company and ride back to the encampment." He turned and tossed Anseth a wary, sidelong look. "But I'll not accept your offer. You're a man of the north, whether you think it or not. You belong with us."

CHAPTER SIXTEEN

Seric Dyre sat upon a barded charger, waiting for the two-drumbeat signal.

He was positioned at the fore of the concealed detachment, Sunburst sheathed at the hip, shoulders aching from the weight of his blackened scale armor. In the distance, the Anirian advance battled against a warband of three thousand Vaskultans, and the sounds they produced all bled together like the crashing of waves against a sea wall. It was difficult to take in these sounds, but these were brave and loyal men in the most honest moments of their lives, and Seric had to remember that.

The push of the Anirian advance was relentless, and under this force the barbarians began to fall back. But this wasn't some disorganized rabble of men fleeing pell-mell; no, the Vaskultans were performing a feigned rout. Truth was, when one sees his enemies tuck tail and run, he becomes fueled by the uncontrollable desire to chase them down and strike them in the back and trample their fallen bodies beneath the iron-nailed horseshoes of his mount. But in succumbing to this desire, one loses the protective organization of his rankmates, leaving himself vulnerable to a counter assault. It happened at Black Gate Pass, when a Serkut rout had suddenly regrouped to decimate the Anirian center. On that fateful day, Seric's adoptive father, Nethan Dyre, had lost his life.

But today, Seric was prepared for the tactic. He'd seen it all in advance, like a soothsayer before a scrying stone. Not only had he seen it, but he'd devised his stratagem for it. So, when the Vaskultans executed their maneuver, when the massive fleeing warband of barbarian horsemen suddenly wheeled about to crush the Anirian front . . . there was no Anirian front to crush, as they were no longer in pursuit. And that was when it happened.

Two drumbeats.

The sound was a death knell shooting through the trees, so sudden and so loud it struck the ears like a pugilist's haymaker. *Boom. Boom.* Two drumbeats. One and then another. In reply flags rose, red as blood, which prompted Seric to crack his horsewhip and lead the charge out of the dark of the forest. The ranks around him roared onto the battlefield like a great gnathic beast, etching fearful surprise onto the faces of the Vaskultans. *They're unprepared,* Seric thought. *For the first time in recorded history the barbarian bastards are unprepared.* They were also staggered and off-balance, and when Seric's detachment struck, the result was a spearing collision that produced a *CRASH* so loud it devoured all other sounds.

The line of barbarian horsemen bowed inward, and moments later they were grunting and shouting and frantically defending themselves with tasseled pikes and steel backswords. Seric had already lost his spear. He couldn't even say how; maybe he'd thrown it, or maybe the impact of the two forces had pried it from his grip. In any case, a second spear sat in his saddle ring, and he pulled it free just in time to stick a charging barbarian rider through the leathered breast. The man grimaced and clutched at the wound, his mount galloping onward, never to be seen again. Sunburst found

Seric's hand a moment later, and with it he slashed at every swarthy Vaskultan face he saw. He took down two, three, four men, then he felt a sudden dump of fatigue, as if his limbs were tied to stones and placed underwater. The Vaskultan warriors appeared and disappeared and reappeared, some slashing at Seric's blackened scales with the blades of their pikes, others taking stabs that came dangerously close to his face. Once a Vaskultan arrow screamed past his ear, but Seric lowered his helmeted head and drove himself forward, knocking a foeman down before wheeling upon the bowman. The barbarian panicked and tried to stab Seric's neck with an arrow, but Sunburst cut off his hand—and then opened his throat. The man fell from his mare, grimacing and gurgling blood as he lay upon the dust-choked earth.

The Vaskultan lines were faltering. Anirian detachments were drilling them from the front, while flankers were hurling pots of pitch from ambush points, causing thick black smoke to billow and bloom and cause widespread panic. Some barbarians continued to stand and fight the bloody fight, while others disengaged and hesitated, unsure of what to do or where to go. The Anirian ranks had them pinned on three sides; Seric could see the distress and uncertainty on their ugly faces. *And what an exhilarating sight it is.* These grim barbarian bastards . . . they were not inhuman. No, they were men, and they were afraid.

The Vaskultan lines went from faltering to folding—and this time it wasn't feigned. Seric urged his soldiers forward, a forcefulness that drove the enemy in the direction he wanted them to go. Stubbornly, willfully, as though they were wise to what was happening, the barbarians resisted, but their attempt to break south was stymied by Wyath's host of infantrymen, who rose before them like an armored blockade. The barbarians then wheeled and galloped east, only to be intercepted by General Zirian and his emerging Zhoulish auxiliaries. A rearmost line of bowmen rained down flaming arrows that set both barbarian and brush alight, causing a redoubled swath of panic to run through the Vaskultan forces. Overwhelmed, they had no choice but to band together and flee down a narrow stretch of land called the Tendril Way.

It was then Seric knew he had them.

Another two drumbeats. *Boom. Boom.* Seric's detachment immediately lifted the pursuit and galloped along a western bypath, while the main forces under generals Zirian and Wyath continued to funnel the Vaskultans through the passage. Flagmen guided them from high vantage points. Flag left to move right, flag right to move left. It seemed an endless journey across the forested reaches before Seric could hear the rumble of the Vaskultan fleers below. He halted the detachment, their position set. The final maneuver to crush the enemy would soon be unleashed. The coup de grâce, as it were.

Seric just needed to wait for the final two-drumbeat signal. Timing was crucial now—every second mattered, and yet, even as the dust-cloud that carried the main Vaskultan body entered the ambush point, the signal did not come. *Where is it? Where is the goddamn signal?* Panic seized his heart. He had to strike now, otherwise the Vaskultans would push through the passage and escape. He waited and waited and waited, but nothing came. *Son of a frog fucker,* Seric thought. *Someone's going to die for this.* He turned to his men and did the only sensible thing he could do. He ordered the charge.

For a moment the soldiers exchanged confused glances with one another, but when Seric repeated the order and started down the rise, the men sprang to life and followed. The wind was screaming in his ears now, the sizzling summer air buffeting his face. *We're coming for you,* Seric thought. *We're coming for you all.* He could smell the imminence of victory, could taste it on his tongue. His charger's hooves pounded the earth with conviction, surefooted in its step as Seric was sure-minded of his strategy. The Vaskultan dust-cloud was dissipating now, and the first hints of the barbarians' tall pikes and boiled leather armor became visible. *We're coming to kill you all.* Sunburst found Seric's hand, its steel tip glinting in the dusky light. *Here we come. Get ready to face your death.*

But no—he realized too late his error. This wasn't the main Vaskultan body but a much smaller contingent. *They decoyed their position,* he thought. *But how?* Then he saw it—riders using branches to disrupt the ground, creating a thicker and more pervasive cloud of dust than what should've been. A few had even tied the branches to their horses' tails to strengthen the effect. *They decoyed their position . . . I don't believe it. They deceived me! I must get the detachment back into position. I moved too damn soon.*

Just then the final two drumbeats sounded. *Boom. Boom.* Seric let out a sound that was half a frustrated shriek and half a tired suspiration. His detachment was too far away now; they would never reach the main body of Vaskultans in time. That realization came to him like the surge of a breaker, and when he and his men charged upon the small Vaskultan contingent, they cut down every northman in sight. Seric lost time during the killing, but when it finally ended, his sword-hand was covered in so much blood he could barely see the color of the skin beneath.

His three generals, Zirian, Wyath, and Madderin, all approached like dogs cautious of a volatile master. The giant Zhoul had streaks of blood spread across the upper plates of his olive cuirass, while General Wyath bore a slight limp from a gash that cracked the scales of his upper left greave. "Your orders . . . the two drumbeats . . . you weren't in position," Wyath said. "Why was your strike premature?"

Seric was breathing heavily, his hands and arms caked with dry blood, his heavy armor filmed in dirt and dust. "What do you think happened? The barbarians tricked me."

"But what of your orders? Any man who deviates will be put to death. *You* authorized this punishment."

General Madderin added, "You said what you said—and now

you have to face the consequences. Otherwise, what sort of leader would you be? What sort of example would you set to—"

Wyath snapped at him to be silent.

The mood became tense, but Seric decided to ignore the insolent general's words. Instead he turned and spoke to Zirian. "Raid the encampment. Rescue my son, kill any who resist, and burn the whole goddamn place to the ground."

Zirian nodded. "What about you?"

"I'll be fine. I won't put myself to the axe. And no one here will demand it of me." His eyes settled on Madderin when he spoke that last part.

Zirian gave another nod and went off, back to his waiting Zhoulish host.

Seric's gaze was left to settle on the skirmish field. He examined the sprawling dead and their discarded decoy branches, and he couldn't help but admire the tactics of the barbarian warriors. Such cunning and poise in the face of adversity; such quickness in executing their deception. With a quiet sigh, he moved closer to Madderin, yet his attention remained plastered on the fallen. He spoke off-handedly. "Did you bed my whore last night?"

It was a strange question to ask in the face of such carnage, so it was no surprise that the handsome general hesitated. "What?"

"Ravia Ravenhair. Did you share your pillow with her last night?"

He shook his head. "The lady never came to my tent. If she had, I would've sent her away. Respectfully, of course, my lord."

"Too bad," Seric told him, "because I'm looking for a reason to take your head."

In a matter of hours, the Vaskultan encampment was reduced to ruin. Anirian soldiers torched their yurts, smashed their tools and equipment, stole their livestock and weapons and women, and slaughtered any lingering tribesmen who attempted to stop them. Seric should've strutted into the encampment with triumph on his shoulders, but instead he slogged in the stiff manner of an overburdened mule. Still, no one had ever routed the barbarians so definitively before, and for that Seric felt accomplished—or he would've, had the bulk of the Vaskultan army not escaped. Not only that, but there was no word of his son's whereabouts. Veldries Dyre was still missing.

That made Seric angry, and, in his anger, he smashed a few things—some old Vaskultan cookery, a few bone tools and bow stands, and half a latticework frame that survived the gutting fires. When that was done and his anger had faded, he ordered Madderin Ruk to drag the Vaskultan captive, Jakken, across the smoldering ground to kneel before him. The small northman's deeply receding brown hair was a knotted mess, and his eyelids seemed so heavy with exhaustion he could barely keep them open.

"My son is not here," Seric explained—calmly, yet with the menace of a master torturer. "Are you playing me false?" His eyes flicked to Madderin. "Ask him."

Madderin did, and the Vaskultan's answer was no. He said he'd spoken the truth about the boy, and then he mumbled something under his breath, something that Madderin didn't translate until Seric ordered him to. "He called you a coward," the deputy general said.

That made Seric smile. "Tell him I just crushed his former tribesmen in open battle. Is that the act of a coward?"

Madderin began to translate the words in the barbarian tongue, but Seric stopped him midway. "Never mind. Take him away for now. I know where to find my son."

"Where?" Madderin asked.

"If this barbarian traitor is speaking the truth, then I see only one sensible explanation. My old friend Ansetheral Athera has him."

"And where is he?"

Seric gave a long pause before answering. "Notify the officers. We march upon Stormhaven."

CHAPTER SEVENTEEN

Rain hammered against the dark cladding of Serpenthold's mournful facade. It was a looming, almost deceptively distorted structure, with uneven battlements and jagged towers that rose some sixty feet high. Vileron described its construction as a mixture of black stone and sundried mud brick, firmly seated on a thick loess base that was divided by scarps of rammed earth. Of course, Miriana Athera knew nothing of masonry, nor did she have any desire to learn, so she nodded politely and feigned interest for his sake. That said, she did take notice when he pointed out the statues of twin serpents perched at each of the four turrets, their eyes glowing a soft green like foxfire on a log of dead-wood. These were the Zythrai, symbols of Raas Dragath's power and prestige—and they were not welcoming at all.

Well, the entire stronghold was a vision of ominous gloom, in truth, and the persistent rain certainly didn't alleviate matters. In buckets it drenched the ragged awnings and the miserable sentries who had the ill luck of standing duty at this time. The wetness glistened against a main gate that bore the likeness of a deep frown, perhaps because of the way the iron bars and knockers were positioned. Still, despite such an uninviting and utterly woeful façade, Miriana wasn't about to turn back. No, she'd been through too much. Raas Dragath was a tyrant and a despot, yes, but he was also just a man. And like any man, he could be swayed by Miriana's charms. *No one is without longing, no one is completely devoid of emotion.*

She remained still and silent as a pair of armed sentries in dark crimson cloaks slogged toward her, boots sloshing through the puddle-soaked earth. To her left, Vileron coughed. A throaty sound, with a low wheeze attached to the end of it. He obviously wasn't getting any better, but fortunately he looked no worse either. Still, once they were escorted safely inside, Miriana would request a physician's assistance at once.

The two sentries were getting closer. Both were on the smaller side, and one was rather plump about the midsection. Admittedly, she wasn't expecting a bright and cheery honor guard, but this seemed a rather low-class way to welcome anyone, let alone a former empress. Still, a sudden thought made her smile. No more running, no more struggling in the wilds, no more fearing the savagery of the land. Soon it would be back to luxurious bedrooms and soothing baths and eager servants. The thought of receiving such lavish attention when she hadn't received any in months . . . well, it was enough to fill her with a joy she also hadn't felt in months. *The nightmare is over,* she thought. *At last, the nightmare is over.*

When they came to a halt before her, Miriana produced an edict with her personal seal affixed, and she held it in their faces before they could ask any foolish questions. "I am the exalted personage Miriana Athera, Empress of the Anir and Lady of Divine Whispers," she stated. "I seek an audience with Lord Raas Dragath."

The sentries bowed, although they didn't seem too impressed, and then they instructed her to follow. She and Vileron were brought inside a side door of the main frowning gate, then beneath a narrow archway of dark stone, which brought them out of the rain along a covered walkway that ended at a studded door. Beyond that was a small and sparse inner courtyard, then another stone walkway that led them to a coiled silver stairway. Up and up they went, to a stone landing and down another corridor broken by several intersections, each lit by scaled patina sconces. As Miriana walked, questions came to her: what kind of guestroom would be arranged, what sort of amenities will be available, where will the feast to commemorate her arrival take place. But when she asked these questions the sentries didn't respond, not until they brought her inside a small stone chamber. "Stay a moment," one told her.

The room was drab and spare, the walls dressed in rough-cut tiles that were held together by slipshod mortaring. A sizable yet empty wooden tub peered out from behind an overlapping triangular screen at the far corner of the room. A bath would be pleasant, but she was expecting finer accommodations, and perhaps a bit of wine and a few dandies to eat. When she asked again for these conveniences, the sentries ignored her and left. Miriana exchanged a disappointed look with Vileron. "Hospitality is lacking."

Vileron was looking around the room. The eerie quiet was broken by his heavy, almost despondent cough. "I don't like this."

In that rare moment she agreed with him, but she wasn't comfortable enough to admit it. "The hour is late. Best not to be hasty about things."

"It matters not the hour. You are Lady Miriana Athera. You deserve far greater treatme—"

The door burst open. A host of red-cloaked soldiers stormed inside, so swift Miriana barely had a moment to react. They whipped past her and bowled Vileron over, dropping him to the floor and piling on top of him like fungus on a rotten stump. She could hear him grunting and struggling, helpless under the Redlander assault. "What are you doing?" Miriana screamed at them. "This man is my escort and protector. Leave him *BE!*"

But they didn't leave him be, nor did they even acknowledge her, not even when she shouted and stomped her foot and reminded them of who she was. The soldiers were talking to Vileron, ordering him to stop fighting and make things easier for himself. After they delivered three more blows, the big man finally submitted, and then gauntleted hands lifted him up and began hauling him out of the chamber. Vileron offered a brief, forlorn look Miriana's way, and then he was gone.

Even as the door slammed shut, Miriana continued her shouting. This was an injustice, an affront no self-respecting woman would ever forgive. But for all her wild ranting, she was just a lone woman in a small dank room, and when her voice turned hoarse, she stopped shouting and sat down. Time passed. The stillness was painful, the silence excruciating. No one came to offer food, dry clothes, or even a simple explanation or word of chat. She sat there, hungry and wet and wholly miserable.

When the cell door finally did open, a lithe and youthful man appeared in the entryway. He moved inside with the fluidic grace of an elder statesman, then he knelt before the lady, tracing the features of her face with a single finger. At last he said, "Your nose looks a little rough, your body could use a wash, but you are as beautiful as I recall."

Miriana pushed his hand away. "We've never met. Who are you?"

"Hiriam Thraves. First general and principal strategist to the Great Zythrai Lord Raas Dragath. And we *have* met before, three years ago, a brief encounter at the Hollow. Do you not remember? Your husband awarded me with a golden plaque for my bravery in battle. It was during the second course of the great Feast of—"

"That's a lie," she said. "We never met. You're *lying*."

His smile twinkled. "Comely *and* astute, I'm impressed. But I have *seen* you before. Though you were dressed a bit more . . . elegantly, I must admit."

"Where's Lord Dragath? I've arranged an audience with him. I bear an official edict."

"Yes, I know, but I had to make sure you are who you say you are. Can't have some imposter squandering our good lord's time now, can we?" He pointed intrusively at her nose. "So what *did* happen there?"

Miriana pulled back. "I was attacked on the road. Brigands."

"How unfortunate," he said. "Were you raped?"

"I would've been, had my escort not protected me."

"I'm not surprised, you are a beautiful creature. The things some men would do to you would make a baboon blush."

"How sweet," she mocked.

"Let's get you nice and comfortable, shall we?" His eyes flicked to his guardsmen, two brawny fellows waiting at the entryway. "Strip her."

Before Miriana could react, one rushed forward and grabbed hold of her. She tried to slip free, but his grip only tightened, and a moment later the second guardsman rose over her, meaty fingers unfastening the clasp of her cloak and yanking it off. The same man seized her tunic next, then used a knife to shear it open. "Get away from me," Miriana shrieked. "What are you—" Within moments the torn remnants of her tunic and trousers and smallclothes fell unceremoniously to the floor, and suddenly she found herself standing utterly naked, with Hiriam and his two brutes staring at her like lascivious drunks, not even attempting to hide their carnal appetites. "Take her back," Hiriam said at length.

They dragged her across the room like a misbehaved mutt. The wide bathtub greeted her behind that triangular screen, in the center of an otherwise unfurnished alcove. No windows, no furniture, just a couple of low braziers, whose black iron stands were forged as rising serpents. "What is this?" Miriana asked. "I will bathe myself. Stop it. What are you doing?"

Hiriam ignored that. "Put her in."

The water hit her with a sharp splash. It wasn't uncomfortable—no, in fact it was rather soothing to her bare skin. Still, alarm drove her clawing for a way out, but the hands on her were too strong. With a series of sharp clangs, the guardsmen shackled her wrists and ankles to the manacles that were attached to the inner walls of the tub. She instinctively tried to yank herself free, but the rusty metal chafed her skin, so she resigned to lay there, hands and feet bound above the surface, while the rest of her nude body lay submerged and spread like a mother-to-be before a midwife.

A bone-thin and hooded fellow came over holding a lidless iron bucket. He set it down beside the bath. Peeking inside, Miriana saw the water was dark and swishing with irregular movement. There was something unnerving about that. *By all the gods, what the hell is in there?* she wondered.

Hiriam stood over the pot, then he bent down to reach into the water. He pulled out a long and snakelike little creature, no longer than the span of a hand, and no thicker than a piece of ribbon. Brownish dots and yellow bands ran along the length of its slender body. "Spineback eels, my lady." Just as he finished saying that, the eel slipped from his fingers, flew into the air, and landed on the floor with a wet *splat*. Hiriam watched it writhe there for a long moment, until the hooded attendant managed to scoop it up and dump it back in the bucket. "Little buggers are slippery, but they're also kind of cute, don't you think?"

Miriana stared at him. *What is this? What are you going to do to me?* Fear and confusion prevented her from asking these questions aloud, but such emotions must've been plain because Hiriam snorted at her like an intellectual amused by a loafer's dimwittedness. "Do you think Raas Dragath so gullible, my lady? Did you think you could come here, with all your beauty and charms, and manipulate us as though we were a rabble of simple-minded miscreants?"

"I came to offer my hand. For an alliance. That is no lie."

Hiriam shook his head pointedly, back and forth, back and forth, while softly murmuring, "No, no, no."

"I fled the capital," she went on. "Abandoned my imperial standing, my *LIFE* of power and privilege. That is the truth. Look at my nose, I was struck by some lowly cur. Do you truly believe my people would've allowed that to happen to their lady and empress?"

"I don't know the truth to that, but I promise you I will find out."

"How? You're just a bully and a lackey, and you have no right to humiliate me in this manner. I demand to speak to Raas Dragath alone."

He ignored that. "Tell me why you left the Hollow."

"Or what? You're going to slime me to death with those stupid eels? They are repulsive, sure, but I've been through worse. Now obey me and remove these shackles at once."

Hiriam sighed, a heavy sigh, like a man reluctant to begin his daily labors. His boyish eyes turned upon the attendant. "Put them in."

The bucket rose and overturned, and a mass of eels slid into the water with a gentle *splash*. Miriana tensed, her mouth twisting to stifle a squeal of disgust. In moments she could feel the nasty things slithering around her, not uniformly, but in a random and unsettling manner, their slimy elongated bodies rubbing against her naked flesh like strands of loose silk. Worst part was, with her wrists and ankles fettered and outstretched, she could do nothing except jerk her hips or wriggle her bottom, but she quickly learned that such movements only attracted them more. Still, Miriana couldn't help herself; she was now squirming beneath their constant brushing and rasping—sharp and sudden sensations, like the prick of very dull thorns. It didn't hurt, not truly, but it was a disgusting, revolting, and humiliating spectacle, and she told Hiriam that, and then she spit in his face.

The youthful Redlander didn't even bother to wipe the spittle from his cheek. He was not an ugly man, though perhaps a little too bright-eyed and innocent-looking for her tastes. "Last chance," he said. "Tell me why you left the Hollow."

She offered up another nasty insult, told him to go get trampled by a horse or something, and then she savored the stupid look on his face. Miriana had been through too much to be intimidated by this fool and his little tricks. No, she wasn't like other women; she was strong as silk, hard as a slab of stone. Let those squirmy little eels rub against her skin; she didn't care. But just as her confidence rose, she realized that Hiriam wasn't finished yet. He offered a nod to the hooded man, who then lifted a wooden stick that resembled a miniature oar. He dipped it in the water, stirring it in a circular motion, to encourage the current. In response, the eels began to dart and dash, their movements more erratic than before.

"You see, the thing about spineback eels," Hiriam explained, "they have this special little ability. A great survival aid in the fast-flowing tributaries of the southern tropics. You see, when the rivers turn to rapids, the eels keep from being swept downstream by burrowing into the smallest crevices they can find. Once inside, they erect little spines to ensure they remain put. Any weedy crevice or mossy hole would do, the smaller the better." He feigned a wincing face before continuing. "Now if it were to erect those spines in a *human* orifice . . . well, I can only assume that it would be very, very painful."

The eels were thrashing now. She felt them rasping at her body, searching the corners and folds of her skin for places to hide. She pressed her backside against the bottom of the tub, but her ankles were shackled too far apart to close fully her legs. A lone eel pressed against her sex, then it darted away. Another followed, and another—rasping, rasping, rasping—until finally, one found its way inside her.

It was an odd feeling, uncomfortable at first, disgusting for sure, but it didn't hurt. Not right away, not until the spines came out. She knew when they did because pain exploded inside her, a pain that raced all the way up her body, past her chest, and up to her eyes. She screamed and screamed for them to take it out—*please, please, please,* again and again and again. *Take it out, take it out, take it OUT.*

Hiriam was disturbingly calm. "Will you tell me why you left the Hollow? I want to know everything. Will you tell me everything?"

"YES," she screamed at him. "YES, YES, *PLEASE.*" *Oh gods, it hurts. It hurts so much.*

Hiriam gave an all-too-casual signal, and then the hooded torturer put down the mini-oar, stuck his hand in the water, and reached between her legs. After a grueling moment, he must've grabbed the eel in a way that made the spines retract, because the pain began to lessen. He pulled the slimy creature out of her and placed something to protect her sex, a plug of cloth perhaps. Then the shackles were removed, hands helped her out of the tub, and someone placed a robe over her. She didn't remember being led to the daybed, but she was lying on it now, shivering from the chill and moaning at the pain that tore at her insides.

At some point Hiriam sat down on a stool beside her. He handed her a bowl of wine and a dish of cured pork strips, but she had neither thirst nor appetite. When he spoke, his voice was quiet yet menacing. "I'm waiting, my lady."

She told him everything. All her underhanded dealings and immoral activities at the Hollow, from her bloody rise to the throne, to her clandestine relations with Seric, and finally her betrayal to her husband. She even detailed the night she tried to murder Zantherei while he lay in a comatose state. Yes, she told him that and other things she'd never expected to tell anyone, and by the time she was done and there were no secrets left to her name, she felt a deeper form of anguish than any torturer could ever inflict.

BOOK III: PRETENSES

CHAPTER EIGHTEEN

The growing autumn wind plastered Szathan Mordall's ragged gray cloak to his back and legs. It was a peculiar wind, not the breezy lightness one would expect from the season's turn, but a warmer one, as if the gods, for some inexplicable reason, had granted the realm an extension of summer. With the first frosts of dawn nowhere to be found, all that remained was a faint glistening of dew along the tips of the grassy sward. The nearby oaks and sweetgums remained virile and clothed, while the maples and ginkgo trees refused to don their brilliant red-gold robes. The willow trees retained their soft green color, but that was expected since they were among the last to turn—unlike the cold weather fruits of hawthorn berries and rosehips, who remained too timid to emerge.

Szathan detached his gaze from the countryside, letting it fall upon the surrounding suburban developments. Longhouses and manors and outbuildings stood in arranged clusters, forming small hamlets that were separated by rows of farmsteads. During the harvest, it was common to see men and women working in the mulberry groves, tending the trees and the silkworm stations, or cleaning and replacing the ground straw. Others would spend long hours rotating crops of millet and soybeans for winter gourds and melons, a rather complex process of planting and interplanting and fertilizing specific plants while making efficient use of the spaces between the trees. But with the weather so abnormally skewed, the harvest had inevitably been delayed, and so the farmers were given no choice but to remain patient, most keeping busy with the menial tasks of repairing granaries and storage pits and ploughs.

Szathan's own patience was at an end, and not because of the cropland. He had been hunting Minister Byort for days now, sifting through the innards of these hamlets and their greater counties without a moment of rest. He'd scoured every roadside inn and hostelry and wine shop, as well as every thatched hall of every outlying village—but he always seemed one step behind the tax collector. Not only that, but his old knee injury began to flare up, which slowed his pace and hastened his frustration. *How can an untrained minister be so hard to pin down?* As disheartening as his search was proving to be, Szathan didn't allow himself to give in to despair. He was too damn angry. What had been done to Lord Alarin was low and sinful; the perpetrator must be apprehended and put in bonds. *I've failed you once, my lord, but I won't fail you a second time.*

After another day of fruitless searching, he and General Thayer Dal retired to their rented room, a tiny nook nestled among the other nooks along the upper story of a ramshackle inn. Its structural shape was oblong and dilapidated, its hallways and common areas thick with the odors of stale millet and rancid cheese. Even with the windows unlatched and open, there was no purging those smells, so Szathan had no choice but to endure and even grow comfortable with them. He spent much of his time enjoying the grand view of the distant city of Stormhaven, his tiny eyes observing how the moonlight caressed the dips and ridges of the outer walls. As towering and impressive as those walls were, they were not impregnable. No, whenever a wall was built, there was always a man who dedicated himself to overcoming it. This time, it didn't take rams or missiles or teams of sappers; no, it was a lone assassin, working from the inside.

Szathan uttered a sound that was half a sigh and half a groan, then he turned away from the window with a gauntleted hand rubbing his forehead.

"Another headache?" Thayer Dal asked. The lanky general was seated at the edge of a lopsided armchair, sharpening a curved dagger with a coarse whetstone. "When do you not have headaches?"

Szathan waited for the scraping to stop before he replied. "When you're not around."

"Did the big man just make a jest? I didn't know you had it in you." He paused, his smile fading. "What's truly bothering you?"

"I let it happen," Szathan confessed at length. "I was sworn to protect Lord Alarin. I let it happen."

"Guilt has no place in the heart, my friend."

"How can it not?"

"Where we failed, the gods allowed Lord Ansetheral to succeed. Alarin would've been on his journey to the next life had his brother not intervened. For that, we both stand in Anseth's debt. He is the redeemer, the one who deserves praise."

There may have been truth to that, but it didn't assuage Szathan's guilt one bit. "I wish my mind was keen enough to foresee this."

"Don't doubt yourself. Of Lord Alarin's officers, you are among the most sensible. His words."

"Lord Alarin . . . he told you that?"

Thayer placed the whetstone aside, then rose and went to stand beside him at the window. He had a nimble way of moving, a soft and slither-like grace. "That he did. Now cast down your misgivings and raise your spirits—we will find this bastard betrayer soon enough."

"I don't know. We've already questioned everyone we saw. I greased palms, I interrogated folk—I even threatened a man to harm. No one wants to speak to me, the monster that I am." It was understandable. Most commoners refused to meet the giant general's gaze, and the few that did seemed flustered or frightened by his disproportionate features and blackened plates of armor. Taloned pauldrons, spiked greaves, high plumed helmet—everything about Szathan Mordall spoke of strength and martial authority. It wasn't hard to see why most were disinclined to share information, and those that did either lied outright or led them to a place where Byort had long departed.

"Do you think I'd survive if I jumped?"

"*What?*"

Thayer was leaning out of the open window so far that his head was almost out of sight. His voice was muffled by the breeze. "If I *jumped* out of this window, do you think I'd survive?"

Szathan shook his head. "Get back inside. I don't know why you'd say something like that."

Thayer pulled back from the window, now sporting the sliest of smiles. He ran a thumb and forefinger against the stubble of his chin, an overly dramatic gesture of contemplation. Everything about him was so theatrical. "The old man . . . you know, the one we met outside the elder's house. He claimed he saw Byort heading north to the monastery."

Szathan shook his head. "Likely a mistake, or a blatant lie. Monks don't pay taxes, there's no reason a tax collector would travel that way. Come now, General, even I know that."

"Of course, silly, but that is why his words struck me as odd."

Szathan turned from the window to face the spindly man.

"Perhaps Byort is seeking absolution," Thayer said.

Szathan continued to stare at him, though now it was more a puzzled look.

"It means forgiveness for one's sins. Perhaps he seeks it for attempting to murder Lord Alarin."

Szathan thought about it. "Byort doesn't seem like the type. In fact, he seems as cold and cruel as the insects he studies." When Thayer didn't dispute that, Szathan gave a long shake of his head. "A lot of uphill hiking for a hunch. Not sure if the effort will be worth it."

"Could be time squandered, yes, but we should exhaust all possible avenues, don't you think?"

Szathan almost shook his head a second time, but when his gaze returned to the open window to view the autumn landscape, he eventually gave a nod. "Leave the horses at the stableyard; we'll head uphill at daybreak."

By midmorning the two generals had reached the outer checkpoint bridge that marked the district's end. Heavy wagons lumbered by, axles straining as wheels rattled and rumbled against stone flags and packed earth, moving in the defined ruts of the many who'd passed before. The day was warm and idyllic, with nary a cloud in a vast sapphire sky. Szathan met the stationed soldiers in the waiting stand and shot a glare to any who dared waste his time with petty proce-dure. A short man with tall hair validated their lead when he claimed to see Minister Byort heading toward Blue Heron Monastery, where he was enjoying a respite from his travel duties. So Szathan and Thayer immediately set off, enduring a lengthy trek through woodsy paths and misshapen hills before they finally came upon the monastery grounds.

An old cobbled path led them through the cloisters, a serene and intimate area that was swaddled by a stand of majestic banyan trees. Tree rodent chitters and frog calls held them in fine company, while the few monks they saw kept their heads lowered and their hands tucked inside the sleeves in their habits.

Szathan disrupted the peace when he pulled one aside and asked about Byort. The old tonsured fellow offered a smile and crooked a dirty forefinger, indicating the north-facing temple complex. It was a tall timber structure fronted by a wide forecourt and surrounded by pathways that led to various gardens and mausoleum grounds and dagobas. The hip-and-gable roof was tiled in hardened clay and ornamented in petal-shaped acroteria.

When Szathan pushed the huge temple doors open, the sound they produced was a long and drawn caterwaul. Rows of monks in tattered habits turned at once, each wide-eyed and obviously displeased by the disturbance. Truly, it was among his most shameful of intrusions, but Szathan had a task to complete, and so he questioned the monks and searched the temple until at last the truth was made plain. Byort was not here.

In silence the two generals exited the monastery grounds and headed back down the wooded hills. *Another day wasted,* Szathan mused. By the time they reached the bottom, the sun was already beginning its western escape, leaving the light of dusk to drench the sky in pale orange. Szathan walked and walked and continued to walk, and only when Thayer called out his name did he stop and turn around. The Wild Goose was standing before the ragged awning of a roadside inn. "Let's stop here, get a drink inside," he said.

"We have a room already."

"I know, but it's still a bit of a ways down the road. I need something to ease the day, something strong. Let's see what sort of spirits this place offers, what do you say?"

Szathan's gaze drifted to the inn. The double-storied building was surprisingly inviting, if a bit quiet at this hour. "Come on," Thayer urged, twice, thrice, before Szathan finally turned and followed with thumping footfalls. A drunk staggering from the opposite direction scowled at Szathan after a near-collision, but when the big general squared his shoulders and straightened his posture, the smaller man blanched and raised his hands apologetically before scurrying off. Szathan's glare didn't waver until the fool was out of sight.

A hand touched his armored shoulder—Thayer's hand. "Easy, big guy."

Szathan ignored that. He climbed a slight incline and stopped in front of the limed oak double-doors. He could hear the rumble of conversation inside. He raised a hand to enter—but at that moment, the door whined open and a man stumbled out. Not just any man— Byort. What a divine stroke of fortune! For all his long hours of man-hunting, Szathan ended up unintentionally bumping into the suspect. The pause between them was brief, a fleeting moment where their eyes met. The bug-eyed minister looked surprised, even a little joyful, perhaps, in seeing a familiar face. "General," he piped up. "What are you doing h—"

Szathan seized the bastard by the back of the neck and drove him to the ground. The man gave a loud *oomph* as he landed hard on his hands and knees. His bodyguards, a thickset pair of protective swordsmen, stepped forward, but when Szathan shot them a glare, they stepped right back.

A moment later Thayer Dal glided in front of them, his fingers touching the hilt of his sheathed blade as a warning. The guardsmen's eyes trailed from the blade to Byort, who made no attempt to fight back, although his mouth was working freely enough. "You big ugly stupid brute—what the hell are you doing?"

"Taking you back to the city," Szathan said.

"For what? I'm midway through my collecting duties, in case that wasn't plain. How stupid are—"

Szathan gave him another shove. "Your duties are over. You're being detained."

His bulging eyes narrowed as best they could. "On what charge?"

"Coordinating a plot to assassinate an esteemed official."

"What? That's rubbish," the minister argued, but he didn't fight back when Szathan bound his wrists in silk cordage. "Which official?"

Szathan wanted to punch his mouth for asking that, but instead he curbed his temper and hoisted the man to his feet. "Lord Alarin Athera."

Byort didn't respond; he simply stared at Szathan, as though he were trying to solve a complex equation in his mind. At length, and with defiant calmness, he spoke. "Where's the emperor's official mandate? Your hands are empty."

"The order has been given by Lord Alarin's brother, Ansetheral."

"The barbarian lord? He has no authority here. The White Fang Council doesn't answer to—"

Szathan palmed the top of the man's head with a single hand. He had to use every ounce of restraint not to crush his skull. And by the gods did he want to. Even still, his grip must've been too firm, because the minister began to panic, soon yelping for help. The nearest swordsman, the thicker (and clearly braver) of the pair, looked as though he wanted to intercede, but Thayer reaffirmed his roadblock of a stance, which caused the guardsman to abandon the notion. Above their heads, candlelight flickered, and silhouettes began to materialize inside the inn's unlatched windows. A small audience was gathering, some pointing and gawking, others talking in loud murmurs to one another. One drunken idiot burst out of the open doorway to demand an explanation. Szathan brought out Nightwing and pointed the spiked head at the man, ordering him to get back inside. That seemed to be explanation enough, but once the man retreated more onlookers appeared in the doorway, and more inquisitive faces crammed the open windows.

"I think it's time to go," Thayer said, his tone as casual as a man ordering a meal.

Szathan nodded and pushed the minister along the hard-packed pathway. Thayer remained behind, apologizing to the crowd for the disturbance—in his own smooth and smarmy way, of course. Still, Szathan didn't care about such courtesies. He didn't care about anything except hauling this conniving bastard back to the city.

CHAPTER NINETEEN

The door opened with a low metallic whine. Miriana Athera lifted her head from the dusty stone floor and shielded her eyes from the sudden outpour of light. When her vision returned, she saw in the entryway the silhouette of a man, obvious by his thickset frame and even thicker beard. He moved inside the cell, neither gracefully nor sprightly, but with a lumbering authority. The oil lamp he set down was a gilded bronze replica of a serpent, with a tail-end that served as a channel for the smoke's release. The constant flickering stole Miriana's focus for a moment, until the man took a seat before her on an old hassock of rushes.

Raas Dragath.

She knew it by his presence, by his look, by the way he carried himself. His face was as cruel as the rumors told, his features broad and flat and curtained by long snarls of silvery hair that dipped past his bushy beard. The two prominent scars on his face were unnerving, especially the jagged one that ran below his right eye.

Of his physique, he was far more robust and muscular than one might expect of a man in his later years. Miriana assumed he was nudging sixty, though he had the resilient look of a man who refused to be throttled by the passage of time. And even though his attire was drab of color, it was not without a certain inelegant charm: waistcoat and scarf and breeches and boots all in gray, along with a ragged bloodred cape that drew the eye like a diamond in a heap of coal.

For a time, the Redlander warlord didn't speak, but his cruel, cavernous eyes probed every inch of her, as though he planned to later describe her likeness to a master artist. It was an awful feeling, having your captor's eyes on you in a dead silence and after a prolonged period of solitude. She wanted him to speak. To say something. Anything. *Stop ogling me and speak!* Everything was so still, so maddeningly quiet.

At last Dragath moved, a single hand that rose to shove something in his mouth. He began chewing, a slopping and slurping noise that echoed obnoxiously within the confines of the cell. Miriana caught a whiff of smoked meat, but it had a spiciness to it that caused her eyes to moisten. He offered her a taste, but she demanded wine instead. That made him chuckle, a deep rumbling sound that lacked cheerfulness. She wanted to ask him why that was so amusing, but her nerve failed her.

"Does it ache?" he asked at last. "Your cunt."

Of course it aches, you crass bastard. In truth, the pain had diminished to little more than a dull throb, which worsened to a sting only when she urinated. Still, she didn't like the way he spoke to her, the utter disdain in his voice. She wanted to cuss at him, perhaps even spit on him, but that would've likely stirred the man's wrath—and if the rumors were true, it was a terrible wrath indeed. Raas Dragath was known to be a volatile man, cruel and crude and crabby, a boil ready to burst at any moment. Vileron once told her that Dragath removed a man's ears and nose for staring at him the wrong way.

"Why not remove the eyes?" she had asked.

"Because he wanted the victim to witness the stares of others,"

Vileron had replied. "And stare they did, at his hideously disfigured face."

Miriana let go of the memory and swallowed hard. Words had to be chosen carefully now, which wasn't an easy task for her, considering how freely and highhandedly she used to speak. She was an empress once, a woman chosen by the heavens to rule over the breadth of the realm. *Now look at me, immured in a cell like a petty delinquent.*

"I asked you a question," Dragath said.

"Why do you want to know if it hurts? Are you planning on sticking something else in me?"

She regretted her words the moment they left her lips, but Dragath's response was another chuckle, as hard and humorless as the last. "You know, I left the Hollow not long before you came to the palace," he said. "A shame fate hadn't brought us together then."

"You didn't leave, you fled. Fled from Demien Mordall's furious vengeance after you failed to murder the former emperor's son in cold blood. From that day forward he was known as the Savior of the Anir, and you were known as a traitor to the highest degree."

Dragath stiffened at that, his meaty fingers curling and uncurling as if deciding whether or not to choke the life out of her.

Stupid woman, don't rile the beast. "I misspoke," she said in her most timid voice.

The finger curling stopped, but Dragath's tone became murderously grave. "You vacated the capital, just as I did. Now here you are, at my doorstep, with promises on your tongue but lies in your heart."

"I didn't"—she paused— "I didn't come to deceive you."

"So I've been told. But there's not a single honest bone in your sweet little body. You really are a wicked whore." He leaned forward, considering her further. "How many people did you have killed? The families of those conspirators . . . over two hundred, was it not? Hiriam said you had Minister Garlan killed while making it appear as though he died of natural causes." His gray-bearded face twisted into a hard smirk. "People think I'm a brute, but you are no different, my lady."

Miriana didn't like where this conversation was headed. She needed to steer it elsewhere. "Where is Cyrille Vileron? I need him. He has served as my escort and protector."

He leaned back. "The man is ill. Smoke has twisted his insides and damaged his respiration. My physician doesn't know if he will recover."

"He *must* recover. I need him alive."

Once more he seemed amused by her response, his deep-set eyes glittering darkly, his bearded mouth opening with the tiniest hint of surprise. Miriana lowered her gaze. *Making demands while incarcerated,* she thought. *You truly are a fool.* She apologized for her impertinence once more, and then she said, "Why treat me so pitilessly? I've come only to offer my hand."

"Offer your hand," he repeated in a mocking tone. "I should take your head. You've been nothing but a thorn in my side, pricking me at every turn. I could've seized the realm with Seric Dyre at my side. One of the finest strategists of our age, second only to my own Hiriam. But it wasn't fated to be, and the blame is cast on you. You took him from me and bent him to your will."

"I needed a man of military strategy," she replied firmly. "If I had known he was plotting against the capital, I would've taken his head myself."

"But you didn't. You opened your pretty little legs and stole him away, and because of that, I lost the Horns of Vermillion, the city of Thornberry, and, ultimately, the Star of the Hollow."

"I can help you win the Hollow. That is why I'm here."

"No, you're here because you betrayed your husband and fled

before he grew wise and put you to the cord. There are no secrets left in you. Hiriam made sure of that."

The very thought of those squirmy little eels made her skin prickle, though she did her best to hide her discomfort. "I came to you. I could've gone elsewhere."

That deep chuckle again, dismissive and demeaning. "You had nowhere else to go."

She wasn't used to being talked to in such a contemptuous way. "Perhaps not in titles or names . . . but I still have much to offer."

"I already employ an adept strategist, I don't need the counsel of an unproven woman. Besides, Hiriam already squeezed every drop of information out of you. What more do you possess—beauty? Yes, you're quite beautiful, but so are the seven concubines who serve me nightly. In truth, our union would mean little other than a public prodding at Zantherei Athera. And while that tempts me greatly, it's just not enough." He leaned in; a thick forefinger reached over to brush aside a lock of her dark hair. "But again, I will admit, you are quite beautiful. Busted nose and all."

A raw chill snaked up Miriana's spine. *Oh no, please don't touch me. You disgusting brute of a man, don't you dare touch me.* She decided to push such thoughts away and slip on her best, sultriest smile. "Provide me a bath, a proper change of attire, and a few simple cosmetics, and I will show you just how beautiful I can be."

"No. I can't do that."

She batted her eyelashes and put a hand to her chest, coyly. "Is the famed Red Terror afraid of a woman?"

His face darkened at that. "I fear no one, man or woman." For a moment it looked like he might strike her, perhaps a swift back-hand, but the moment passed, and he continued speaking. "My advisors are always telling me to conceal my emotions and not be so quick with violence. A difficult thing, perhaps akin to telling a wolf not to hunt. It's just . . . natural for me."

Natural for a madman, she mused.

"Your husband has mobilized his army; he's furious with me for shoving my sword down his little brother's throat. Vengeance . . . it is becoming too commonplace in this realm. But while Zantherei marches to strike me down and spit on my corpse, here you arrive, wanting to join me, yet unable to tell me what I truly need to know."

"And what do you truly need to know?"

"Zantherei's military plans. His numbers, his formations, his positions. Not only do I want to know how many men will stand against me in open battle, I want to know the names of his regiment generals, what they ate for breakfast, how much they love their wives and children, and how much respect they've earned from their corps commanders and lesser squadrons. I want to know all this and more, but apparently Zantherei was wise in withholding military intelligence from you."

Yes, in military matters Zantherei kept me in the dark, as though I were too slow to understand. "I can still help . . . I—"

He cut her off. "You can't help me." With that, he shot to his feet, scooped up the oil lamp, and turned for the door.

Panic rose in Miriana's heart. "*Wait,*" she shouted. The bearded brute halted, without turning. Miriana spoke softly. "He has fire."

It sounded so silly when she said it. And of course, he looked uninterested, and rightly so, since fire was a common tactic in warfare. But Miriana went on, "Not just any fire. The strangest fire you'll ever see. Black as a shadow, hot enough to burn through the earth and melt the thickest steel. Darkfire, it is called."

He turned around to face her, a motion that seemed to say, *Go on.*

"The creation of these fires may be linked to a wrathful summoning of the sun god. Perhaps they are the cause of this prolonged warm season."

He was still staring at her, a long and hard look, as though carefully digesting her words. "You've seen this fire?"

She nodded. "In the lower forges, deep in the bowels of the Hollow . . . there you'll find pumps and burners and beakers and cauldrons full of strange, scalding liquids. The darkfire is given life through some kind of alchemical process, an admixture touched by the foulest, most wicked of sorceries. Zantherei's planning on using it against you, a secret weapon." She raised a hand. "I know the mastermind behind it. I can help you."

Raas Dragath snorted. "No such sorcery exists."

So that's it? You're simply disregarding my words? What sort of closed-minded fool does that? She shouted at him to wait, even though he hadn't yet moved. Then she said, "Please—you can't just leave me in here. You can't keep me locked up. *PLEASE.*"

He moved so fast. One moment he was by the door, the next he was in her face, staring at her, following her eyes like some deranged animal. "You still don't get it, do you?" Hot breath struck her face. She turned her head to the side, but he grabbed her chin and brought it back. "I can beat you, I can violate you, I can cut off your fingers and use them to scratch my rump. You're mine, you snobby little whore. You understand me? *MINE.*"

He rose and stormed out of the cell. Miriana winced as the door slammed shut. She was alone again, alone and frightened and terribly disheartened. *Cyrille was right,* she thought. *Raas Dragath is not a man to be reasoned with. I've made a terrible mistake.* Suddenly she felt very homesick.

How could Dragath disregard her words so thoughtlessly? She was reminded of a conversation she'd had with Seric nearly a year ago, on the day he'd told her how to defeat Raas Dragath at the Horns of Vermillion. He'd mentioned the warlord's arrogance as his greatest flaw. It was true then, as it was true now. Seric was so clever and insightful—why couldn't he just remain faithful to her cause?

With a sharp clang the door reopened. Something flew into the cell, a heavy object that smacked against the far wall and landed with a dull thud on the stone floor. Dragath's voice floated in from the entryway. "Here, something to occupy your time." The words were spoken casually, almost gleefully, but when the cell door shut, it was with malicious force. Swiftly the darkness returned, but Miriana didn't need light to know what she was looking at.

Vileron's head.

CHAPTER TWENTY

Ansetheral Athera was staring sidelong at a man gnawing on his own arm when the chamber door groaned open. He turned away from the morbid painting to see General Szathan Mordall lumber inside, one giant hand wrapped around a much smaller fellow who was undoubtedly Minister Byort. It was peculiar sight—humorous even—the way Szathan carried the man, as though he were hauling an armload of kindling. With minimal effort, he dumped the councilman on the patterned floor tiles in the center of the room's waiting area.

Byort's protruding eyes remained fastened on his giant captor, even as Anseth came to stand before him. To remedy that, Szathan seized the back of his neck and forced his gaze forward. Now Byort had no choice but to acknowledge Anseth and the multitude of faces around him—from the Vaskultan guardsmen to the gray-black Anirians; to Kirik and Ikara, both broad-shouldered and proud and undoubtedly intimidating; to General Thayer Dal, rangy and smirking and clad in full-plated battledress; and lastly to Chamberlain Rennerin Rothar, who was rubbing at his white temple with a nervous finger. Byort offered the old fellow a pleading look, perhaps a silent request for help, but Rennerin only looked away.

Anseth cleared his throat before speaking. "Are you Minister Byort Belthor, Senior Tax Collector, Second to the Chief of Finance, Master of Entomology, and Fifth Seat of the White Fang Council?"

Byort's eyes flicked again at Rennerin.

"He can't help you," Anseth told him. "Look at me."

The man did, though it was a begrudging effort. "I have more titles."

Anseth didn't want to make any presumptions about this man, but years of commanding Vaskultans made him quite adept at judging others, and to him this official reeked of hubris and snake oil. He also seemed devoid of character, a mediocre man born into nobility and blessed by nepotism. Even his physical attributes—the bug-like eyes and defiant scowl and puckered nose—were unfriendly to the eye. Still, Anseth couldn't publicly condemn a man based on his appearance or upbringing. He wanted a confession. "I believe you," he said. "Do you know who I am?"

"Lord Alarin's brother, and the leader of those northern savages." His head cocked to the side. "You're smaller than I expected."

Anseth didn't let the jab rile him. Nothing he hadn't heard a hundred times over. "I've lived with the northmen for nearly a decade. In that time, I've crossed swords with enemies and created blood-bonds with friends. I've risen through the ranks to personally serve their chieftain, and when he passed I became the chieftain myself. Now you can call them savages if you choose, but one thing Vaskultans do not suffer is a man who schemes in the shadows."

"That's because they're dimwitted," Byort replied with a snort.

Anseth must've evinced his surprise because Kirik asked what was said. With a quick motion he warded off his bondsman's question and directed his response to Byort. "Schemers, deceivers, betrayers—they are called *ruzolek*, shadow rats, to my people. Do you know how these shadow rats are punished? They're not put in cells, they're not fed, and they don't have their shit pots emptied. Do you know what my people do to them?"

"Enlighten me."

"They strip them bare, peel their flesh, cut out their insides, and present each piece in a ritual of consumption. The brains go to the shamans, the stomachs go to the warriors, the genitals to scorned lovers, the hearts to childless parents, and the rest goes to the dogs. The only organs left uneaten are the eyes. Those are boiled to ensure the offender's soul experiences an eternity in the Great Void."

Byort's narrow face paled, but his defiant expression remained unchanged. "You can intimidate me, you can threaten me, you can beat me and have me hanged. But I will never give you the truth of what happened . . . because I know nothing. I am as innocent as a fruit fly."

Anseth leaned over and shouted in the councilman's face. "An *ASSASSIN* entered my brother's chamber. An assassin *YOU* hired."

Byort winced. "A falsehood. I hired no one."

Anseth was so close he could bite the man's cheek if he wanted to. But he chose instead to withdraw an arm's length, and in a calm and uncaring voice he said, "Yes, well, we shall see about that." He turned to Chamberlain Rennerin. "The master torturer should be here. Why isn't he here?"

Rennerin looked down before he replied. "Forgive me, the master has pleaded illness. He offers his sincerest apologies and he understands the penalty that may result in his absence, including the full revocation of his certification."

Anseth felt his jaw tighten. *Illness? You mean he didn't wish to torture a trusted colleague. I see how these privileged fools all stick together.* "Fine, but where is his standby?"

"I couldn't find a suitable replacement to appease a man of your caliber."

"Of my caliber . . . what does that even mean? You know I'm not above eating pig innards." His sigh of frustration was pronounced. "Never mind, I'll do it myself." He wasn't an experienced torturer by any means, but he was somewhat familiar with certain Vaskultan techniques, most of which were administered to pry information from the captured or kidnapped enemies of rival tribes. And while he'd hadn't performed any such techniques himself, he was confident that he could make a man like Byort confess.

He gestured to Kirik; the bondsman approached and handed over a spiked war club. It was a one-handed anti-armor weapon, slender at the base yet sturdy at the head. Anseth didn't point it in any specific direction, just allowed the accused man to see it, acknowledge its presence. He spoke with a professional's coolness. "Long have the other councilmembers known of your dissatisfied heart. Long have they heard your disgruntled mutterings toward my elder brother's policies."

"I spoke my mind, yes," Byort admitted.

"You despised the changes Lord Alarin made to the palace district, the way he stripped you of your extravagant furnishings and overindulgent lifestyle."

"Yes, I did."

"You made your displeasure public when you threatened him at the council meeting."

Byort objected to that. "A mere warning, I didn't intend to—"

"You *threatened* him."

Byort winced and looked down, a preoccupied stare, as if there were something extremely interesting about his shoes.

"You wanted him dead, and you organized a ploy to make it happen."

"I did nothing of the sort, you must believe me—*please.*"

"Liar." Anseth raised the club over the councilman's left kneecap . . . steadily, steadily. Byort stifled a fearful cry, his large eyes slamming shut. Anseth's arm tensed, and then—

"*ENOUGH.*"

Anseth froze. The voice came from beyond the waiting area, at the far end of the room. *Alarin?* He spun to see his elder brother standing at the foot of his bed, one hand clutching the wooden bedrail, the other gripping his cane for support. His balding head was a mess of what little hair remained, and his tattered gray robe was unbound and open, revealing the dressings that Master Penry had applied to his midsection. "Let him go," he uttered, his face grimacing with every word.

Szathan released his grip from the back of Byort's neck, though it was a reluctant effort. His tiny dark eyes gazed with concern at Alarin. "My lord, you shouldn't be up. Please, you're in no condition."

Alarin's focus was on Anseth. "You cannot treat the councilman this way."

Anseth didn't like what he was hearing. "The man spearheaded a plot to murder you."

Alarin gave him a tight-lipped look, like a father disappointed in his son. "And where is the corroborating evidence? You have nothing."

"I heard how he threatened you at the council. Do you not recall—"

"You *heard?* You cannot present hearsay as fact. It is no better than scuttlebutt."

"I was there," Thayer Dal cut in. "You know that, my lord."

"I am aware, General, but harsh punishment without irrefutable proof is the foundation of a legalist society. Do you not remember the malicious Emperor Thurlain of the Third Dynasty? He punished men and women without fair treatment of the law, causing fear and discontent to spread like a virus through the land. You must not allow your emotions to cloud your judgment. That goes for all of you."

A cold moment of silence followed. Anseth looked down. *Alarin's right—my lack of judgment has been shameful. What have I done? They must think me a cruel savage.* He opened his mouth to speak, but Byort's voice rang out first: "You have my thanks, Lord Alarin Athera. Your wisdom knows no bounds."

Alarin ignored that and spoke to the guards. "Escort the councilman out, please."

Szathan and Anseth both stepped back, allowing the councilman to rise. The bug-eyed man casually brushed his robe free of dirt and dust, then offered his most disapproving glare at the small group of onlookers. "You disrespected me. All of you. You brought shame to my house and name." His eyes turned upon Szathan. "And you, Ogre, never touch me again."

Szathan's gapped teeth clenched so hard it looked as though they might shatter. It was clear he wanted to wrap his meaty hands around Byort's neck and squeeze the life out of him, but Alarin put a halt to that idea when he gave a swift motion to the guardsmen, who promptly escorted Byort out.

That done, Alarin spared a few moments to adjust and readjust his balance, grimacing and groaning and shooing away any attendant who attempted to help him. At last, he continued speaking. "I know you all want revenge—and believe me, I do as well. But I was once accused of a crime I didn't commit. I saw firsthand the corruption of our system. Miriana Athera . . . she wielded power far beyond her limitations, accusing and mistreating me without undeniable evidence. When I escaped her clutches, I swore I'd never allow such an abuse of power again. Not in Stormhaven. We must be certain of his culpability. Only in rewarding do you value the small. In punishing, you must value the great."

Anseth thought long and hard before responding. "And if he flees the city?"

"It will be difficult to see that as anything but an admission of guilt. If it happens, I will have His Majesty issue a mandate for the councilman's captu—" Alarin stopped.

His eyes were fixed on something beyond the waiting area, and when Anseth turned he saw his principal Vaskultan scout, Urryk, standing in the entranceway. Kirik moved to speak with him, but whatever information Urryk divulged made the bondsman visibly upset. Anseth demanded to know what was wrong, but Kirik had trouble spitting it out in a coherent manner.

He sounded out of breath, yet the words flew from his mouth in an angry blubbering, so fast Anseth had to calm him down. "Relax. Breathe. That's it. Now tell me."

"The river encampment was decimated, our Vaskultan brothers and sisters shamefully defeated. Severak and the bulk of the main force have survived the onslaught, but only by a last-ditch effort to outwit the enemy."

"Who's behind this?" he demanded of Urryk, even though in his heart he already knew the answer. "Who attacked my people?"

"The one we defeated at Amber River," Urryk replied. "Ser-ric Dyy-rre. His army moves in a southbound march. Three columns, full wings. Seven thousand men, at least seven thousand . . . maybe eight. Heading directly for the gates of this city."

He's coming for his son, Anseth thought. *He's coming for revenge.*

"What is amiss?" Alarin barked from across the room. When Anseth turned and translated the report in the Anirian tongue, Alarin's old wounded body immediately rose in stature, a strength brought to life by urgency. His reply was an authoritative boom that resonated across the chamber, a sound not unlike the days in which he was a powerful general: "Move the civilians inside the city and bar the gates. It's a siege. *Prepare for a siege.*"

CHAPTER TWENTY-ONE

A veritable sea of gray-black banners bristled in the balmy autumn breeze. Rows upon rows of Anirian soldiers were assembled beneath them, cavalrymen and infantrymen and auxiliaries alike, all armed and armored and stinking of days of arduous travel. The arrangement was one of veteran efficiency, with numbers nearing nine thousand in all, and that didn't include the divisions of noncombatants: the commissary teams and armorers and physicians and priests and clean-up crews.

Seric stood at the fore of his army, eyes affixed to the imposing outer walls of Stormhaven. It was a warm, white-cloud day; the late afternoon sun shone affectionately on the farmsteads behind them. Most smallholders and their families had fled for the safety of the walls, but those that hadn't were left unmolested, and their homes were spared from invasion and the torch. This was all done by Seric's command. After the crushing of the Vaskultans, his officers didn't hesitate to obey. Even that cocky fool Madderin.

Alarin Athera appeared from behind the upper parapet, a tall man with a head as balding as Seric had remembered. It was diffi-cult to see his facial expression with the distance between them, but his posture looked rather hunched and frail, as though he were suffering from illness. The man was draped in his usual Anirian rags, which were accentuated by the seal of office fastened around the neck. The seal of the Lord Regent, no doubt. Alarin stared down at him, a knowing stare that Seric didn't like. *The cripple didn't poison the wells or raze the crops of his own land,* he mused. *He must've realized that I intend to win the populace in order to stand against a much larger foe in Zantherei Athera.*

"It's so nice to see you again, Lord Alarin," Seric called up. "Don't think I've forgotten about the letters you posted all across the realm. You slandered my name, tarnished my reputation."

"I exposed the truth."

"A truth twisted to fit your own needs."

Alarin said nothing.

Seric's gaze turned back to the city walls, so tall and seemingly impregnable, with projecting turrets and wooden hoarders and machicolations that were manned by keen-eyed soldiers. Seric could only speculate at how many arrows and bolts were pointed at his heart. Not that he was deterred or even fazed by the notion. "Is this how you greet an old friend? Abandon your fields and bar your gates?"

Alarin didn't take the bait. "To march upon the sovereign ruler's house is a crime that stands above all others. Abandon your campaign and your proposed kingship—and acknowledge the true emperor of the Anir."

Seric made sure his chuckle was heard. "You may have the Imperial Seal, and some silly rumors about magical flowers, but you do *not* have the true emperor."

"It matters not what you think. Be gone, Seric. Return whence you came."

"Oh, but I cannot. Not until I see that little barbarian brother of yours. Where is he? It's rather urgent."

Again, no answer.

A scowl tugged at Seric's face, and without warning he began to shout: "Show yourself, *Anseth*. I know you're here. I know it because you weren't among your rabble of savages. I'm sure you've heard, little Anseth. Your Vaskultans have been smashed, and it was *I* who smashed them."

A moment passed, a moment so long that Seric no longer expected a response . . . but then, a figure appeared on the battlements, a longhaired man much shorter than Alarin, but with a similar hard-boned face.

"There you are," Seric called. "Good to see you again, old friend. Sorry to get reacquainted under these circumstances, but I do believe you have something of mine, yes?" He raised a hand and held it horizontal to his nose. "About this tall, olive skin, dimpled chin. Looks very much like me."

"Your son is here," Anseth said.

"Well, I pray that out of compassion toward our past friendship, you will release the boy."

"Is that the same compassion you showed our childhood friend Emeron Mathius?"

"He betrayed me, and you inspired his betrayal. The man deserved a much worse fate than what he received. Now release the boy."

"The boy is not my captive. You abandoned him, Seric. After falling in defeat to my 'rabble of savages', you wept on the banks of the Amber River, wishing for death. Is that the mentality of a master strategist? No, that is a child's mindset, at best."

Seric couldn't stopper the anger rising in his throat. It was viscid, like bile. "Lies. You've filled his head with lies. Where is he?" He began calling out his son's name, loud and urgent. "Veldries. *VELDRIES.*"

"I'm here, Father."

Veldries's youthful face appeared on the battlements above,

standing beside Anseth, yet half a head taller. He looked handsome and unabused, his skin clean and his chestnut hair shiny and brushed. Of his attire, all Seric could see was a short black mantle worn over a stitched linen tunic—nothing fancy, but nothing that resembled a prisoner's garb either. "It's true," the boy said. "Uncle Anseth hasn't kept me against my will. Not in a way that one is usually detained."

Seric went to reply to that but a woman exclaimed from nearby, startling him. He turned just as Nyvia pushed past him and called out her son's name. "Damn it, woman," Seric growled. "I told you to wait—"

"Alarin and Ansetheral, my *brothers*," she cried. "I wish to speak with you both." She took a few more determined steps forward, as if she planned to break through the gates herself. "And I wish to see my son."

Alarin gazed long and curiously at his sister before answering. "The eastern edge of the promontory, a boatman will be waiting to take you through the river gate. Come alone."

Nyvia agreed and went off at once, and from above Veldries withdrew from sight. Alarin and Anseth spoke a few inaudible words to each other, before they too vanished from the wall. Seric was left looking at stones and slits and sentries, until the sun slipped out from behind a cloud and blurred his eyesight. He turned away to watch Nyvia in her gull-gray gown head off east, and then he motioned to his officers to retire and break camp. It'd been a long day of marching, and the men were famished and footsore and in desperate need of rest. Thankfully, the autumn air was still rich with warmth, despite the growing push of the wind.

Seric moved inside his commander's tent. A pimply squire with a greasy head of hair was preparing cuts of pork for a blood soup. Ravia was sitting nearby, but Seric ignored her and instead spoke to General Wyath, who had followed him inside. "She moved too quickly. I told her to wait."

Wyath's narrow face wore a doubtful expression, and it wasn't hard to understand why. "Do you think the lady can be trusted?"

"She'll do what is best for her son, which means she'll get the intelligence I require while proposing a contest of might. Champion against champion. Zirian Revil against their best, which I'm assuming will be Szathan Mordall. It's the only way to avoid a lengthy and grueling siege." Seric gave a pointed nod, as if convincing himself of his own words. *Don't foul his up, Nyvia.*

CHAPTER TWENTY-TWO

Ansetheral Athera burst inside the vacant Rosebud Hall and hustled to his elder brother's writing desk. It was a heavy structure of dark knotty wood, one leg off-kilter enough to make it dip forward when he pressed his weight on it. Scrolls and parchments and other loose paperwork covered the surface, so many that Anseth didn't know which to examine first. *You were never this messy, Elder Brother. The Alarin I remember was as organized as a bookman. Has your mind also deteriorated since losing your leg?*

To his left, Kirik was speaking about Nyvia, asking silly rhetorical questions such as: "Was that truly your sister?" And awkward compliments such as: "For a pale one she has a sweet face, and big beautiful eyes."

Anseth scowled at him. "We're not talking about my sister, so put an end to those thoughts right now. Here, hand me that leather satchel."

He did. "I'm just saying . . . she's quite a feast for the eyes."

"Not many would agree. Hold it open. Wider." Anseth grabbed any incriminating papers, anything that might expose Alarin's military plans, and shoved them into the satchel. "There, now close it up."

The bondsman obeyed. "Why are you doing this?"

"Because I don't trust my 'sweet-faced' sister." He sat down on the chair, then retrieved a blank scrap of silk paper from a lower shelf. He spent the next several minutes writing spurious words on it, and, when he was done, he placed the brushpen back onto its holder and massaged his wrist. It'd been years since he'd written anything, and yet it surprised him at how neat his penmanship turned out to be. He positioned the false document on top of a paper pile, in a somewhat natural yet difficult-to-overlook way. That done, he muttered to himself, "Forgive me if I'm wrong, Nyvia, but I can't take any chances. Not now."

Kirik spoke from behind him. "Are you finished? I still don't understand what you're doing."

Anseth stretched out his legs and rose, adjusting the fit of his light Vaskultan longcoat. Kirik scratched at his half ear as he examined all the smudges and marks that Anseth had jotted down. Vaskultans had no written language, so to communicate in such a way must've seemed odd to him. Still, that didn't mean Kirik was unintelligent. In fact, he was among the sharpest Vaskultan warriors, which was probably why Anseth preferred his company. "I need you to sneak Urryk out of the city," Anseth told him. "Tonight."

The bondsman shot him a wary look.

"Have him track down Severak and the surviving warband. Tell them to regroup, rearm, ride south, and strike Seric Dyre from the rear. He'll not expect it. Trust me."

Kirik's wary look turned to an understanding nod. And with that, the two men moved toward the grand double-doors of the hall's exit. Anseth didn't even spare a glance at the magical cloud-falls in the far alcove. "We must hurry," he said. "Before we are seen."

The ferrule of Alarin Athera's blackthorn cane thumped against the floor tiles of the western wing. Nyvia's softer footfalls padded between those thumps, along with Veldries's heavier taps, which blended with the clangor of the surrounding gray-cloaked guardsmen. The reunion between mother and son had taken place just outside the river gate, on a gentle embankment before an exposed culvert. It was a tearful moment, but Alarin cut it short when he urged Nyvia and Veldries inside, and now he was leading them to the Rosebud Hall.

The corridor he hobbled down was dimly lit, narrow of space, and full of dancing shadows, and when Alarin turned the corner he barely saw the onrushing figure. He flinched, his cane slipped from his fingers, and his balance faltered—yet even though the wall was there to keep him upright, the heel of his wooden limb slammed hard into it, causing a streak of red-hot pain to shoot from his stump through his pelvis and into his wounded chest.

The nearest guardsmen went to Alarin's aid, but as expected he was brushed off. "I'm fine," Alarin said. "I don't need your help." He grabbed his cane and readjusted his footing with an obvious grimace, then his eyes turned up at the careless individual who'd nearly crashed into him. It was Anseth—who apologized both immediately and profusely. Alarin told him not to fret, that he wasn't hurt, and then his tone took a downward shift toward the accusatory. "Brother, what are you doing? Why were you in the Rosebud Hall?"

Before Anseth could reply, Nyvia came forward and threw her arms around him. A long embrace, a reunion of brother and sister ten years overdue. *Much more heartfelt than my own reunion with Anseth,* Alarin mused. *Or maybe I didn't make a worthy enough attempt.* Whatever the reason, Anseth was clearly more receptive to Nyvia's affections. He even raised a hand to brush a lock of hair from her face, and afterward the two siblings stood apart and spent a few moments commenting on appearances, as kin are wont to do after a lengthy absence. And when they were finished, Anseth's bodyguard moved forward to offer his barbarian greeting to the woman. Kirik, his name was, and though he probably hadn't seen more than twenty-five summers, he still looked as fierce and experienced as any man could look, courtesy of that rawboned face, protruding lower jaw, and half-torn ear.

The courtesies completed, Anseth turned back and apologized once more to Alarin. "I must've lost my bearings. I suppose I'm not yet re-accustomed to the confines of these intricate structures. I meant to head to the center courtyard to apprise my company of our current predicament."

He's lying to me, Alarin thought. *But why?*

"He tends to do a lot of wandering," Veldries remarked. "Must be the nomad in him."

Anseth flashed the youth a taunting, playful smile.

Alarin gave his brother instructions to the courtyard, and then he turned and motioned to Veldries. "Go with your uncle. I need to speak with your mother in private."

Veldries nodded and gave Nyvia a brief hug. "We'll talk later, Mother. Later, all right?"

With that, Veldries joined Anseth and his barbarian bodyguard, and together they disappeared down the dim corridor.

Inside the Rosebud Hall, Alarin limped across the grand empty space that was once festooned with ribbons and decorated with dozens of exquisite sculptures. Nyvia followed him into the far alcove where she gazed at the tiers of puffy white cloudfalls and listened intently as Alarin detailed how their late brother Merio would pontificate about them, and how they later shined for young Silas Mordall. After that, he brought her back to the main chamber, and together they sat down at an old trestle table that had replaced its fancy burgundy-black predecessor. By this point, the pain in Alarin's leg had flared up so intensely that it made his wounded upper body ache, and he could no longer hide his grimace.

Nyvia observed him with big piteous eyes, as though Alarin were a lamed horse soon to be put down. "Are you sure you're all right? Maybe we should fetch your physician. I already lost one brother. I can't lose another."

"You won't lose me. Master Penry is good at what he does. Although he does have a strange, almost halfhearted way of going about it." He pushed down the bitter ache that rose from his chest; it was like the burn one feels after eating spicy food. "It saddens me to see you under the Whitecrow banner. Seric has always been cruel to you. The man is a liar and a cheat. How could you stand with him?"

"I came to him as an envoy of the Hollow, but I stayed for my son. I want to take Veldries back with me, and I want you to come as well. Forsake this drawn-out charade, Alarin. Denounce the false emperor, give up the Imperial Seal, and return with me to the Hollow. You are Zantherei's elder brother; he will forgive you, that I promise. He will even reinstate you as his Imperial Advisor. You don't know how much he needs you. Zantherei is not the same without you. Without Anseth either. Our clan must unite for the realm to prosper. You *must* return."

He sighed. "I'm not going anywhere with your former husband's army at my gates."

"Seric will be dealt with when the time comes—when we are strong. But for now, he wants his son released. You must give him what he wants."

That made Alarin snort, despite the pain it brought him. "If I give him what he wants, he won't lift the siege. He wants the city. He wants to expand his power."

"He will leave. To prove it he's offered a proposal. A contest of arms. His champion against yours. If Seric's man is victorious, then my son is to be released. If his man is defeated, then Seric will lift the siege and depart."

Alarin cocked his head in thought. "An interesting proposal. I assume he will be putting Zirian Revil up to the task? The Mad Wolf is a formidable beast. He took on two generals at Howler Pass, and Aldebron Pentagath and Wyath Silth are no ordinary generals."

"Yes, but Zirian suffered an expected fall during the march, and now he's nursing an injured leg. He's nearly hamstrung." She looked squarely at her brother. "Use that to your advantage, Elder Brother. A powerful man like Szathan Mordall can beat him."

Alarin thought about it for a moment, then sighed quietly to himself. "You are kind to divulge this secret, but even if General Szathan is victorious and the siege is lifted, I can't go back to the Hollow. The true emperor is here, in Stormhaven. The cloudfalls deemed it so."

"You're wrong, Elder Brother. The true emperor is he who unites the six major provinces, and to do that brothers must squash bad blood, and enemies must simply be squashed. Raas Dragath is a cancer to the realm, an unruly flame that needs to be snuffed out. His assassins murdered Emperor Thavian Siven and severed the remaining thread of the dynasty. Death is too kind a punishment for him—but we cannot stand against him if you continue to stand against your brother. So swallow your pride and return to his side and service. Together we can revive the Anir and rid the wrongs of the realm."

Alarin studied her. She had changed a bit since last he'd seen her. Her face, known for its plumpness, appeared thinner now, and he wasn't sure if it was in a healthy way. Her body had lost a little weight, too, which gave her the look of her younger years, even though her frilled gray gown was as mature and tasteful as ever. A memory came to the forefront of Alarin's mind, so he decided to share. "The day after your wedding to Seric, when we paraded gaily through the Imperial Garden . . . do you recall the hag who stopped and scolded you for neglecting to feed her pond fish?"

Nyvia's face brightened. Of course she remembered. An elder noblewoman had mistaken her for a lowly attendant, even though she wasn't dressed in homespun attire. "She yanked me aside, nails tearing at my fancy white gown," she said. "I *loved* that outfit. All long and fanned out, trailing behind me like the tail of some arctic animal. Anyway, the woman kept shouting, 'Look at how thin they are! Look at how thin they are!'" Nyvia giggled at the memory. "The look on the guardsmen's faces . . . oh, I'll never forget it. And when the poor woman was kindly informed of her error, she nearly fainted from shame. I pitied her, but I could *not* stop laughing."

Alarin couldn't help but laugh himself, though his was strained with ache. "You were kind not to punish her."

"The court gossiped about the incident for weeks to come. I think the lady's embarrassment was punishment enough."

"Perhaps. Others would've taken her head."

She shrugged a single shoulder. "Well, I'm not like others."

"That is true, you've always been so kind. So compassionate." For some reason Alarin found himself moved by remorse. He held her pale hand in his, squeezing tenderly. "Forgive me."

"For what?"

"All these years, I've been so cold to you. Please forgive me, Sister."

She didn't seem concerned, or maybe she hid it well. "Pain changes a person. When our uncle was suffering from gout, Father said he turned from a kind and caring man to a mean old fellow."

He shook his head to ward off her attempt at consolation. "I was cold to you before my accident."

Her face softened into an expression of sympathy. "Oh, Alarin. It's not your fault. Father was always hardest on you. You were the firstborn. You were his pride."

"That's no excuse," he said. "I have regrets, Sister. Many regrets. I regret the way I treated you. I regret how, after my accident, I shirked my duties and hid from the public. I regret being absent for Father's funeral. I regret letting Merio march after Raas Dragath with rage in his heart. I regret . . ." Alarin stopped, fighting back the ache in his chest and the moisture that suddenly touched his eyes. "So much."

"Elder Brother . . . it's unwise to dwell on the past. And you couldn't have stopped Merio. His choice was already made." She removed her hand from his, not disrespectfully, but also with an unfamiliar firmness. "You should see the physician, perhaps he'll administer something to help you rest. I believe the pain is turning your emotions loose."

Alarin spoke quietly. "I suppose I am still out of sorts." He grabbed his cane and slowly rose. "A guest room has been prepared for you. Would you like to see it now?"

"Not yet. I think I'll stay and sit with the cloudfalls some more. Perhaps it'll bring me closer to Merio. Then I'll spend the remainder of the day with my son. Thank you for treating him so kindly."

"You should thank Anseth. I had little to do with it."

"I will. Is that your desk over there?"

"Yes, it is." The hinge of his wooden leg groaned as he turned toward the exit. "I'll post a pair of guardsmen at the door. They'll escort you to your chambers when you are ready." He paused. "Thank you, Nyvia. For being the sister that I needed, and probably don't deserve."

"Don't thank me, I am only doing what is best for our clan, and for the realm. Oh, before you go, do you have an answer regarding Seric's proposal?"

"Let me think more on it. I will let you know."

Alarin departed then, and after a long and strenuous walk back to his private chamber, he removed his wooden leg and slipped into the downy sheets of his featherbed. The stout and owlish Master Penry immediately came to his side, and for a time he worked on changing Alarin's bandages and offering encouraging words and doing all the things an exemplary physician does for his patient. Alarin's eyes soon closed, and the world began to grow quiet, yet no matter how forcefully he told himself to sleep, sleep just wouldn't come.

A short while later, his eyes reopened and he sat up in his bed, and when he heard Penry nearby, he called the man over and spoke in a low voice. "Do you know anyone with a mind for dreams?"

"Dreams, my lord?"

"Yes, well, visions specifically. This may sound silly but during an early stage of sleep I would sometimes experience visions of future events. But now, all I see is fire and darkness."

Penry's face scrunched inquisitively. "These visions . . . did they come randomly, or were you able to conjure them yourself to some degree?"

"I had no control over them, though perhaps an expert can help change that. Someone obviously wants me dead, and I'd like to know who that someone is."

That made him think for a moment. "When I was younger—and thinner—I served as an apprentice for a man who claimed to have the ability to tap into the subconscious mind at will. To do so, he would sit alone and in a meditative state, eyes closed and hands holding two glass spheres as he let his mind drift away. You see, there is a line between the waking eye and the otherworldly plane, and this man used to walk that line by tapping into the subconscious without losing himself to the unconscious. If he drifted too far and lost his physical, his muscles would relax, the glass spheres would drop, and the shattering sound caused him to wake. By this method he was able to enter a state where he could see what his regular eyes could not. Perhaps this is the same state in which your 'visions' live. Sounds strange, I know."

"This man, who is he?"

"He's an oneirologist by trade, or what laymen call a dream-scaper. He uses stones and spheres to decipher an array of abstruse topics and theories ranging from disjunctive cognition to precognition. He is undoubtedly the expert you're looking for."

"Good, I'd like to meet him."

Penry held up a wrinkled finger. "Ah, my—"

"What is it? You know coin is no object."

"He's a wanderer I'm afraid, an eternal itinerant. He could be anywhere from here to the Deadmoon Vale, if he's still fit to travel."

"Well, find him. Send the word out to our agents and trackers. I'd love to talk with this 'dreamscaper'."

"As you command, my lord."

Alarin thanked the physician, and a few moments later he rolled over and closed his eyes. He spent the next three days recovering in solitude, and on the fourth day he rose and informed Nyvia that he accepted Seric's proposal, and then he summoned General Szathan Mordall to arms.

CHAPTER TWENTY-THREE

F our days had passed and Nyvia still hadn't returned to the encampment. That meant four days of idle puttering, with soldiers who were restless and twitchy and consumed by boredom. It was hardly an appealing sight, a soldier without purpose. He became more agitated by day, until his mind finally descended into a storm of unbridled aggression, which left him killing wildlife for pleasure and antagonizing the locals for the release of pent-up emotions. Seric Dyre had to take the heads of two soldiers for crimes against civilians. One was rape, the other murder. He did it grudgingly, and he silently blamed Nyvia for it.

Seric otherwise spent those four days perched on an uneven plateau that overlooked the city, which itself was perched on a promontory that presided over a wandering arm of the northern river. The city gates remained closed, including the massive water gate, and the watercourses that snaked around it remained devoid of any activity—no river-going boats or sampans or merchant junks to be seen in any direction. The outer wall, a mortared hunk of fat gray bricks that sat upon a base of soils and slurries, certainly looked sturdy and impenetrable enough, but it was what lay *beyond* those battlements and machicolations that held Seric's attention. No doubt the enemy had anti-siege weaponry in due preparation.

Seric's own preparations had been thorough. He commissioned labor men and engineers to assemble the dismantled pieces and parts of mangonels, catapults, and other torsion siege engines. Others constructed temporary earthwork fortifications and arranged defensive posts and positions. Seric did not want to decimate or demoralize the Stormhaven populace by violently breaching the walls of their city, but if that goddamn cripple Alarin didn't accept his proposal of combat, then by the gods he would have to do just that.

Where are you, Nyvia? Seric thought. *Where the hell are you, my dear former wife?* His eyes drifted lazily around the area. To the left, a clustered mass of branching broadleaves stood tall and firm in the balmy spring haze, maples and hickories and willows all towering over the lesser shrubbery. Above, a crow cawed mid-flight, only to be chased off by two smaller grackles. Lower, leaf litter rustled under the furtive movements of an unseen ground rodent. It was proving to be another sluggish day of wasted energy, which would only further dampen morale.

General Wyath was beginning to think Nyvia might never come back at all. Seric had been spending a lot time with the narrow-faced general as of late, perhaps too much time. He often knew what the man was thinking without even sharing a word, and right now, Wyath's look said it all. A tight-lipped, tight-cheeked, lost-stare sort of look—which Seric despised. It made him want to explode in anger, truly, but Seric had enough sense to remain calm. If not, his negative emotional state would pass down and infect his officers and soldiers, and Seric couldn't risk that.

At last, on the fifth morning, the skiff reappeared, and when Nyvia stepped back onto land, the rising sun heaped its golden rays upon her shoulders like a gilded shawl. Her movements were a sort of half-saunter, half-stride that Seric found annoying given the urgency of the situation, and when she reached the commander's tent, she stopped to casually adjust the fit of her long gray cloak. Beneath that she wore a high-collared blouse and a matching outer skirt, both the color of an old potato skin, and both likely given to her by some snooty high official of Stormhaven. Gusts of wind threw her long locks of hair into her face and mouth, and with a single finger she pulled them free.

Seric stared at her while holding open the outside tent flap. She looked self-assured and rather pleasing to the eye, even though she deserved a good throttling. He didn't hesitate to mention the latter either; in fact, it was the first thing he said to her when she joined him inside. That and: "*Five days?*"

What made matters worse was that she just shrugged him off in a way that suggested she were only an hour or so late. Seric was so angry he almost seized the nearest cooking pot and flung it. Not to hurt her, just to get her attention. Still, he had more self-control than that. "Five days and you return without a word. What news of my son?"

She looked him dead in the eye, as if to say, *our son,* then she sat down on a low stool beside a brazier. It wasn't particularly cold, but she seemed to appreciate the warmth nonetheless. "Alarin has agreed to your terms. Champion against champion."

"And Zirian's 'injury', did you mention . . .?"

She flicked a nod. "I said he agreed, did I not?"

Seric leaned against the tent's support pole in relief. *Poor Alarin, you crippled old fool.* His eyes went back to Nyvia. "What else do you have for me?"

"The defeated Vaskultans have fled to rejoin their northern brethren. They've abandoned Anseth."

"Marvelous news," he said. "You have my gratitude."

She spoke after a pause. "So I did as you asked, Seric, and now you must do the same. When the contest is over, the siege is to be lifted, and my son is to return with me to the Hollow."

Seric nodded. "My dear former wife, I know I've let you down in the past. But this time, you have my word."

———————

Szathan Mordall emerged from a wicket door beside the city's main gate, clad in full blackened battledress. He marched down the bridal ramp with noisy steps, and when he emerged onto the open field, he could feel the watchful eyes of the protective sentries on the parapet above. If they were meant to provide any comfort they failed, for in his heart Szathan knew he was truly alone.

Well, no, that wasn't entirely correct. The Mad Wolf Zirian Revil was waiting for him about fifty yards away, a towering vision of invincibility even from so great a distance. He was strapped from calf to crown in dark olivine armor—greaves, bracers, skirted cuirass, a fierce lupine halfhelm—and yet it was his giant crescent-bladed halberd that truly commanded attention.

To lesser men he must've cut an intimidating figure, but Szathan wasn't like other men—and he certainly wasn't afraid. Still, he felt his body tighten when the Mad Wolf stalked forward, yard after yard in a subtle limp that seemed to confirm his leg injury. Szathan waited until they stood no more than ten yards apart, and then he displayed the flat of his figured halberd, Nightwing, and said, "She's here for your head, Zhoul."

Zirian seemed amused by that, though his left eye remained half-lidded and inert. "You try," he said in broken Anirian.

Szathan lowered his hips and leaned forward, assuming a halberdier's stance, and slowly the two men began to circle each other, like a pair of dueling actors in an open-air theater. In the distance, feather-cloaked soldiers watched motionlessly, while the surrounding landscape, as if sensing the impending clash, made not a sound. No bird calls, no rodent chitters, not even the slightest hint of an autumn breeze—nothing.

And then the Mad Wolf charged.

His first strike was a predictable overhead arc, but it came so fast and so fluid that Szathan almost failed to block it. *Clang*— Nightwing juddered in his gauntleted hands, down to the tips of his battle-roughened fingers.

He whirled to counterstrike, but Zirian turned it aside, and then he baited a low strike but came up high. Szathan parried that and another, and now the strikes kept coming, high then low, low then midlevel. Haft pounded against haft, *boom, boom, boom,* and when steel kissed a rush of sparks sprayed the air. For every move executed by the Mad Wolf, Szathan was prepared with a counter-move, and this went on until Zirian's first onslaught of strikes came to an abrupt end.

The giant Zhoul pulled back, his breathing a little heavier now. Szathan twirled his pole arm in a show of confidence. Somewhere, dozens of yards away, a man began to shout. It was Seric Dyre. He told 'Ogre' Mordall to throw down his weapon and concede defeat, or keep fighting and die brutally at the hands of the Mad Wolf. Szathan didn't let the words distract or unman him; no, he was far too experienced for that.

Nightwing shot forward; Zirian's blade rose in defense. A sharp *clang*, and another, and now Szathan was pressing the attack, moving forward, imposing his will, showing the Mad Wolf just how formidable *he* was.

Attack combinations flowed out of him, maneuvers and tech-niques that were practiced countless times and in countless different ways. A low sweep became an overhead slash. *Whoosh, whoooom.* Two side thrusts ended in a mid-torso slash. *Skrrrrt, skrrrrt, clakk.* Scales snapped, sparks flew, and the Mad Wolf backpedaled.

He was off his footing now, his injured leg slow to respond, his speed greatly hampered. Szathan had him. Another thrust, and another. *That's it, I have you now, I—*

Szathan didn't know what happened. One moment he was weaving and thrusting and chopping away with Nightwing, and the next he was on the ground, the breath sucked out of him, blood streaming from some wound he didn't realize he had.

Zirian's weapon must've ripped into his midsection, because the scales of his armor were smashed, the padding and flesh beneath torn open. When Szathan looked up, he saw Zirian standing with unhindered poise and balance, his feet planted firmly in the earth. His expression was curious—a tiny, deceitful smile. And then, the truth hit Szathan like a blow to the brain: it had been a trick, the Mad Wolf wasn't injured at all.

Anger drove Szathan to his feet, but he found himself immediately on the defensive, raising and lowering Nightwing against the powerful slashes and sweeps of Zirian's long crescent blade. Szathan lost more ground with each parry, more and more until his feet crossed and he fell on his rump.

Zirian's massive weapon came screaming for his head. Szathan rolled; the blade *thrummed* past his ear and cleaved the earth beside him. *Boom.* Szathan scurried backward and staggered to his feet, his breath coming in forceful pulls.

He was still holding Nightwing, but it felt as useless as a flyswatter in a child's hands. Zirian Revil was simply too skilled and too strong. Szathan could hear laughter from the enemy's spectating lines, laughter that could've only come from Seric Dyre. It was a goading laughter, dripping with derision.

"Looks like the ogre got a taste of the wolf's true power," Seric barked, "and he doesn't like it at all."

This time it wasn't so easy to shrug off the insult. Probably because Seric was right. Szathan's gaze trailed back to the city walls. Beneath the pale afternoon sky, he could see a row of figures watching him. Among them were Lord Alarin, Lord Ansetheral,

General Thayer, Chamberlain Rennerin, and of course little Emperor Silas and his little timid eyes.

I can't let them down, Szathan thought. *Not again.* He turned back, tensed his arms, pointed the top spike of his weapon at the Mad Wolf . . . and then he charged.

Their halberds clashed once, twice, and then Szathan was back on the defensive. The Mad Wolf demonstrated a master's level of precision and patience with each of his two-handed strikes—and his power felt like nothing Szathan had ever felt before. *His talents are beyond mortal. Did I ever stand a chance?* Back and forth they exchanged strikes, back and forth and around and around, with Zirian always getting the better of the exchanges.

Nightwing worked furiously, but Szathan's arms were growing heavy and slow. And yet the Mad Wolf was still fresh, still fast. Did he ever get tired? An overhead slash just missed, one that could've cleaved Szathan's skull neatly in half, but before he could retaliate, a follow-up backslash almost took Szathan at the neck. He backpedaled a bit, but Zirian only peppered Szathan with flicking jabs, poking and prodding him from a fair distance.

Szathan could feel the warm blood leaking from the cracks in his armor. He wasn't the aggressor anymore; he had no strategy to achieve victory. He was simply trying to survive.

The moment he realized that he knew the fight was lost—and that was exactly when Zirian closed the distance and delivered a nasty over-the-shoulder chop that stole Szathan's balance and knocked Nightwing from his hands. Szathan was left on his knees, spitting up wads of blood and choking on smatterings of dust, his great taloned shoulders slumped over in defeat.

He refused to look up, but he could see the Mad Wolf's elongated shadow creep into view. The crescent-bladed halberd came up to dispense the deathblow. Szathan's eyes slammed shut. *Forgive me, Lord Alarin . . . forgive me, all.*

But no, it never came.

Szathan opened his eyes. The Mad Wolf was no longer focused on him. He was gazing to the west, at a rugged forestland of maple and hickory and willow. *What are you looking at?* Whatever it was Szathan couldn't see—but then he heard it. A rumble. A deep, unmistakable rumble.

At the fore of the spectating lines, Seric Dyre began to shout. A call of alarm to the troops. Moments later drumbeats blasted to life, with feathered Whitecrow flags waving frantically as Seric attempted to put his lines into position.

While this was happening, a murder of crows wheeled into the pinkish sky, cawing and shrieking and beating their dark wings. Below, the rumble continued to pulse louder and louder—and then, in an explosion of twig and leaf, horsemen roared out of the woods, hundreds of them, likely thousands, all moving at a blazing gallop.

An ambush, Szathan realized. *But by whom?* The mass of sun-beaten men were clad in boiled leather armor and lightweight long-coats, with forerankers armed with deadly pikes that snapped forward from an upright position. These were northmen. These were Vaskultans.

Seric Dyre's ranks scrambled for order, but they were ill-prepared and out of time. *CRACK.* The collision of opposing forces was like the snapping of a thousand saplings, a reverberating bawl that felt as though the world had imploded within itself.

Once the initial shockwave passed, the landscape melted into that familiar vortex of violence. Seric's disorganized ranks were plowed over by the charging Vaskultan front. Steel clashed and war horns blasted and men wailed, with all sounds mixing together like the rush of white water. The fighting was everywhere now, the blood spilling every which way. Vaskultan riders thrust their pikes through enemy infantry, while in return the Whitecrow soldiers slashed and hacked at horse legs and barbarian legs. Wooden shafts snapped and broke, but the Vaskultans continued their onslaught with single-edged backswords.

Szathan didn't so much as join the fray as he was thrown into it. He had been running along the frontlines, chasing the Mad Wolf, when a number of feather-cloaked soldiers unintentionally hurtled into him.

Nightwing immediately went to work, cutting through armor and flesh and tearing through cartilage and bone, but as one body dropped another rose in its place, and soon Szathan was wearing his enemies' blood and bits like a red smock. Yet as fearsome as he must've appeared, more and more foemen continued to surround him, and now there were too many to slip away from.

But Szathan didn't want to slip away. He whipped Nightwing around, thirsty for blood and hungry for glory—but then a host of Vaskultan horsemen careened into the circle, scattering the enemy.

Szathan met the dark eyes of one allied barbarian, a hawkish fellow who offered a slight nod that seemed to say, *you're welcome, friend*. With that, the Vaskultan was gone, pike braced forward as he plunged back into the fray.

To the north, the city portcullis began to open, a slow screech that draped itself across the battlefield like a funereal shroud. A column of Stormhaven cavalrymen sallied out in a tight wedge, galloping onto the battlefield and piercing the Whitecrow flank like a great harpoon.

The punctured enemy line began to deflate and bow inward, trembling and trembling like a wall about to collapse. Then it did collapse, and suddenly there were feather-cloaked men running this way and that, with many colliding into or trampling one another to escape. Outside the chaos, banners waved and drumbeats pounded, but Seric Dyre's Whitecrow forces would not find order again.

The Vaskultan riders didn't give chase; instead they dropped their pikes, unfastened their bows from their shoulders, and launched a screaming fusillade of arrows that pierced the fleers in the back and legs and head. Bodies tumbled and crashed and fell spinning to the earth, limbs streaming red and mouths twisted in agony.

Szathan didn't see the Mad Wolf again. The Zhoulish commander had rallied his auxiliaries and fled through a narrow bypath with the rest of Seric Dyre's feather-cloaks. In response, victorious pennants and flags rose from the city walls, and the prevailing Vaskultans began to topple the enemy's defensive barriers and smash their half-built siege engines in celebration.

Some of the Stormhaven soldiers joined in, while others raised their weapons and their voices in triumph. Szathan observed it all impassively. *Another battle won,* he mused.

As the fighting spirit fled from his body, the physical pain began to surface—the gashes along his midsection, the cut on his mouth, the long-injured knee, the terrible exhaustion . . . and all that was accompanied by the mental anguish of losing the contest to Zirian Revil.

In his heart, Szathan knew he should not be alive.

CHAPTER TWENTY-FOUR

Beyond the uneven plateaus and down the valley trails was where the defeated Anirian army retreated, regrouped, and re-provisioned. It had been a terrible slog back to safety, with men trudging through injury and misery as they attempted to re-establish the encampment and restore military order. Like whipped and beaten dogs they labored, while morale dripped lower than the old gunk on a keg bottom.

Inside the commander's tent, Seric sat on a roughhewn stool, alone save for the two Zhoulish guardsmen idling by the entrance flap. The one to the left seemed to enjoy complaining about his foot blisters, while the other seemed to enjoy teasing him about it. Seric himself was nursing his big toe, which he'd reinjured dismounting from his charger after the frantic battlefield flight. He wasn't surprised; his whole foot had been tender since the day he'd twisted it on the scree-covered slopes outside of Aster Falls.

That was many moons ago, when Veldries had still been with him; Aldebron Pentagath too. After descending armorless from the cliffside, they'd surprised and trounced Emeron Mathius's deceitful forces. Victory had tasted so sweet then. To overcome adversity and prevail in the face of defeat was the most glorious nectar a man could taste.

But today was different. Today the taste was bitter and nauseating, like the foulest snake wine from the coastal south. *I've made a fool of my name and my title. How can a strategist of renown fall to such an obvious deception? My legacy will suffer because I trusted the word of a mistrustful woman.* He raised his other hand and nibbled on a hunk of day-old millet bread. It was stale and hard, and he didn't have much of an appetite, so he ended up tossing it on the ground. The thoughts circling his mind were heavy and inflexible. *Nyvia told me the barbarians were miles away, tucking their tails from the defeat at Tendril Way. So I retracted my border guard and fell to the most basic of tent-room tactics: feign softness and strike hard.*

Throughout the day reports came and went. Death tolls, wounded counts, the soldiers that were lost to defection or capture, and those that were simply lost. Abandoned siege parts, razed granary stores, stolen supplies, and smashed equipment—everything that came with the burden of defeat. At one point, a bleary-eyed physician came to look at his foot, but Seric sent the little man scurrying off with a shout. *Don't you dare take away my pain,* he thought. *It's all I have right now, and I need to feel it. I deserve to feel it.*

The pain made him angry, and being angry was like a balm for his wretched doubts. And by the gods did those doubts gnaw at him, gnaw and gnaw with their unyielding cynicism. *Has Nyvia truly betrayed me, or was she deceived just as I was?* He needed to confront her, to find out the truth—and so he summoned her.

But when she finally entered the tent, the sight of her round little face made him apoplectic with rage, and next he knew both hands had wrapped themselves around her neck, and he was squeezing and squeezing and choking the life out of her. That tiny, innocent expression she wore had transformed into one of sheer panic, as eyes bulged and lips quivered under the constrictive pressure.

Seric could feel her frantic fingernails gouging the flesh of his arms, but that only made him squeeze harder. He wanted to kill her. To strangle her until her last breath left her lips and her body jerked the way it does upon death's embrace. But no . . . he couldn't. Not while there remained a smidgen of doubt, a tiny, tiny speck of uncertainty that niggled at his heart. And so he let her go, and when he did she stumbled back, hands thrown over her chest, wheezing like a goat after a mauling from a mountain cat.

Before she could make sense of things, Seric began to yell. He didn't know why, but all of a sudden he was screaming at her, screaming and screaming like a resentful master at a disobedient slave. Accusatory shouts and angry imperatives and whatever random thoughts filled his head. Even sinister jussives such as: *You should DIE!*

Perhaps it was the physical pain, perhaps it was the emotional distress, but Seric could no longer control his tongue. All he could do was yell at her, and as he did Nyvia recoiled in fear, a fear so pure it was like the cowering of wounded prey. For some reason Seric wanted to choke her again—and he almost did, except a sudden hand from behind landed firmly on his shoulder, *thump,* withholding his advance.

Seric spun. Fist still upraised, he *almost* struck General Zirian Revil. *Where did you come from?* He hadn't heard the huge general enter. But by the gods he was glad he didn't strike, because for one, Zirian was still strapped in his heavy armor, so a miscalculated punch might've left Seric with an injured hand to go along with his injured foot; and two, and more importantly, the Mad Wolf had a baleful look in his good eye, a look so cold it could freeze piss.

Seric had no choice but to bury his hostilities, wipe the spittle from his mouth, and step away from his former wife. He paced the length of the tent's inner chamber a few times, then sat back down on the stool and rubbed at his toe a bit more. Nyvia attempted to storm out, but a quick motion by Seric placed the two Zhoulish guardsmen before her. She tried to push past them, but these men were brick buildings that would not be moved, so in the end, she simply turned back around and accepted her situation, eyes lowered to the floor.

Seric didn't address her then; instead he flung his gaze at Zirian. The general's face was bruised along the cheekbone, a fat maroon welt that looked like someone smeared dirt on him. There was also a crusty scrape that ran below his left earlobe to his chin. Lower, the scales of his cuirass were dented and chipped across the upper torso, and also at the shoulder. His battle-cloak was marred by a tear deep enough to fit a man's head through, leaving its outer fringes black from filth and dry blood. "Steady yourself, my lord," the general said in the Zhoulish tongue. "A leader who cannot control his impulses is no leader at all."

Seric almost shot back a snarky comment, but he decided to let the matter drop. Zirian was right, of course, and yet Seric wasn't ready to verbally admit it, so he offered the most cursory of nods instead, after which he said, "You are wounded. You need to be seen by a physician."

The general didn't answer right away. "I won the contest. I had the ugly man on his knees."

"I know." There was a pause. "I'm told your auxiliaries suffered few casualties, thanks to your swiftness in establishing rallying points."

"It was more General Wyath. It was his direction that helped us escape."

Seric nodded. "He is an exemplary follower of the three major points of military action: swiftness under pressure, boldness under fire, and decisiveness over hesitancy. Examples of such wisdom are found within the pages of the *Wits and Wiles of War,* if you care to know."

Zirian acknowledged that with an offhanded grunt, and in the brief quiet that followed Seric's eyes trailed down to the hunk of millet bread on the ground. It lay beside a small rectangular wash-basin, whose waters shined dully under the light of the brazier. Seric couldn't help but lean forward to view his reflection; it was faint, and his features were darkly distorted, but he could see the exhaustion plain as day.

His hair, once thick and brown and full of life, now hung in sweaty tangles, unkempt and thin and ugly as hog bristles. And his face . . . that healthy olivine skin tone had receded into a pale, sickly one. *You look awful.* He touched his dimpled chin with a hand that had been trembling since the battle's end. *Get some sleep, Seric Dyre,* he told himself. *The gods know you need it.*

But no—not before he dealt with his dear former wife. When he reaffixed his gaze on her, he realized she'd been staring at him this whole time. Staring with those big, deceitful eyes of hers. "I don't know why you still have your head," he muttered, in a tone that dripped venom.

"Seric, I had no knowledge of—"

He flicked a hand to shut her up. Such petty attempts at manipulation would not work on him. "Hundreds dead, hundreds more wounded. A significant number of my army, either mauled or mutilated or murdered by those barbarian bastards. Barbarians that were reported, by you, to have fled back to the north."

Her eyes seemed to struggle between looking Seric directly in the eye and looking directly at the ground. For a moment Seric pitied her. She had been his wife once, and together they had made a son, and now that son was being held by the enemy. With a sigh, Seric buried the anger in his heart and looked at Nyvia more closely, studying her timorous stance and slumped, defeated shoulders.

He wanted to believe her, but he was no fool. *I had them. Zirian was standing over Ogre Mordall, blade in hand, ready to end his life. And with that, my son, Veldries, would've been freed.* His eyes trickled down once more to that hunk of bread lying on the ground. *But I fell victim to another deception perpetrated by the old Athera clan.*

Nyvia's face suddenly brightened with recollection. "Ansetheral. I passed him in the corridor, just outside the meeting hall." She swallowed, a hollow sound. "He must've known, he must've tampered with the documents on Alarin's desk. He must've—"

Seric motioned for his two guardsmen to escort her outside. Nyvia tried to finish her thoughts, but Seric turned away to deliberately shun her. *Leeches,* he reminded himself. *The entire clan, all bloodsucking leeches. Nyvia included. When will I ever learn?*

———

The field before the city of Stormhaven was littered with the dead. Of the Vaskultans there weren't many, perhaps a hundred at most, but these men were to remain where they'd fallen, to allow their fatal wounds to bleed into the dirt in reverence to the Landforger. Clean-up crews under Seric Dyre's Whitecrow banner maneuvered around them, picking out their own dead to haul back to the oxcarts.

Teams of collectors followed, snatching up any strewn weapons and equipment left by their fallen allies. When one would accidentally disturb a fallen tribesman or attempt to loot an item not of his own, he would receive a fierce rebuke from a watchful Vaskultan, and more than once a good thrashing was needed to dissuade those especially greedy crewmen.

Ansetheral Athera wandered along the outskirts of the field, his senses taking in the aftermath of battle. Always that same smell permeated the air whenever a lot of men killed a lot of other men—and always was it a tangy mixture of scraped metal and old blood and body sweat. His sharp eyes examined each fallen brother they came across, and with care he noted their expressions: often an expected grimace, sometimes a wide-eyed stare of shock, and occasionally a (strangely) serene look.

The slender General Thayer Dal approached from the rear left, the scales of his blackened armor creaking in the still air. The man was clearly ignorant of Vaskultan customs, as evidenced by his frivolous questions: "No retrievals? No burials?"

"No," Anseth said.

"Not even a dirge or elegy?"

"Nothing."

"But they are just lying there. Soulless husks for flies to bloat and crows to dine on. Why not burn them at least?"

Anseth's next words were spoken slowly and evenly. "The flesh descends to the Landforger, the spirit rises to the Skybringer."

Thayer shook his head in an overdramatic fashion. "Silly, silly."

Anseth turned at the call of his name. Not his Anirian name but his Vaskultan appellation, Lord Revek. His eyes found the hawkish-faced Severak Bonesplitter advancing toward him leading a coal-colored mare. The commander looked unscathed and strong and sturdy as ever, though a small smile betrayed his usual stoniness.

"My heart is glad to see you again," Anseth said.

His eyes shifted slightly to study the gangly Thayer Dal, but his reply was spoken in Vaskulti. "You are our chieftain and our brother; we'd not leave you in peril. The scoundrel"—he did his best to pronounce the Anirian name—"See-ric Dy-er decimated our encampment and outwitted our warband at the pass. For that, vengeance was the only option."

Anseth was about to reply but his attention was stolen by the passing of several horsemen. They called out Revek's name while holding up crude little wreaths garlanded with bloody pairs of dangling eyes, and just like that they rode off, leaving Thayer Dal to mutter, "The hell was that about?"

"Just a little victory ride," Anseth replied in the Anirian tongue, then he looked purposely at Severak and his odd little smile. "Or is there something more I should know about?"

"News from the northern front," Severak said. "The Nidrak tribe was overwhelmed just north of Iron River, at Sickle Hills. Commander Kaigon baited them into a surrounding depression then picked them off one by one as they emerged. Some managed to escape, but most either surrendered or died. The victory is crucial, lord."

Anseth nodded at that. "So it appears the Gray Plains will finally stand as one. Under the Vaskultan banner, just as Lord Volduk had envisioned."

Severak's eyes trailed down to the Earthstone tied around Anseth's neck. He spoke while looking at it. "It's time to return to the north."

"Not just yet, but soon. Very soon."

Severak nodded. "You must join us in tonight's celebration. Drink some blackmilk, down some blood sausage, rattle a few anklebones, perhaps laugh a little. You *do* remember how to laugh?"

Anseth smiled even though he didn't intend to. "I remember."

Later that night and under a fiercely waxing half-moon, Anseth did join the Vaskultan festivities—and what a night of merriment it was. Massive bonfires raged while leather-clad females danced to the sounds of the male throat-singers, whose gravelly voices surely made the distant Anirian listeners wince. There were flutes too, shinbone flutes and flat, disc-like flutes that sounded heavenly. Two goats and a rare drop-tine buck were slaughtered as offerings to the Skybringer, and later their cooked heads were staked at the foot of the fires to be picked cleaned by hungry revelers.

They took a break from the food and dancing for moonlight archery and horse racing contests, which led to a lot of cheering and stomping and waving of yak-tail banners. After that a crude bone cage was erected, not for a blood challenge but for tests of strength and wrestling among the veteran warriors. When that was done, the bonfires blazed anew and the drinking and dancing and debauchery returned in full. It was a warm, welcome night, despite the dark mist that swirled like tentacles in the night sky.

At some point Anseth found himself draped in little more than a bone robe, which is exactly how it sounds: a long gown of haphazardly glued animal bones (along with the occasional ungulate hoof). When he moved the bones rattled, and so with torchlight in hand he whirled and danced and capered like a pixie in a forest. So cheerful was his spirit, so carefree was his mind, he even decided to take a woman that night, a thin Vaskultan broad who lured him playfully into her private yurt. Anseth enjoyed caressing her sweet skin and fondling her firm breasts, but he was too intoxicated to enjoy much else. Still, despite the growing wooziness, Anseth couldn't recall the last time he'd had such an entertaining evening. Come morning, he would likely suffer a splitting headache and swear off drink altogether, but for now, he gladly savored life's simple pleasures. He deserved it; he was the Vaskultan chieftain, after all.

———

Moonlight swept the battlefield like a pearlescent fog. Thayer Dal crept across it, absently listening to the peeps and hoots of the surrounding nocturnal denizens, which seemed to commingle with the distant hum of the Vaskultan celebration. Over vacant hillocks he paced alone, boots flattening the low weed grasses and patches of white clover. Around him lay dozens of deceased Vaskultan warriors, men and women who remained where they'd fallen, their bodies strewn like discarded playthings. Dead—and yet they beckoned to Thayer. *I hear you,* he told them. *I hear you all.* An especially grisly corpse lay behind a nest of undisturbed bramble. *Yes, you'll do. You'll satisfy the void's call, won't you?* Thayer paused, stole one last glance around the area, then knelt down for a closer look.

The barbarian's arm was folded behind his back, his head mushed into the earth sideways, as though stomped by a boot. The visible part of his face was pinched and gray, with half his cheek shorn off and dangling like old meat trimmings. *A short blade did this,* Thayer mused, *carbon-infused steel, serrated in edge. An officer's weapon, no doubt.* He leaned a little closer. *Did you have the honor of being killed by an officer? Yes, I believe you did.*

The man's eyes were still intact, preserved by some strange gel the barbarians must've slathered on to prevent crows or other scavengers from plucking them out. Seemed a rather futile effort, since decomposition would eventually win out, but Thayer wasn't about to question a barbarian's theological beliefs. *Not that I could even converse with them to better understand.* He leaned closer to study the expression on the dead warrior's face . . . it was the *only* expression that was true in this world. Someone once told him that, someone aged and wise.

The unmistakable smell of death rose to tickle Thayer's nose. He embraced the odor, even breathed it in, a great big inhalation, drawing in every last whiff of that malodorous sweetness. So strong it burned his nostrils, a good burn—exhilarating even. *So pure, so proper.* His hands went to work. *Sorry, but I must relieve you of your attire.* It was a difficult process, as dead men seemed to weigh thrice their living counterparts, but Thayer was no weakling, and despite the pull of late-night fatigue, he outmuscled the corpse and stripped off its lightweight coat and under-tunic, then draped the garments over himself. The cut was adequate, the fit loose and comfortable, and the scent . . . well, the scent was utterly divine. Like the fragrance of a schoolboy to a pederast, or the musty odor of old coins to a skinflint. The void's call whispered into Thayer's heart, a breathless, will-o'-the-wispish call that could not be ignored or cast out.

He sprang into motion. Running, running, running through the night, overdressed in a dead warrior's attire, arms extended like a great gyrfalcon in the sky. Thayer may not have been blessed with the broadest upper body, but his legs were solid and powerful, and with them he ran and ran and continued to run, and only when his heart pounded from exertion and his calves stiffened with ache did he slow to a walk. It was a strange, almost leisurely stroll through a field of death and decay, like a wayfarer who'd left his cares in the wind. Then, at some point, when he finished sightseeing, he stripped off the dead man's clothes and wandered back to his quarters in the barracks, celebrating the stench of unlife that wrapped itself like a smile around him.

CHAPTER TWENTY-FIVE

I t was always looking at her . . . the head.

The one that was once attached to the body of her escort and protector and friend. The one that used to speak, to have opinions, to be annoyed at Miriana's willful pigheadedness. Now it was just a head, a rotting and rupturing thing, its once vulturine expression long twisted into a ghastly grimace. Truly a disgusting sight. But worst of all was the smell . . . that horrible, horrible smell. Like powdered sulfur rubbed on unwashed flesh.

The hollow chill of the spacious cell seemed to slow the rate of decomposition, and strangely enough, there were no maggots to be found. *Am I too far underground?* She had so many questions. How long before liquefaction would begin? How long before all that was left was cartilage and bone and random globs of decay? Miriana didn't wish to see that, so she tossed a few handfuls of loose straw and hassock over the head, but even beneath such coverings she could feel those empty sockets gazing up at her, a long and lonesome gaze. *How long will it remain here?* she wondered. *Will I witness a complete skeletonization, perhaps months or even years from now?*

Time passed in a peculiar manner. Not in a forward series of events, but in a disconnected, almost ethereal stutter in which night and day had neither bearing nor meaning. Without significant external changes, one day became no different from the last, and moments had an almost backward mentality, an endless perceptional tug of war. *How long has it been? Days? Weeks? A month— has it been a month?* She had nothing with which to entertain herself, nothing but the occasional thump from some upstairs commotion, and every so often she heard the distant echoing bark of a hound. She'd often count the faint but frequent sounds of a *drip, drip, drip,* and sometimes she would try to predict when the drips would occur, and once she correctly tallied two hundred and seventy-six consecutive drips. An achievement, for sure.

The crushing solitude was occasionally broken by meal deliveries, congees of millet or soybean that were passed through an open slat at the bottom of the ironbound door. Less frequent was the removal of the chamber pot, which was actually more of a rusty bedpan. This was all done in a very cold and taciturn manner, without a word spoken or even a meaningful look. She tried to communicate with the turnkeys, but her words always went unheeded. *Am I even here? Am I even alive any longer?*

The bulk of her time was spent thinking about ramming her head into the cell walls. They were constructed of uneven stone and held together by a mortar of lime and clay and likely rice flour. She assumed the latter because it looked and felt exactly like the mortar of the second parapet of the Star of the Hollow's eastern district wall, the one that had eroded so deeply they had to commission an emergency crew for reparations. She remembered the head mason informing her how the infusion of rice flour would aid the bonding process of the mortar—and, as it turned out, he was right.

The Hollow. *Oh, what a word to have stuck in the heart,* she mused. *I'd give anything to return to my city. To return to my home. If I could go back, I would gladly take my chances with Zantherei.*

Perhaps she had overestimated his vindictiveness; perhaps she would've received mercy for her schemes and depraved dealings. Perhaps they might've even gone on as husband and wife, as emperor and empress even. As cold as he was, Zantherei had his moments of reason. His trust and favor could be recaptured. Yes, she *could* convince him to forgive her. Perhaps . . .

No. Miriana shook her head dismissively. *It's over now. Your choices have been made, and now you have to live the rest of your short, miserable life with them.* That revelation stung, a debilitating pain. It was much easier to deny the truth, because denial had a way of soothing the heart—even if one knew the consequences of lying to oneself. Still, in her mind, the only truth was that Cyrille Vileron had been right . . . yes, he'd been right all along.

The head had somehow shrugged off its covering of straw and was staring at her again. Empty eyes burrowing into her heart like the claws of two sand fiddlers. She couldn't bear it any longer. It was as if those eyes were judging her, mocking all her poor decisions and wretched foul-ups. Those two terrible voids, staring, staring as if to say, *I was right, my lady. I was right.* The head kept repeating those words, over and over, every moment and every drip, until Miriana had no choice but to yield to the admission herself. "You were," she murmured at last, her voice weak and thin, like the stretching of a salt-hardened rag. Vileron's head seemed pleased to hear that. *I told you Raas Dragath is a cruel bastard, a man not to be trusted or trifled with.*

"You did tell me . . . but I didn't listen. A sound ruler always considers the counsel of those who aided her ascent. Always."

But you didn't, and now look at me. Look at what's happened to me.

"I know." Miriana turned away. She curled up on the floor and wept silently to herself. Alone, despairing, without a single sympathizer in reach. Again, her thoughts trickled back to the Hollow, her heart desperate to latch onto better times, anything to evade the present darkness and dolor. The status of being an empress, the authority and near-omnipotence of enthronement . . . it was an ambrosia, a wine to sate even the richest of palates. Every want and every whim were tended and tailored, every command met by servile attendants who scurried to assist. Courtiers and stewards would vie to win her favor, scorning and slandering each other all for a chance to bathe in Her Majesty's good graces. By the gods the realm was hers. All of it, anything and everything, from the earthly to the divine and all the details in between. It was all hers for the taking.

And now it was gone. Gone because she failed to end a single man's life.

She wondered what he was doing now, the great Storm of the North. It wasn't a stretch to assume Zantherei Athera was planning a military campaign. The man lived for war, and he was good at it, and war made the economy thrive, and himself rich. But were his eyes set on his traitorous brother Alarin and the false child emperor? Or were they aimed here, at vengeance against Raas Dragath? Or perhaps he was looking to the north, to deal with Seric's betrayal. There were enemies at all corners of the realm, pretenders and claimants whose actions were keeping the realm divided.

Miriana sighed to herself. *What does it matter?* She would die here, alone and afraid and filled with remorse. Tears blurred her vision. She wiped them with the sleeve of her homespun robe. A filthy thing, the material so coarse it made her itch, not to mention how unpleasant it smelled. Her fingernails were filthy too, the same of her palms and the soles of her feet. Grime ran in streaks up her limbs, leading to a lathery sweat that irritated her thighs and under arms. She could only imagine how her hair must've looked. Once so clean and black and arranged in styles that varied by mood or day, but now it felt like a mess of filthy knots—surely a hideous addition to her busted nose.

Vileron's head was still looking at her. *You should've listened to me, my lady. You should've listened.*

"I'm sorry," she said plaintively. "I said *I'm sorry,* all right? What would you have me do? I can't change what happened."

You should've listened to me.

"You shouldn't have come. I told you not to come. Gods know I tried to send you away."

You never would've made it without me. Those brigands would've raped you, robbed you, left you for dead.

"So? A better fate then what lay ahead. But you . . . you could've lived."

I could've, but you didn't listen.

"I know." It was all she could think to say.

You should've listened.

"I said *I know.*"

The head began to repeat itself. *You should've listened. You should've listened. You should've listened.*

"Stop saying that. *Please.*"

But you're not listening. Why not? You should've listened. You should've—

"SHUT UP!" Miriana sprang to her feet, weak and wobbly, yet still angry enough to shake a fist at Vileron's head. "I'm *DONE* listening. How about I smash your festering skull into the stones? Hmm? Then you will talk to me no—"

There was a sound. A low rumble, a subtle *booooom,* but it was far away, somewhere in the outer reaches of the stronghold. She heard it again, moments later. *Booooom.* This time it was followed by a sharp *crack.* It sounded like something large had split apart, some sort of support structure perhaps. Miriana listened closer. She heard the same rumble again. Then again. Suddenly it was growing more frequent, and louder, like claps of thunder from an incoming storm. But no, it wasn't thunder at all.

BOOOOOM.

The walls shook, dust and debris shooting out of the cracks and crevices. Again. *BOOOOOM.* Miriana lost her balance, nearly tripping over her own bare feet, before she lowered herself to the ground and shielded her head with upraised hands. Above, the shored-up ceiling trembled and groaned and spat chunks of clay and mortar. Another *boom* and another, and now the ceiling was buckling even further, with hand-sized bricks dropping to the floor with terrible *thumps*. One landed far too close, forcing Miriana to scramble away. *What is this? What is happening?*

It was then the ceiling, as if in answer, decided to collapse.

In segments it broke, almost a methodical process. First the leftmost partition cracked, and this crack rippled all the way to the middle of the shoring, dislodging everything around it. Huge slabs of mortared stone came crashing down, a clattering so loud Miriana slammed the palms of her hands against her ears. More bricks fell, bricks of all different sizes and shapes and edges, and these were accompanied by a showering of grit and gravel.

When it was finally over, Miriana lowered her arms and stole a cautious look around. Mortared dust and chunks of stone covered the cell like a funereal shroud. Looking up, she saw light punching down from where the ceiling used to be. Not a bright light, but a dull smoky kind, thick and unnatural. She heard sounds too, strange sounds, a mass of people yammering all at once, like a busy market square perhaps. But no, these were urgent sounds, of men and women screaming for aid. An assault—it must be an assault against the stronghold.

You need to get out, Miriana told herself. The wall to her left was partially gutted, exposing a jagged rise of broken brickwork that Miriana could use as an improvised stairway. Yes, that was her way out—her *only* way out. All she had to do was climb. She placed her bare feet on the cold stones, one at a higher elevation than the other, and then she paused to take one final look below. Vileron's head lay upended on the floor. It wasn't staring at her any longer; it was just a dead, decomposing husk, voiceless, eyeless, and half covered in fragments of lime and clay.

Miriana didn't bother to say goodbye. Instead she turned back, reaffirmed her footing, and began to climb. One light step and then another, slowly and cautiously. *That's it, Mir, keep it steady.* Loose bricks wobbled under her weight, forcing her to work and rework her position. Without proper footwear and climbing gloves, everything she touched threatened to prick or slice her. There were too many jagged edges, too many uneven corners.

Steady, Mir, keep it balanced and steady. Up and up she went, higher and higher toward the grayish light. She could hear the pounding of drums now, along with the unmistakable clamor of conflict. Every few moments the drums vanished beneath another explosive *boom,* and for a moment Miriana thought the stronghold itself would come crashing down, much like her own cell had. But the floor above seemed to hold . . . well, for a time anyway. And then it didn't.

BOOOOM. Miriana lurched forward. *CRACK.* Her body whipped sideways, her rear foot sliding off the makeshift stairway, leaving the other to teeter precariously on the ledge. She redirected her momentum and threw herself flat upon the uneven bricks, then watched in horror as a great fissure ripped through the upper landing.

She had to move. *NOW.*

Hands scrabbled for purchase. She could feel the fresh cuts in her fingers and feet, but she didn't care. She had to get out. Up and up she went, up and up as the walls crumbled around her. *Hurry. Hurry. HURRY.* She latched onto a slab of semi-collapsed stone and pulled herself through the gaping ceiling hole, just as the stairway fell away. *BOOOOM.* She was free.

When the dust settled, she found herself in a vacant, lopsided corridor. The tiled ceiling was split by a sidewinding gash that bathed her in that strange, smoky light. Miriana dashed for the tall double-doors at the far end. Another explosion sprayed clay shards and bits of plaster in her face. She lowered her head and kept moving. A twin-serpent statue toppled in front of her, shattering into a thousand pieces. She veered around it, then dodged the wall sconce that fell and vomited embers on the floor. *Almost there, almost out of this nightmarish place . . . but what awaits outside?*

She was moving so fast she nearly slammed into the double-doors in an off-balance slide. Throwing her hands flat against the red-lacquered wood, and after summoning all her muscle and all her grit, she heaved the doors open. And then she froze. *By the gods . . .*

Serpenthold's center wall was under heavy assault, ramparts and battlements breaking apart like toy blocks. No, they weren't breaking, they were . . . *melting?* Shadowy black fires clung to the fortification like an army of aggressive ants, overpowering it, weakening it, eroding it away as though it wasn't stone but something as friable as sand. The smell of this destruction was not so different from the one Vileron's head gave off in the cell, only this was fouler and more prevalent, like the stench of a giant over-cooked carcass. Even Miriana's impaired olfactory sense wasn't immune to it; in fact, she recalled having smelled this very scent before. At the Hollow, down in the depths of the covert workshops.

Darkfire.

As if on cue, the massive base of the center wall *cracked*, a terrifying sound that left the entire structure struggling to remain upright. Turrets and hoardings wobbled and snapped, while buttresses and brattices fractured and rattled. The wall took on an odd, downslope shape, as though sappers had compromised it from an underground tunnel.

It was then Miriana saw a spear-like missile scream across the sky, directly over her head. *BOOOOM.* A black crater opened along the corbels of a rectangular tower, and within moments the support brackets melted, and heavy stones slid burning from its crown, speeding groundward with an enormous howl. Miriana leaped for cover. *Ohhh gods—*!

Stones met earth in a tremendous roar, an unearthly, almost incomprehensible sound. Dust billowed and great tentacles of black smoke reached out to seize anything and everything in sight. Miriana was smothered by it, her senses dulled and dizzied. *You have to get out of here!* She tried to move, but a sudden fit of coughing betrayed her, and when she finally overcame it her ears were assaulted by the horrific sounds of armed men killing and dying and burning alive. In the midst of this, another ballista missile struck the wall, and the great *boom* that followed rendered all other sounds insignificant.

You have to run, Mir . . . RUN now!

This time her legs obeyed. She ran and ran without any notion of which direction she was actually running; east or west, north or south—nothing made sense in this giant whirlwind of black smoke. She heard the pounding of booted feet all around her, but no one paid her any mind. She was like an invisible nymph stealing through the mist, except this nymph was scratched up and half clothed and utterly terrified.

The darkfire was everywhere. Scorching everything it touched, shoving its poison into the lungs of anyone who dared breathe it in. It was nothing like the wildfires she'd encountered months ago; no, this was a much more putrid and powerful blaze, difficult for the mind to digest. Hard blocks of dressed stone melting like buttery cream? It just wasn't possible. *And that smell . . . it's so awful, so frighteningly awful.* She begged the gods for a way out. She begged Azrial the Protector to whisk her back to the Hollow and drop her safely within the confines of her private bedchamber. *I want to go home . . . please, gods, I just want to go home.*

But Azrial and the other gods must've disregarded her pleas, because she remained trapped in this hellish nightmare. Redlander soldiers lay all around her, writhing and moaning as the darkfire devoured their scale and lamellar armor and feasted on their flesh. She saw the skin of a man's face melt away like runny egg whites, leaving a smiling skeleton briefly in its place, before that too dissolved into ash.

Nearby, a fallen horse succumbed to a mass of searing black blisters that leached through its protective barding and consumed the tissue beneath. Another man's hands liquefied like hot candlewax to the wrists—even more frightening was the poor bastard's horrified expression as he examined the twin stumps. Miriana couldn't do anything to help him, and yet she couldn't take her eyes off him.

You won't end up like that, she told herself. *You won't. Not you, Mir, you're strong. You were once an empress.* Redlander non-combatants were fleeing past her in frantic waves, unarmed men and frightened women and crying children all desperate for salvation. Miriana tried to fall in line with the traffic, but these poor, panicked folks were as lost as she was, sprinting every which way, some right back into the darkfire's path, where they met gruesome ends.

Miriana branched out from the crowd and hustled in the direction her gut told her to go, and when the smoke eventually cleared, she found herself at the stronghold's perimeter, standing before the tall Sadralen banners of the assailing forces. These were Star of the Hollow soldiers and judging by their blackened steel armor and serrated gray-black cloaks, they were the elite forces of the empire: the Bristled Boar Regiment, the Blood Thrasher Regiment, the Black Pine Regiment, and more. Symbols on their frayed standards identified powerful generals such as Aldebron Pentagath, Sabriel Soffin, and Gilberon Brehems. *But what about my husba—?*

Miriana froze. *There.* She could see him now: the Storm of the North, the Emperor of the Anir, the one and only Zantherei Athera. He was standing beneath his personal ensign and clad in his full imperial battledress and plumed halfhelm.

The very sight of him pushed Miriana's heart up her throat. *Stay calm, Mir. He doesn't see you. Just walk away.* She tried to do just that, but her feet were like two stone slabs mired in a bog hole, and all she could do was gaze fearfully at her husband. So stern and hulking and self-possessed he appeared, especially now at the head of his military campaign, a place in which he'd always been most comfortable. It was an intimidating sight . . . the way his underlings scurried around him, the way he held command over the siege officers and artillerists at his sides. He was pointing at the stronghold's walls now, undoubtedly indicating where he wanted the next volley of darkfire to loose.

Turn around, Mir, turn around and walk away before someone sees you. Her legs lifted from their petrified state and obeyed, but between the screens of smoke and the mass of armed soldiers, she found herself circling around and ending up at the same place, as though Zantherei were a ravenous vortex intent on sucking her in. She was panicking now, feet darting this way and that—but no matter where she went, she couldn't seem to find a safe exit.

Eventually she stumbled out somewhere to Zantherei's left, maybe twenty paces before a line of siege ballistae, huge military devices built on wheels and manned by busy crewmen. At the head stood a man dressed in ember-colored battle robes. The war hammer in his dark-skinned hand was narrow and flat and faded like weathered patina. *I know you,* Miriana thought. Yes, it was Nanjen. Nanjen the Sijian and Nanjen the master alchemist—and he was looking right at her.

Miriana's eyes dropped. She turned her head and hid behind the lengths of her ratty hair. *Did he see me? Did he recognize my face?* Her feet shuffled into movement, taking small, discreet steps across the dusty earth. Each step was agonizingly slow. She could *feel* the man's eyes on her. *Don't call out to me, don't call out to me. Don't—*

A shout rang out; Miriana burst into a run. She wasn't even sure if the shout was meant for her, but she bolted anyway, a wild, clumsy effort, like a drunk blundering down a midnight alley. She ran and ran and just when she thought she'd gotten away, someone caught her arm by the crook of the elbow.

A voice murmured in her ear, a soft yet masculine voice. It told her to stop struggling and follow. For some reason she obeyed, perhaps because she was tired of running, or perhaps because she was tired of all this blood and fire and death. The figure led her past the siege engines and past the files of soldiers and conscripts and squires. No one stopped them. A few soldiers even stepped aside. Her guide didn't acknowledge anyone—he only spoke to her. "Keep your head down. Don't look up."

Wait a moment. Miriana knew that voice. Yes, she may have been disoriented and exhausted and congested with black smoke, but she *knew* that voice. And when she looked up, she saw a familiar face, pale and narrow and partially concealed by a black halfmask.

It was the face of her brother, Vylas Voren.

BOOK IV: DESTRUCTION

CHAPTER TWENTY-SIX

Alarin Athera hadn't forgotten.

Not when Seric Dyre and his Whitecrow forces had laid siege on Stormhaven, not when the Vaskultans had stormed the field and driven off the enemy, and not when the season had turned and a new threat from the southwest emerged. He hadn't forgotten, nor would he ever forget, that someone in this city had tried to kill him.

Winter's presence was no more threatening than autumn's uncharacteristic warmth. The trees bared their leaves seemingly out of habit rather than necessity, and the air lacked that crystalline crispness of the usual heartland clime. If the farmhands and plowmen found it peculiar, they didn't express it, and as their crops continued to thrive they toiled blissfully through the shorter days.

Still, there was something unsettling about the lack of chill. Aberrant weather affected everything from harvesting gourds to discerning tide tables, and even the most experienced recorders of this age were having difficulties establishing meteorological patterns both earthly and beyond.

Alarin groaned as he turned away from the unlatched window of his private chamber. Despite the passage of time, the tightness in his upper torso never seemed to fade, and somehow it had become an unwanted companion to the phantom pain of his missing leg. Every little move sparked some sort of ache in him, and on certain intolerable days (like today), he wanted to free himself from this bodily vessel altogether. But Master Penry had been a patient and attentive caretaker, and under his expert guidance Alarin was able to put his mind at ease.

But he hadn't forgotten.

The plotter behind the assassination attempt was still roaming these halls, still sipping his or her morning tea, and still whistling blissfully throughout the day. That didn't sit well with Alarin. His intuition leaned toward the bug-eyed Minister Byort, but Alarin couldn't detain a man on the account of a hunch. No, commands should never be issued without due consideration; to do so is to create a seedling of doubt. And when that seedling grows and grows and finally rears its ugly head, the entire authoritative structure falls into question.

With that in mind, what if Byort wasn't to blame? In quiet moments faces would appear in Alarin's mind, faces of the other White Fang councilmembers. He replayed conversations they'd shared, little snippets and oddments here and there, in the hopes of discovering an overlooked clue. Lowering the status and removing the finery of the upper nobility was a difficult transition for some, sure . . . but Alarin didn't expect to be *killed* over it. How do you focus on your civil duties when your would-be murderer remains at large?

Alarin slept, as one would expect, rather poorly. Harmful thoughts and inactivity threatened to drag him back into that old familiar pit of misery. It was a comfort in a way, like the lure of a destructive ex-lover you just couldn't seem to resist.

Living as a recluse and a layabout was much easier than facing the truth of what he'd become. But no, Alarin refused to allow those old habits to ruin him. He was a stronger man now. Still, the latest reports of a terrible black magic were working hard to undermine that strength.

"Surely you don't believe it, my lord?" Chamberlain Rennerin asked, later that day. The bald man was reclining on an old gray settee, moving his crossed feet back and forth while cleaning the wax from his ear with a metal pick. "It's just rumormongering. Idle chatter. That's what people do. They talk, they embellish, they hyperbolize. Could very well be misinformation spread by Zantherei Athera's own agents."

"Perhaps, but we should still take measures."

"Why? No such sorcery is known to man."

"Many believe the same of the cloudfalls," Alarin told him. "Many believe they never gave a voice to the young Silas Mordall. The proof is standing right before them, and yet they choose not to believe."

"Yes, well, that is different. Some say the cloudfalls are nothing more than a natural luminescent remedy. But this . . . this darkfire that men speak of. How can something be so utterly unnatural? It sounds too farfetched, too made up." He removed the ear pick and turned his head toward Physician Penry, who was preparing his herbal extracts and tinctures on a nearby cubby table. "Master, surely you are blessed with greater insight. Tell us your thoughts, won't you?"

The stout, owlish man cleared his throat like a professional orator before a speech. "Just because something is not understood doesn't make it unnatural. The darkfire is rumored to be the product of a purple pyrotail, a flowering plant found in the far reaches of Sijian's arid jungles. Such a clime seems contradictory, I know, but naturists and explorers have proven its existence. Anyway, it is said this plant produces a certain bioluminescence that combines with specific gases in the environment and results in an exothermic reaction. When this reaction is soaked in a type of linseed resin it releases a tiny black flame, in a sort of thermal encapsulation. It is quite possible that the elements of this plant were somehow extracted and used as a coating for the purposes of siege warfare."

"Fascinating," Rennerin said, though his enthusiasm was lacking in sincerity. "And perhaps you are right. But to me all this talk just screams of hooey and hogwash, spouted forth by wannabe occultists and their bat-blind followers."

"I don't disagree with you, Lord Chamberlain," Alarin said, "but only a short-sighted man dismisses sound reason and logic, just as a careless man dismisses the threat of danger. Regardless of the truth behind this 'darkfire', I've received reports from my spies, and these reports do not lie. Serpenthold was decimated by a siege assault from the Hollow. Walls were smashed, defenders were crushed and burned. The tyranny of Raas Dragath has ended. In subjugation the Redlands now lies, its territories seized north as far as Lakewood, east to the Azure, and south to the borders of Sijia. All of it now belongs to Zantherei Athera. With the aid of magical fire or not, my brother has reaffirmed his grasp on the realm, and now his boots are marching east. This is a threat we cannot ignore."

"I agree," Rennerin said. "But what should we do?"

Alarin didn't respond. He let his eyes drift to the far waiting area, where his younger brother Ansetheral had been standing for the past several minutes, his eyes affixed to the *In the Shadows of Deceit* painting. Alarin cleared his throat before calling across the room. "What do you think, Little Brother? Can you tear your eyes away from that morbid slab of nonsense for a moment?"

Anseth's face softened as he turned and approached. "Forgive me. The Vaskultan people . . . we create no works of art."

"This is known," Alarin said. "But you were raised in the Hollow, you've seen plenty of paintings hung in its many halls and hallways."

"Yes, but nothing like this one. This illusory style." He gestured behind him. "The subtle wisps of the brushstrokes, the misleading tones and misdirecting shadows. From one angle it's a cityscape bustling with life; from another it's death and darkness. The dichotomy between truth and deceit is rather intriguing, I must admit." Anseth ran a pale hand through his knotted dark hair. He didn't speak again for a long moment. "I will investigate this dark-fire myself. A small company is all I require. No harm will come to me. My Vaskultan riders will make sure of that."

Alarin looked his younger brother up and down, a thoughtful look, and then he nodded. It was a nod that said thank you, and a thank you that extended to Anseth's efforts in thwarting the assassin and setting the ambush that freed Stormhaven from Seric Dyre's forces. The nod was returned in kind, and with that, the barbarian lord withdrew.

Alarin sat down on the end of his featherbed and removed his wooden leg, grimacing away the ache in his stump. "The unguent, hand it to me," he said to the physician. "My pain persists today. I don't know why. The weather hasn't changed."

Master Penry retrieved the leather-wrapped jar, but instead of handing it over, he opened it and began applying the soothing lotion himself.

"You should be tending to Szathan, not me," Alarin told him.

"Lord Szathan's wounds healed with no lingering effects. It seems he's as resilient as he is large."

Nodding, Alarin turned to address Chamberlain Rennerin, still reclining on the settee. "And where is His Majesty?"

"In the conservatory hall, preparing his speech."

"His *speech?*" Alarin didn't like the sound of that.

Rennerin didn't seem to notice. "Tomorrow at high sun, on the grand terrace of Tower Tempest."

"The boy's thirteen at most. In no way is he ready to deliver a speech. Whose asinine idea was this?"

"The high ministers, my lord. They petitioned His Majesty, advised him to reach out to the populace and address the threat of darkfire. And why not? The fear that began with Seric Dyre's unexpected siege is continuing to spread. Folks are evacuating the city for the safety of the mountain hamlets."

"He cannot make that speech. He's not ready." Alarin knew what he had to do, but the thought of it made him sigh. "Tell His Majesty to be present, but I will address the populace myself."

"My lord, your wounds," Master Penry cut in. "You're still—"

"I'm fine. I'm not strapping on steel plates and riding into battle; I'm just speaking." His gaze turned back to Chamberlain Rennerin. "I will be ready tomorrow. Inform His Majesty and make the official announcement."

The sky at high sun was dreary and dull, but the breeze was vigorous from where Alarin stood on the tower terrace. The darkened underbellies of the clouds teased rain, while wisps of finger-like fog curled around the city walls like gray wreaths. Closer, in the main square below, civilians stood clumped together like sprouts on a stalk. A few were in movement, little busybodies with places to go, but most gazed collectively up at their lord and regent and provincial governor.

The wind tousled what little hair remained on Alarin's head. His chest rattled with every breath, his missing leg constricting from the pressure of altitude. To his left, General Thayer was leaning so far over the low terrace railing he looked like a gangly gargoyle. Were he to slip, it was a forty-foot scream down, then *splat* upon the hard cobbles of the city square. Alarin hissed at him. "I've seen men fall from higher and survive, but I don't suggest you try it, unless you wish to end up a cripple like me. Now step back, you're making me uncomfortable. Please."

The general obeyed. *That one needs to get his head checked,* Alarin mused. *He's one egg short of a clutch.* To his left, Emperor Silas Mordall sat on a lacquered seat that replaced the fancy throne-like chair that once served Lord Merio. The boy looked quite regal today, his face of good color, his posture erect, his bearing touched with uncharacteristic confidence. A long outer robe of ashen gray enhanced his midnight blue sash, matching silk shoes, and of course the adorned Imperial Seal—an intricate cut of five intertwining Sadralen inlaid in silver and black jade. In his left hand was a small pelletdrum, the one he'd acquired during his travels many moons ago. He was just holding it, not fidgeting or playing with it, and when he met Alarin's gaze, his youthful eyes glistened with worry. "Even with the ability to speak, I still don't know what to say."

"I'm more than honored to speak on your behalf, Your Majesty."

He cracked a bashful little smile. "I'll never get used to that title." His voice was a murmur in the breeze. "There's so many people. Are you prepared to address them?"

"No orator makes a public appearance without some degree of preparation."

"What will you say?"

"I will alleviate the concerns of the people by speaking the truth. Our granaries are full, our weapon racks are stocked, our stations are manned, and are defenders are well trained. We will crush the Hollow forces just as we crushed those of Seric Dyre."

"I like that. But how do you know?"

Alarin gave a slight bow, the most his broken body could concede without causing too much ache. "Because heaven's appointed ruler stands under our wing."

Silas blushed, which made Alarin smile inside. *Such a pure boy, so removed from the pull of politics and the struggles of war.* It almost pained Alarin to know that he would one day become embroiled in the complex decision-making process of a sovereign. But the cloudfalls had chosen him. They'd granted him a voice. *Something about the boy must please the gods.* Or maybe Rennerin had spoken true; maybe the cloudfalls were not of the divine, but simply a natural, curative phenomenon.

Still, it was Alarin who had placed the Imperial Seal over the boy's neck, so it was Alarin who was meant to protect him. And to protect him was to allay his doubts and fears, so when it was Alarin's time to move to the center of the terrace, he did so with courage and aplomb (and a little bit of a limp), and, sweeping his gaze across the silent city square, he steeled himself and began his speech.

The words flowed like wine from his lips, a judicious combination of timing and transparency that would've made even the finest rhetoricians take notice. Alarin always had a knack for public speaking, his skills honed over the many years of service as a commander and advisor. At the Battle of Bearblood Pass, his impassioned speech had rallied his beaten men and launched an upset victory against a ruthless clan of highland barbarians. On that day, his father had awarded him the commanding cord of the Black Pine Regiment, the finest crack soldiers of the empire.

But that was long in the past, the glorious years before Alarin had become a cripple. And yet, as the words flowed from his heart, the crowd observed with rapt attention, as though he were the commander of old.

He spoke about security and prosperity, incentive and reward, honor and disgrace, propriety and policy. He spoke words that made the people applaud, others that brought them to quiet contemplation, and some that even produced tears. He offered praise to the worthy, condemnation to the evil, and the wisdom of understanding each. He spoke of control and restraint, of commitment and command; he spoke and spoke and made sure his speech would affect all members of this great body of spectators, be it merchant or moneylender or minister or military mind.

It was a beautiful feeling, a glorious one at that, but before he could end the speech with an inspiring conclusion that would send the crowd into a frenzy of cheers . . . something strange happened. He tasted blood in his mouth, and when he looked down, he saw flecks of it spattered across the railing. A wave of dizziness overtook him then, and next he knew he was lying on his back staring up at the dreary gray sky. The boy emperor and General Thayer and other frightened faces crowded around him. Someone shouted for help, and Alarin knew no more.

CHAPTER TWENTY-SEVEN

Brothel tents clung to their military counterparts like ocean barnacles, their coarse canvas flaps rustling gently in the breeze. Most stood along the rear fringes of the encampment's perimeter, where they were monitored by watchtower eyes and protected by tall stake walls. The nearby grounds were bustling with activity, as soldiers and sutlers and scullions moved to and from their duties, along with the panders and procurers and of course the courtesans, who were dressed in tightfitting gowns and caked in cosmetics.

The tent Miriana followed her brother into was as far away from the hubbub as one could get. Inside was dim and cheerless and stuffier than a pile of mildewed linen. Vylas motioned for her to sit down on a dusty canework stool, and as she did her eyes were drawn to the odd contraptions and furniture cluttering the inner chamber: curved chairs and undulating cots and back-and-forth seats for engagement in various sexual positions. An open bin of play instruments sat casually against the far wall, everything from feathers to goose quills to pleasure balls and lubricant flasks. Nothing she hadn't seen before, but nothing she cared to see either.

There was also a motley assortment of clothing, feathered robes and silk slips and chemises either hanging from wardrobe pegs or slung across a rack somewhere. And—to her utmost revulsion—lying on the floor half-covered by loose linen was the largest double-headed artificial penis she'd ever seen. *Is that jade? Ugh, these women are shameless.*

"Let's take a look at you." Vylas lowered himself and his good eye squinted in examination. Although he looked rather bedraggled and worn out, he was still the same black-haired, bony, and effeminate man she walked out on months ago. His halfmask was frayed a bit along the lower edges, ruining the tracing of smoky filigree, and his long gray-black robes were stained and torn beyond the usual Anirian style. In contrast was the cord and seal of his imperial position as privy counselor, which hung about his neck with spotless pride. "Your nose . . . did that happen on the road?" At her nod his teeth clenched in sudden anger. "Sister, you—"

"Don't say it, I don't need your counsel. Not now." *Gods know you want to scold me for leaving you, Vylas. But you must understand . . . I couldn't take you with me, not after what you did.*

His pale hand rose to gently touch her hair. "This won't do. It's lovely, but—"

"It's filthy. *I'm* filthy."

"Don't worry yourself, I'll prepare a bath." He turned and moved off.

"*No bath!*" Miriana shouted, and with such urgency that Vylas gave a start. The look on the uncovered part of his face was a mixture of hurt and shame, as if Miriana were denying his request because of his past sexual advance. She had to alleviate those doubts, and quickly. Vylas was the only 'friend' she had right now, as pathetic as that sounded. "I was tortured in a bath . . . by Raas Dragath's men."

His expression softened at once. "Sister, I . . ."

"It's not safe here. I have to leave, I have to—"

"This is the *only* safe place for you. Rangers patrol the outer wilds; if you try to escape they'll catch you, question you, and dump you at Zantherei's feet. Only if you blend and blur will you be safe. Hiding in plain sight."

"Fine, but I'm not going back to a life of prostitution. I was the Lady of Divine Whispers and the Empress of the Anir. I once sat upon the Imperial Throne, horns spiraling behind me and carved Sadralen heads beneath my palms. I counseled and commanded the highest of the high nobility—celebrated men such as Minister Thomen and Minister Korval and Minister Garlan. No, I won't go back to that life. I *won't*."

"Sister." He raised his hand in a reassuring way that only her brother knew how to do. "Nothing will be asked of you." He gave a pause before continuing. "Where's Cyrille Vileron? The captain served as your escort, did he not?"

"Dead. Raas Dragath killed him." She didn't give her brother a chance to respond. "Is there a washbasin? If you want me to 'blend and blur', I'll need to be free of this grime."

He didn't answer right away. The news about Vileron seemed to affect him deeply. "Of course, give me a moment." He fetched an empty pail and exited the tent, returning shortly after with the vessel gripped in both hands, water sloshing as he walked bow-legged to fill the basin.

"Who is the madam of this station?" Miriana asked.

His breathing was slightly labored when the task was done. "Madam Faria is strict but not unfair. Her bawds are clean, her servants are loyal, and her staff is well trained. She has agreed to traffic you—an undisclosed friend of mine—for a substantial fee."

"And what is my bawd name?"

"Camellia, does that suit you?"

"Fine. I suppose I'm a flower then. What if Zantherei sees me? That is how we first met, you know, I was but a lowly courtesan in the army's baggage train."

"He has no interest in the brothel tents, so there's no need for concern. But we'll have to dress you up nice and handsome, so you fit in with the others. I'll also have to cut your hair. Make it more form-fitting, to better conceal your face. A bob cut will serve, you'll see. I am quite handy with a pair of cutters. I once toiled for weeks under the old livestock manager, shearing sheep and goats, when a spell of influenza laid-up his labor men."

"Brother, I'm not a farm animal."

"Yes, but the principle remains. And it is a simple cut, and you have easy, manageable hair. Wash yourself first, and then I'll have a look. Be quick."

She rose and moved behind the screen, then doffed her filthy rags and knelt on the floor. The water in the washbasin rippled from the vibrations, tiny bubbles clinging to the corners. She grabbed a nearby washcloth, soaked it, and scrubbed every nook and cranny of her filthy body. Thankfully, Vylas attempted nothing untoward. From beyond the black-paneled screen, she could hear him cleaning up the strewn crockery. He was always a stickler for tidiness.

"Are you hungry?" he called. "You must be. I'll have an attendant fetch some wheat cakes from the canteen."

She thanked him, and he paused from his cleaning but didn't answer. By now the basin water was black, so she rose and dried herself with a threadbare towel, then slipped into the garments Vylas had thrown over the screen for her. The slightly oversized chemise was patterned in silk and dyed pinkish-red—a color derived from what the southerners beyond the Black Sands call cochineal. Beautiful to behold and beautiful to touch; Miriana admittedly felt like a woman again. The outfit was completed by a red chiffon scarf, a pair of mink fingerless gloves, and heeled fawn-skin sandals called embades, whose leather thongs rose to wrap around her shins like vines.

She moved to the center of the room and held out her hands to display her attire. Vylas's good eye brightened, his thin-lipped mouth opening slightly. "You look . . . like your old self."

She pointed disappointedly at her nose.

"It's a boon," he said. "It'll serve to help your disguise. Now come, sit down." He gestured to a nearby stool, then leaned over and began searching through a rattan basket. "Oh, where the hell are they? This place is a mess. Goddamn it—oh, here they are." The cutters were cast in bronze, with a double-loop center handle to provide flexibility. Vylas chewed his lip as he trimmed and trimmed her hair, and then he paused to examine his work, before trimming some more. Finally, when he was done, he straightened his lips and gave a nod, as if to say, *I've done well.*

He handed her a look mirror, then his fingers went to his mouth for some habitual nail-biting. Miriana raised the hard-shell object and gazed at her reflection. It was an acceptable haircut. Short in the back while the front angled down to rest by the chin . . . and it was layered and defined, and it would cover her face whenever she needed it to. With her busted nose and new hairdo, no one would recognize her.

"Well, Sis—I mean, Lady Camellia—what do you think?"

"It will suffice, I suppose."

"Good." The cutters returned to the table with a low clang. "Now it's time to meet the madam. Stay here." The one-eyed man turned away.

"Vylas."

He paused.

"Thank you . . . for doing this."

The unconcealed part of his face softened. "How could I not?"

"This is my burden . . . I fled the capital."

He seemed to reflect on that a moment. "What choice did you have?" When she didn't answer, Vylas offered a small nod and left the tent.

. . .

Miriana remained on the stool for a time, fiddling with her mink gloves while listening to the noises outside the brothel tent. The typical *stomp-clang-stomp* of passing soldiers, the collective buzz of conversation, the infrequent call or order of command. Once a silhouette loomed by the entrance flap, but just as quickly it withdrew. *Hurry, Brother, hurry.* She feared at any moment Zantherei would storm inside, identify her to his guardsmen, then watch as they hauled her out by her stupid haircut. She didn't want to get caught this way; she didn't want to die by the command of her own husband.

Another stomping of boots passed, then another. *Hurry, Brother, hurry.* A second silhouette appeared by the entrance. Only this time it didn't depart. Miriana heard herself gasp as a man's hand pulled aside the tent flap. Eyes peered inside, like a predator staring into a ground hole. "Are you new?" The voice was deep and unfamiliar.

"Me?"

He cleared his throat and spoke slowly, as if Miriana were a simpleton. "Are *you* new?"

Screw off. No one talks to me like that. "I don't know you, so I suggest you begone."

That made him laugh. He stepped inside, boots stomping. A broad, bulky figure, or maybe it was the armor that made him look that way. His cloak was gray and serrated, and his halfhelm was embossed and decorated with striations along the cap and nasal guard, which indicated he was an officer of some kind. Perhaps a squad leader? Or a subdivision commander? She wished she'd paid more attention to military insignia. His eyes were piercing and sharp, but his face was quite ugly, features droopy and scrunched like those of a seal. "Tell me your name." When he spoke, a gauntleted hand rose to scratch the stubble beneath his halfhelm's cheekpiece.

"It's not your business."

He moved another two steps closer. *Stomp, stomp.* "Everything is my business. Do you not see the emblem on my cloak? I am an officer of the Anir. A second deputy of the Bristled Boar, the realm's premier regiment of flying cavalry. Spear-heavers we are, the scourge of the weak and the wicked." He made a few hoglike grunts for good measure.

"Would you like me to be impressed?"

Laughter again. "You've got some lip on you, lady." He moved closer. *Stomp, stomp.* He was so close she could smell the funk of his body. "Here, why don't we put it to better use, gods know you want to."

"Go to hell."

A hand reached out, seizing her hair. He gave a fierce yank, and immediately she was on her feet, punching and clawing at him. Fingernails met only steel and scale, and between the awful scraping sounds, the man started to laugh once more, a harsh, mocking laugh.

He took her in his bulky arms and held her close like a dancer leading his partner. She tried to knee him in the groin, but the man's protective lames absorbed the blow. He told her to calm the *fuck* down, but when she didn't his hold began to tighten. She cried out, then reached up and raked her fingernails across his face. The officer yelped and released her. His left eye was bloodshot and bulging. "You stupid, *stupid* whore." He rose over her, raising a gauntleted fist—

"*STOP THIS.*"

An older woman was standing inside the tent, tall and dignified despite the plumpness that comes with advanced age. Her gown was long and lacy and gray, her silvery hair pinned up in loosely flowing curls that were accentuated by gilded peafowl feathers. Behind her, Vylas moved in quick steps, like a minion before his queen. He halted before the officer and glared with his good eye, pale fists balled at his sides. "Who are you? You need to leave before I have you stripped of your rank. Do you hear me? *Now.*"

The officer squared up to the much smaller privy counselor. "This is a military campaign. You robe-wearing kinds don't hold authority here. So fuck off, you scrawny one-eyed prick."

"Get out, Johm," the old woman said. "Please."

She must've held some measure of the man's respect, because Officer Johm put his heels together and offered a slight but sincere bow. "Madam," he announced quietly, and with that, he turned about and stomped out of the tent.

Madam Faria glided nearer to Miriana like a lily in a pond. Up close, her skin was gently wrinkled, and her outfit was exquisitely detailed—tiny intricate lines of scrollwork along the lacy, elbow-length sleeves, with more along the jeweled neckline and matching silk shoes. "Let's take a closer look at you, shall we?" She bent down to examine Miriana's face, a routine and coldly professional action that was done while humming to herself.

"My lady, are you hurt?" Vylas asked.

Miriana opened her mouth to respond, but the madam cut her off. "Oh my, your nose looks awful. Downright, downright awful. What caused this? Did you anger or tease a client?"

Miriana suddenly felt very meek under this authoritative woman's questions. "No, it was a brigand . . . he punched me with his cestus."

"His *what?*"

"It's a glove . . . like a gauntlet, but leather and spiked."

Her lips tightened; a look of mild disappointment that seemed to come easy for her. "So sad." Her tone lacked the slightest touch of compassion. "How many summers have you seen? Subtract three."

Miriana thought for a moment. "Twenty . . . two?"

"Still a bit too old. Let's make it twenty-one. Understood?"

She nodded.

Madam Faria concluded her examination and rose. "I have twelve girls here and we run this station tighter than a dead clam.

Sheets washed and warmed after every client, incense coils relit, fragrance stones replaced. Do you have any talents?"

"Madam," Vylas interjected, "Lady Camellia won't be entertaining any clients. You agreed to this."

She nodded, then gave Miriana that same disappointed look. "A shame . . . you are a woman to make many men salivate." Her voice had a cold, detached politeness to it. "I usually don't harbor competing trulls, but Vylas has been very convincing. Yet I must warn you, these soldiers like to drink, and when they drink, they get randy. Some will barge inside with coin in one hand and their tool in the other, like our friend Johm here. And if a man of substantially higher military rank wants to purchase you, I might not be able to stop him."

"I can handle myself."

"Fine." She used a finger to brush aside a lock of hair in Miriana's face. "All right then, stand up. Remove your clothes."

"*What?*"

"Go on. Remove them all."

"Why? What for?"

The old madam pursed her lips. "Flower check. Come on. Off with it."

Miriana's eyes drifted to Vylas, who promptly intervened. "Madam, we already discussed this. She won't be for sale."

"I know, I know. Still must be done. There are no lice or rashes among my girls, and I intend to keep it that way."

"It *will* be that way."

Her lips became even tighter, if possible. "Don't insult me with your false guarantees, I'm not a naïve young woman. I have to be sure."

"But she's been through enough, don't you think she should—"

"What is the problem? I am an old woman. Hurry up. I've got places to go, bawds to tend. Lady Iris needs help with the seam of her new dress. It's form-fitting, which isn't good since the girl won't stop eating. I'll have to widen the fabric at the waistline . . . maybe gusset the shoulders."

Vylas exchanged a sympathetic look with Miriana, then murmured, "I'll wait outside." At her nod, he exited the tent.

Miriana rose before the woman, blowing out a nervous sigh. Slowly, the clothing came off, one garment after another, until she stood there, naked as her day of birth. The madam's commands came freely: lift your arms, lower your hips, spread your knees, turn around, bend over. And when it was all done, when the madam nodded and turned away, Miriana re-clothed herself, timidly, the same way she'd done after that horrible eel bath.

"Welcome to the Blush and Bloom," the old madam said, with a rather unceremonious smile. "It'd better be a brief stay."

"It will," Miriana said.

CHAPTER TWENTY-EIGHT

L ord Alarin Athera lay once more on the physician's
sickbed, a pale and fragile shell of his former self. Szathan
Mordall couldn't bear the sight of him: face withered and
pale, lips fat and green, mouth hanging open like that of a ghoul,
nose leaking snot and blood. For each shallow breath Alarin
inhaled, a weird hiss replied in exhale, as if his soul were screaming
for release.

Nearby, the normally placid Master Penry worked hastily,
clinking and clanking his bowls and prongs and tubes and other
medicinal instruments. Occasionally he would remark on Lord
Alarin's toughness and durability, but the compliments seemed
insincere, and his spirits did not seem high at all. "A tripartite
toxin," he stated. "Laced in his morning cruller."

"I'll question the baker," Szathan said.

"I'm assuming the poisoner was clever, in which case the conta-
mination occurred in the storage pantry, long before it ever hit the
kitchens. So ask your questions, but neither he nor the dough
puncher or scullery maids may know a thing."

Lord Alarin's body convulsed suddenly, a spasmodic twitch of movement that drew Penry's full attention. The owlish man looked so discouraged. "This is a terrible poison. I don't know if it can be bound or reversed."

"Try."

"I am, but this time the damage is more than just an imbalance of body and spirit. I'm administering an antitoxin and force-feeding a restorative agent to aid in blood flow, but . . ." He gave a long pause. "But it may not be enough. Not this time." He stopped what he was doing, his small-featured face leveling a hard look at Szathan. "You need to find out who did this."

"I *know* that."

If the physician took offense at Szathan's curt reply, he didn't show it. "I mean it's on you and you alone. Lord Anseth is off scouting the southwestern threat, and the White Fang Council cannot be trusted, or any nobles for that matter. It is incumbent on you to find this schemer."

Szathan didn't know what incumbent meant, but he understood the physician's gist. He pressed an oversized fist to his forehead. Once more, his world was crumbling. He wished he were adept at handling such underhanded intrigue, like his brother Demien had been. *Too bad you've long departed from this realm.* Szathan's sigh was so deep it was like the seismic rumble of a cavern, and when he spoke his voice was like the growl of a bear living inside said cavern. "What else can you tell me?"

"The concoction used is a highly concentrated venom-based poison, an advanced compound crafted from the toxins of three separate creatures. In this case, scorpion and centipede and fireback spider, all shoved inside in a small container and left to devour one another, which in effect combines their essences into a single concentrated force."

"This three, is there any significance to it?"

"There certainly is, my lord. The three is reminiscent of the Old Way. It represents the attributes of the gods: omniscience, omnipresence, and omnipotence. Or creator, redeemer, and sustainer. The oldest clans before the Anir believed that the number three was the first true number. To them it represented the past, present, and future. Birth, life, death. Beginning, middle, end." He paused to consider his next words. "The remains of the three creatures were ground into a fine powder and laced with other nasty additives, including a masking agent to remove any hint of odor." The physician's solemn eyes blinked curiously at Szathan. "The Old Way is not studied by many. An antiquated, if not intriguing twist on our theological and philosophical ideologies." He paused. "What if a man told you exactly how he would die? Say, by an attack of the heart or hemorrhage of the brain. What if a man explained to you in detail his coming death, and then he died that very way. Would you say he correctly predicted his death, or do you think his mind made it into a reality?"

"I don't know, I'm not the scholarly type. What does this have to do with the poisoner?"

"Well, I dare say our perpetrator is a learned man, most likely highborn, and certainly knowledgeable about the creepy crawlers of the realm."

Szathan could only think of one name. *Byort.* Minister Byort Belthor with his stupid face and protruding eyes and puckered nose. Yes, it had to be Byort; only he had the gall to arrange two assassination attempts on Lord Alarin. *But we couldn't prove it then, and we can't prove it now.* So what then? Szathan wouldn't waste his time questioning him; no, he needed to take matters into his own hands.

A muffled sob made Szathan turn. It was the boy emperor, Silas Mordall, standing at the far end of the room, legs planted in an awkward knock-kneed stance as though too afraid to move them. A satchel was cradled in his hands like a sickly newborn. *Poor little liege,* Szathan mused. *He will be lost and frightened without Lord Alarin,* and *understandably so, since it was Lord Alarin who had proffered the Imperial Seal and named him emperor.* Szathan approached the boy and lowered himself to one knee. "I am going to get this traitor, I promise you that."

The boy didn't seem to hear him. "Why didn't you protect him?" He was so timid; nothing like the previous emperor Thavian Siven, who was brash and hotheaded and full of typical teenage angst. "You didn't protect him, Uncle. Why didn't you protect him?"

Szathan wanted to say that he'd been recuperating from his battle against the Mad Wolf, but the words would've been hollow in the somber air, so he remained silent.

"Father would've protected him," Silas went on. "Father would've prevented this from happening, just as he single-handedly prevented all those traitorous officials from murdering the emperor's son years ago." He released a hand from the satchel and clutched the cuff of Szathan's tunic. "He can still help us. We just have to find him. I know he's still out there."

Szathan pulled away from the boy. "Not this again. Demien's dead, boy."

"He's not dea—"

"Accept it, little one, accept it or you will insult the very legacy he left behind. When those we love are dead and gone, the living must carry on. Don't lose yourself in false wishes. Lord Alarin is our only concern now."

The boy's hand returned to the satchel. His mind seemed to be moving frantically, in several different directions, but when he spoke his voice was surprisingly calm. "You're right. Forgive me. You said you were going to get the traitor . . . well, please do it. Right now. *Please.*"

Before Szathan could respond, the boy crossed the room and stood before Master Penry, who paused from his duties to bow deeply to his lord and sovereign. Silas pulled out something from the satchel—a handful of white flowers. Cloudfalls? Yes, they were dull and dirty and uprooted, but they were undoubtedly the cloud-falls from the tiers in the hall. "I need you to stone grind these and administer them to Lord Alarin," the boy said.

The owlish physician accepted the flowers, though he looked unsure about doing so. "Your Majesty, these have been tested by expert herbalists. There's no way to extract the healing properties—"

"Just do it. *Please*."

The master physician nodded his solemnest nod, then he proceeded to do his lord's bidding. Szathan remained there for a long moment, quietly observing the boy who was desperate to save his bedridden regent and protector, then he spun and stormed out of the chamber, boots stomping down the palace hallway like the pounding of a chef's mallet.

Moonlight spilled inside from the upper windows, highlighting a pair of nightshift sentries who didn't hesitate to scurry out of the way. Szathan barreled past them and moved from one hallway and wing and courtyard to the next, until at last he reached the minister's private bedchamber. Three blows from Nightwing's haft weakened the door, and a final kick sent it whining open. Cresset fire flickered and flashed, momentarily darkening a room that was draped in faux cobwebs and full of dusty bookshelves.

Minister Byort was sitting upright in his bed, quilted coverlet drawn to his lap, eyes squinting angrily at the armed intruder. "What the *fuck* is this?"

Szathan stormed forward, seized the man's forearm, and yanked him out of bed. Byort clawed and kicked like a willful child, but it was a wasted effort since Szathan was in full battledress.

He dragged the man out of the room, past another pair of sentries (who also scurried out of the way), and then down the long hallway. Byort was hissing and grunting and demanding to be released, but Szathan didn't oblige him. Yet instead of bringing him down to the lower cells, or up to the tower cells, he hauled him outside into the foggy evening drizzle, across the forecourt of the main palace, down the center courtyard, and into the outer kennels.

Hounds barked and snarled, some rattling the bars of their houses. The kennel master came to investigate but took no action when Szathan dumped Byort inside a vacant kennel. With a sharp *clang* the wrought iron gate slammed shut.

Byort lifted himself to his knees. He was caked in mud, his embroidered sleepwear ruined. The look on his face was priceless, however; especially those bugged-out eyes. Szathan regarded him with a growl. "If you want to lie like a dog, then you will be treated like a dog." He turned to the kennel master. "Lock it."

Done. Not a single question was asked.

A short while later, when Szathan returned to his lord's private chamber, he found that an act from some divine agent had taken place. Alarin's vital ethers had gone from weak and erratic to strong and steady, and not only that, he was conscious and even in good spirits. "His recovery will be quick," Master Penry commented, a tiny smile lifting his normally solemn face. "His Majesty has quite a bond with those white flowers. I must say it is beyond what we might call 'natural'."

Silas was standing beside the physician, eyes blissfully bright. Szathan immediately went to him, and like father and son the two shared a warm embrace.

CHAPTER TWENTY-NINE

There is a permeating sadness to the inner workings of prostitution, one that Miriana Athera had intentionally forgotten since her former days as a courtesan herself. But now she was knee-deep in the thick of it, yet for the most part she remained contented and unbothered.

A few looks were cast her way, a few harassing or derogatory comments, but so long as she kept her head lowered and her eyes averted, no one paid her much mind. And with the army in constant movement, there was little time for meaningful connections. Always was she at the urge and whim of the baggage train enforcers, who were fair but prickly as rambutans.

Vylas would come to her intermittently. Mostly to ensure she hadn't been roughed-up or mistreated or solicited for sexual purposes. It hadn't happened, nor had she asked for his protection, but whether she wanted it or not, Vylas was back to being her slightly overbearing brother again. *Almost as if nothing's happened between us.* And yet, Miriana wasn't displeased by that. She needed her brother by her side. She needed Cyrille Vileron too, but his life was taken at the cost of her own foolishness, and for that she would never forgive herself.

On a particularly mild winter afternoon during a particularly long day of marching, Miriana found herself encumbered with a rucksack of cooking supplies as she struggled to keep in line with the baggage train. The earth around her rumbled under the persistent pounding of foot and hoof and axle wheel, and the air was alive with whinnies and clangs and loud bawls of conversation. Ahead, the columns of soldiers stretched out along the eastern base of the Agate Mountains, a variegated cluster of crags and canyons and chasms with paths of friable earth and old rottenstone. Miriana had to tread carefully here; the winding declines and unfriendly rock pits threatened to snag her balance with every step. Still, it was hard to focus when you were exhausted, and it was hard not to drag your feet when your muscles ached all over. At least it wasn't winter-cold today, more like autumn-crisp, and while the sky was placid and cheerful, the alpine air was tinged with the foul smell of rubbed limestone, a smell not unlike rancid eggs.

Condors emerged from their roosts in high rock ridges, huge beasts with rippling bald heads and white-banded wingspans. They circled the rear of the columns, zeroing in on any scraps that might've been left behind. So persistent they were, and so majestic as well, a roc's little sibling, freeborn and unfettered. Miriana often stared at them, and, in her mind, she soared vicariously along, with only the firmament above her. *Take me there, gods, please. Take me away from all of this misery and war and death.* She wanted to feel the liberation of a bird in flight. *It's not so much to ask, is it? Not so much . . . not after what I've been through.*

A marksman shot one from the sky just after high sun. It was a challenging task; the man had to position himself on a pinnacled ridge and nock a specific flight arrow with smaller fletching for a greater cut through the wind. But with a perfect stance and grip he made the shot, and as the poor bird jerked and screeched and spiraled to the ground, the spectating soldiers raised their hands and cheered. Miriana wanted to strangle them all, and she would've done so had she still been in power. *Maybe one day I'll get my chance again.*

Vylas came to check on her shortly after. The hood of his cloak was pulled over his head, concealing a face that was already partially concealed by a black halfmask. When he saw Miriana struggling with her burden he immediately reached out to help, but she switched the heavy rucksack to her far shoulder so he couldn't take it from her. "Don't draw attention to me," she told him.

Vylas nodded soberly, then stole a long glance behind him. He spoke at length. "We're deep into Riverwind now, third district north of the border." He stole a second glance around, this time much quicker. "Stormhaven is the primary target, but we will be halting our advance east of the mountains, along the fringes of the Shaded Plains. There a blockade awaits in the form of Whitecrow soldiers, so that must be dealt with first."

"Whitecrow? You mean . . .?"

"Yes, Seric Dyre. The terms of submission have been sent via envoy." He gave a sigh. "If Seric doesn't agree to them, I fear it will be a terrible slaughter."

She scoffed without realizing it. "A terrible slaughter? Do you think so little of Seric Dyre? The man is twice as cunning as Zantherei. You know this, Vylas, you've campaigned with him."

A pair of passing soldiers on horseback drew Vylas's attention. He waited—while biting his nails—until their gray cloaks diminished into the distance. "That I have, but I do believe you are overrating the abilities of your former Imperial Advisor, while underrating the power of the darkfire." He gave a pronounced shake of his head. "Even the greatest strategists of the age won't be enough. It simply does not matter."

"Why doesn't it matter?"

Vylas's fingers returned to his mouth to resume biting. She

smacked his hand away. "Stop doing that. Tell me, why doesn't it matter?"

His saliva-coated fingers remained in the air for a moment, before he withdrew them. "You know why. You were there, in Serpenthold. You saw the stones blacken and burn. No force can withstand the darkfire. It is more than magic; it is a warhead coming to annihilate the realm."

"Even still, I can't let that bastard husband of mine reign supreme. I have to stop him."

Now it was Vylas's turn to scoff, though the soft-spoken man immediately apologized for it. "I don't doubt your abilities, Sister, but just how do you propose to do that?"

"The Sijian is the key. Nanjen. He's the mastermind behind the darkfire."

"I heard you had a talk with him before you left the Hollow."

"I did."

It was a long moment of trudging before Vylas spoke again, and when he did his voice had become so quiet she could barely hear it. "What will you do?"

"For now, I will keep my head down and continue the march to the Shaded Plains."

"And then?"

"And then I'll make my escape."

———

The Hollow envoy was an impressively built man, but his self-righteous manner, tacky ermine-trimmed frock, and fancy skewbald horse were enough to make Seric Dyre despise him on the spot. *And the terms!* The goddamn terms he delivered so smugly made Seric want to execute him right then and there, and only the remonstration of his former wife had prevented him from doing so. Eventually Nyvia managed to draw him away to speak privately inside the commander's pavilion. Seric was pacing the room now, displeased and huffy and making no attempt to hide it.

"Look at these terms, just *look* at them," he said, but instead of showing her he raised the scroll eye-level and began to read aloud: "*The civil and military officials of Whitecrow Province will acknowledge the true emperor of the realm by prostrating themselves and proffering their allegiance to me. Those who comply will be spared and given rank suited to their skillset; those who refuse will be put to death. The Zhoulish auxiliaries will hereby be exiled from this land, and the traitor mongrel Seric Dyre is to turn in his cord and seal and face an execution by the very blade he has stolen from me.*" Seric crumpled the scroll and flung it on the ground, then he shot a glare at Nyvia. "I'm not some meager vassal to be bullied into submission. Who the *hell* does he think he is?"

"I told you what would happen," Nyvia snapped in return. "I told you the Red Terror will fall, and I told you what would happen next. Why didn't you heed my words?"

"Because I don't believe in black magic rot."

"It's not rot, Seric."

Seric flicked a hand to dismiss her statement, then his eyes lowered to the crumpled scroll on the ground. After a long and pensive moment, his fingers drifted to the hilt of his sword. Nyvia took a step back. He didn't mean to frighten her, and he told her that as he unsheathed and leveled the blade.

It was a beautiful amber-hilted design, with a chromium-plated steel edge that ended in a shimmering point. "I'll not give it up," he said at last. "Not the blade that has subjugated the Zhouls, defeated my blood father, slain traitors, crushed the Vaskultans, overcome adversity at Aster Falls, and conquered a sizeable chunk of the northern realm." He paused briefly. "I'll not give it up."

She gave an indifferent shrug. "You should write a song about it. You still have your lute, yes?"

Seric sheathed the blade and smiled wanly at her poor attempt at wit. His voice was detached when next he spoke. "Zantherei also demands your immediate return."

"As expected. I will be gone at dawn."

"Always a minion to your brother's beck and call. What about Veldries?"

She looked down, her doe-like eyes searching the ground as if she'd dropped something. "My son will be returning to the Hollow with me after all. I've . . . made arrangements."

"I want to see him first."

"You can't. Not now." She gave a long pause. "I must obey my brother's command. I've no choice. Zantherei cannot be stopped."

Seric snorted. "I disagree. Fire may have destroyed Serpenthold and rooted out Raas Dragath, but fire is nothing without the influence of wind. And if you consider where we are today, in the low point of winter, you will notice that the prevailing winds carry only from the north. Any attempt to burn us out will fail. The flames will blow back upon Zantherei's own ranks."

She gave another shrug, a noncommittal, blasé gesture, as if Seric were a toddler trying to explain an intricate theory. That set him to anger, though this time he didn't express it. Instead he absently rubbed the scar beneath his neckerchief, then bent down to pick up the crumpled scroll. He unfolded it slowly and somewhat cautiously, as though a scalding liquid might spray out at him, and then he reread the terms, even though he knew it would only upset him further. Once finished, he spoke to his sister in that same detached voice. "Fine then, run back to that tyrannical prick. I don't care."

With nothing left to say, she turned and started off. Seric told her goodbye, and half a watch later, he climbed the camp tower and observed her being escorted out by that stupid envoy and his wretched honor guard.

Seric spent the evening at his military table, ruminating over the enemy's position and the corresponding details that had been reported by his many spies and scouts. He searched for weaknesses in the ranks, missteps in the chain of command, deficiencies in logistics and organization. At first glance the Hollow forces seemed unconquerable, but experience told Seric there were always cracks in the plaster, always rust in the patina, if one knew where to look.

Still, nothing seemed evident to him, and in truth, the sheer force of Zantherei's army was intimidating. How had Raas Dragath's stronghold fallen so easily? A battle against the Hollow should've been a bloody deadlock to drag on for seasons and even years. But no, Serpenthold was destroyed suddenly and swiftly, like a wick flame squashed between two fingers. *What sort of critical error has the Red Terror committed?*

He put no weight on the rumors of magic fire. Gossip and speculation were always rampant during wartime; just today he'd heard a dozen or so tales that ranged from the slightly believable to the absurdly ridiculous. Such buzz was generally created as a way for people to make sense of difficult situations, but fire was simply fire. There were many destructive ways to wield it, but there was no magic in it. A more plausible theory would suggest that sappers undermined Serpenthold's main wall from subterranean tunnels. It is no secret that war is ruled by deception, and only the most capable of strategists can outwit and outmaneuver their enemies on every terrain and in every situation.

You're drifting, Seric, get back to the facts at hand. Zantherei had an impressive number in his rank-and-file. Nearly twenty thousand (more than twice Seric's own forces), and these men weren't slouches but tough-minded soldiers molded by countless hours in the Pit. Not only that, but Zantherei also commanded a handful of powerful officers, including Aldebron Pentagath, who had once served Seric faithfully in the campaign against Aster Falls. *I'd love to win the lionhearted general back,* Seric mused, *but I don't know how just yet.*

Ravia rolled over in her sleep, drawing Seric's eye. He liked the way her pale face was limned by the soft glow of candlelight, but the way her mouth hung open was anything but flattering. Still, she looked peaceful enough, lying outstretched in a tangle of bedroll blankets like that.

Seric thought about slipping under the covers with her, gods knew he wanted to, but he couldn't sleep until his plans were set. As usual, the fate of many rested on his shoulders. And it was a great weight. If Seric submitted to Zantherei's terms, then he would die, his auxiliaries would face exile, his officers would face incarceration, and Ravia would likely be sold as a slave or concubine. No, he couldn't allow that. He had to fight, and he had to win. And in order to do that, he had to focus. *Yes, focus, you bleary-eyed numbskull . . . what do you see in these maps?*

Zantherei's forces were deployed in three divisions, and each was moving along a rocky and uneven course that abutted the foothills of the Agate Mountains. Seric could certainly take advantage of their restricted movement and inevitable fatigue from his position on the Shaded Plains. Could it be a bait trap? No, Zantherei didn't know these routes well enough to execute such a precise tactic.

But Seric did.

I will employ a basic principle of warfare: catch the enemy right after he crosses difficult terrain. He placed a small paper point on the map. *The enemy is susceptible here. Two divisions will squeeze Zantherei's center and left, trapping his men in a bloody pincer, and removing the distance the ballistae need to fire.* His eyes drifted to the small wooded area to the southwest of the battlefield. *A detach-*

ment of auxiliaries can be hidden here, to sweep the enemy's right and cut them down in surprise. Yes, this could work. A much larger force could be overwhelmed this way.

Seric rose to empty his bladder, and when he was done, he ladled himself a goblet of wine from a lobed silver container on the floor. The aroma was rich, and the taste was slightly tart upon first sip, then gathering in sweetness as it settled on the tongue. Satisfied, Seric returned to the stool and spent the remaining hours of the evening going over his plans, again and again until he was certain of every detail of every possible outcome. Seric would defeat this Athera clansman and the next, and when the realm was finally rid of these leeches, he would raise his banners and affix his seal and rule the breadth of the realm, north south east and goddamn west.

Two days later he set his plan into motion. Drums pounded and cymbals crashed as a host of eight thousand Whitecrow soldiers stormed forward in pincer formation, their spirits roused by Seric's earlier speech. Zantherei's forward army met them at the base of a rocky piedmont. It was incredible to see how disciplined and dauntless they stood in the face of an ambush, but the troop positions, the rank-and-file columns—it was all as Seric had predicted. The ballistae were unready and too poorly positioned to fire, and the enemy was tired and at the mercy of Seric's scissoring charge. *Surprise! I'm here to crush you all.*

Sunburst in hand, Seric led the advance, boots churning across the dusty flats, feathered cloak plastered to his back under the strong northern wind. His body was heavy, especially his eyelids, yet he was miles away from sleep. The enemy was too close, the air too thick with tension.

Seric's heart was like a barbed pendulum that swung back and forth with rabid energy, while the wind was a phantom that screamed alongside him. The combined effort created an urgent impetus of beating and blowing, like the coming of a powerful storm. *Yes, we're coming,* Seric thought. *The gods are on my side, and together we will crush you.*

But before a single weapon was lowered upon a foeman's flesh, the wind changed direction, suddenly blowing in Seric's face, as if by a shaman's earnest supplication. Just then, something was lobbed into the air from behind the Hollow's frontlines. At first Seric thought them arrows, but no, they were certainly too close for such a shot, and these were not slender missiles but small black spheres. They traveled with the wind, like locusts in the sky, and strangely enough, their trajectory was on course with Seric's front. *Son of a mother-raping . . .*

He gave the order for a full defensive brace, bodies down, shields up. The black globules hit them like a spattering of paint, splashing the soldiers and those in a ten-body radius. The struck soldiers merely looked at one another, confused and disgusted yet seemingly unhurt. *What the hell is this shit?* Seric wondered.

And then there was fire.

CHAPTER THIRTY

The black blaze spread through the Whitecrow ambush force like sharpened claws through flesh. The left and right pincer collapsed so quickly it was almost as if the ground had split into a gaping fissure and dropped them inside.

Men shrieked and shouted and shied away from the black fire, many pushing and pummeling each another for a chance at freedom. Great billowing plumes of smoke rose in all directions, some thin and fingerlike, others thick as the breath of an elder basilisk. In an eye's blink chaos had overtaken the land, a rampant and ravaging chaos that destroyed all sense of rational thought.

Ansetheral Athera observed the devastation from a vantage point half a furlong up. This wasn't a battle but a cookout, with Seric Dyre's forces writhing and withering under a great winding-sheet of black fire. It was difficult to watch a man melt—flesh, armor, weapons, and all.

He saw a horse dragging itself forward with only its forelegs, as its hindquarters were scorched to stumps. He saw a soldier's face melt like hot wax, and another whose lower legs liquified beneath him as he ran. He saw an officer whose eyes burned like two coals, and all he could do was scream and scream until his mouth melted too.

To Anseth's left, Severak Bonesplitter stood with a grim look on his hawkish face, his black longcoat discolored by dust about the shoulders. Kirik was beside him, scratching his half-torn ear. He spoke in an unusually shaky voice. "What in the Skybringer's bowels is that?"

"It is our death unless we flee," Anseth replied, and without another word he was off, galloping astride his frosty mare, the gray ground passing beneath him. Dread and anxiety were like dragging weights, and the wind was cold and ashy and intent on thwarting his progress. Nevertheless, he rode and rode until he reached the empty farm fields and vacant crofter houses outside of Stormhaven's wall, and once inside, he dismounted and rushed to the main palace. A few corridors and courtyards later he reached his elder brother's private chamber.

The *In the Shadows of Deceit* painting seized his attention at once. He couldn't help but stare at it, at all the little morbid details and woeful representations of human darkness. It made Anseth angry. So angry he drew his backsword and slashed at the painting, cutting through the wooden frame and tearing through the canvas. Like a cracked mollusk shell, it broke apart and clattered on the tiled floor, leaving Anseth to sheathe his blade and continue into the chamber.

Chamberlain Rennerin approached with caution; Anseth didn't stop to greet him. "We have to leave the city. Evacuate. At once. Is my elder brother still abed?"

The old man made a bewildered gasp. "Leave the protection of the city walls? I don't think—"

"Walls will do nothing against what I've seen." The inner chamber was dark, and a quick glance at his elder brother's feath-erbed proved it was empty. "We need to evacuate this city at once, and—"

He stopped. Standing by the western window was Lord Alarin Athera, blackthorn cane in hand, looking healthier and more robust than he had in quite some time. Others were in the room with him— the wild-eyed General Thayer, the timid boy Silas, and the waddle-walking, owl-faced physician Penry—but it was Alarin who commanded attention. He was wearing the typical Anirian gray-blacks, yet his face was of good color, his balding head unlined by stress, his dark Athera eyes focused and strong. Behind him, a wash of light from the unlatched window danced on his shoulders like a phosphorescent glow. "Elder Brother . . ." Anseth said. "What's happened to you?"

"I was poisoned, but as you can see, I am alive. Better than alive. I am revitalized." His attention turned to young Silas. "The boy has a certain way with the cloudfalls. Commands them like a master herbalist with a flair for wizardry."

Anseth fixed his gaze on the young emperor. He looked formal enough in his deep blue mantle and dark gray underrobes, but it was the five intertwining Sadralen of his black jade Imperial Seal that gave him an air of sovereignty. He certainly wasn't the tallest lad (despite being the son of Demien Mordall), but he'd likely surpass Anseth's stature within a handful of years. Still, he was noticeably timid, and thrust with sudden attention the boy took a small step back. Maybe he was afraid of Anseth's hardened face and fur-and-felt barbarian attire, or maybe he was nervous without his usual protector nearby. Anseth's eyes drifted across the room. "Where is Lord Szathan?"

"Off fixing a mistake," Alarin said. "I expect him to return posthaste." His left eyebrow rose slightly. "There's urgency in your voice, Brother. What is it you saw on the plateau?"

Anseth took a moment to gather his thoughts. "I saw fire. But it was a black fire . . . blacker than any blaze I've ever seen. Like shadowy tendrils controlled by an unnatural wind. Zantherei must have an adept sorcerer under his employ. Sounds harebrained, I know, but what I saw was a nightmare come alive, and I don't reckon we can stand against it. We must evacuate."

"I'll not abandon this city. Not after all I've done. The promises, the hope, the happiness . . . I won't give that up."

"You're too concerned with the ruck, Elder Brother. None of that will matter when those siege ballistae roll up and spit darkfire upon our walls. I promise you that."

A moment of grim silence passed before Alarin replied. "I cannot run. And not just because I'm a cripple. I cannot run because I am a man of principle and faith. Do you think Father would've tucked tail so easily?"

"Father's dead. It doesn't matter what he would've done. Merio too. What matters is what *we* will do to prevent mass casualties."

Alarin sighed. "You are so certain of the outcome."

"I saw the darkfire burn through steel armor like acid. I saw it melt boulders and bore holes through granite like worms in fruit flesh. Rammed-earth walls with limestone cladding stand no chance. I know this is difficult to believe, but for once the rumor-mongers have spoken true. Seric Dyre's forces were obliterated by incendiary weapons of the occult, and if we don't evacuate, our fate will be the same."

Alarin had that bullheaded look on his face, the one that used to frustrate Anseth when they were young. More frustrating still was his eventual reply. "Everyone knows the tale of how the First Emperor's sight was restored by the shining of the cloudfalls. But few know about an incident during the third year of his reign in which his private hall was cast aflame by an arsonist. Now this fire should've killed him while he slept, yet he not only lived, but his inner apartments remained unscathed."

"Are you suggesting that the cloudfalls protected him?"

"That is exactly what I'm suggesting."

"Even if that were true, it's not the same as darkfire."

"The cloudfalls will protect." Alarin adjusted his cane as he turned to the boy emperor. "Just as they have restored, they will protect."

This is ridiculous. Anseth shook his head, as if freeing himself of some foul notion. "I do not doubt His Majesty's connection to these flowers, but they are just that—flowers. Even if they can restore a man's vital ethers, that doesn't mean they can defend against the darkfire. And I don't believe they are a thing to command at your behest."

"You're wrong," Alarin said in a near-whisper. "The boy *feels* them, sounds strange I know, but the same magic that has given him a voice also continues to communicate with him, like the unspoken counsel of a god."

It was then Chamberlain Rennerin cut in, although his normally cheery voice sounded oddly flat. "Forgive my candor, but this reeks of recklessness. Can His Majesty elaborate on this . . . feeling?"

The boy spoke with a soft, timorous voice. "I . . . I don't much understand it, but I know it's there. Inside me. A beacon of faith I can't explain. I know I'm only a boy, but I'm certain the cloudfalls will protect us. If we allow it of them."

The room fell silent. Anseth lowered his eyes. He realized his hand bore a small gash between the forefinger and thumb. *Must've happened when I slashed that stupid painting.* It didn't hurt, but he regretted allowing his temper to get the better of him.

Kirik, to his left, was also looking at Anseth's hand, but instead of commenting on it, he asked for the details of the conversation. When Anseth provided a brief summary in Vaskulti, the bondsman's long, reptile-like face frowned. "So, these magical flowers will protect us how? Do we just stick them in our hair like barrettes?"

Anseth had to stifle a chuckle, but it was a valid question. He turned to the boy and switched to the Anirian tongue. "How do we do as you say . . . how do we 'allow it of them'?"

The boy gave a meek little shrug.

"My lords, if I may intervene," Master Penry said. "There are fragrance oils, as you know, lavender, lotus, and many others taken from botanic sources. We could do the same, extract the oil and apply it to the wall as a protective coating. It's an uncomplicated but rather tedious process called enfleurage. Lard is heated and the vegetal matter is stirred in them. After repeated straining and replacement the fat becomes saturated with the oil, preserving both substance and fragrance."

"Lard in itself is highly flammable," Anseth countered. "How do you suppose this will work? If anything, it will do the opposite and attract the fire."

The master physician didn't disagree.

"The cloudfalls will protect," Alarin said.

Penry's jowls receded as he tightened his lips. "As far as the extraction, yes, I don't see why the process would be any different for cloudfalls. But even to speculate that such a mixture would repel the darkfire is logically unsound."

"About as unsound as those flowers purging the poison from my body?" Alarin shot back, then waited a moment before speaking again. "The cloudfalls will protect."

Anseth offered his elder brother a measured look. The crippled man certainly had a renewed sense of strength and focus, that much could not be denied. "As much as I want to believe you, we cannot set this theory into motion without first testing it. Appoint an infiltrating force to steal a small amount of darkfire powder from Zantherei's camp. Only then can we be certain that a cloudfall extraction will protect. Now obviously this is an exceedingly dangerous operation, and, to be plain, I don't rightly know who'd be stupid enough to lead—"

"I'll do it."

Anseth turned to the speaker. General Thayer stood lank and gangly and proud, his mismatched eyes glittering like two polished gems. "Appoint me."

"You're a prized general, among the most decorated in this city.

The risk is too great. We need a lesser officer who can command a company of skilled yet expendable men."

"Appoint me," he repeated, like a child stubbornly asking for permission. "I can do this, my lord. I want to do this."

Anseth sighed. "If you are caught, you will die brutally at the hands of my brother Zantherei."

The general seemed undeterred—hell, he seemed *excited*. "Appoint me. My Jackalmen and I are up for the task."

Anseth, in the end, could only nod. "You really are a mad bastard."

Thayer smiled. "The maddest."

———

Szathan Mordall stood back as the attendant unlocked the kennel door and pushed it open with a rusty whine. Byort was inside, sitting on a filthy patch of straw bedding, reeking of dog shit and looking as miserable as one would expect. "You're free," Szathan told him.

Byort took an unnecessarily long moment to rise to his feet. His bug eyes were like two stone drill bits boring into the much larger general. "Do you regret locking me up like a dog? You should." He stumbled out of the kennel, the top of his head not even reaching Szathan's shoulder. "You know, I used to have a brother. He bullied me, badgered me, never treated me with an ounce of respect. And now, well . . . I don't have a brother anymore."

Szathan turned to fully face the councilman. "Did you just threaten me?"

Byort gave a small, unconcerned shrug. "Ah, very astute. And here I thought you were the simplest of brutes."

CHAPTER THIRTY-ONE

Ashes.

They itched her skin like glasspaper, stung her eyes like dust, burned her lungs like subzero weather. Jagged gray flecks drifting aimlessly through the air, like the mist and mizzle of a gentle spring morn. They stole her vision like a fog wall and made blotchy the ground like a field of wild garlic.

Ashes.

They were all Miriana Athera knew now, after having made her escape from her bawd station during the darkfire assault at the Shaded Plains. Ashes, ashes, ashes. They clogged the air and stained the land, and like tendrils they snaked around the blackened heaps of dead soldiers. Faces were unrecognizable; bodies were nothing more than burnt meat-sacks that occasionally rattled and puffed black air. Steel weaponry remained attached to lifeless hands, some so melted they appeared as goopy treats of cream and cacao.

An unpleasant way to enter the next life, Miriana thought, as she raised the hem of her cloak to step over a particularly large mound of melted flesh. *Terribly unpleasant indeed.* She stepped over another corpse, and another, and just as she crossed the next, something caught her ankle from behind. It was a hand, a half-melted hand, and its owner was groaning with a half-melted face.

Miriana screamed; she pulled her leg free and ran, but she must've tripped, because next she knew her balance was gone, the ground was rushing up, and *boom*, she found herself lying face down in a pile of ashes.

There was no pain, but on her tongue, she tasted something foul, and when she lifted herself back to her feet, she found herself wearing a head-to-toe garment of powdery gray crud. She didn't wipe it off; she wanted to, dearly, because it was smelly and itchy and likely the remnants of poor dead men. But no, she wore it like an evening robe and continued on her way. *Be strong, Mir, be strong and welcome the disguise.*

Ahead, she spotted the tail-end of a mass of Whitecrow soldiers fleeing through the forest bypaths. It was a desperate and disorganized retreat, with exhausted and wounded men moving in whichever direction was the least clogged at that particular moment. Zantherei's forces pursued in organized detachments, stabbing the backs of their foeman like expert spearfishers in a shallow lagoon. From somewhere behind, Miriana could hear Vylas calling her name—well, not *her* name, but her bawd moniker, Camellia. When she turned her brother appeared through a screen of smoke, his scrawny frame outlined in dust, his booted feet slogging across a ground of smoldering cinders.

He called out to her again, and she told him to follow her voice, and when he finally found her it wasn't with joy but with an exhausted frown. "What are you doing out here? You're going to get yourself killed. Zantherei's advance parties are combing these fields."

She gave him her most matter-of-fact tone. "I'm covered in ashes. What better disguise do I need?"

His pale hand reached out, but he must've reconsidered, because it withdrew before touching her. "Sister, this isn't a good idea. We should return to the station."

"I'm done being a meek little wench. I need to find Seric."

"Seric *betrayed* you."

Her eyes became heavy things that only wanted to look at the ground, and in a small voice she said, "There's no one else."

When Vylas didn't respond, she started walking, and he scurried after her.

There were more bodies near the forest's outer edge. The ash had settled thicker here, appearing as black as crushed obsidian or those faraway beaches of volcanic sand. Steel weapons and human bones lay fused to the ground or to burnt flesh, like candlewax spilling and hardening.

At Serpenthold she'd seen the darkfire enkindle men before her eyes, but there was a certain revoltingness in observing its lingering effects. Still, Miriana averted her gaze and pressed on, and as the twilit sky faded into night, an eerie and foreboding darkness rolled across the land. The paths turned ever quieter and ever spookier, and occasionally, in the distance, she could hear the passing gallop of riders, which was usually accompanied by the glow of torchlight. Even less frequent were her encounters with incapacitated White-crow stragglers. One reached out to her as she passed, but this time she kicked away his blackened hand and left him moaning in the darkness.

You're strong, Mir. Strong as silk.

Inside the forest, her surroundings became a shadowy tangle of branches, most leafless and black like the frostbitten fingers of a giant. Clematis vines rose here and there, most clinging to the trunks of trees whose surface roots reeked of loam and leaf litter. It was hard to see, harder to breathe, and nearly impossible to figure out which direction to go. And yet Miriana pushed on, searching and searching for the only ally she might have left in this world. And even that was uncertain.

———

Seric Dyre led his defeated soldiers through the trails of the dark forest. Bloody men, burned men, battered men, all dragging themselves along, some with makeshift walking sticks, others discarding armor or weapons to ease the burden of travel. When a soldier collapsed in weakness or hunger, the sound of his body hitting the earth was heavy on the heart. Only thing worse was the sight of the fallen man's rankmates looting him for anything of use.

Chargers were also stripped of their burdensome bridles and saddles, but even then, only a few could keep up. The hard-going travel became even harder when the temperature decided to take a plunge for the colder, as if to further salt their terrible wounds. *This is the Amber River revisited,* Seric mused. *And that was a defeat I swore I'd never let happen again.*

Of course, it wasn't just the weakness and despair that hampered his retreat. Zantherei had sent detachments to harass him along the way. By day and night, at any given interval, drums would pound and cymbals would crash, and suddenly Hollow soldiers would pour out of the thicket, and Seric's men would have to flee or fight them off. By the third day of this, what few men he had left were so exhausted they could barely stand. Seric ordered General Madderin Ruk to lead a company of riders to cut down any Whitecrow laggards and conceal the bodies along the paths. Despicable work, sure, but they had to remove their trail.

Later that day, it began to rain. Not a gentle rain but a frigid winter downpour. More complaints arose, more cries of misery. *This is the truest test of a man's fortitude,* Seric thought to himself. It was hard to look at his officers after such a one-sided defeat. *I was supposed to be a strategist of no equal. I was supposed to be the greatest ruler this realm had ever known.* He shook his filthy head. *But now look at me, weak and weary and faced with another humiliating defeat.* Yet this time, there was no room for self-pity, no hole to crawl into and hide. To do that would be a death sentence, simple as that.

They marched through the chill of the night, stopping briefly to rest on the cold earth, concealed by entangling thicket and fragrant spruce and fir. Sunburst remained in Seric's hand at all times, like an irremovable prosthesis. Ravia never left his side either, but she was so distant, and Seric was too demoralized and fatigued to offer words of compassion. *I let her down, I let my soldiers down, I let my kingdom down. Where does this mongrel lord go from here?* What little sleep he did get was plagued by visions of that horrible darkfire . . . men melting before his eyes, their faces twisting like old rags of oilskin. After each vision, he'd awake with a start, his face sweaty despite the cold, his mouth dry despite the rain.

The next morning, they came to a muddy waterway with no viable workaround, so Seric passed orders to gather stones and branches and twine to create a crude bridge. The men obeyed, but the strenuous labor took a terrible toll on their already exhausted bodies. A few collapsed right there in the mud, never to rise again. Others simply labored around them, which caused the fallen to inadvertently become part of the bridge.

When at last the work was completed, Seric led the soldiers across, a dreary footslog through the mud and the chill and the ever-present misery. The complaints didn't cease. *So much crying and moaning and bitching!* Seric had heard enough. Upon next complaint, he spun and menaced a glare at his underlings. "You can either rest when we reach Aster Falls, or you can rest here and die in the cold." That didn't halt the grousing for long, so Seric ordered the next person to complain would be cut down by the Mad Wolf. That shut them up.

By midday the rainstorm had finally receded, and the cold went with it. Seric observed the late-winter scenery, the broad, beautiful vistas, the thick conifers and tall broadleaves, and the surprising number of wildlife rustling among them. The forest was alive with rodent chitters and woodpecker calls and the unmistakable quacking of wildfowl, and by afternoon, songs of woodlarks and other birds became commonplace, along with the occasional *twit-twoo* of tawny owls. Just before dusk, Seric gaped at a massive flock of starlings whirling through the reddish sky as a unified entity, the flapping of their wings producing a sound not unlike the crashing of ocean waves.

Seric welcomed the sights and sounds; they reminded him that the world was still here, that it knew nothing of his defeat. He listened to it in silence while the remnants of his men sat down around him like hogs in an undercrowded pen. He'd set out with just over eight thousand; now he'd be fortunate if he had a fifth of that number. And what a miserable lot that fifth was.

Generals Zirian and Wyath joined him later in the evening. The Zhoul looked as towering and stoic as ever, but there was a touch of sadness in his eyes—well, in the eye that wasn't half-lidded. He was cleaning his teeth with a dogwood twig, but once done he spat a wad of phlegm and spoke in the Zhoulish tongue. "We've risen from defeat before."

"Not so harrowing a defeat as this."

"There's no shame in losing to sorcery," Wyath said in Anirian.

The word was bitter on Seric's tongue. *Sorcery.* It sounded preposterous and even silly—and yet, how else could those fires be explained? Truly, he knew nothing about them, which meant he knew not how to stop them. "I fell to my own conceit," Seric admitted at last, then gave a forcible shake of his head. "You know what bothers me the most about all this? Zantherei beat me. That rotten prick beat me. I cannot live with that. I just cannot."

"From what I can tell," Wyath replied, "you've lived with it your whole life."

Seric couldn't help but nod. "Yes, I suppose I have."

————

Miriana followed Seric's retreat by all the discarded equipment and fallen bodies and endless mishmash of footprints, but as the days passed the tracks eventually lessened and lessened and then altogether vanished. Miriana found herself at an utter loss—until she spied a company of dismounted riders ahead.

Vylas grabbed her cloak and pulled her down into the brush. Miriana emerged only a few seconds later. Vylas hissed at her to get back down, but she ignored that and said, "Those are Whitecrow soldiers."

"What are they doing?"

Her eyes followed a particularly handsome man with a plumed helmet—a Whitecrow general no doubt—approaching a wounded soldier resting against a hollow log. At first, she thought he was going to help the man, but the general lowered his spear and shoved it through the hapless fellow's breast. Then, he gave the order to dump the dead body deep in the brush, and his underlings swiftly obeyed. "They're cutting down slackers," Miriana said. "And hiding the dead."

"This is Seric's doing," Vylas said. "Is that the man you want at your side? A man who kills his own soldiers? We can go elsewhere; there are plenty of other allies. Hey, are you listening? Where are you going?"

Miriana was moving toward the Whitecrow company. It took a moment for the general to notice her, but when he did his body turned in a slow, unconcerned manner, as if a lone, ash-covered woman wandering through the forest was a commonplace sight. Vylas hissed at her one last time to return, but she ignored that and continued forward, one step after another until she found herself standing face-to-face with the handsome Whitecrow general. Without any form or gesture of greeting she said, "You have to take me to Seric Dyre."

His brooding eyes narrowed at her. "And who might you be?"

"Seric Dyre knows who I am. I need to see him. Now."

The man removed his helmet and brushed aside the loose strands of honey blond hair from his eyes. His jaw was rigid as pale marble, and his expression seemed a cross between annoyed and amused. "I am not some errand boy, my lady. I am Madderin Ruk, third general and regiment commander of the Whitecrow army. Now you will tell me who you are and what your purpose is, or I will slap a pair of manacles on your wrists and drag you back to our prison camps."

She gave him a hard look, one that said she would not be intimidated by his words.

"If you are a bawd wishing to enlist in our campaign services," a soldier chimed in, "then I suggest you visit the—"

"I am not a bawd," she shot back. "I am Miriana Athera, Lady of Divine Whispers and former empress of the Anir. Now take me to Seric Dyre."

The general's brooding eyes looked her up and down. There must've been something about Miriana that made him seriously consider her, likely her confidence and poise. At last, he nodded, and next Miriana knew she was riding with the Whitecrow company through the dark paths of the forest, north and south and east and west, until at last the small makeshift encampment was in sight. And when they finally brought her to Seric Dyre, her heart jumped at the sight of his handsome but weary face, and she couldn't suppress a smile of relief. Yet in return he offered an absent glance, which was followed by a dismissive wave. "Don't know her," he said.

General Madderin Ruk caught her arm. "Come away, you lying wench."

Miriana yanked herself free. She called out Seric's name, again and again, and when she received no response she shouted, "You heard the tale of the deaf maiden and immediately ran out to purchase the most expensive lute in the city."

That made Seric pause, and after a long moment he turned to stand before her. A hand came up, brushing the chin-length hair from her face. "Mir?"

The way he said her name made her heart soar, as though the heaviest burden had just been lifted off her. "Yes, Seric, it's me. It's me."

He held her pale hands in his, and even though hers were shaking, he didn't seem to notice. She couldn't help but stare at his green eyes and dimpled chin and lovely olive skin, and when he spoke it was with a voice softer than she'd ever heard from him. "Your hair . . . and your—" His jaw tightened as he studied her busted nose. "*Who* did this to you?"

"I survived, Seric. That's all that matters."

He took her in his arms then, and their embrace was warm and magical and seemingly endless. Miriana wasn't ashamed to admit how safe she felt with him; in fact, it was the safest she'd felt in a long time. And when it was done, when at last they stood apart, Miriana glimpsed the approach of a tall, dark-haired woman at Seric's left, and she was wearing quite the angry little scowl on her long face. "Who the hell is this?" the woman demanded.

CHAPTER THIRTY-TWO

Under the cover of darkness, Thayer Dal skulked through the enemy encampment, flanked by his Jackalmen raiders. The nine-man crew had used spycraft and subterfuge to overcome each outpost and gateway, and now they stood just west of the imperial pavilions—huge things with double-stitched linen walls and thick roofs of heavyweight canvas.

Zantherei Athera was undoubtedly inside one, and he was undoubtedly sitting on his rump, either shoveling gruel into his gob or sipping rice wine or doing whatever the hell a self-proclaimed emperor did on his downtime. Thayer felt a call from those pavilions—a whisper that begged him to burst inside and slit Zantherei's throat. How quickly would the guardsmen cut him down? He would have only seconds to escape. The very thought excited him.

But no, his task was to the north, where a half ring of artillery tents fanned out beneath the dim twinkle of the stars. Thayer crawled to the outermost one under a concealment of low juniper shrubbery, his nose tingling from the rich, peppery smell. It was neither windy nor cold, but the two sentries posted near the entrance looked unhappy all the same. Couldn't have been a more odd-looking pair either: one tall and tidy, and other short and scraggly. They rarely spoke to each other, but when they did, it was in a disdainful manner, as if one had sold the other's mistress to slavery, and somehow the gods forced them to stand duty together.

Yurin Grayheart was crouched at Thayer's left, his broad, caprine face staring patiently through the brush. A pair of daggers occupied his hands—slender, serrated blades, not of pure steel but an alloy of iron and jadestone. Both were of expert craftsmanship, with midnight-dark hilts and lightweight pommels to aid in balance and fluidity of movement. Beside him was Rander the Ripper, the baldheaded and granite-faced man who was built stocky like a ratel, and next over was Keven the Unkind, along with the five remaining mercenaries.

Thayer gave a quick motion of the wrist and Rander and Keven withdrew into the darkness. There was no sound, not a whisper of movement nor the tiniest rustle of leaf litter. Next, Yurin rose to his feet and—in plain sight—began to leisurely walk toward the artillery tent. He was disguised in the Hollow's gray-black attire, so the two sentries allowed him to approach.

Yurin bowed and said hello. Very calm, very casual, very confident. The sentries greeted him cordially enough, but their expressions turned to shock when two moonlit shadows seized them from behind.

Steel and blood burst from their chests, one and then the other, precise thrusts that immediately ended the lives of both men. The stabber on the right, Keven, must've struck the man's spine on the way in, because the *crack* of bone was like an arbalest's twang in the still air.

Thayer winced. His eyes searched the area until he was certain no alerts were raised. Yurin flashed a signal and the two corpses were dragged away. The intent was to hide them in the shrubbery, but along the far-side of the tent rested a stack of wooden crates, so they opted for concealment there instead.

When that was done, Yurin seized the tough linen of the secluded sidewall, and with his dagger he cut it open like the belly of a game animal. With that, he offered a grandiose gesture of welcome, and the Jackalmen slipped inside.

Now this wasn't a small tent but a huge multi-sectioned area, with thick dividing curtains and towering support poles that were occasionally dressed in pongee. All appeared quiet and vacant until they crossed paths with a lone, dressed-down fellow who was shambling forward while rubbing the sleep from his eyes.

By the time he realized what was happening it was too late— Thayer and his men had bowled him over, then Rander drove his knife through the poor bastard's skull, and that was the end of that. Thayer signaled for the group to split up, and he alone headed into the easternmost chambers, where he found heaps of dusty and rusty siege engine parts strewn on small and tall tables. He moved closer to investigate but paused at the sound of another man being stabbed nearby, a sharp, unmistakable *squelch*, followed by the dull *thud* of dead flesh hitting the ground. A raider clicked, signaling that the threat was dealt with, which prompted Thayer to return to his search.

There was so much to examine. Springs and pulleys and capstans and cantilevers, along with various lengths of sinew and skein and cordage. On the floor lay other mechanisms of iron and wood and steel, likely the unbuilt parts of mangonels, catapults, and, of course, those darkfire-spitting ballistae. Some were as thick as a man's thigh, others were so small they sat in a collection bin among a hundred others. Thayer sifted through it all but found nothing of worth, so he moved through the dividing curtain into the next chamber. Nothing here either. Frustration fell upon his shoulders like a dead weight. He needed to get his men out of here—but wait, just as he was about to call off the search, he spotted a narrow walkway that led to a larger storage area, where a double-row of powder kegs stood on racks like wine barrels. He moved closer. The symbol branded in the wood was a black tongue. This was it. Dark-fire casks.

He brought out a small bow drill, which was little more than a few shafts of wood, some string, and a steel bit. He plunged it side-ways into the wood casing, boring a small hole to drain the granu-lated powder into his unhooked belt-pouch. He only needed a small amount, a beggar's bit, but every second of pouring seemed an eter-nity of waiting. And just as he was finished, his ears picked up a commotion from somewhere outside the tent, and this commotion grew more noticeable as he made his way back to the main area. Regrouping with his Jackalmen, he made a quick motion to follow.

The eight men exited the tent, slinking away like rats through the underbrush. *Don't mind us,* Thayer thought. *We're not impor-tant, thanks.*

They made it about thirty yards before the hue and cry of alarm rang out. It was a horn blast, a tremendous *ooooOoOoOOOO* that sent a chill down Thayer's spine. He turned to keep his men calm, but it was too late—they had already bolted. *Goddamn son of a—*! He was off then, his booted feet battering the ground and kicking up gray dust and debris. The exit was close. Twenty yards. Fifteen. Torchlight flashed all around him, some close enough to blur Thay-er's vision. When he blinked the spots away, he saw shadows closing in. *Perimeter watch, has to be, but how are they moving so fast?* Just then he heard the terrible snarls, and he realized they weren't men at all. They were dogs.

GRRRUSH. One latched onto Thayer's armored forearm. He managed to remain upright, even as his body was yanked violently groundward. *You're strong, doggie, but I'm sneaky. Watch this.* The beast gave a second pull, but this time Thayer moved with it, one foot pivoting back to create distance, the other turning as he drove Bloodless into the beast's forechest.

Its jaws fell open at once, and with a bloodcurdling yelp it flopped back and scurried off. Thayer turned to aid his fellow

Jackalmen, but Yurin Grayheart and the others had made short work of the beasts, cutting down three or four before the rest swiftly fled.

Still, the hounds had done well in slowing their escape, and now a host of spearmen circled in from the left flank. Thayer brandished his blade while flashing a madman's smile. "Hi there!" The armored spearmen returned the greeting with a fierce charge, but the lighter, faster Jackalmen weaved and bobbed and slipped their strikes while moving in to pepper the enemy with dagger thrusts.

It was swift and skillful counterwork, and for a moment it looked as though the raiders might overcome their foes—but then a heavily armored bruiser stormed into the fray, a massive man with a massive battle-axe and an even more massive mane of wild hair. *Who the hell are you?* Thayer wondered.

The big armored bastard didn't waste a single breath in greeting. His battle-axe blasted through the nearest Jackalman's chest, shattering his lightweight lamellar armor and cracking his breastbone like an egg dashed. *Oh shit, that was Rander.* A second blow to the shoulder dropped him to the grass, where he writhed like a snake with a squished tail.

Thayer must've made a sound, perhaps an expletive of disbelief, because the wild-haired killer turned on him next. In a flash he'd closed the distance, and now Thayer was reeling back, fumbling to find a defensive stance. The axe-head *screamed* at him—an overhand butcher's chop that just missed splitting Thayer's head open. Off-balance and overmatched, Thayer tottered backward, one trembling step after another, until he was safely out of the axe-wielder's range.

The big man simply watched him, porcine nostrils flaring. He wore a single lion-headed pauldron that glinted beneath the moonlight's glow, and when he spoke, his voice was like a demon's growl. "Come back."

Thayer hesitated, and the wild brute let himself get distracted by other targets. He smashed a Jackalman's skull with his axe haft, then whirled and hacked another man's head clean off. His next victim—Keven the Unkind—was cleaved down the shoulder, so forceful that the poor man's clavicle burst from his skin like deer prongs, the gash frothing blood like ocean spume. And just like that, three more Jackalmen were dead.

Yurin's voice was full of urgency. "Goose, we have to go."

Thayer ignored the request, and instead waded forward, Bloodless in hand, eyes fixed on the huge general. The void pulled at him. *What a challenge you are.* Thayer was excited to take this beast down or die in the attempt. *I just need to close the distance, to render your axe useless and take away your strength.* The big man tossed him an amused smile, to which Thayer replied with a cocksure grin of his own, and then he rushed forward, feigning a low thrust and lunging at the midsection.

It was a swift and skillful maneuver—but the bullish man read it with exemplary ease. He ignored the feint and parried the mid-level strike with his axe haft, then smashed down with such force that Bloodless flew from Thayer's grip. *Gods he is strong, and much quicker than he looks.* Thayer staggered back; he wanted to charge the man barehanded, but a hand clamped his shoulder from behind. It was Yurin, who shouted in his ear while pointing at the exit. "We have to *GO.*"

Thayer scooped up Bloodless and started running. Tangles of grassy shrubs threatened to snatch a foot, while sinewy roots crisscrossed his path like tripwires. When his balance was stable enough to look back, he saw the musclebound brute hadn't pursued. Instead he stood there, mane bristling and eyes ablaze, staring the runners down like an angry bullock behind cage bars. "Who the *hell* was that?" Thayer shouted.

Yurin's breathing was ragged with exertion. "General Aldebron Pentagath. Not supposed to be stationed here . . . yet here he is. Know the name?"

Thayer grunted. "The general who helped subdue the Mad Wolf, and later led the cliffside assault on Aster Falls." He paused to catch his breath. "So that was Pentagath? Fucker was huge."

"And goddamn lionhearted," Yurin added.

Whitecrow squires were waiting with horses outside the rude timber stakewall. Thayer and the few remaining Jackalmen mounted and galloped off. For a long while, all he heard was the pounding of his own horse's hooves across the hard-packed forestland, then softer across the boggier peat.

His wrist ached from when Pentagath knocked Bloodless from his hands, but he was otherwise unhurt. Yurin had a gash in his shoulder that penetrated his armor, and another that ran down his opposite arm like a centipede. Four raiders were dead, maybe five, Thayer wasn't even sure, but he knew Rander and Keven were among them. He looked down and patted the pouch of powder fastened to his belt. At least their deaths would not be in vain.

Upon his return to Stormhaven, the powder was rushed to the private workshops, where Penry and his assistants had already been toiling and tinkering for days, melting pork and beef lard onto wooden frames and adding the cloudfall petals. The enfleurage pomade was prepared, and when it was applied as a coating to a small stone slab, the lit darkfire powder burned black but the stone didn't dissolve. The physician pulled it out of the reinforced brazier and held it by a corner.

"It appears we have our darkfire repellent," he said with a satisfied nod.

CHAPTER THIRTY-THREE

After decimating the Whitecrow forces at the Shaded Plains, Zantherei Athera had stormed across the heartland, blasting through counties and plundering hamlets and raiding homesteads. Farm owners scorched their crops and poisoned their wells before fleeing once more for the safety of Stormhaven's walls, but Zantherei dispatched advance parties to slaughter them and steal their women.

There was no end to his cruelty, and as a result, fear and discord spread through the civil and military officials of Stormhaven. For the second time in a span of five lunar months, the city was facing the threat of besiegement.

The White Fang ministers petitioned to abandon the city and flee upriver, but Alarin rejected that and pledged to stay with the people. If they were to die here, then Alarin would die with them—but not before doing everything in his power to prevent that.

Defenses needed to be bolstered, able-bodied men needed to be armed, food shortages needed to be resolved, and loyalty needed to be re-affirmed. To accomplish this, Alarin personally visited various districts and addressed the people. It was long and exhausting work, but Alarin was no longer hampered by the phantom pain of his missing leg, so he was able to make the necessary effort.

Emperor Silas often accompanied him, and always under the protective wing of Szathan Mordall. The boy did his best to stand as proudly as an emperor should, but there was always a touch of timidity holding him back. Often, during downtimes, he'd sit in silence, absently toying with one of his old knickknacks, be it that old figurine or curry comb or whatever else he'd acquired last year.

Alarin pitied the boy; Silas had never asked for such sovereignty, nor was he prepared for it. By the gods, the boy had been a mute his entire life. Still, as of now, these were lesser concerns— Alarin's focus needed to be on the imminent arrival of his brother Zantherei.

Two days later, Alarin stood behind the stone merlons of the high parapet, the midmorning sky yawning above him like a stretch of old gray fabric. Below, laborers had just finished removing the scaffolding from the defensive wall, after having covered it in animal hides treated with the fire-repellent cloudfall concoction. At Alarin's side was Ansetheral, or Lord Revek, as his people called him. The small-statured chieftain was dressed in his usual barbarian longcoat, a darkened wool garment trimmed with wolf fur and clasped at the shoulder with rounded nodes. The nearby Vaskultan guardsmen were dressed in similar fashion, and the young one, Kirik, looked to be entertaining the others with some sort of pantomimed gestures. He had a peculiar energy about him, a child-like vigor despite the toughness of his features.

Anseth cleared his throat before speaking. "I am loathe to denounce our brother as a traitor."

"We can't dither about it," Alarin said. "Not because of familial compassion. Zantherei must recognize the true and rightful sovereign of the realm."

Anseth's pale fingers tapped on a stone merlon and his eyes drifted to the open landscape of the promontory base. A small smile found his lips. "The day after the annual Steel Gauntlet, when you claimed top honors in the grappling competition . . . I remember when Zantherei came to you, all flush with wine and wounded of pride, demanding a private rematch against you. Did you ever give it to him?"

Alarin nodded. "I outwrestled him behind the royal hedges, and I outwrestled him again at the edge of the imperial pond. I must've outwrestled him four times that day, and then two more the next. Merio kept a tally of each bout, even sketched diagrams showing the lifts and reversals and clinches that were used to achieve victory. And after every bout, he would flash the diagram in Zantherei's face and cackle like an overexcited child. But Zantherei wouldn't give up. He'd strap on his headgear and scuff his foot in the dirt, issuing another challenge. I could've outwrestled him a hundred times and he *still* wouldn't have been satisfied. But that's Zantherei. He was always so stubborn."

Anseth gave an agreeable snort, and a long but comfortable silence spread between the brothers. Alarin closed his eyes and let the crisp winter breeze touch his face, his thoughts flowing like endless meandering rivers. So fleeting was the essence of time . . . so strict in its passage and so cruel in manner. One moment you are young and vigorous, the next you are aging and full of memories. It was difficult to watch it go, in truth. To realize your life is nothing more than the wisp of a cloud, or the tiniest raindrop in an unending storm.

Alarin's eyes reopened. He wished he could go back and mend his failures—to go back and save Merio and save Zantherei and save the empire and then save himself. He wished he could go back and save everyone, as foolish as that sounded.

Anseth finally spoke, a soft, subdued tone. "He will be suspicious if we don't check his army at the base of the headland."

"No. His confidence is soaring now. He will merely think me afraid."

The question came after a beat. "*Are* you afraid?"

Alarin's reply was slow and hesitant. "I've been fearing this day ever since Demien Mordall smuggled me out of the Hollow."

Spotters reported sight of the enemy force just after midday. Alarin held his nerve as the mass of man and horse and wagon approached like an inexorable mudslide. The center was an impressive column that ran many bodies across and many more deep, and these soldiers were fully clad in blackened steel armor and fringed with wings of heavy cavalry.

Near the front, mounted men waved the gray-black flags of the Hollow, while cymbalists crashed their instruments together and drummers pounded the rhythm of the marching army. In the rear rolled the heavy siege engines, most intimidating of which were the darkfire-spitting ballistae, which looked like giant crossbows mounted on wheeled platforms.

The army broke camp on the widened base of the promontory. Tents were pitched and barricades were erected as soldiers and squires and supplymen moved like buzzing insects. Zantherei had always been an efficient logistics officer, so it wasn't surprising to see how quickly a small company of horsemen detached itself from the encampment and rode toward Stormhaven's walls. They looked tiny from where Alarin stood on the upper parapet. "That's him," he said. "Don't let him beguile you with talk of sorcery. And never outright accede to any of his demands."

Anseth cocked his head, his knotted black hair curtaining his high cheekbones. "Do you take me for a clod?"

"Just do as I say. Zantherei is not the same man we once knew."

"Neither am I."

Fair point. Alarin tossed a long look at his younger brother. "When this meeting is done, I want you above the central barbican, at Tower Tempest. Your Vaskultan bowman and their keen eyes are needed there. Szathan will secure Tower Rainfell, Thayer will be given Tower Thunderstone, and I will hold Tower Snowblind. These four points are Zantherei's primary targets. We need not fear an amphibious assault; the water gate is impenetrable, and the bulk of the city is protected by the headland. Besides, the Hollow has always lacked a strong naval force. Do you understand?"

"Yes, Elder Brother."

Alarin shifted his focus to the approaching Hollow riders, who began to dismount before the wall. He recognized the center figure at once. After two long years of bad blood and unanswered missives, there he was, the Storm of the North, the Warden of the West, and the self-proclaimed emperor of the Anir: Zantherei Athera.

Time for another family reunion, Alarin mused, *and this one is long overdue.*

Zantherei was dressed rather trimly—not so flashy as Merio's garb, but certainly a bit regal for someone so accustomed to the ragged grays. His cloak was dyed a deep imperial blue and edged in black mink, while his brigandine coat was fitted with hexagonal plates of shiny black lamellar. Lower, he wore knee-high fawnskin boots over heavy winter leggings, and on his head sat the most ridiculous headdress Alarin had ever seen. It looked like a noncombat ceremonial helmet with its oversized Sadralen horns, and not only was it distasteful, it also stunk of overcompensation for the one object that was noticeably missing from his attire: the Imperial Seal.

Without a word, Zantherei moved forward and stood directly below the wall, under Alarin's scrutinizing gaze. The man's roundish face of forty years appeared withdrawn and off-color, but that was expected considering his prolonged battle with poison. *How long has it been since we last spoke?* Alarin wondered. *Wait, I remember. It was two years ago, at the Pit, where we argued about*

*Governor Tavarin Valayne and his many grievances. Gods, that was
a lifetime ago. So much has changed since.*

"Look at you, Elder Brother," Zantherei said with a snort. "Up
and about during the middle of the day." His head turned to
examine the outer wall, scrutinizing its length as though making a
mental note of each moss-filled crack or uneven chunk of mortar. It
was hard not to notice his slightly off-center gaze, just as it was
hard not to notice how ugly that horned headdress was. "Is this how
you greet your beloved brother?" he said. "From behind stone and
steel?"

"I can't talk to you with that thing on your head," Alarin told
him. "You look ridiculous, Brother. It's not the Anirian way."

Zantherei menaced a glare at him, but a moment later he
removed the headdress and handed it off to a young squire. As the
lad withdrew, Zantherei removed a glove and pushed a hand
through his tangled crop of short brown hair. He spoke offhandedly.
"What do traitors know of the Anirian way?"

"*I'm* the traitor? After all you've done. How risible."

Zantherei's scowl could chisel through stone. "I liked you more
as an embittered slugabed. You were less ambitious then."

"And I liked you more when you didn't attempt to claim what
wasn't yours."

A vein bulged in Zantherei's forehead, but he quelled his temper
enough to disregard the insult. For a brief moment, silence stole the
air, then his dark eyes wandered to the smaller figure beside Alarin.
"I see the barbarian lands have not been kind to you, Little Brother.
You look like hell."

Anseth's voice was firm. "My heart is glad to see you, too."

His cold eyes narrowed. "I mourned you, Brother. I thought the
barbarians had gutted you at Black Gate Pass." His eyes flicked to
Alarin, but only for the briefest of moments. "You're standing
behind the wrong sibling. Submit to the true emperor of the Anir,

and all transgressions will be pardoned, and you will be given the cord and seal of command, as our father would've wanted."

Anseth looked down, his sharp eyes lost in knots of black hair. He seemed to have a difficult time finding his tongue, but when he did reply, it was with unexpected strength. "The true emperor of the realm resides here, behind the walls of Stormhaven."

"The Mordall stripling is a fainthearted mute, nothing more," Zantherei said. "And don't waste your breath speaking of magical flowers. I've listened to the rumormongers, but it's all tommyrot. The only magic is that which I possess, and those who wrong me will suffer a most horrible fate. Your spotters reported the ruin of Seric Dyre's forces, yes?" He didn't wait for a reply. "That is the fate of all who oppose me."

He made a curt gesture, and a dark-skinned fellow draped in an ember-hued robe stepped forward. In his hand was a crude wooden pike with a leather sack tied at the top. With his other hand he cut the cords with a curved knife, and then he pulled away the fabric to reveal a man's impaled head. It was a gruesome thing, features grayed and twisted by the horrors of decomposition, but even then, there was no mistaking that bushy silver beard or wide, cruel face: it was the head of Raas Dragath.

Zantherei took the pike and thrust it skyward. His voice was loud and full-throated, a general's voice, one that he'd used many times to command many men. "The southern tyrant Raas Dragath has committed a towering list of atrocities. He used sedition to undermine the ruling house, he used chicanery to gain allies, and he used an assassin to murder Emperor Thavian Siven. His offenses have been fulfilled by death, and his stronghold has been purged from existence. And with that, our brother Merio has been avenged."

He handed the pike back to the ember-cloaked man, but the fool must've mishandled it, because it slipped from his fingers and landed top-first with a *thump*. There was an embarrassed chuckle or two from the surrounding soldiers, but Zantherei ended that with a sharp look. At length, his cold eyes drifted back up to Alarin. "So, you never responded to my letter."

"Does that mean you've come for my head too? Perhaps for some crime I never committed, which will surely echo the baseless accusations your lovely wife, Miriana, once laid upon me."

"Do not speak of her," he growled, face darkening. As stern as Zantherei was, he could never mask his emotions well—at least not in Alarin's presence. "In my name a new dynasty has begun, a new era of rule to be documented in the annals. Laws are being promulgated and policies are being dictated as we speak. For you I had but two simple demands: return the Imperial Seal and offer your unwavering subservience. You ignored both. Recall my words in the letter: 'deny me and you will be considered an enemy of the realm.'"

"He is your elder brother," Anseth cut in. "He is your blood. You would break the familial bonds and declare him an enemy?"

Zantherei's eyes remained focused on Alarin. "*Any* who oppose me are enemies, blood or not." His tone made it obvious that Anseth wasn't excluded.

"You are mad," Alarin said. "You are mad with power. You have no claim to the throne, nor do you deserve it. Do you recall what happened when you attempted to subvert Emperor Thavian Siven's rule and secure the throne for yourself? You were poisoned. By Sydrian Rane, loyal Imperial Steward and longstanding servant of the empire."

"Sydrian Rane was a snake and a coward, and he died as such, along with his co-conspirators and kinfolk. A rightful end. Now I ask you once more, will you open your gates, hand over the Imperial Seal, and prostrate yourself before the true emperor of the Anir?"

Alarin stared at him for a long, tense moment. "Sorry, Brother."

Zantherei's scowl grew ever deeper. "Then I've nothing left to say." He spun, motioning to his guardsmen to fetch his horse. Once mounted, his hard gaze rose to acknowledge Alarin one last time. "You will regret your decision, Elder Brother. You will regret it and you will beg. Oh, by the gods will you beg . . . when the darkfire comes for you."

CHAPTER THIRTY-FOUR

The darkfire came for them the very next day.

This is not the end for us. This is not the end. Ansetheral Athera repeated the words in his mind, again and again, like the morbid mantra of the terminally ill. He was crammed inside the square-shaped commander's quarters and facing a full onslaught of catapult and ballista fire. *BOOM. BO-BOOM. CRACK.* Volley after volley of darkfire missiles slammed into the walls of Tower Tempest with the fury of a thunder god. *BOOM. BO-BOOM. CRACK.* Brickwork crumbled like old bark paper, spraying dust and mortar and loess into the air. *BOOM. BO-BOOM. CRACK.* The sound was so loud Anseth could feel his skin vibrating beneath his boiled leather armor.

This is not the end for us. This is not the end.

Vaskultan warriors moved around him like caged wolves, pent-up and restless and afraid. Some were climbing retractable ladders that led to the tower's uppermost story, where protection was provided behind the battlements and under the pitched roof.

Anseth watched them absently, his mind a fast-moving whirl-wind of slow-motion thoughts. Oddly enough, he couldn't stop thinking about how much manpower and brainpower would be wasted in the destruction of the wall. How many laborers and quarrymen worked themselves to the bone to erect these structures? How many builders and engineers were commissioned for their painstaking mathematical calculations? Such thoughts were senseless, Anseth knew, but they didn't stop until he forced his mind to refocus on the situation at hand. *This is not the end for us. This is not the end.*

Another missile struck the wall. *BOOM.*

Anseth braced himself against a shower of shattered brickwork. For a moment he feared the entire structure would collapse. *Are the oiled skins working? Are they halting the spread of the darkfire?* He lifted himself up, dirty fingernails clinging to the stone sill as he gazed out of the arched window. *I can't see anything.*

Noxious fumes struck him like a club, burning his nostrils and leaving him coughing and retching and coughing some more. To his left, Kirik was speaking, but the words were soundless in the chaos. *What the hell are you saying?* Anseth decided to give the order to return fire, and within moments the Vaskultan bowmen took aim through the room's loopholes and loosed. Despite the haze, their arrows appeared to have some measure of success, but that only drew the enemy's full attention—and wrath.

"Get *down*!" Anseth shouted.

BOOM. BO-BOOM. CRACK.

Masonry shifted and dirt sprayed and ceiling bricks crashed to the floor. Vaskultans hunkered down beside each other like children in a sandstorm, waiting . . . waiting . . . waiting . . . and just when the danger seemed to pass, a massive bolt screamed through an arched window, skewering not one but two Vaskultans.

The force was so great it carried the men across the room and nailed them to the far wall, and Anseth could only shudder in horror as gravity pulled their lifeless bodies to the floor, where they lay in a bloody, contorted heap. Globs of liquid darkfire began to drip from the bolt, forming crannies and craters in the stone floor, like animal prints in an oversaturated ground.

"*SMOTHER IT*," Anseth cried, and two hefty Vaskultans wasted no time in throwing a treated animal hide over the bubbling black fire, extinguishing it at once. Anseth gave a praising nod to the pair —Ikara on the left, Severak beside her. The war maiden looked as broad-shouldered and formidable as ever, but by the gods Severak was barely recognizable—and not because he was covered in grit and dirt from boot to black wolf hide, or that his left cheek was shredded of skin and smeared with blood. No, it was his eyes . . . Anseth couldn't recall the last time Severak Bonesplitter's eyes had looked so hopeless and out of sorts.

This is not the end for us. This is not the end.

More darkfire missiles struck, more earth-trembling catapult *booms* and ballistae bolt *cracks*. Anseth and Ikara and Severak dropped for cover, but a nearby Vaskultan hadn't been so quick. A flying slab of stone struck him directly in the diaphragm, and with a breathless grunt he doubled over, his legs folding inward as he sank to the ground.

A second Vaskultan tripped over his prone body and crashed down on his hip, while a third crawled past them both, moaning about how he couldn't see. Anseth tried to help the poor blinded man but a bolt screamed past his ear, so large and so heavy it was like a sharpened tree limb. It speared a Vaskultan several feet away, and when it slammed into the already weakened wall, stones crumbled and nearly stole Anseth's legs out from under him.

He hopped and bobbed across the room until he could regain his footing, then he took a moment to paw at the dust in his eyes. A hand touched his shoulder, and a familiar voice—Kirik's voice— asked if he were all right. Anseth turned to his friend and gave a grunt. Somewhere to the left, a man was screaming an awful scream. Kirik moved his head to look—then a flying stone smashed into it.

It was so quick, the merest blink of an eye. One moment Kirik was standing at Anseth's side, the next he was lying ten feet away, limbs sprawled out and stiff like those of a dried-up sea star. The blow had knocked his leather helmet clean off, and the face beneath was twisted in a semiconscious grimace, while his body tensed and untensed as though shivering from some immeasurable cold.

Anseth rushed to him, fingers working at once, feeling, feeling, feeling his head for the wound. A slippery indent just above his half-torn ear, hidden by hanks of ratty hair. When his fingers withdrew, they were slick with blood, but thank the Skybringer there were no bits of skull or dashed brains.

"Kirik. Kirik." He kept saying his name, over and over until the man's eyes fluttered open . . . open and then closed, and finally open once more. "Kirik, can you hear my voice?"

His elongated face looked bewildered, and when he spoke, his voice was a croak, no stronger than a whisper. "Lord Revek, what hour is it? Did you summon me?"

Anseth tore a strip of linen from his tunic, then fished inside a small pouch for a bit of pulverized alum, an effective coagulant. He pressed the cataplasm to the man's head, but another missile struck the tower and he was thrown on top of his friend. Kirik groaned as though sucker-punched in the gut. He tried to sit upright but Anseth put a hand on his chest. His look of bewilderment twisted into irritation. "What's wrong—why are you crowding over me?"

"Listen to me. Kirik. Do you know where you are?"

Kirik blinked. "In . . . in my yurt."

"We're in the central tower of the outer wall, in the Anirian city of Stormhaven. We're under heavy assault by enemy siege engines. You were—" Anseth had to wait until the blasts died before continuing. "You were struck by shrapnel, likely concussed. Don't get up. Stay here for now."

He didn't try to fight it, thank the gods. "Oh, is that true? I don't—"

Another salvo of missiles struck the wall.

BOOM. BOOM. CRACK.

The sounds were like a herd of stampeding wildebeest, a rapid stuttering of explosions, again and again and again. Anseth threw himself protectively over Kirik. *This is not the end for us. This is not the end.* Another fusillade followed, then another. Wood snapped and dust sprayed in every direction. Anseth feared the foundation would buckle and the stones would slide free and descend, taking his world with them.

CRACK. BOOM. CRACK.

More missiles and more explosions and more madness. Anseth couldn't see, he couldn't hear, he couldn't think or breathe or even move his body. *Gods, please don't let this tower collapse. This is NOT the end for us.*

This is NOT THE END!

. . .

The barrage ceased . . . and the world became still. A warm breeze passed through the tower, the air thick with embers and smoke. Anseth crawled to the sill and stuck his head out of the arched window, eyes drifting to the battlements and the semicircular enceinte, then farther along to the crenellated wall-walks.

There were jagged depressions in the brick face, smashed and broken cladding, and disrupted layers of rammed earth—but the structure remained intact, and the cloudfall-treated animal hides had impeded the spread of the darkfire. Oddly enough, there remained a faint aura of white light over the wall, serene and soft, like moonlight on a lake.

It was beautiful.

Alarin was right, Anseth thought. *The cloudfalls did protect. By the gods old and new, Vaskultan and Anirian, I've just witnessed a miraculous event. I will never doubt you again, Elder Brother. Never again.*

The stillness was broken by the stirring of heavy machinery.

Amid the smoke and the wreckage, the wheeled ballistae, catapults, and other torsion engines withdrew from the battle, and in seeing this many Vaskultans gave a great rousing cry of victory. *The sky above be glorified, the land below be lauded.* Some decided to throw imprecations and execrations at the fleeing enemy, while others flashed lewdly their rumps and privates. The euphoria of victory was as pure as honey, and no less sweet.

Anseth let himself enjoy the moment, before his gaze returned to Kirik. The bondsman was propped against a wall of the central room, nodding as Severak spoke to him, no doubt clearing up all the confounded questions a man has after having his senses taken from him.

Kirik may have been wounded, but he was alive, and that was all that mattered. *This was not the end for us, and for that I am grateful.* He turned back to face the landscape. A single crow appeared in the sky, weaving around the plumes of dark smoke, its harsh cawing heard over the Vaskultan victory song.

It was an ill omen, Anseth knew, an obvious gesture to Zantherei. Ten years removed or not, they were still brothers, and in his heart Anseth knew just what that meant. *Zantherei will not give up so easily,* he mused. *The battle for Stormhaven has only just begun.*

CHAPTER THIRTY-FIVE

Szathan Mordall stood on the upper story of Tower Rainfell, his giant gauntleted hands resting upon a ledge of broken brickwork. Above, the waxing crescent moon lay on its side, partially cloaked by a stretch of stringy gray clouds. The evening breeze, rich with the coming of precipitation, lifted his mid-length tousle of unwashed brown hair. *The air is cold enough for hailstones or sleet,* he mused, *but I pray we get neither.* Szathan's gaze wandered down to the treated animal hides that checkered the outer wall. Most were punctured and torn and burnt of edges, but by the gods' good graces, they had succeeded in preventing the spread of that nasty darkfire. The other front-facing towers also remained intact, even the center Tower Tempest, which had taken the brunt of the artillery fire. Ansetheral's barbarian forces had mustered an effective return of arrow and arbalest fire, but not without sustaining casualties in the process.

Reports flew from tower to tower, detailing the extent of the damages. The dead were buried honorably while the wounded received aid in the physicians' quarters, with those burned by the dark-fire treated in a separate, quarantined chamber. For the unscathed and able-bodied, there was much to be done. Debris to be removed, loopholes to be cleared, barricades to be repaired, weapons to be replaced, torsion coils and ropes to be tightened or replaced. It was mindless, menial work, and it went on through the deepening chill of night.

A coyote yipped from somewhere beyond the wall, stealing Szathan's attention. He couldn't see the creature, so his eyes inevitably drifted to the open sward near the forest's edge, where enemy torchlight flickered across a perimeter of military tents and barriers and breastworks.

There was no shortage of fierce generals under Zantherei's command: General Sabriel Soffin, General Aldebron Pentagath, and most concerning of all, General Gilberon Brehems. Under no circumstance would Szathan ever draw steel against his former deputy commander. They'd been on too many campaigns together, had stood side-by-side through too many sorties and skirmishes. Brehems had always been a good and loyal friend, even when Szathan was an ugly, disliked youth in the Pit.

A hand rose to rub the bridge of his nose. He was filthy and he was exhausted, and his shoulder ached, even though he didn't remember injuring it. Soldiers were bustling along the wall-walk around him, many setting down chaff mats for a bit of rest under the drab evening sky. A physician on his rounds handed Szathan an unguent of lavender and eucalyptus oil for his pain, and shortly after a reedy squire working a double shift offered a bowl of rice gruel. Despite looking old and stale, the meal was rather tasteful, and after washing it down with a hollowed-out gourd of wine, Szathan had the squire fetch him some blankets. He would've preferred a fire and a bedstead with a comfortable thatched mattress, but this would have to do. He lay down and stretched himself out before the starlit sky, his mind free to roam and ramble like an uncaged bird.

Not a moment after his eyes closed did a meek voice bring him out of sleep. "Uncle?"

Szathan sat up, gazing at the youthful face of Silas Mordall. The boy wasn't dressed in his usual imperial raiment but a homelier gray robe with loose sleeves and a handful of dark jadestones sewn at the collar. The cord of his Imperial Seal was visible around the neck, but the object itself was hidden beneath an embroidered stole. "You shouldn't be here," Szathan told him. He forgot his courtesies for a moment, then added, "Your Majesty."

The boy lowered his head, timid as ever. He usually carried some sort of knickknack; today it was a small pelletdrum he'd acquired during his travels to Stormhaven. Szathan fixed his gaze on it while he spoke. "Your place is in the palace, with your guardsmen and advisors and attendants. It's too dangerous out here."

Silas nodded but made no motion to leave, and that only prompted Szathan to sigh. He flicked his wrist, motioning the boy closer, and when he obeyed Szathan put a hand on his shoulder. It was so big it covered the entire upper arm, and the weight of it made the boy slump to the side a bit. "I once thought that being so pure of heart would only lead to pain," Szathan said, "but now I am starting to see the wisdom in it." He looked down for a moment, as if gathering his thoughts. "It was you who repelled the enemy today. *You* saved our city, just as you saved Lord Alarin's life. Without your otherworldly bond with those cloudfalls, Stormhaven would've been reduced to a smoldering heap."

Silas smiled a meek little smile, and that made Szathan shake his head. "Listen, boy, I'm not the wisest man, but I do know that shyness is unbecoming of an emperor. Others will see it as a weakness in you, and unless your intent is to purposefully deceive, there is no reason for it. Allow yourself to feel the confidence that stirs inside you. You are not a mute little stripling any longer; you've been given a voice and a purpose. Heaven itself has chosen you as its sovereign. Let that purpose shine forth."

The boy's chin rose slightly in response. "If I do as you say, will I not suffer the same fate as the former emperor?"

"Thavian Siven died because the gods willed it."

"But he shouldn't have died. I didn't want him to die. I don't want *anyone* to die. Not Lord Alarin, and not you. Few have treated me kinder."

"Don't worry about losing me. This oversized galoot isn't going to die."

The boy's expression softened. "Good. It hurts too much. Like my father. Even though he didn't have the warmest heart, I still loved him. And I know you don't believe me, but he's not dead, I just kno—"

"Enough of that. Your father's alive in your memories. He will always be there, until you meet again in the next life."

The boy looked down; he was silent for a long time. "I may have saved the city today, but the enemy hasn't retreated. They are preparing to strike again, aren't they?"

Szathan's aching shoulder tensed at that. "There's no need to discuss the intricacies of siege defense with you, Your Majesty, but we do have countermeasures in place. It's best if you return to the palace and get some sleep. We'll talk more after the city is secure."

Silas gave what appeared to be his most confident nod. He seemed to want to raise his arms and embrace Szathan, but the moment passed, and the boy turned and withdrew.

The storm arrived just after daybreak. What began as a soft drizzle became a thick, semi-frozen downpour that glazed the wall-walks and overstayed its welcome. Szathan spent much of the day squinting into the cheerless gray mist that rose before the city, and in the quiet of the early evening he could hear the echo of enemy laborers chopping trees or hauling timber or performing other tasks of drudgery. That night the racket didn't cease until the fourth watch, which was well past the midnight hour. Lord Alarin had sent saboteurs to disable contraptions and disrupt workflow, but that resulted in Hollow horsemen riding up and tossing their severed heads on the ground.

Szathan spent the next few days patrolling the wall, waiting, waiting, waiting. It wasn't easy. His sore shoulder and long-aching knee made him grouchy, and the halved rations and heavy armor made him grouchier still. The posted soldiers were suffering from boredom and unease, which meant that some fell to wrongful activities such as excessive carousing or mischief making or minor instigating. Still, he was hesitant to punish the offenders, as most simply wished for the siege to end so they could allay their fears and return to their loved ones.

Szathan's own wife and sons were currently stationed in the inner city, behind three impregnable district walls and under the protection of handpicked guardsmen. It was hard not to miss them —especially his wife. She was a petite and patient woman with a compassionate heart that never once criticized Szathan for his freakish build and oversized head. Some had teased their initial courtship, passing whispers that he was too ugly to take a wife, but she never paid any mind to such gossip, and for that he treasured her.

A long week later, three mobile enemy assault towers were spotted in the distance, but their advance was at a slug's pace, no more than a hundred feet a day. Still, they were massive things, four or five floors of crisscrossing beams with sloped roofs and protective animal pelts, and by the gods were they louder than an army of oxcarts.

Closer, they began to eat arrow after arrow from the Stormhaven bowmen, but like juggernauts they roared dauntlessly forward. Well, except for one. It must've suffered poor workmanship or construction, because it suddenly bucked and wobbled and halted, its rollers broken and left immobile. In the middle of the field it sat, absorbing arrow after arrow from the wall until eventually a smaller, hide-covered penthouse rolled to its aid, and a host of laborers emerged to begin the treacherous work of repairs under missile fire.

That's one down, Szathan mused.

As the two remaining assault towers moved closer, a swarm of Hollow scaling parties flooded around them, men advancing upon the wall with giant wooden ladders. Stormhaven bowmen and slingers attempted to turn them with a hail of missile fire, but the scalers pushed through the assault and worked in unison to slam the ladders upright against the wall.

Szathan watched the enemy ascend, the haft of his great figured halberd clutched in both gauntleted hands. Bowmen at his flanks fired with abandon, while others dumped pails of hot oil and broken glass on the scalers. One team was rolling giant stones off the wall ledge, and these were so heavy they landed with massive *thumps* that opened crater-like holes in the earth. From below shouts and groans could be heard, along with the occasional drawn-out scream of a plummeting man, but the enemy kept coming.

Szathan held his breath and closed his eyes, allowing himself to fall into a detached state where all he did was listen to the violence of the escalade. He absorbed those sounds, took them into his lungs like oxygen. The enemy was close now; the first of the scalers had reached the topmost rungs of the siege ladders, and now were attempting to climb through the crenels. Szathan opened his eyes and put Nightwing to work, chopping at any hands or heads in sight. Blood spurted from slashed limbs and smashed helmets, like the yolks of dashed eggs. Szathan worked and worked and worked, but after splitting the fourth or fifth assailant's skull and wrenching his blade free, he suddenly gave pause.

An enormous assault tower came to a halt before the curtain wall. Moments later its windlass groaned, lowering a great draw-bridge that landed with an enormous *boom* on the parapet wall.

The enemy's calculations must've been a few degrees off, because the result was a rather steep downward angle, and this caused some balance issues when the Hollow soldiers poured out. A few stumbled, a few tripped, and one poor sot fell off the side and plunged fifty feet to the hard winter ground. Szathan rose to meet the enemy charge but was forced to find cover when bolts suddenly zipped overhead, fired by crossbowmen perched on the assault tower's uppermost floor. He could hear the furious *clink* and *clank* of projectiles slamming against the defensive barriers, and when at last they stopped, Szathan peered up to see a throng of gray-cloaked Hollow soldiers crowding the wall-walks, swords and polearms whirling, steel edges shimmering in what little moonlight the cloud cover allowed to pass through.

Time slowed to a crawl. The clash of soldiers was like a slow-motion effervescence, as though the battle were taking place under-water. Nightwing whirled and took a man by the throat, then Szathan used the butt-spike to stab another in the breast. When he dislodged the weapon, the soldier doubled-over and collapsed, trip-ping a third attacker who was helplessly unprepared to defend against Nightwing's overhead chop. It was an awful blow. The man's face nearly split in half, a vertical gash that left him shivering in agony as blood and tissue and broken teeth spewed onto the flag-stones beneath him.

More enemies vaulted over the battlements. They wouldn't stop coming. Stormhaven defenders attempted to cover the main breach with a wheeled barricade, but the Hollow soldiers overturned and disabled it. Once more, Nightwing went back to work. But the moment Szathan cut one man down, another sprang in his place, then two more, then another two. Soon his world had descended into a mad, gruesome place with neither escape nor reprieve.

Men, friend and foe alike, were being stabbed and sliced and battered, and many of the fallen were trampled beneath the rush of booted feet. Szathan saw a man's face raked by the metal cranequin of a turret arbalest, while another unfortunate soldier had his groin pierced by a stray arrow. Others were thrown head or feet first off the wall. For a moment it appeared as though the Stormhaven defenders would claim the upper hand, but for every siege ladder knocked down, another would rise in its place, and for every grapnel that was severed or unhooked, two more would fire up with fury.

The enemy just wouldn't stop coming.

It mattered not. Szathan Mordall was a giant monster of a man who would not be discouraged, and as he dropped foeman after foeman to the bloody flagstones, others began to take notice and back away. This boosted Szathan's bloodlust ever higher, and with a berserker's rage he pounded his fist to his chest, once, twice, three times, and then he roared like a bull-demon. The Hollow soldiers scattered like gadflies. Some stumbled, others shoved, but the slowest were hewn down with a hearty swing of Szathan's halberd. "*RUN* from the ogre," he shouted, to no one and everyone at once. "*RUN* before I eat you *ALIVE*."

Still, for every soldier that did run, there was another brave sot who dug in to fight. But again, it mattered not; Szathan's figured halberd whirled and parried and struck with unrivaled precision, his mind *feeling* the maneuvers more than seeing them, in a way that only years of experience could give a man. He cut down one foeman and then the next, trudging deeper and deeper into the fray until the shouts of some unknown enemy commander caught his attention. *Please be Gilberon Brehems,* he thought. *Please be Gilberon Brehems.* Szathan could end this bitter siege if he could only speak to his old friend, but if it were Aldebron Pentagath or Sabriel Soffin or even Zantherei Athera himself, he would have to fight his way to victory. *Gods, please be Gilberon Brehems.* Szathan strode forward and cut down the next foeman, and then the one after that, and then another and another until at last he broke through the inner ranks and squared-off against the enemy commander himself.

It was Gilberon Brehems.

Szathan shouted his old friend's name, though he didn't know why—he already had the man's attention. Brehems looked as beefy and barrel-hipped as ever, though the beard he'd begun to grow in Thornberry was much shaggier now. And his eyes had certainly changed; they no longer looked upon Szathan with amicability. "Szathan Mordall, you old piss-cutter." His voice was a throaty huff. "Dandy to fucking see you, but a damn shame it's from opposing sides."

"I serve the rightful emperor," Szathan told him. "The *true* emperor. Not a self-proclaimed and self-serving tyrant."

An armed Stormhaven soldier emerged aggressively from the nearby fray; Brehems reacted at once, backhanding the poor sot with his wolf-toothed mace, a movement not unlike the swatting of a pesky bee. The soldier dropped to the flagstones at once, and Brehems spat in his direction before replying to Szathan. "Did you say the same when you crooked the knee to Raas Dragath?"

"That wasn't the same. I had no choice."

"There's always a choice."

"And I made the honorable one, but you were already gone. You shouldn't have defected."

Brehems shook his shaggy head like a bear shaking the wetness from its fur. "I did what I—"

There was a tremendous *crack,* so loud and thunderous that Szathan's balance nearly faltered. His eyes rose to the enemy's second assault tower, which had just collapsed at the foot of Tower Tempest. Great rings of dust plumed into the air, spreading outward like ripples in a boggy lake. The surviving Hollow soldiers were exposed and panicking, easy pickings for the Vaskultan bowmen above.

That's two down, Szathan thought.

He turned back to see Brehems backpedaling a bit, one slow step after another. Hollow soldiers were rushing around him, moving in every direction. "Return to my side, Gil," Szathan shouted. "Serve the rightful ruler and I will deputize you once more." When Brehems didn't reply, he raised a gauntleted hand, a gesture of friendship. "The siege is lost. The darkfire was repelled, and your assault towers are breaking. It is heaven's will."

Brehems gave a defiant snort. "I wish you weren't wrong, old friend." He retreated to the edge of the battlement and climbed over, hands grasping the rungs of the wooden ladder. Szathan moved forward, but he made no attempt to stop him. No, he couldn't do that. Brehems was more than just an old friend and deputy commander; he was like a brother. But there was something odd about Gilberon's departing words. *How am I wrong?* Szathan wondered. He tried to ask that very question, but Brehems had already shinnied down the ladder and vanished into the gray haze.

The answer came shortly after, when the flagstones beneath Szathan's boots began to rumble. The rumbling swiftly turned to quaking, and this quaking grew and grew until it was so intense that Szathan had to brace himself against the stone ledge.

He wasn't the smartest of men, but suddenly the truth of the situation seemed painfully clear. *They fired a mine,* he thought. *The assault towers were a distraction . . . to allow sappers to fire a mine from below.* Just then the main wall's foundation groaned, as if pulled inward by an enormous weight. Szathan could feel the wall-walk buckle like an overburdened hay cart. *I must get to Lord Alarin. Gods, please don't let this wall collapse. I'm not ready to die.*

CHAPTER THIRTY-SIX

Thayer Dal grunted as he raced across the hard flagstones of the wall-walk. Broken brickwork and jagged rubble threatened to twist an ankle, but the Wild Goose moved with a nimble caution that seemed to defy his cognomen.

He couldn't help but observe the fallen men along the parapet, some slumped over the open crenels, others stacked in bloody heaps against the stone barriers. It was a dreadful sight—yet exhilarating all the same. Agony and fear were expressions that did not lie, and on some of these poor bastards the truth was plastered for the world to forever see. But where had the souls of these empty husks gone to? Would some minor god drag them to his netherworld, or would they be reborn into another life? Thayer wanted to know all that and more, but most of all, he wanted to know what it was like to cross over.

Stop daydreaming, you're in the middle of a siege. He realized the void was pulling at him furiously right now, an enticement not of whispers but of loud, urgent commands. *Fling yourself off the wall or run headfirst into a spike barricade or bash your head against the stone ledge. Choose one and do it, do it, do it.* Yes, any of those would be a thoroughly emphatic way to go. Thayer shook his head feverishly to free himself of such thoughts, then his eyes drifted back to Tower Rainfell. The split was a few degrees off-center, yet wide enough that it could buckle inward and drag down half the curtain wall with it. But that didn't happen, so either the load-bearing arches did their job, or perhaps the enemy sappers had been negligent, or maybe this was all just the whim of the gods.

Still, there was a rift in the wall, and it was just wide enough for two or three Hollow besiegers to squeeze through at a time. And that was exactly what they did—or tried to do, had Lord Alarin's defending forces not been there to repel them.

Mined from below, Thayer thought bitterly. *How did our watchmen not see this ruse?* It was easy to conceal the tunnel entrance, a simple screen of thatch would work, but it was nearly impossible to conceal all the excavated earth. There would've been mounds of it, heaps three times as tall as a man. Far too much to go unnoticed by watchtower eyes. *Zantherei, that clever dog . . . he must've used darkfire to disintegrate the haul.* Thayer shook his head once more. The tower was close now. Soldiers were rushing past him with the frantic swiftness of birds. Gray cloaks, black cloaks; were they friend or foe? He couldn't even tell anymore. The haze was too thick and disorienting.

He found Lord Alarin on the battlements just outside the tower. The fringes of his outer cloak were shredded, and his lower body was smeared with gray dust, but he otherwise appeared uninjured and unwearied. Several guardsmen and officers encircled him, the most noticeable being Szathan Mordall, who stood head and shoulders above the others. The general looked even more mountainous in his black plates of burnished mail and taloned spaulders. His figured halberd, haft as thick as a man's arm, was clutched in his gauntleted hands. *Gods, he's covered in blood,* Thayer thought. *The blood of those foolish enough to stand against him.*

Lord Alarin was leaning on his blackthorn cane while arching his back to speak to the huge general. "You can't go. I need you here, I need you at the breach."

Szathan opened his mouth to protest but Alarin cut him off. "Organize a reinforcing division to aid the breach defense, but don't hold that hole. I have another tactic in mind. The squires and conscripts are constructing a barricade. Caltrops and chevaux de fries with antipersonnel arbalests perched behind them. Once the enemy floods inside, they will be forced into the arched gateway beneath the ramp, which leads to the western courtyard. Two detachments of bowmen will be waiting along the higher parapet, trapping the enemy between the outer and inner walls."

Szathan nodded and hurried off. Alarin then turned to address his barbarian brother, the mousy Ansetheral Athera, who had been standing to his left like an overlooked child. The two exchanged a few quiet words, then Alarin's gaze fell at last on Thayer. He began to give instructions, but Thayer already knew what they would entail. To defend the foundation of the main curtain wall, and to prevent the enemy from digging directly into the compound, there was only one practical solution: a countermine.

The next few hours passed in urgent motion. A force of about fifty soldiers—Thayer and Anseth included—toiled alongside every able-bodied laborer available, and these men dug and dug under the supervision of engineers who analyzed and reanalyzed and shouted their updated calculations. The toiling was tedious and taxing, and Thayer's hands quickly became raw from the spade handle, even with his old pair of dog-skin gloves. Still, discomfort and pain were minor inconveniences—what bothered him more was having to grub out a hole in the rear compound while the main wall was under assault. He was missing out on all the fun.

The first tunnels were tight little spaces that ran in parallel lines, their purpose to deduce the proximity of the enemy's location. It wasn't difficult to narrow their search since the earlier firing had cratered the surface and pushed out the subsoil. But time was still required to dig out all the mud and dirt and grit, and when at last the company burrowed into the enemy's tunnel, Thayer found himself in a musty place that reeked of sweat and shit and dirt-covered death.

It was then the soldiers discarded their digging tools and took up arms, and in a tight column they delved into the subterranean passage. Thayer took the fore. Torchlight revealed an earthen passageway whose floor was occasionally layered with duckboards and whose ceiling and sidewalls were revetted with wooden slats and frames. The going was tough; the tunnel was sloped and skewed, and rarely could the men move in a position other than an uncomfortable stoop or crablike crouch.

The lack of air was like a jolt to the lungs, but it wasn't long before the tunnel opened into a larger, breezier cavity, perhaps the size of a minor lord's bedroom. Enemy sappers had underpinned a second section of the wall, and now were propping timbers for a second firing.

Some were wrapping the timbers in pitch-soaked linen, while others were stuffing brushwood and livestock carcasses and other combustibles beneath the woodwork. It was all very filthy work, but Thayer wasn't bothered by the sights or the smells or the congestion of the tunnel, nor was he unmanned by the possibility of a cave-in. With a smile on his face, he lowered a hand to his double-wrap sword belt, and then Bloodless came out to play.

His first victim was lumbering mindlessly along, his face a mask of mud and muck, with only the white sclera of his eyes visible. When he spotted Thayer, he froze and blinked a heavy blink, as though stunned by this new visitor yet too exhausted to react in any meaningful way. It mattered not, since Bloodless did all the talking.

The blade sang a downward sweeping cut that tore through half the man's nose and most of his cheek. The poor bastard fell, soundless as blood streamed down his filthy face, a comingling of dark on dark that appeared as some grisly application of camouflage.

The sappers nearby didn't even take notice. It was almost as if they were deaf-blind automatons beavering away in the dark. Not that it mattered; these men were not known for their close-combat expertise, so when Thayer's company fell upon them, they panicked and spun to flee but found themselves bottlenecked before the egress chute. Sadly, perhaps even a little humorously, they ended up shoving and squeezing one another like shiners in a cask hole, fighting for a way out. The chamber itself began to tremble, as though a collapse were imminent.

Thayer wanted it to collapse. *Yes, yes, YES.* He wanted to feel the helpless agony of pounds upon pounds of dirt crashing on top of him. *Buried alive . . . yes, what a magnificent way to leave this world.* He thought about that as Bloodless whirred and worked, shredding the enemy's fleeing bodies like a razor through rice paper. Torchlight flickered and flashed, highlighting his bloody handiwork. He slashed and stabbed until the bulk of the sappers finally pushed through the chute and escaped down the tunnel beyond. Thayer led his company after them. He wanted them all dead. He wanted the underground area littered with enemy corpses, like a field of trampled wildflowers.

A pair of Hollow soldiers emerged from some unseen alcove, but even their heavy hide shields weren't enough to stop the momentum of the assailants, who bowled them over like twigs in a storm surge. Thayer didn't look back. He continued his bloody charge through the seemingly endless tunnel, and only when he realized the enemy sappers were no longer running did he stop. *What are they doing?* The men were clustered behind a giant appa-ratus, a sort of piston bellows with a large frontal nozzle that was pointed in Thayer's direction. A rather muscular fellow leaned over to pump the piston. Thayer backed up a step. *Oh shit, I think I made a boo-boo. I—*

A great cloud of black smoke burst from the bellows, flooding the entire tunnel. Thayer shouted the retreat—or he tried to, but the air was ripped from his lungs. Next he knew, he was crawling through the blackness on his hands and knees. *They're smoking us out,* he thought. *How bloody rude.* It was a slow-going ordeal, but he and his soldiers eventually snaked their way out of the manmade passages, coughing and wheezing from the oxygen-deprived air.

When the surface rose up to greet him, Thayer dug his black fingers into clumps of grassy earth and inhaled the freshest, most inviting scent in the world. At last he was free of that subterranean nightmare . . . free once more to feel winter's chilly embrace. Anseth was standing over him, hands on his hips, the crescent moon reclining in the sky above his shoulder. The small man gave a disappointed shake of his head, and then he said, "Collapse it all. Bring the entire mine down."

More drudgery in the evening darkness. More backbreaking work, more dirt and filth and musky, irritant fumes. Thayer labored so hard he barely knew where he was. By the gods the enemy could've walked right up to him and he wouldn't even have noticed. After hours of digging and calculating and more digging, they had finally undermined the enemy's tunnels with their own works. The charges being planted were the typical combination of sulfur, charcoal, and saltpeter, mixed in irregular parts to create an effective explosive radius. Once set, Anseth raised a single, soot-covered hand. "Light 'em up."

The explosion was a thing of beauty, a wide-ranging and far-reaching camouflet that brought down the network of enemy tunnels in a shower of mud and wood and subsoil. Thayer's ears rang and his body vibrated as though from an earthquake, but at last it was done. Without sparing a moment, Anseth led the soldiers back to the breach of the inner wall, where the aboveground battle still raged amid the breaking of dawn. Thayer Dal was exhausted, but he never felt more alive.

CHAPTER THIRTY-SEVEN

I t is unwise to employ a direct attack on a city. Such a feat should only be attempted when all other methods of warfare are exhausted. Too many lives will be sacrificed, too much unnecessary destruction will result.

Alarin Athera remembered the day his father had spoken those words to him. He was no more than twenty then, an ambitious young man with a seemingly endless number of tomorrows stretched out before him. Never would he have envisioned himself, some two decades later, embattled against his own brother and mired in the very situation his father had forewarned.

Lasarin Athera was right in what he said, and he was right simply because the Anir were a people of walls. It was in their blood and bones. Ramparts, bulwarks, barriers, stockades—the walls were everywhere, and they were dividing everything from compounds to wards to districts and counties. To attack a city meant one had to overcome these walls, and that was neither a simple nor straightforward task. And yet, Zantherei had found a way. Even though his underground mine had collapsed, the damage to the curtain wall had been done, and now his forces continued to push their way inside.

Once more Alarin was in motion, hobbling up the wide ramp that flanked the main courtyard and rose to the outer wall. An arrow screamed past his head, no more than a handspan away, but Alarin was so exhausted he barely mustered the energy to react. After nearly a dozen trips up and down this ramp, he was no longer sure what was keeping him up. *Probably this cane.* But he couldn't rest, not while the strongpoints above and below were in danger of being overrun. Should they fall to the enemy, the entire city would soon follow.

Armed men were rushing past him in a continuous blur of motion. Defenders, conscripts, taskmen, supplymen, and firefighters —there was little order, and even less logic. The enemy was nowhere and everywhere at once. Through the gap, at the barricade, in the courtyard; perhaps even on this ramp. It was just after sunrise —*and the fighting had started when? Last night?* Alarin was so tired, he could barely discern an hour from a day, or a dawn from a dusk.

A crack in the ramp snagged his cane. Momentum drove him forward, and he stumbled and flailed and nearly toppled over. *How embarrassing. I hope you all saw that.* No one did—or if they had they pretended not to. It was just a cluster of sweaty bodies, rushing up and down and to and fro, shouting, clanging, stomping across stone. Alarin had no guardsmen. They'd fallen behind and became lost in the chaos. It mattered not. He readjusted his cane and carried on, eyes narrowing at the faint metallic squeak of the ankle joint of his wooden leg. *Well, that sound is new.* It must've been a loose catch or hinge, but he had no choice but to ignore it and push on. *Damn it, don't break on me now. This old cripple has much to do.*

The moment he reached the upper level his eyes went to work. Scrutinizing, analyzing, prioritizing, memorizing. In the courtyard below, the enemy was caught in a deathtrap of clogged bodies. Easy targets all, but the hundred or so bowmen positioned along the high inner wall were firing hectically and haphazardly, and this allowed small bands of Hollow soldiers to regroup and return fire, which accounted for the stray arrows whizzing over the ramp. Staff slingers whipped their arms in overhead arcs, throwing darkfire bullets onto the high walls. When the projectiles struck a slab of unprotected stone they immediately began to melt, and teams of firefighters would rush over to smother the flames with tarps or hides treated with cloudfall oil.

A group of Hollow soldiers raised up a spiked board to shield a group of batterers at the inner gate. Alarin responded to that by realigning the archers and redirecting their salvos. Bowstrings twanged and arrows screamed like diving eagles, puncturing feet and hamstrings and calves. The batterers had no choice but to scatter. Alarin then issued orders to reinforce the upper squadrons and replenish the supply lines. That done, he was off again, hobbling down the ramp, back to the inner wall to ensure the breach defenses remained in place.

A grapnel latched onto the outer side of the ramp, startling him. Alarin swung his cane like a polo stick to dislodge it. *That wasn't thrown from the courtyard side—how did it reach over here?* Another landed with a deft *clang,* no more than a yard from Alarin's wooden leg. He gave that one a smack too, but that only deepened the embedment, so he had to bend down—hinge squealing—and give it an earnest yank.

The grapnel fell away, a man cried out, and Alarin continued on. *The enemy is all around me.* His free hand unsheathed the saber on his opposite hip. It felt unexpectedly heavy. *You can still fight. Just because you're a cripple doesn't mean your sword arm doesn't work either.* His pace slowed to a cautious limp. More bodies clogged the ramp, more and more until they grew so thick Alarin had to push his way through. *Goddamn it, move, move, MOVE.*

It happened so suddenly. A Hollow soldier in a gray-black cloak rose over him, curved sword clutched in his upraised hand. Alarin panicked and swung his own blade in a clumsy arc. He didn't feel the impact, but he certainly felt the warm blood splash his face and drip down his eyelids. He pawed the wetness away and watched his foeman's body tumble down the ramp. *By the gods, that was too close. How are they getting those grapnels over here?*

When he reached the second story and looked over the side, the answer came to him.

The barricades and the caltrops and spiked frameworks . . . they were all being torn down and smashed to bits. The Stormhaven defenders who attempted to interfere were being overwhelmed.

Beneath the fluttering of great banners, Alarin saw General Sabriel Soffin, a tall man with a cherubic face who was dressed in a silvery mail that matched his silvery hair. He was barking orders near the breach, telling the men to push the center, to push and push and *push.*

Another Hollow general, the powerful Aldebron Pentagath, was battling nearby, hewing men down with his great battle-axe. *I was a fool to think this would work,* Alarin thought. *Not with such elite generals under Zantherei's banner.* He dispatched all available squadrons to reinforce the center, and then he scanned the bloody havoc for Szathan Mordall. *Where are you, General? Did you fall or flee?* No, he was still there, fighting . . . thank the gods.

Szathan Mordall blasted through the enemy ranks like a rockslide down a mountain, his bloodlust rising with every Hollow soldier slain. Steel blades and stray arrows scraped and pierced his armor, but he absorbed the damage like an impenetrable golem, a vision so frightening it caused his foes to pale and falter. And when a company of reinforcements joined him in defending the center compound, Szathan grew so bold that he glared upon the enemy, slammed the butt of Nightwing on the ground, and roared, *"I AM SZATHAN MORDALL OF SEVEN LAKES. WHO DARES FACE ME?"*

The throng of combatants seemed to fade away, like ghosts dematerializing into an evening mist. Only one man remained: Aldebron Pentagath. Szathan wasn't good with words, so he didn't waste time with greetings.

He charged forward—only to halt midway, in a simple feint to gauge the man's reaction. The wild-haired general didn't flinch or give any ground; he simply twirled the massive axe and gestured Szathan forward. "I respect you, Ogre," he growled. "I will cleave your great big head from your great big shoulders, but I respect you."

Szathan raised his grip on Nightwing's haft and took a single step forward. The ground beneath his booted feet was slick with old sleet and puddles of gore. "I've clashed with greater warriors than you, General. You are nothing to me."

The wild-haired man sneered, spat, and lunged forward, his massive battle-axe screaming as it cut through the air. Szathan moved with the attack, rolling his shoulders and deflecting the blade with his own. *Clang.* His gauntleted hands juddered like a struck gong, but he managed to retaliate with a deft backslash. *Clang.* Somehow the spike of the halberd became stuck in the hollow of the axe-head.

Szathan leaned back to pull it free, but Pentagath's forceful tug drew him closer. The wild-haired general was a bit shorter, but that allowed him to drive his helmet into Szathan's chin, *wham,* the impact so hard it knocked Szathan's own halfhelm askew.

His world became a dizzying place, but Szathan managed to grab hold of the general to prevent a clean follow up strike. He knew Pentagath was an aggressive fighter, but he didn't expect him to be so *strong.*

The two men continued to work at close range, with Szathan adjusting his holds while Pentagath maneuvered to free himself. The wild-haired man's strength seemed to flag for a moment, but then, without warning, he exploded into a full thrashing, like a grouper caught in a net. Szathan couldn't defend the onslaught of arcing windmill strikes, and when one clobbered the side of his halfhelm, just above the eye, his vision blurred and his grip broke. The blows kept coming. *This is bad, this is bad,* Szathan thought. *I have to get out of this.*

He lowered himself to a knee and drove the big man forward, but Pentagath was so quick and so strong, and instead of flailing backward he straightened his posture and grabbed Szathan's hips and flung him aside. The two men finally came apart.

His infighting skills are superior, Szathan thought. *I need to avoid him there.*

Pentagath scooped up his weapon and allowed Szathan to do the same. Both men resumed a fighting stance. "Men speak of your clash with the Mad Wolf," Pentagath growled. "Heard you fought honorably . . . until you lost heart."

"No different from how you fared against him at Howler Pass."

Pentagath's broad face twitched at that. A smattering of blood painted his left cheek, but Szathan could tell it was his own. Around them, soldiers were rushing to and fro, some fighting to escape the fray, others joining the deadlock at the breach.

In any major conflict it was imperative not to focus on one specific object or opponent; instead one needed to detach a part of their senses and observe their surroundings as a whole. And in doing that, Szathan observed a man standing to Pentagath's rearward right . . . a lesser officer by the looks of him. Szathan didn't like the nervous excitability in his eyes, or the way his brandished saber twitched in his hand. *Telling signs,* he mused. *He plans to sucker-strike me. Even I'm smart enough to see that.*

Pentagath came forward once more, but Szathan spun away and thrust his weapon into the chest of the lesser officer, who at the very same moment had tried a lunging stab from the flank. The skewered man was left wobbling for a clumsy moment, before Szathan removed the blade and watched him drop headfirst to the hard flag-stones. Aldebron Pentagath's musclebound frame turned toward the fallen man. "That was my deputy officer."

"Your deputy officer was an honorless wretch," Szathan told him.

Pentagath grumbled under his breath, readjusted his grip on his battle-axe, and thundered forward. But this time Szathan remained on the outside, and after Pentagath overextended his advance, Szathan peppered him with two jabs from the end-spike of his halberd. Pentagath walked through the first, but the second poked him just below the armpit, halting him.

He smiled, but that sort of smile usually meant the blow had hurt. His next attack was a ferocious overhead swing, but Szathan slipped away and returned with a counterstrike that cracked Penta-gath's single lion-faced pauldron and sent broken bits of lamellar to the ground.

The wild-haired general pounded a fist against his armored-plated chest. "*Stop* running from me, Ogre. I promise to make it quick."

Szathan didn't take the bait. He continued to circle the outside, eyes fixed on his opponent yet careful not to lose his footing on the blood-slick stones. *He's frustrated. You can beat this man. Just stay calm and stay on the outside.* Pentagath lunged with an overhead chop, but Szathan backpedaled and retaliated with a thrust that ripped through the tasset of Pentagath's upper thigh.

That made the man grimace. He began cursing at Szathan, calling him a coward and a runner and a lily-livered puss, but before he could say anything more, a man slammed into him from behind, knocking Pentagath to the ground. For a brief moment the supine general looked helpless, limbs reaching skyward like a beetle on its back, but then he righted himself, snatched up his battle-axe, and rose to his feet.

His assailant was the squat, compact, and heavily bearded Gilberon Brehems. *My old friend, you've come to my aid after all. Thank the gods.* Brehems offered a friendly but wan smile to Szathan, as if they had just shared their last tankard of mead together. That done, he turned back to Pentagath. "That's my comrade you're insulting."

Pentagath scowled in response. To his left, a tall man in silvery armor approached amid the waving of gray-black banners. This man was General Sabriel Soffin. His jowls were a little heavier and his hair a bit grayer than Szathan remembered, but his posture and bearing were as stern as ever for a man well into his fifties.

Szathan did not want to fight him. After all, it was Sabriel who had Demien Mordall buried with honors, and it was Sabriel who subsequently had Demien's son and the Imperial Seal smuggled out to Szathan. Were it not for him, Silas Mordall would still be a mute little nobody.

Aldebron Pentagath pointed the head of his axe at Brehems, but when he spoke it was directed at General Soffin. "I want this one, the traitor. Ogre Mordall is yours."

Sabriel Soffin gave a nod. His eyes locked onto Szathan's but he didn't speak. Nearby, a small crowd of soldiers couldn't help but observe, despite the constant push and pull of battle. In the rear, a rallying warband of Vaskultans were ripping through the Hollow left, with the powerful Severak Bonesplitter leading the bloody charge. The dead lay all around him: crumbled in heaps on the ground, impaled on framework spikes, or slumped over woodwork like broken string-puppets. The scent of darkfire smoke was revolting to the nose, an acrid, almost bludgeoning odor.

Szathan fixed his gaze on Sabriel Soffin. "I won't stand aside for you, General."

"I don't expect you to. But I'm too old to rebel. And I won't put aside military duty for personal sentiment."

"I don't expect you to." Szathan raised Nightwing to a readying position. "Should I fall to your hand, please honor me like you honored my brother."

It was a simple request, but for some reason it made General Sabriel Soffin hesitate. That was peculiar. *When Demien died you had him interred near our home village of Seven Lakes. Is that not what you said to me?* Szathan repeated the question aloud, not once, but twice before Sabriel finally nodded and said, "Like I honored your brother."

With that, their arms clashed, and the siege carried on.

CHAPTER THIRTY-EIGHT

"Y ou're not just a little unbalanced," Physician Penry said. "You truly are frog-hopping mad."

Thayer Dal grinned a devilish grin as his fingers continued to work. His armor had been removed and he was wearing only a ragged gray loincloth, and when he applied the cloudfall oil he did it topically and liberally, all over his body. The sensation was strange—a tingly, itchy, almost burning numbness, like an herbal compress of extra-potent eucalyptus. Penry continued watching him for a long moment, then his old, oval head turned to peek out of the soldier's alcove, where the battle thundered in the central compound. "You will accomplish nothing," the physician said at length. "Apart from an agonizing death."

Thayer reached down to scoop up the oversized robe at his feet. The garment was rough to the touch, the fabric homespun and coarse. He rose from his stool and slipped it on, fastening it closed with a sash at the waist. "These are Hollow soldiers. Men of little fear, men who earned their bruises and blades at the Pit. To turn men of such high talent, extreme measures must be taken."

"Lighting yourself on fire and throwing yourself at the enemy is not what I would call 'extreme measures.'"

"The cloudfall oil prevented our main fortifications from melting, so I reckon it will do the same for me."

Penry jabbed a finger at the nearest wall. "That's stone and mortar and dirt. You're a mortal man of flesh and bones."

"Does it matter? It should still protect, no?"

The physician gave a bewildered shrug. He was usually a calm and composed fellow, but the clash in the central compound was clearly pulling at his nerves. His head kept flicking in that direction, his owlish face taut with distress. "To me it seems a senseless sacrifice," he said. "The soldiers will not lose heart and run, not with Aldebron Pentagath as their leader."

"That's why Aldebron Pentagath is my target. If I turn him, the battle is won."

"But why is igniting yourself the only way to do that?"

Thayer took a moment to adjust the fit and fall of his black cloak. The fabric itched his skin, but he didn't want to scratch for fear of smudging the oil. "As a child Aldebron Pentagath was wild and unruly, so his father warned that all children who misbehaved would be burned alive by a demonic spirit called the Firewalker. Supposedly, the tale frightened him straight into obedience."

"That was a long time ago, and he's not a child anymore. How did you come upon this story?"

"When you're a famous hero of the realm like Aldebron Pentagath, it's difficult to hide your past." He flashed a smile that was probably more unnerving than comforting. "And you're right, he's not a child anymore, obviously. But I believe that somewhere inside him is that same little boy who still carries that same fear. I intend to use that against him."

"And if it doesn't work," Penry said, "what then?"

"I suppose I'll die."

Penry frowned. "What you're planning to do here . . . it's

lunacy. You'd be of much more use at the barricade, fighting beside General Szathan Mordall and his defending host."

"Maybe." Thayer stood tall and spread his arms like a black-feathered roc, allowing the tatty sleeves to hang low and loose. His breathing came in short ragged pulls, but he wasn't afraid—no, he heard the call of the void, and it was exhilarating. "Now get on with it, my rotund little friend. Light the darkfire and set my robe ablaze."

Physician Penry wore a deep frown, but in the end, he gathered his equipment and did as he was told.

From the ramp's upper slope Alarin watched the battle heave and hurl like an unrelenting storm. The bulk of the Stormhaven defenders had fallen into disarray, with each armed unit forced to fight through injury and congestion and impaired vision.

This was the truest test of a man's mettle; to endure in this haze of violence required a level of equanimity and durability that not all possessed. Still, Alarin did not lose faith. These were disciplined and determined soldiers, and they were not about to give up their city. No man fought with more courage than the man whose back was against the wall.

Everywhere one turned, everywhere one looked—there was only violence. Men were being hacked and skewered and thrown upon spiked blockades and broken brickwork. Bodies appeared and vanished in a welter of steel and blood. Alarin watched a soldier ram a foeman's head into a stone wall, then that soldier collapsed when an arrow pierced his calf. A few paces away, a downed Hollow officer was using a knife with a broken blade to stab the boots of passersby. And near to that, a man had half his face sheared off by an axe. Alarin winced at that, then again when he saw an armored soldier plunge from the sky and crash down upon a broken barricade. *Where the hell did you come from?* A dust-cloud immediately swallowed the man up, removing him from sight.

Alarin's eyes shifted to the massive Szathan Mordall, who was engaged in single combat against the silver-haired General Sabriel Soffin. Steel kissed and poked and prodded, and for every stab and strike of Soffin's long-handled saber, Szathan's halberd was there to deflect and counterstrike.

Up-slash, down-slash, overhead cut—their blades sang in harmonic dissonance, like twin serpents in a ritualistic dance. Nearby, the wild-haired Aldebron Pentagath fought with far less grace. He drove his great axe upon Szathan's old deputy, Gilberon Brehems, and while the shorter man was quick to evade and parry, Pentagath was an unrelenting and untiring beast. When a blow from his axe haft caused Brehems to stumble back, Pentagath gave chase and barreled into him like an angry bull.

Alarin tensed; he'd never seen someone lift such a rock-solid man like Gilberon Brehems off his feet with such ease. Pentagath even carried him a few steps before throwing him down. Brehems landed hard and scrambled to protect himself, but he was hurt and confused and vulnerable. Pentagath stepped forward to deliver a fatal blow, but Szathan rushed over to intercept, and now he was alone and squaring off against two of the Hollow's finest generals, Aldebron Pentagath and Sabriel Soffin.

This is a fight he can't win, Alarin thought. He turned and snapped orders at anyone nearby, anyone he could see, or grab hold of. "Help him, help your commander." But the soldiers either ignored him or wrenched free of his grasp and ignored him, and the few that did acknowledge him looked unwilling to intervene. *Damn it all, I must do this myself.* He burst into movement, limping down the ramp while silently cursing himself and his soldiers. Upon reaching the bottom, he made a sharp turnabout to face the tangle of broken barricades and bloody corpses. The carnage hit him like a metalsmith's mallet.

Don't be discouraged. You were once a great general . . . a man of power and prestige and principle. You must *be that man again.* He absently lifted his saber and took a long look at it, studying the carved Sadralen pommel, the fine silvery inlay, and the dressing of blood from its earlier labors. It was a weapon he once treasured, but after years of disuse and neglect it now felt alien to him.

He gave a sigh, then lowered the blade. All around him was an excess of gore, a macabre vision of dismembered limbs and loose entrails and dashed brains. He could hear the tiny, intimate nuances of battle: the low wheezes of the wounded, the withered groans of the dying, and the grating of steel as it pushed through mail and entered flesh. He could hear it all, could see it all, and without warning his thoughts began to scream at him: *You can't do this—are you insane? You're a goddamn cripple. You can't fight, you're just going to get yourself killed. Do you understand? You're going to—*

Something rushed past him. It came from behind, perhaps from the second or third arched gateway beneath the ramp. It moved so swiftly Alarin barely saw it, and when he did manage a look, he couldn't believe *what* he saw. *A great dark . . . what?* It appeared to be a robed figure engulfed in black fire, a frightful yet mesmerizing sight, like some strange aberration of sorcery. All Alarin could do was stand there, mouth agape, while this figure charged the enemy horde like a boulder down a hill.

Hollow soldiers spread out at once, all save one unfortunate victim who was too slow to react. A black-flamed hand seized him by the throat. The soldier reached up to free himself, but his gauntleted hands melted like molten cheese, and so did his neck.

For a split moment Alarin caught a vision of his head bobbing without any muscles to support it, then the soldier dropped like a stone, *boom,* smacking the ground like a piece of rotten fruit. No one spoke, just wide eyes and trembling lips all around. Then the shadow-thing turned, a quick movement, to focus on its next target: Aldebron Pentagath.

The wild-haired general's face turned pale as a cloud. He took one look at the melted corpse of his fellow soldier, then another at the black-flamed figure . . . and then he bolted. The other soldiers followed at once, and suddenly the world became a stampede of men, with boots stomping and armor clanging and voices screaming for protection from the gods.

Greenhorns and veterans, conscripts and crack troops, it mattered not. They all fled. Alarin watched, dumbfounded. *They're breaking . . . I don't believe it, they're breaking.* It was an army of fleeing fools, each shoving and squeezing their way out of the breach, until all that remained were the defenders and the dead and all the blood and smoke that stood in between.

And just like that, the siege of Stormhaven was ended.

CHAPTER THIRTY-NINE

By twilight's approach, the enemy train was retreating toward the southwest horizon, leaving the city of Stormhaven in a bereaved and battle-weary silence. The four frontal towers had all suffered extensive damage: Tower Rainfell with its broken brickwork and merlons, Tower Snowblind with its collapsed turrets, Tower Thunderstone with its shredded sand-and-slurry base, and Tower Tempest with its gutted facade and smashed parapet. The breach of the curtain wall exposed the structure's inner earthworks, but just minutes after the battle's end saw stone masons and laborers being assigned for repairs.

Ansetheral Athera hadn't seen the catalyst to the enemy's break, but both reports and rumors spoke of a great black fireball that charged into the fray and melted every Hollow soldier it touched. Anseth was skeptical of course, but whatever it was, it had succeeded in running off not only the foot soldiers, but the great and powerful generals Aldebron Pentagath and Sabriel Soffin. Now with all the stories being passed around, Anseth was curious about what truly happened, but he would have to wait until he spoke to Alarin and heard the official reports.

Severak Bonesplitter found him on the wall-walks near the partially destroyed Tower Tempest. Anseth didn't fully turn to greet the big Vaskultan commander, though he could tell the man was nursing an injury by his slow and unsteady gait. The two spoke casually for a time, first about the darkfire, then about the speculation surrounding the enemy's retreat, and lastly about the details of the siege defense. When that was finished, Anseth asked about Kirik.

"He'll be fine," Severak said. "Got his head bashed good, but all he needs is a few days of rest and some recuperative herbs. I'd rather one of our shamans tend to him, but that plump little pale man seems capable enough."

"Physician Penry is capable indeed," Anseth said with a nod. A brief silence followed, and Anseth's gaze drifted off to observe the Anirian retrievers, rugged men who were hard at work picking up weapons and armor and dead Stormhaven soldiers. Of the Vaskultans, they were left where they'd fallen as customs dictated—but that didn't sit well with Anseth. Not here, not on this hard stone. "I want you to organize a hauling crew to carry our fallen brothers to the foot of the mountain."

Severak protested at once. "Lord, such an action defies the precepts of our—"

Anseth cut him off. "What would you have me do? Leave them lying here like discarded playthings, to decompose fifty feet above the ground? They belong on the soil and sand, to be claimed by the Landforger below and the Skybringer above."

Severak didn't offer a reply, so Anseth continued speaking. "Be sure to keep the dead in their final anatomical positions, so they remain pure and unspoiled. And don't forget to post sentries. Looters and scavengers are drawn to our dead like flies on rot."

Once more, Severak didn't reply, so after a quiet moment Anseth had assumed the big Vaskultan had withdrawn. But the moment Anseth himself started to walk away, Severak spoke. "You off somewhere, lord?"

"Scouts reported a wounded Hollow officer hiding out in the northwest forest. A Sijian, no less."

There was a pause. "I'll come with you."

"No." Anseth wasn't sure how to express his desire to do this alone. There was no accurate Vaskultan word in that specific context. The closest was *rekarei*, which meant alone—but alone by circumstance, not by choice. Vaskultan people were as socially interwoven as their fabrics; there was no other way to survive the harsh north. "I just . . . I need to walk."

"To walk?"

Anseth finally turned to meet his commander's eye. The big man looked battered and drained, his black longcoat ripped at the shoulder and ratty about the edges. He had a dried laceration on his cheek and a smaller cut along the jaw, but it was the dark stain beneath the fabric of his left shoulder that held Anseth's attention. He gestured to it before speaking. "The blood is fresh, better have it rewrapped."

Severak looked down and touched the wound, coming away with red-stained fingertips. He used the cuff of his longcoat as a wipe, and with that, he bowed his head and withdrew.

Anseth did a lot of walking that night. His injuries had all been minor and above the waist—a scraped forearm, a bruised rib, a strained shoulder cuff—so he was grateful to walk without much constraint. And as he walked, his eyes drifted away from the destruction and up to the midnight slate sky. It was a lonely sky, pockmarked by a smattering of dark clouds that edged the glimmering gibbous moon. Anseth sighed when he looked back down. The aftermath of battle often carried a silent, almost dreamlike aura, and even though the adrenaline and fear and bloodlust had all faded, the blasts and blows and shouts were still fresh in the mind. It was a strange, almost stifling transition, and one that Anseth never seemed to get used to.

He broke away from the wall and moved through the outer suburban dwellings. Torches flickered like tiny fireflies, and the scouts and sentries who carried them were busy surveying the land and shooing away trespassers.

To Anseth, they neither stopped him nor spoke a word, and so he continued west along the periphery of the open field, where the Hollow besiegers had hastily decamped. The remains of their visit were obvious and plentiful: smashed mangonel and ballista parts, burnt and broken soldier tents, dead horses, dead hounds, dead men. Anseth drew his backsword to scare off a bare-chested little man who was stripping the horseshoes off a fallen charger, then he hissed loudly to drive an overly inquisitive owl into flight.

The debris and destruction lessened as Anseth moved farther west, and soon a stretch of untouched wilderness dominated his view. Clusters of spruce and fir and the occasional cypress rose like mammoth gray fingers, their crowns glistening under the moon's angelic glow. It was a beautiful and pristine sight—but Anseth was more focused on the trail of blood along the low shrubs. He followed it through the dark of the forest to find a wounded Sijian man seated against a rotted-out stump. He was a Hollow officer by the look of his uniform and discarded helm, but his skin was dark, and his battledress was of an unusual reddish hue, like the embers of a dying fire. Anseth decided to observe from the shadows for a time, before circling around and approaching from the north.

At the rustle of leaflitter the man lifted his head weakly, and when his eyes locked onto Anseth's he smiled feebly. He wasn't a handsome man, but a man of narrow, shrew-like features beneath a messy mop of head hair. A glop of fresh blood covered his left ear, and a band of purple welts covered his upper left cheek. His hand was bruised too, and with it he began searching through the nearby grasses for his discarded war hammer. Anseth walked over and kicked the weapon away, and the dark-skinned fellow offered a quirky half-shrug. "Oh shit, ah, you got me. I was never particularly good with that thing anyhow."

"You're Nanjen, I reckon."

He nodded, sharp eyes squinting. "And who might you be? Some pesky little barbarian rogue with a knack for the Anirian tongue. You *are* one of those barbarians, are you not? You're dressed like one, but I didn't know they recruited runts." His laugh was more of a fizzled cough.

Anseth didn't like the way he said that. Reminded him too much of the cruel Dariok. But he didn't act on his irritation; no, instead he glanced about the area, making certain they were alone. Once satisfied, his eyes settled back on the wounded Sijian. "Your darkfire failed."

He grunted. "Yeah, so, what are you waiting for? Bind my wrists, haul me in, I'm your captive, am I not? I'm a rather important fellow, you see, director general of the west and second advisor of defense to Emperor Zantherei Athera himself. So yeah, there are poems about me."

Anseth looked around once more. "Yet here you are, abandoned and alone."

"I brought shame upon the heavenly house, this I know." He spoke in an off-beat manner, as if everything he said was of minor importance. "But a single loss in war should not determine the loss of one's head, should it?"

"With Zantherei, you're only given one chance."

The man spat. "Well, aren't you the priceless fucking scholar. Who are you to be so brazen, as to pretend to be privy to the ways of my lord and emperor?"

Anseth glared at the man. "Zantherei is my brother." His hand reached down to unsheathe the dagger from his belt.

"*Wait*." The man held up a dark hand; thin strands of grass were stuck to his fingers. "Wait, wait, wait. *Please*. Are you truly His Majesty's brother? You do look a little too pale to be a northman . . . and you speak the Anirian tongue exceedingly well." His eyes grew larger, as if touched by a sudden epiphany. "Forgive my manners. If you are truly the brother, then perhaps you can help me. We can help each other."

"I will help you . . . into the next life." A gloved hand seized the hair at the back of Nanjen's head. The man squealed, arms flailing clumsily, eyes impossibly wide. Anseth gave a good yank to hold him still, and then he took a moment to steady his own hand and swallow the lump in his throat. "I'm sorry," he uttered, then his blade ripped across the man's throat, opening the dark skin in a burst of bright red. From Nanjen's lips there was a long tremulous groan, and when his eyes dulled and his mouth slackened, Anseth released his grip and watched the man fall face-first to the leaflitter. Anseth spent a few moments over the corpse, wiping the blood from his blade with the edge of his longcoat. That done, he rose and exited the forest.

The night had grown chillier, as if suddenly aware of the cold-blooded act Anseth had just committed. The moon too—it hovered closer and larger, like a great observing eye, and the wind puffed in stern wisps, pushing Anseth's long black hair into his eyes. *I need a bath,* he thought wearily. *Yes, a bath, a hot meal, and perhaps a companion for the night. It's been too long since my wife left this world, and I grow tired of being alone.* He looked down at his gloved hands. Were they even capable of tenderness anymore? He wasn't sure. *Nine years of waiting and hoping . . . and for what? To come home to nothing but deceit and despair and death.*

He heard a sound—a sudden whistle of wind—and next he knew a spell of weakness had overcome him. Not the general weakness that one experiences after the moil of battle, but an urgent one, a forceful pulsation in his chest. He looked down. An arrow shaft protruded from his midsection, dug in through the flesh between the lower ribs. His hand rose to touch the fletching, but then he faltered and resigned to stare in disbelief. *When did this happen? H-how did I not see this?* He wondered if Nanjen had somehow stabbed him before he died—but no, that wasn't possible. The man didn't have an arrow.

No . . . this just happened. A small ring of blood formed around the puncture, staining his Vaskultan garb. *I need to sit.* He dropped onto his rump, drawing ragged breaths, one after another, like an overworked boar. *I don't understand . . . how did this happen?* Through blurred vision and the blurriness of night, he glimpsed a shadowy smudge approaching from the far-off fields. Then Anseth immediately knew. *I was shot by a sniper . . . and this sniper is coming to finish me off. Ugh, I'm too weak to run, but I can try to buy myself some time.* He leaned over and wiped the blood from his midsection onto his lips and inside his mouth, and then he waited.

It seemed forever before that smudge became the figure of a man, and though small of build, he walked with the confidence of someone much larger. Anseth saw him wrapped in what appeared to be a Vaskultan longcoat, though the darkness made it difficult to tell. The man spoke while sauntering closer. "Wow, look at that shot." His voice was bright and boastful and tinged with mock disbelief. "Over one hundred yards away and . . . *thunk,* right in the lung. What remarkable precision that was." He stopped and stood over Anseth, his face hidden in shadow. "Did you see that shot? Of course you didn't . . . but you *damn* well felt it."

Anseth deliberately coughed, spraying flecks of blood. "Do I know you?"

The man snickered. "Told you I'd come back."

It was then Anseth recognized the assailant's voice. *Jakken.* Anger rose like bile in Anseth's throat. He tried to rise, but his legs were like two blocks of jelly. He ended up staggering and stumbling around like a calf on ice before falling back down. *My dagger, where's my dagger?* It was no longer in his hand. He reached for his backsword, but Jakken yanked it from his sheath and tossed it into the brush. Then he made a *tsk-tsk* sound.

"Where's your mighty bondsman? Oh no, don't say he fell at the siege." He bent down and put a hand on Anseth's chest. "I'll take this now." With a yank the Earthstone talisman broke free of its cord. Anseth gave a low groan. He tried to take the object back, but his arm was too weak to make an earnest attempt. Jakken seemed amused by that. "Don't strain yourself, lord. I struck a vital lung, I can tell by the blood in your mouth. I should let you suffer here in the grass until your last breath, but I've got people to return to. The stink of the south has clung to me for far too long." His knife glimmered in the moonlight. "Lie still, and let it come quick." He leaned forward.

I'm going to die, Anseth thought. Well, a thousand thoughts came to his head, and it seemed he had a thousand moments to think them all. But one persistent thought just wouldn't leave his mind. *I'm going to die, and all my dreams and desires and everything I've ever wanted will die with me.*

But the blade never struck—no, instead a series of nearby shouts stole Jakken's attention, and without warning he cursed and shoved Anseth aside and bolted. The man's footfalls rustled through the undergrowth before fading into quiet. Anseth remained on his back, looking up at the tangle of black branches overhead. At length he turned his head to the side, then swept the hair from his eyes. He could hear the Vaskultans rushing to his aid, could hear Severak calling his name from the fore. Next he knew, the big commander was kneeling at his side, studying the wound and calling for a shaman.

"It was Jakken," Anseth grunted, then made a point to wipe the blood from his mouth. "It hurts like hell, but it's not a mortal wound. See?"

Severak's expression softened with relief. "Shrewd thinking, lord. I'm sending a company after him."

"*Don't*," Anseth growled. "He stole *my* Earthstone, and he must die by *my* hand."

BOOK V: RETRIBUTION

CHAPTER FORTY

Miriana Athera had visited Aster Falls during her dark days as a traveling courtesan, so there were few surprises when she returned to this bright-eyed and bustling port city. It was a place known for its proud sea traders and uppity marketplace and grand interlacement of canals and bridges and stone-paved streets.

The waterways were crowded with slow-moving flatboats and gentle sampans and heavier barge-crafts, while a constant hum of activity from burly seamen and surly deckhands rose from wharf and dockside. The air was rich and ripe and briny, and the waterfront boardwalks and promenades were warm and welcome in these early days of spring. Gray-winged gulls surveyed the passersby atop stout wooden beams, while small brown pipers bathed themselves in sandy curbside pools. In merchant shops, sea crabs clacked inside half barrels and holding tanks, ready to be sold for supper.

It amazed her to see just how cheerful and courteous the civilians were. Sellers and stallholders and shoppers—they all had a certain charm in their voice, a certain zest in their step. Maybe it was the feeling of early spring, a feeling of rebirth and renewal that was as evocative as it was intoxicating. But once Miriana's escort took her beyond the main district walls, she found herself surrounded by the same snobbish palatial officials that one might find in any city. Still, to her, an unknown traveler, they were pleasant enough, although to Seric they groveled like hungry old mutts, clinging to his side and flattering him with unnecessary praise.

Miriana found it all mildly amusing. Admittedly, for the first time in a long while, she felt safe. *Safe . . . with Seric Dyre. Or is he King Seric Dyre now?* But uncrowned king or not, he was quite receptive to her needs.

Upon the first night of her arrival, Seric had arranged for her a private chamber in a secluded wing of the main palace. It was a rather luxurious little suite, walls bedecked with expensive arras and elegant plaques and embossed mirrors, while the floor-space was decorated with silk screens and lacquered basketry and twin couches adorned with floral antimacassars. A silk-and-down bed sat against the north wall, surrounded by a fine onyx washbasin and stacks of fish-scale boxes and clamshell trays, most inlaid with mother-of-pearl.

Such finery was enough to make her heart sing, but when she opened the ceruse oak wardrobe, she nearly wept with bliss. Outer robes and inner robes and blouses and skirts of all fabrics and shapes and cuts. She spent a long moment thinking about what she might wear in the following days, but for now she chose a simple linen robe for comfort.

A lone attendant delivered a hot dish of pork bits and bean curds. Miriana accepted the fare before sending the meek little lady out. Despite her hunger she only managed to eat half the portion, but the tart hackberry wine was downed in full. When she was good and tipsy and brave, she stood up and examined her nose in the suspended wall mirror.

It was still the same busted thing she'd come to despise, but at least the swelling was long gone, and the crookedness was no longer *that* noticeable. And her olfactory and gustatory senses had returned in full. She ran her fingers through strands of oily black hair. She needed another bath, but she opted for a quick scrub in the washbasin instead.

When that was done, she opened the bedcurtain and crawled into the coverlets. Her eyes closed without any effort, and she slept through sunlight and darkness and all the lost moments in between. When she awoke, she thought she was back in that nasty prison cell, but then she felt the silk fabric and exhaled in relief. She slept some more before rising to break her fast and visit the privy, and while urinating she wondered just how much time had passed. She returned to the chamber and from the wardrobe she chose a lightly feathered garment with short blue sleeves and ruffled shoulders, which she complemented with coiled silver armlets and openwork hairpins that allowed her to up-style her hair in a loosely braided bun.

Seric came to her early in the evening. He was dressed in black woolen trousers and an earthen dark tunic that brought out the green of his eyes. Of his face he looked as comely as ever, but of his temperament he seemed a bit restless, disjointed, impatient even. His posture was a little slacker, as if his burden had grown considerably these past few months. *Is this the same man who once so eloquently charted the course of the realm?* He was walking around the room, fiddling with things, all while absently asking if her accommodations were adequate, if this or that or whatever mindless little comfort was acceptable to her.

She said it was fine, everything was fine, and they talked for a while longer, small, insignificant words. But when he tried to deepen the conversation, she would steer it another way, but somehow, it would always wend its way back to topics of higher importance.

"My spies just reported—"

She cut him off. "Seric, I don't wish to discuss it. Not now."

"Forgive me, but you need to know. Zantherei was repulsed at Stormhaven. The darkfire failed him, his sappers failed him, and the Sijian sorcerer Nanjen was found in the forest with his throat slit." His tone turned softer, almost pacifying. "Your husband's no longer a threat."

"My husband will always be a threat," she shot back, but then she was silent for a long moment. "I should've done what you had asked of me. Back at the Hollow, I should've killed him with the Mists of Midnight poison." *I tried, but I couldn't . . . I was too weak. I thought I was strong, but I was weak.*

Seric came to stand before her. Closer, she could see the hollowness of his cheeks, both a shade lighter than their usual olivine hue. His eyes held a certain longing, deep like the gaze of a lovelorn hermit. Miriana had trouble meeting those eyes. *I wonder what I must look like to him.* He tried to touch her hand, but she pulled back. If he were insulted by that he didn't show it. "My lady, I . . ."

She raised a finger to silence him. What was there to be said? Miriana didn't want to hear some lackluster explanation as to why Seric did what he did. She certainly didn't want to hear an apology. "That little scheme you played with Raas Dragath . . . you betrayed me. You betrayed the capital."

"As did you."

She didn't expect such a bold reply. As much as she'd distanced herself from her old life of imperial power, she was still accustomed to responses that came with forethought and finesse, neither challenging nor questioning her. Perhaps it was these luxurious accommodations that brought back her old mindset. "I did what I had to do to survive."

"As did I."

She should've let that go, but it was too offensive to leave untouched. "What you did was *only* to satisfy your own unremitting ambition."

"As did you."

"*Stop* doing that."

"It's true, my lady. Fault me for my ambition, fine, I will accept the blame for that. But don't reprove me while turning a blind eye to yourself. It's hypocrisy, my lady, don't you see that? Yes, you left to survive, but you also left to find a way back to power and privilege. Unfortunately, seeking refuge with Raas Dragath wasn't the most sensible choice."

She offered her meanest mug. "And I suppose you think you were the better option? You must know I can never trust you again."

His next words were spoken without a drop of wryness. "You're trusting me now."

Because I am desperate, she almost blurted, but wisely held her tongue. Another bout of silence. She shifted uncomfortably in her fancy floral seat. Seric was looking at her oddly, his green eyes almost probing her likeness, as though she had food smeared on her face and he was unsure how to tell her. "You've changed," he said at last.

She took offense to that. *Is he talking about my appearance?* She demanded that he look elsewhere, but he didn't obey. "Why? You look as beautiful as ever."

A sudden crest of emotion came over her, eyes blinking and burning as if ready to burst into tears. *He still cares for me.* Still, it pained her to hear Seric's compliment, simply because it wasn't true. *I'm not the same strong woman I was before.* For some reason she told him how her charms didn't work on Raas Dragath, but he only smiled—he had such a warm smile—and said, "Your beauty is unchanged."

He tried again to touch her, this time her cheek, but again she pulled back. His hand remained in the air for a moment, but instead of bringing it down, he withdrew it to untie his silk neckerchief, letting it fall to the floor. The scar on his neck was jagged and rather unsightly, but Seric didn't seem self-conscious about it. "See? We all bear reminders of the past."

Miriana looked down. She didn't reply.

"You should've come to me sooner." His voice was steady, unfazed. "I understand why you didn't, but you should've. If you had"—a forefinger rose to touch the bridge of his nose—"this could've been prevented."

"*This,*" she shot back, "wasn't from Raas Dragath. This happened not a day's ride from the capital."

"What of your escort? Tell me you had an escort."

She shook her head. "Too great a risk. I traveled only with Cyrille Vileron."

Seric never liked Vileron, and his face made that plain. "Sounds like he didn't fulfill his oath as a protector."

That made her angry. "He was a fine protector, far more capable than any other man, including you, Seric."

Her mocking tone made Seric shrink a bit. *Good,* she thought, *you deserve to be mocked.* But when Seric finally spoke again, his voice was relaxed. "Well, where is the gallant protector now?"

"Raas Dragath cut off his head."

Seric took a moment to absorb that tidbit, then he leaned over and poured himself another goblet of wine. He didn't drink. "Raas Dragath too is dead. Your husband had his head paraded before Stormhaven's walls, up and down like a vendor peddling a meat-stick. Serpenthold lies in a heap of melted stone and darkfire ashes. The Redland forces have all been absorbed, save the traitors and defectors who have been put to the axe. The borderlands cities south of the Agate Mountains down to the Azure have since tendered their allegiance to the capital, but upon Zantherei's recent defeat, public opinion has swayed a bit." That made him chuckle. "Amusing, the minds of the common-ers, don't you think? They only love you when you're the victor." He paused, and this time he did take that drink. "Anyway, Lord Boris Balim of Willowsea and the Black Rend of Lakewood have openly criticized Emperor Zantherei, and the southern cities of Sundark and Sandstead are currently mired in indecision."

"You intend to win those cities and place them under your banner?"

It was clear that Seric wanted to, but something was inhibiting that. "I can't, not now, not with the Thunder of the North and his barbarian brother holding the eastern heartland. Alarin's bold siege defense has only further cemented his power and brightened his standing, which of course will pass to that talking brat who wears the Imperial Seal. Fools and followers are already trickling in to crook the knee to the crippled lord and his boy emperor." Seric frowned. "And here I am, stuck between two warring brothers in the north. Alarin Athera is truly a thorn in my rump. And Zantherei, well, I'd wager retaliation is a remote notion with the heavy casualties he's suffered."

Miriana's gaze lowered to the floor tiles. She couldn't help but think about all she had seen and done; from the day she fled the capital to her frantic escape from the burning Serpenthold. When at last she spoke her voice was small, almost a whisper. "If Zantherei finds out I'm here . . ." Her mouth remained open, but she said no more.

Seric's voice softened, became tender. "I will protect you, my lady."

He still cares about me. She told him thank you, that it was fine, that she was strong, but the truth was, she felt weaker than ever. After all she'd gone through, after all her trials and torments and tribulations, she expected to have gained a greater degree of toughness—but no, quite the opposite was true. She felt frail, beaten, overwhelmed by the mere thought of her past. And not just the journey from the capital to the Redlands, but everything from her early days as a mistreated courtesan to her arduous rise to sovereignty. If she were forced to do it all again, she would've chosen a different path.

There was a knock at the door. Three hard raps followed by a woman's inquisitive voice. Seric gave a start, his face reddening just a touch. His eyes were still attached to Miriana, but his hands began rubbing down the length of his trousers, up and down, either irritably or nervously—or perhaps both. "Forgive me," he whispered, then moved to open the door.

There was a bit of talk in hushed tones, a bit of arguing, some objecting, and even a few witticisms on Seric's part. Miriana couldn't hear all of what was being said, but when she readjusted her position and peered through the semi-open doorway, she saw the same tall and shapely woman who had confronted her when she'd first reunited with Seric.

The woman was dressed in a black studded blouse and gray waist skirt, and while she was dark-haired like Miriana, her face was a bit too pointy and asymmetrical to be considered handsome. *You again . . . who are you?* It was obvious that she was a courtesan of some kind—Miriana could tell just by her proud carriage and sensual mannerisms. And this courtesan, while arguing with Seric, was stealing looks inside the room, and her eyes narrowed to dagger-points when they met Miriana's.

At length, Seric's voice rose to a jarring volume, and with the turn of his wrist the door slammed shut. *Boom.* Silence returned, but this time it was awkward and uncomfortable, and when Seric walked back to Miriana, his head was lowered, and his shoulders were slumped. Without a word, he sat down.

It was a long moment before Miriana spoke. "I see you still haven't quit your whores."

Seric's face twitched. "She's nothing to me. Just a harpy with claws too big for her hands. You needn't be concerned."

"I never said I was concerned." *Am I supposed to care? To feel a pang of jealousy? You and I shared a dalliance, nothing more.*

Miriana wanted to believe that. She truly did. *I know how you are, Seric, ambition over loyalty, self-preservation over goodwill. I know that because I was cut from the same silk cloth.*

"My lady, I know as a half-Zhoul I can never make a legitimate claim to the imperial throne, but I do seek to reunite the realm. To clear it of all the ill-suited functionaries and to snuff out all the bad blood. I would like to do it with you beside me. Give me your hand and swear to me your fealty, and you will rule once more."

He tried once more to take her hand, but she didn't allow it. "Rule beside a mongrel king? Seric, you are mad to bestow such an exalted title upon yourself."

"My father was a king—my birth father."

"A king of Zhouls. Barbarians."

"A king is a king. Race or lineage matters not." He gave a frustrated sigh. "We live in a time in which warlords call themselves emperors without any ties to the royal house. Why bother adhering to outmoded policies now? True boldness doesn't consider morality before it takes action. Do you remember Emperor Tyvan of the Ruan dynasty? A lowborn man tainted with Cothil blood, and yet he ruled briefly during the breaking of the four kingdoms. My lady, I have what is required of a ruler. Strength, cunning, wisdom, and decisiveness. Do you not see how my city flourishes? Stand with me and I promise you will—"

There was another knock at the door. Seric gave a grunt, then rose and saw to it. To Miriana's surprise, it wasn't the same courtesan, but a military officer, a tall and fleshless man with sharp eyes and sharper features. He spoke to Seric briefly and in a hushed voice, before the door slowly closed and Seric returned to Miriana. This time he had a bit of vim in his step, a vigor that prevented him from sitting. "I have to go. My son has returned to me. He just passed through the city gates." He looked even comelier when he smiled.

"Go on then. We'll talk later."

He nodded his thanks. "You're safe here, Mir. You do feel safe, don't you?"

"I do." It was the truth.

He nodded once more, satisfied. "Are you in need of anything? A softer quilt, some tidbits, a massage perhaps? We have plenty of experienced hands here. They can touch you the way you like, the way that Sijian girl used to touch you."

"I don't want to be touched in any way. I just want to see my brother. Has he arrived yet?"

"By tomorrow, my lady, his escort is still en route."

"I pray he makes it, Seric. I'm aware you two aren't the fondest of friends."

"Vylas served me well during my campaign in Silver Leaf. I bear him no ill-will."

Miriana gave a nod, and with that, Seric turned and exited the chamber. Alone again, she doffed her fancy clothes and crawled back into bed. It was so quiet only her own breathing could be heard, a soft and light susurrus, again and again. How long had it been since she was ensconced by such warmth and comfort?

Here, in this luxurious little private chamber, she felt an empress again, perhaps an empress without an empire, which must've felt like a mother without a child. She thought about everything she'd just learned . . . about Zantherei's loss at Stormhaven, about Raas Dragath's death, and Nanjen's too. And of course, she couldn't forget about Cyrille Vileron. She still saw his dead grimace, staring up at her no matter where she tried to escape to.

It was all too heavy for her heart. She wanted to be strong, but she had no strength left.

After failing to find sleep, Miriana rose and slipped on a robe and padded across the tiled floor, heading toward an archway that led to a small terrace. She was on the third story, so when she stepped outside, a sudden gust of chill tickled her skin.

Nightfall on the waterways was a beautiful sight, especially with the arrival of spring. Moonlight twinkled across the crisscrossing canals, highlighting the dark waters with shimmering ivory ripples. The main district of the city was quiet and at rest. Miriana stood there, enveloped in its splendor, and thought about the words Seric had said to her. *Give me your hand and swear to me your fealty, and you will rule once more.*

CHAPTER FORTY-ONE

Seric had thought of so much to say to his son when at last they reunited, but in the end, he only managed to utter two trite and meaningless words: "You've returned."

Veldries rightfully gave him a look that wavered between mockery and confusion. "That is plain, Father."

The reunion took place in the small palace hall, the two men enveloped by the moody ambiance of flickering sconce-light. The smell of overcooked meat all but strangled the air, courtesy of an amateur chef who had botched the beefsteak delicacies. Still, it made no matter, since Veldries declined his portion and addressed his desire for rest. Seric gobbled down a few charred morsels himself, then escorted his son to a suitable guest chamber while picking the foodstuffs from his teeth.

Once inside, Veldries was greeted by a meek pair of male servants. They removed his old filthy garb and scrubbed his hair of dirt and grime, and after dressing him in clean apparel, the young man looked more mature and handsome than Seric had remembered. Thick locks of brown hair, unblemished olive-tinged skin, sharp eyes like two polished jadeites. His once youthful face now bore the hardness of experience, along with an ever-present hint of dissatisfaction. "Our great emperor disrespected me," he said without preamble. "Zantherei is nothing but a bully."

"Disrespected you?"

"He struck me."

That made Seric snap to attention.

"Outside the barracks of the Pit, he struck me with the metal chape of his scabbard. In front of everyone. The officers, the cadets, the instructors—even my mother."

"What cause was given?"

Veldries looked at him as if he'd stoned a kitten. "You think *I* gave him cause? He struck me because he is an unstable man. A wrathful, foolish, unstable man. I refused to tolerate such an affront from anyone, emperor or not, so I left."

"And Nyvia?"

"I didn't tell her. I knew she would've tried to stop me. She knows the truth of her brother, even if she won't admit it. Zantherei is a quick-tempered fool who treats worthy men like dogs. From the day I arrived at the Hollow he's kept me under his watchful finger, staring at me as though I were a traitor. Well, stare long enough and I will become one. I'd much rather serve someone who appreciates my talents. I wish to serve you, Father. Do you accept?"

Seric could feel his heart smile. "Of course, my son. You needn't ask."

"I want to be a part of this," Veldries went on. "As I was during the battle of Aster Falls, when we roped down the cliffs and crushed Lord Emeron's forces. He betrayed us, and so we punished him, and I'm glad we did. I want to punish Zantherei as well. Mother will understand. She knows I don't belong in the Hollow. I was too hard on you, Father. Ridiculed you for your minor losses, when I should've realized that true victory only matters in the long-term. A man shouldn't be judged by his latest conflict, but on the full scope of his achievements. I know you have great plans in mind. I want to serve you. I want to rise through the ranks and stand as your top general."

So much ambition in this one, Seric mused. *I wonder where he gets it from.*

"You're smiling again, Father, like you did when Lord Alarin destroyed that bridge. You're smiling and I know not why."

"I'm smiling, my son, because with you at my side, I will be unstoppable."

Veldries nodded, his shoulders squaring up a bit. "We will stand against Zantherei and all those who have grieved us."

"We will, but we must be patient. First, we need to deepen our roots here in the northeast, while looking south to the cities that were affected by the breaking of the Redlands. Best to seek out their support before making our move elsewhere. The task won't be easy, I reckon. I'm a half-Zhoulish, self-styled king who happens to be surrounded by enemies."

"You will succeed, Father, I know it." He was thoughtful for a moment. "Since you are a king, does that make me the prince and heir apparent?"

"I suppose it does."

"Good, because I'm tired of being treated as anything less."

"Listen carefully, my son, the truest test of a man's character comes when he is given power."

"What does that mean?"

"It means you must be careful of how you act. Be firm and authoritarian over your subjects, but also be fair-minded and decisive. Cruelty is only to be employed when cruelty is necessary. Remember, common men and kings are made of the same flesh and blood. We all live and die."

Veldries deflated a bit. "You make everything seem so difficult. I don't want to concern myself with all that. I just want to stand among the greatest heroes of the realm. Is that too much to ask?"

That made Seric laugh. "Of course not. But it would behoove

you to learn the finer points of military strategy. I have a few tomes I'd like you to read. Insightful writings from legendary figures of historical dynasties. My adoptive father made me memorize many passages when I was no older than you. It helped me understand, just as it will help you understand. Listen, why don't you rest for now, and tomorrow we'll break our fast and set to study."

Veldries thanked him once more, and after a brief exchange of departing words, Seric turned and was off. Wyath was waiting for him outside the chamber. He had a wry look on his narrow face, his sharp, probing eyes ever focused and thoughtful. Seric moved past but allowed suitable space for the man to walk beside him. He already knew what Wyath was going to say, but he let him say it anyway. "You must take caution."

"He's my son, General."

"That he is, but he's also your weakness. Do you not think Zantherei might exploit that? We must consider the possibility that your son has come to—"

"To *what*, General?" Before Wyath could answer, Seric said, "He's my *SON*. Do you think he has the heart for patricide?"

"His father did."

Seric gave him a sharp look. "An unfair blow, my friend. My Zhoulish father was a ruiner and a raper. I did what I had to do. You know that."

Wyath conceded the point with a nod. "Still, I ask that you not be so trusting."

"I would like to be alone, General."

"At least assign additional guardsmen to your—"

"Just go. I'll be fine."

Wyath was off then, and Seric moved alone down the hallway toward his own chamber. He paused halfway and decided to take the long way around, and once outside he stopped at the scenic waterfront veranda where the evening air was fresh and invigorating. *My son has returned to me, and in good faith.* There were not many times in Seric's life in which he could say he was genuinely pleased, but right now, he was.

Not only had Veldries returned, but Miriana as well. *My dear sweet Miriana.* The thought of her made his heart flutter with joy, but that was offset by how distant and withdrawn she appeared to be now. Despite that, she was still the same beautiful Miriana, broken nose or not. In fact, he rather preferred the way she looked now, and so long as she had doubts about herself, she wouldn't be so quick to leave him. An awful thought, he knew, but it was the truth.

He moved along the veranda and stopped beneath a wooden arbor, his fingers grasping the latticework as he stared at the distant ribbons of moonlit water. Soft spots of light glowed from the lanterns of the night fishermen who moved along the muddy banks with gigs in hand. Seric lost himself in those lights, his mind focusing on all the decisions that led to his taking command of this city. *The wheel of war ever turns, and from the depths of defeat I will come to rise again. My foes, both to the west and south, will fall to their knees and proffer their lands to me. I will elicit a new order, a new kingdom under a new ruler, and it will be done with my son and my queen at my side. Together, and only together, we will make our enemies suffer.* He smiled at the thought, eyes still lost in the distant lamplight along the waterways. *No more fucking mistakes, Seric Dyre.*

When he returned to his room, he found Ravia Ravenhair waiting for him. She was sitting on an upholstered chair, arms in her lap, pale fingers interlocked, body draped in a silk taffeta gown—of Zircian origin surely—which was tightly woven and dyed black with gray lacings. She didn't look pleased. Seric glared at her, making it known that he wasn't pleased either. He spoke quickly, before she could. "You shouldn't be here."

Her gown rustled when she stood up. "Who is she? That little whore with the busted nose—the one you coddled away like some child of illegitimacy. Who is she?"

Seric brushed past her. "None of your concern."

She caught him by his tunic sleeve, but Seric wrenched free of her grasp and assumed an aggressive stance. "I don't think you want to do that."

At first, she seemed cowed by his threat, but when he continued walking to his desk, the bitch quickly collected herself. "I want to know who she is."

"She's just a friend."

"Then why do you treat her as something more?"

Seric began looking through his tomes. His desk was a mess of crinkled silk papers and scrolled parchments and jade paperweights and wolf hair brushpens. He'd been meaning to tidy up. "I don't have time for this. My son has just returned. Do you know what that means? My son has returned to stand with his father."

"You never have time. Not for me. Do you think I'm just some lonesome mistress, always here at the stamp of your foot?" She moved closer to him, close enough that he could smell her subtle perfume of vetiver and vanilla. "I want to be your queen."

Seric only laughed at that, though he instantly regretted it, given the scowl that erupted on her face. "Why not? I *should* be queen. I've been through too much not to be."

Everyone wants a piece of the world, Seric mused. *No one is satisfied with what they have.* He stopped searching and turned to face her directly. "You are a harlot and a harridan. I would never ask for your hand."

Her back straightened and her hands withdrew to her bosomed chest. She looked hurt, yet she remained tremendously defiant. "That woman, you would make her your queen. You love her, it's obvious by the way you look at her. I can tell. I can these things."

He didn't hesitate. "So what if I do? You and I are nothing."

She spoke with a scowl. "You scum-sucking leech. I regret ever meeting you."

"Good. Likewise. Now get out of my sight, or I'll have you hanged in the garden we used to frolic in."

"I don't bel—"

"*GET OUT.*"

Ravia flinched. A stern silence fell upon the room. Her eyes soon dissolved of their anger, and her expression became cool and distant. Without another word she gathered her skirts, raised her head high and proud, and stomped off, leather heels pounding with every step. When the door slammed behind her, Seric lowered his head and cursed quietly to himself.

CHAPTER FORTY-TWO

The hour was midday, but the granary's inner chamber was so dark a quartet of cressets had to keep it alight. Not that Alarin Athera wanted to see all that much. Where once bushels and baskets and bales of dry grain sat, now lay the injured victims of the darkfire. Burned bodies sprawled out on linen tarps and canvas cots, rows and rows of them, like the ghastly exhibit of an overly productive pyromancer. Limbs were blackened and encrusted and sometimes fused together, while arms and elbows were occasionally melted into torsos and bellies.

Some soldiers were so badly desiccated their bodies appeared as those of children, yet their heads remained very large and very adult. The moans of these unfortunate men, and many others, wafted across the dimness, commingling with the bustling of the many physicians and their assistants.

More distressing was the fully charred and bedridden man at the far end of the makeshift quarantine. This man was General Thayer Dal—or what had become of him. Three weeks had passed since the siege's end and Thayer remained in a catatonic state, showing no signs of conscious life.

Witnesses had long conjured up a handful of new epithets for him. The Siege Shadow was probably Alarin's favorite, although Thayer Nightskin had a certain charm to it. Still, looking at him now . . . seeing how hideously ruined he was, it was difficult to feel anything but sadness. The man looked like a giant lump of over-cooked meat, his hair and eyebrows singed entirely off, his limbs and torso barnacled with untold nastiness.

Physician Penry was in the process of changing Thayer's wrappings, a menial task that was done once a day, sometimes twice depending on the extent of the seepage. As if the mere sight of Thayer's ruined flesh wasn't revolting enough, the skin would sometimes ooze from the body, like cheese melting in the summer sun. Strangely enough, it never oozed enough to expose muscle or bone, which led Penry to believe it was somehow reutilizing or recycling itself. A rather odd theory, but right now there was no time to ponder odd theories, because something extraordinary had just happened in the confines of this little makeshift quarantine.

Thayer Dal moved.

It was the slightest flick of the wrist, followed by the twitch of two fingers, fore and middle. From the medics and scribes a hubbub arose, and soon they were gathering to describe and transcribe the details. Alarin was fortunate enough to witness the spectacle, but Emperor Silas didn't arrive until shortly after, and with a small caprine figure clutched in his left hand, he gazed down at Thayer with an adolescent's nervous eyes.

Chamberlain Rennerin Rothar stood behind him, his old, plump hand hovering protectively over the boy's upper arm, as if ready to take hold in the event of a fainting. Silas looked more sad than woozy, however, and that was especially true when he murmured that he had no cloudfall salves left to administer. "I don't want him to die," he said after, but Physician Penry then told him that the darkfire had somehow emulsified with the cloudfall oil, creating a most peculiar relationship. Whether or not this relationship proved beneficial, well, none could say. Penry also admitted that nothing had been able to heal Thayer; at least, no medicine of earthly origin.

Silas begged him to keep trying. He didn't want Thayer to die, he didn't want anyone to die, and he made sure everyone knew that. Penry nodded and obeyed, but only after noting that his herbs and salves and compresses were designed to treat ordinary burns, not this type of anomalous searing. "I hate to sound insensitive," Penry said, "but his fate is with the gods now. Whatever strange, twisted fate that might be." That was enough to send Silas out in tears, and so Alarin ordered Chamberlain Rennerin to see His Majesty safely back to his private hall.

The mood turned ever somber, and Alarin tossed Penry a grave look before turning it upon the shadow-skinned man who was once a respectable general. Alarin couldn't say how long he stared, but Penry broke his concentration when he said, "He risked everything for your city, my lord."

Alarin didn't agree. "He risked everything because of his reckless obsession with death. He wanted this."

A grim silence devoured the room. Penry wasn't the type to engage in small talk, but right now, he seemed uncomfortable with the quiet, so he began to ask about the city. Out of courtesy Alarin obliged the man. Yes, yes, masons, builders, designers, mathematicians, laborers—they were all working hard to reconstruct the outer walls and make them as grand as they once were. Grander, even.

Alarin also briefly detailed the constant influx of civil issues that required his attention, a never-ending to-do list that stretched from issuing proclamations to overseeing the burial services for the fallen. When all that was said, Alarin returned with some questions of his own. Have the victims of the darkfire responded to any sort of treatment? What other types of experts have been summoned? "Coin is of no consequence," Alarin reminded him. "Just make sure to find the best in their field. Occultists, herbalists, soothsayers, even experienced brewers—whoever you think might know something about General Thayer's condition. I'm trusting your eye on this."

Penry was using an angled knife to scrape some gooey ointment across a slab of soapstone. "As you command, my lord."

Alarin turned toward the exit. He could hear the low moans of the wounded, along with the quick scuffling feet of the physicians and medics. "And Master," he said without looking. "Keep Thayer alive. It's in your hands, not the gods."

"As you command, my lord."

"You don't have to be so formal. We know each well enough."

"As you comm—forgive me. Yes, of course."

Alarin started off, but Penry stopped him not a moment later. "My lord, I forgot to mention. I received a visit from the oneirologist."

"The who?"

"The dreamscaper. You'd asked me for help regarding the cessation of your visions. I told you I knew a man who specializes in the matter."

"Oh yes, I remember. What news of it?"

Penry approached and placed something in Alarin's hand. "He called it a celestite dreamstone, my lord."

Alarin looked down. It was an odd-looking object, oblong and semi-transparent yet blue as the summer sky, with tiny hints of abstract lines like marks of wear in leather. It was pretty, but it didn't seem to be anything beyond that. "Is this a jest? This is a stone. How am I supposed to use it?"

Penry just shrugged. "He said all you need to do is hold it up to your eye like an optic lens, and the dreamstone will alter the face of the deceiver."

"That's it?"

Penry nodded, then shrugged once more for good measure. "I'm sorry, my lord. I wanted to arrange for you to meet him, but you were busy with the siege preparations, and he ended up leaving in quite a hurry."

Alarin examined the stone a moment longer before closing his hand. "Well, thank you, Penry." With that, he turned and left.

As the day wore on, Alarin was looking forward to retiring to his private chamber and removing his wooden leg. There had been something different about his stump ever since the cloudfall treatment. It wasn't overtly noticeable, but it was just something that felt . . . *different*. Or maybe he was just overtired. Good, solid rest was a rarity these days, and even though his phantom pain had long diminished, that didn't mean he had the energy of a man half his age. *Forty and three is still relatively young,* he mused. *And I'll never again be as young as I am today.*

General Szathan Mordall came to him with unexpected news just after supper. Alarin's stomach was fighting off a minor bout of indigestion, so he was happy to have a reason to be up and moving, and in his speediest limp he followed Szathan's long strides through the palace grounds until at last they'd come to the soldier barracks. Inside a small corner room, and amid a stuffy interior haze, was the captured Redlands strategist, Hiriam Thraves.

If you looked past the filthy face and exhausted eyes, you could see that Hiriam Thraves was a younger man, most likely shy of thirty. His ankles and wrists were bound with cord, and yet he was wearing a quaint expression of mild disappointment, as if he were only slightly inconvenienced. Alarin had met the man only once before, and that was years ago, so seeing him now didn't mean much, but Szathan was clearly battling with his emotions, and with good reason. Before Hiriam had defected to Raas Dragath, he had served as Szathan's prized officer in Thornberry.

Szathan was glaring at the traitor as if that betrayal had just occurred, but when he spoke it was directed at Alarin. "Scouting parties found him holed up in an abandoned southern redoubt, him and a small host of ex-Redlander soldiers. They've all been rounded up."

Alarin nodded. "So it looks like justice has been meted out after all." He paused, then turned his head to address the young general. "I must admit, I didn't think you survived the destruction of Serpenthold."

Hiriam lifted his hairless chin and raised his eyes, a gesture of undeniable defiance. "My abilities are always underestimated and underappreciated. Is it because of my sweet and innocent face?"

"I should rip off that sweet and innocent face with my bare hands," Szathan growled. "You're a double-crossing worm and you don't deserve to live."

Hiriam's posture shrank, now playing the coy victim. He was such a snake. "You should take my life. I know I deserve it. But if you're a man of any sensibility, like I believe you are, then you should at least grant me an ear, if only for a moment."

Szathan grumbled under his breath. "You always know what to say."

Hiriam took that as a compliment. "I'm a survivor."

"You're a goddamn—"

Alarin took a step forward and put a hand on Szathan's arm, both to calm him and to show that he would take over the conversation. "General Hiriam Thraves, your crimes and indiscretions have risen beyond the firmament itself. You abandoned your position, betrayed your commander, and served as chief advisor and strategist to the traitor Raas Dragath." Alarin paused. "What could you possibly say to me?"

"Your brother Zantherei destroyed my home and murdered my lord, and for that, I wish to see his reign of tyranny come to an end."

Alarin gave him a square look, as if to say, *I'm listening.*

"My lord, even though you've repelled Zantherei's forces, the thought of his eventual retaliation must consume your thoughts.

And rightly so. Your brother is a stubborn and volatile man, but he is not a fool. Vengeance he will undoubtedly seek, and this time he won't rely on supernatural fire, but a much more tactical effort."

Alarin shook his head. "This is all plainly known, no matter how eloquently your silver tongue puts it." He shook his head. "I'm afraid you are of little worth to me."

"Misdirection is your best strategy," Hiriam said quickly. "You need to draw Zantherei's eye to the peripheral, away from the fundamental, by offering him another target. This will grant your city the time it needs to regroup and rebuild, while the Hollow forces will only become more taxed and depleted."

"Another target? If you're referring to Seric Dyre, then you're grasping at clouds. Zantherei has already crushed Seric's forces at the Shaded Plains. He has no reason to pursue a second assault."

"That's why you must *give* him a reason."

"I cannot produce that which doesn't exist."

"That's true," Hiriam said, then left it at that.

Alarin stared at the bound man. *What are you driving at? Is this some sort of attempt to string me along and stall your inevitable death?* Alarin decided he'd heard enough. He readjusted his footing and slammed the ferrule of his cane on the floor tiles. "Tell me what you know."

"And if I do, what will become of me?" He gestured at Szathan. "Will this one here rip off my face all the same?"

"He should. You deserve it. Not only for your dishonorable defection, but for your hand in the wedding deception that led to Cathia Athera's murder. I suspect that even in his next life, Lord Merio won't forgive me for that."

Hiriam attempted to respond, but Alarin flicked it away with a curt hand gesture. "You are in no position to bargain. Tell me what you know."

"Spare my life and I will."

Szathan banged a mailed fist against the wall, but Alarin

ignored it and continued speaking. "Tell me what you know, and I will consider leniency. That's the most you will get from me. You are lucky your head is still sitting on your shoulders right now."

Hiriam's nod was slow and docile, an unexpected response from such a confident and intelligent young man. "It's Zantherei's wife, the lovely Miriana Athera, former empress of the Anir." He paused briefly and thoughtfully, as if to manufacture suspense. "After Serpenthold burned to the ground, she escaped in Zantherei's supply train and later reunited with Seric at the Shaded Plains."

"And you know this, how?" Szathan demanded.

"Because I too followed Zantherei's army for a time." His face couldn't resist that cocky smile. "Like I said, everyone underestimates me."

"I still don't understand," Alarin asked. "How is Lady Miriana the misdirection? She gave up her rank and power when she fled the capital. She's inconsequential now. Zantherei wouldn't organize a campaign against Aster Falls just to get to her."

The former Redlander general's posture became straight as a bamboo stalk, and his voice turned coldly ominous. "He will when he finds out what she's done."

CHAPTER FORTY-THREE

The trail wound its way north in the form of torn fern leaflets and finger-dusted stones and urine-stained bushes and abandoned cookfires. Apparently, Jakken hadn't bothered to conceal his tracks, nor did his footprints reveal anything but a steady walk, almost leisurely in stride. Ansetheral Athera liked his overconfidence; it made for an easy pursuit.

The wilderness was a serene escape. It'd been quite some time since Anseth found himself alone, and he certainly felt the weight of that solitude, so much so that after the sun had fled before night-fall's embrace, he swore he heard someone whisper his name. Strange, it sounded like the glottal Vaskultan accent, but the whisper wasn't his title of Lord Revek; instead it was his Anirian birth name Ansetheral. *An-seeth-er-all.* He twisted his head around, but no one was there. No one was anywhere. Uneasy, he looked back down, ruminating on what he'd just heard, until at last he dismissed his overactive mind and continued dauntlessly the hunt.

The puncture wound he'd suffered at Jakken's hands had been dressed before he set out, but the constant motion prevented the blood from fully clotting. Anseth didn't feel any pain, or maybe he was too tense and angry to feel it. Regaining the Earthstone was the reason he went after Jakken, but he also needed a temporary reprieve from the city and all its burdens. The recent siege still pressed deeply on his mind, the terrible destruction and the near death of his bondsman Kirik. It was strange not having him at his side, and there were a handful of times in which he half expected the witty young man to appear out of nowhere and say hello, but of course that never happened.

The terrain that opened before him was unfamiliar yet manageable. West of the Amber River was a marshy mess of lakes and ponds and streamlets, muddy and oxygen-poor places that were devoid of most aquatic life. In the trees, wrens and crossbills chittered gleefully, while along the banks sedges rose as high as Anseth's waist.

Sphagnum mosses and shrubby growth covered nearly everything underfoot, often forming ringlets around the surrounding pools that made it difficult to judge where to step. But for all its boggy bravado, the wetlands dwindled as quickly as it had arrived, and next Anseth knew, he was climbing shelf-like plateaus that were home to great carpets of wildflowers that could draw even the most unappreciative eye. Sunbaked oranges, lagoon-bottom blues, volcanic reds . . . Anseth couldn't recall having seen such a magnificent array of colors, not even before the nine years he'd spent in the northern wasteland.

People were scarce in this region, which meant no hostelries or roadside inns to visit. Anseth didn't need them; survival came easily enough with hunting spears and deadfall traps, and the land provided plenty of game. But what puzzled him was the audacity of some of these creatures. Often, he'd espy hares and marmots and even small wildcats emerging unafraid from the underbrush, some no more than five paces away.

Once a lone wolf was so intrigued by the campfire, Anseth had to wave a torch to frighten the beast away. He feared drawing the attention of its natal pack, so he extinguished the flames and climbed the oversized bough of an oversized maple for safety. That evening he didn't sleep much, but he was contented to peer through a net of branches and view the waxing moon, bright and curved like a tusk of ivory.

While the night proved to be an uninvited stranger, the morning was a welcome friend. After breaking his fast on smoked jerk and half a skin of blackmilk, Anseth rose and continued through a meadow of stubbly grasses toward a forest of old growth. The foliage here was dark and shrouding, with wide, robing conifers jostling the tall broadleaves for space.

Recent wildfires left their smoldering mark in one place and another, but it was the sight of an especially charred tree trunk that brought haunting visions of the darkfire to Anseth's mind. The way it had melted everything it touched . . . the way it had turned stone and steel and flesh into a soupy black ooze. Anseth disliked himself for what he'd put his Vaskultans through. They were warriors of the open steppes and plains, not stationary defenders of walls and cities. So many casualties could've been—*should've* been—avoided. *I was their chieftain, they trusted me. They still trust me. I cannot risk losing that trust again.*

The next day, Anseth lost the trail. He was traveling in the shade of a looming maple grove, lost in the crisscrossing black boughs and five-lobed leaves, when suddenly the spoor had vanished—no faded footpaths or disturbed foliage or even the slightest breakage of grass.

After an hour of circling and retracing and doubling back, Anseth was ready to give up. His arrow-wound had reopened and was beginning to fester, and the abundance of ragweed was making him sneeze and sniffle. Not only that, an outbreak of hives had laced up his right arm, likely caught from a sumac shrub back in the wetlands. When he'd made the mistake of scratching a bony cheek with bare fingers, his entire face became swollen and irritated.

So here he was, the Supreme Lord of the Gray Plains, conquered by the unassuming wilds of his former homeland, like a conscript on a campaign without a lick of training.

If Kirik were here he'd laugh and call me a quitter and a milksop. Anseth would probably use logic and sensibility to justify himself, but his bondsman would only fire back with his usual comical banter. Such thoughts made Anseth sigh.

When he took another sip of blackmilk, something caught in his throat and he coughed, the sudden outburst rousing a few passerine birds into flight. That only made Anseth laugh, and after a fit of half laughing, half coughing, he couldn't help but feel a great weight of despair settle on his shoulders. Here he was . . . lost and alone and having second thoughts about the pursuit. How much longer could he fight the fatigue and hunger and pain?

Until I find the bastard and cut the eyes out of his head, he decided. *I didn't spend years and years clawing my way up the barbarian ranks for nothing. I didn't kill Dariok in the bone cage for nothing. And I won't allow some little upstart traitor to get away with stealing my Earthstone and nearly murdering me in the process. I am the chieftain of the Vaskultans, and I will have my revenge.*

And with that, Anseth continued the search.

Alarin Athera sat at his writing desk, brushpen in hand, eyes gazing down at the edict whose ink was drying under an old oil lamp. The Rosebud Hall was imperceptibly quiet, the only sounds rising from the gentle rush of a floor sweeper making his rounds, along with the footfalls of the incense collector and brazier tender.

It was late and Alarin was tired, so the minor commotion was a bit irksome, but not enough for him to interrupt their duties. Truth was, he welcomed their company, for despite the recent victory, Alarin was feeling rather alone and despondent.

Chamberlain Rennerin entered to personally invite Alarin to an intimate evening banquet at the Iris Hall. A kind gesture from a kind man, but Alarin declined his offer and dismissed him all the same. He preferred to stare aimlessly down at the letter he'd written, and to ponder all its implications once it reached the hands of his brother Zantherei.

The revelation of Miriana Athera's treacherous designs and terrible misdeeds would come to light, from her bloody ascension of the throne, her scandalous tryst with Seric Dyre, her devious attempt to eliminate Zantherei, and finally to her fleeing the capital to ally with the southern Redlands. It was all there, just as Hiriam had revealed, every known act of deceit and skullduggery committed under her false reign. A lineage broken, an empire burned to the ground, and the single woman who had her filthy hands in all of it.

And now Zantherei would know the truth.

Alarin folded the letter and pressed it with the hot wax of his official seal, then he slipped it into the sash of his outer robe. *Brother, this will make you mad with vengeance.* But it was necessary; the misdirection would work, just as Hiriam had promised. It was the only viable tactic. So why did Alarin feel so uncertain about it?

He remembered the days he'd spent as a boy with his brothers: stern Zantherei, scrappy Ansetheral, sociable Merio. They were all rough-and-tumble lads, all vying to win their father's attention and approval, and even though they quarreled and tussled often, their fraternal bonds had always been strong. But not anymore. How had everything fallen so far into disharmony? Merio was dead, Anseth was a coldhearted barbarian, and Zantherei was a false emperor and outright villain.

The world was ever changing, and yet, it was growing increasingly difficult for Alarin to keep up. Time and solitude were essential for reflective thought, and reflective thought had not come easily these past few months. That made Alarin sigh. *Come on, you old goat, what are you even getting at?*

Something still niggled at his brain. Before Zantherei had laid siege upon the city, there were two assassination plots against Alarin, one by blade and the other by poison. This was an internal threat, and one that still loomed large. *I need to know who was behind these intrigues. No more conjecture, no more false accusations. Just the truth.* Alarin reached across his writing desk to scatter some papers and pick up the celestite dreamstone, but in the process he knocked a brush holder over with a low-hanging sleeve. He shook his head and set the holder upright before examining the small blue object. *'The dreamstone will alter the face of the deceiver. The dreamstone will alter the face of the deceiver.'* Alarin gave another sigh, this one deeper. *Perhaps I should make an appearance at this little banquet after all.*

He closed his fingers and squeezed the object in his palm, then with his free hand he grabbed his cane and rose, hobbling across the room to exit beneath a long archway. Outside, he caught sight of two sentries mocking a scrawny night-soil worker. Alarin scolded the pair of buffoons at once, threatening to strip their ranks and have them bucketing out the privy chambers of the soldier barracks. The men straightened up and shut their mouths, although the taller of the two wore a slimy little frown that Alarin didn't like.

He continued along the uneven cobbled path, which led him to the hall's forecourt, a raised and gated area that was expectedly vacant at this hour. For a while the only sounds came from his own limping across the paved bricks, foot then cane, *thump* then *clack*, not unlike a wounded animal dragging itself to its den. He stopped at a carved limestone bench and sat down, resting his cane beside him. A hand reached down to tighten the straps of his wooden leg. There was no pain, but the fitting on the stump continued to cause discomfort. *I'll have to ask Penry to take another look at it; perhaps he can make the necessary adjustments.*

His eyes rose to the looming Iris Hall. It was a marvel of architectural beauty, from its floral colonnade to its low tapered eaves and heavy wooden framework. Along the roof, a line of statuettes once rose over the lower courtyards, but that was before Alarin had them removed. He remembered them vividly enough, mammalian guardians armed and armored in fine detail, each marked with one of the five cosmic symbols that governs the people of the Anir. Without the statuettes, the roof looked rather plain, as did the city's inner wall without those lewd relief sculptures. *I suppose I can iterate my point about the Anirian way, but perhaps I've gone too far. Even the Hollow had a touch of character to it; this city just looks dull.*

Through the tall open windows of the Iris Hall, he could see the illuminated outlines of the many men and women at leisure. Alarin observed them for a while, silent and pensive, before rising and heading toward the building, dreamstone clutched in his hand. *Something tells me this will be a waste of time,* he thought. *But I must try.* Inside, he was met by a roar of conversation and a cluster of moving bodies. Courtiers and military officials and dressed-down soldiers all standing in tight conversational circles on the tiled floor, laughing and carousing and reveling in their recent victory. On a raised platform to their left, a quintet of string musicians serenaded the hall with a joyful melody, though it was barely heard over the clamor.

A young and effervescent serving girl approached to offer both a seat and a meal, but Alarin declined, opting to stand unobtrusively against the far wall. To his right a hunchbacked veteran was trying his best to *not* appear drunk, while the courtesan he was engaged with was trying her best to appear interested. Alarin observed their little dance for a bit longer than he'd wanted, then his eyes turned to the lacquered table at the end of the room.

The White Fang ministers were all there: Byort, with his dark attire and bulging eyes; Dobbin, with his glossy robe and wisps of white hair; Fallon, with his deep frown and elongated ears; and Elisa, with her age-inappropriate blouse and heavy arm bangles. Alarin held the semi-transparent dreamstone over his eye and stared pointedly at each minister's face. Nothing happened. *This is a sham.* Alarin turned to view the lesser known councilmembers, then to anyone and everyone he could see, every single civil and military official in sight. But nothing happened. *I am a fool to think it would be this easy.* He wanted to throw the damn thing. There was no connection to the subconscious mind, no magical revelation of the deceiver. It was just a worthless, stupid stone.

"There he is, the glorious man in his most glorious hour." It was the voice of Chamberlain Rennerin Rothar, who had emerged from a nearby alcove to approach with steps too lively for such a stout and aging man.

Alarin was still looking through the dreamstone. He was about to lower it—but then he stopped himself. Rennerin's face . . . it was *different*, but not in a way Alarin could readily explain. The man's features were smudged and distorted, like a watercolor portrait gone awry. Alarin recoiled at once. "What's happened to your face?"

"My lord?" Rennerin questioned, his voice still full of pep. The sight of him was so off-putting Alarin had to lower the stone and look away. "I'm glad you've decided to come after all," Rennerin went on casually. "Forgive me, I was in the larder showing the kitchen staff how to properly season a stew of beef tenderloins. You'd think they'd not be as green as mold by now—the staff I meant, not the tenderloins. Anyway, a thousand pardons for missing your illustrious entrance."

Alarin didn't respond. He tried to remain calm, but his thoughts were racing at a pronghorn's pace. Rennerin himself seemed rather tipsy, so he was less inhibited and more talkative than usual (if that were possible). "Come join us, my lord. Welcome, welcome! Join us in the grand celebration of a grand victory. Hello, I am speaking to you, my lord!"

Alarin didn't answer. All he could think about was the celestite stone, warm in his palm. When he looked down, he saw it was emitting a subtle yet unmistakable glow. He stared at it, frozen and with head lowered, while the garrulous man rambled on about this and that and everything else. It was only after a long while did Rennerin's voice lose its exuberance. "Something amiss, my lord?"

It was at that moment the raw truth hit Alarin like a fist. It made him want to laugh, it made him want to weep, it made a hundred different emotions assault him at once. "It was you," Alarin croaked at last. "It was you all along."

Before Rennerin could respond, the ferrule of Alarin's cane struck him in the mouth. *Thwack.* The impact spun the stout man and dropped him to the floor, where he made a sound like a stifled sneeze. Alarin stood over him, hands wrapped around his cane, lungs pulling heavy breaths. Blood was dripping from Rennerin's mouth. He gave Alarin a troubled look, a look that begged to know *why,* but Alarin ignored it and ordered the nearest guardsman to bind and arrest the fallen chamberlain.

CHAPTER FORTY-FOUR

The nights she spent with Seric were warm and familiar, and despite their nonphysical nature they mirrored a closeness once shared at the Hollow. For the first time since abandoning the capital city, Miriana Athera felt a sense of belonging. Not to say she could ever bring herself to fully trust Seric Dyre again, or that she could ignore the probing eyes of his disgruntled whore, Ravia. For the latter, Miriana would've liked to have protection. Her spiked cestus glove was confiscated upon her capture at the hands of Raas Dragath, and she regretted the loss ever since.

The bronze wall mirror was kind to her today. In it she saw a face that was youthful and proud and sharp-featured, not one defeated by time and hardship. Of course, her nose was still crooked, but she otherwise remained that same attractive woman who once ruled over the realm. Especially when she fastened her short hair in a simple updo, drawing the focus to her neck and shoulders.

Of her attire she rifled through a few outfits before settling on a plaited overdress of pale blue, embroidered and laced and draped over a raincloud gray underskirt. The cool undertones matched well with her skin, which was pale and smooth as a polished gemstone save for the soft spray of freckles on her shoulders. She looked handsome, so very handsome, but no one was around to tell her that. At the Hollow she had countless fawners and flatterers to compliment her at every moment. Here, aside from a single semi-bashful attendant, she had no one. Well, she had Seric, but she only saw him in the evening.

He was a 'king' now, and being a king meant having a diverse cavalcade of followers to surround him during most of the daylight hours. Miriana quickly came to know many of these followers. Seric's personal guardsmen were always around, and these were lumbering, blockheaded fools that towered over most others. The Zhoulish officer too, Zirian the Mad Wolf; he may as well have been attached to Seric as a limb.

The other military general, the thin one named Wyath . . . Miriana wasn't sure what to think about this man. He was undoubt-edly intelligent, and he seemed to serve as Seric's counselor—in wartime and out—and he seemed to do it better than any other offi-cial. He was young yet, perhaps only a handful of years older than Miriana herself, yet his plain-featured face had a touch of sagacity to it. Seric seemed to trust the man implicitly, which was strange since he seldom trusted anyone.

As for Aster Falls, it was a true romantic's city, and tonight, as she stood on the high terraced garden, she couldn't help but admire the view of gorgeous esplanades and rustic boardwalks and beaches of red clay. The city itself was blanketed by a soft, calming light, a gossamer glow that cradled every district and ward and backstreet and market square. Seric eventually joined her at the wooden scroll-work railing, and together they stood in silence, the wind pushing through their hair, the soft grasses brushing against their bare feet. It was spring, the weather was warm, and the air was full of passion.

But for all his attempts to woo her, Miriana refused his tender touch, courteously yet firmly. It was a difficult decision; a part of her *did* want to succumb to his advances, to lie back and make love to him under the bright half-moon, wreathed by the night and the gentle murmurs of the lower cityscape. What about this man made her heart flutter? Perhaps it was his courage, or perhaps it was his relentless and unflinching desire to reach the pinnacle of his ambitions. Perhaps it was just his comely looks, those warm green eyes and rugged half-Zhoul features and fine tousle of medium-brown hair. He'd grown a bit of stubble on his face, with the tiniest hint of gray along the sideburns, so now he looked distinguished as well as handsome.

Still, she knew she couldn't give herself to him. Not now, not like this.

"I'm a persistent man," Seric told her. "And the gods generally reward persistent men with that which they crave. They've already seen me fit to rule a portion of this shattered empire, and now they've given me back my son and my queen."

"I'm not your queen."

"No, but you want to be."

"I didn't know the gods have also granted you a telepath's insight."

His smile was one of wry amusement. "I am confident, that's all. A man is nothing without confidence."

"Confidence or conceit?"

He seemed to enjoy what he perceived as kittenish banter. "Regardless of semantics, I know you wish to stand beside me. I know your love for me has never diminished."

She studied him. *That may be true, but unlike you, my emotions don't determine my decisions.* Still, she knew this man was as magnetic as he was persuasive, but tonight he didn't push his advances as much as she'd expected. No, he spent a strange amount of time flattening the creases of his silk tunic and rubbing the skin beneath his neckerchief. When she asked what was wrong, he gave a long sigh and cleared his throat before responding. "I received word from the northwest today, from the governess of Silverleaf."

A pang of apprehension touched Miriana's heart. She misliked that devious little governess. Lady Perilia Valayne once manipulated Seric into an alliance based on her carnal needs. Did he enjoy lying with the woman? Probably. Still, Miriana was well past caring now. *Aren't I?*

"Her husband Lord Tavarin is dead," Seric went on. "Suffered an attack of the heart while he slept. A peaceful passing, so the lady says, and the city has endured a peaceful transition as well. Perilia now sits upon the governmental seat. With the support of her civil and military officials, she aims to rid the realm of the false emperor and seditious tyrant Zantherei Athera. She also wishes to tender her aid to my campaign. Her city and her garrisons are mine to command."

"And you believe she speaks true?"

He didn't hesitate. "Lady Perilia has no cause for deceit."

"All women have cause for deceit."

"Yes, perhaps you're right, but she bears as much ill-will toward Zantherei as her husband did, and as I do."

"She just wants to play her little vixen games with you. The lady's as shallow and small-minded as they come. No greater vision for the greater good of the realm. She is not someone to be trusted."

"I know what kind of person she is, I don't need you to counsel me." He seemed to regret speaking so sharply. *I must remember he is a 'king' now,* Miriana mused. *Or maybe it's because of how I look? Would he have talked to me this way were my nose not crooked?* Miriana didn't wish to conjure up such negative thoughts, but here they were, ripe and rancorous.

"So, will you go to her?"

Seric seemed to consider her question for a while, and for a while the only sounds were the rustling canopies of the far-off trees, and the faint lapping of the distant rivers against the stone banks.

The air had a moistness to it, a mossy and mushroom scent, not unlike the rich smell of the earth after a downpour. "No, I will use spies."

"Spies?"

"Knowledge, my lady, specifically advance knowledge, is the key to any enlightened ruler's success. We of the realm all know this, we all employ spies, but an enlightened ruler knows that in every area there must be *good* spies, and by the gods, I employ good spies. They are everywhere, mind you. I have spies in my own encampments and branches of office; I have spies in the lesser towns of the surrounding heartland; I have spies with fancy titles wandering the halls of the greater cities—the Star of the Hollow, Stormhaven, Silverleaf, Willowsea, Thornberry, you name it. And all of these spies are passing information to me, every day. And every day I comb through these reports, and I take what is useful and discard what is not. My lady, to know the true situation of the realm and its players, one must have eyes in all facets of civilization, in all corners of the realm. So as I've said, I will use spies, and I will wait." He leaned closer to her. "And I hope I can spend my time waiting with you."

Seric's words remained in Miriana's mind long after she'd returned to her private chamber. She moved behind an eight-panel, room-dividing screen, doffing her fancy attire and draping herself in a homelier outer robe. When she finally emerged, she padded barefoot over to a bronze washbasin to remove the touches of cosmetics. Vylas visited her shortly after. The one-eyed man had arrived at the city days ago, and he seemed to have no trouble adjusting to his new surroundings. Right now, he was doing his best to tend a sputtering brazier. "You see, it's all about the principles of combustion," he remarked. "You have to balance the right amount of coals with the right amount of oil. Like this, see?"

Miriana shook her head and made a comment about Vylas's fastidiousness, and when the one-eyed man agreed with her, they both shared a laugh. Afterward, she looked once more at her face in the mirror, then her eyes drifted to the length of her private room. The stylish décor and convenient amenities made her smile inside. *It'd been too long since I've known such luxury.*

Finally, after sitting down on a couch of rich mahogany, she decided to speak her inner thoughts. "Do you think anyone knows I'm here?"

Vylas looked up at that, scratching an uncovered cheek with a soot-covered finger. A streak of black was left on his skin. "What do you mean?"

She gestured at the stain on his face, then nodded when he wiped it with a sleeve. "Here, in Aster Falls," she said. "Do you think anyone knows about me?"

His one-eye narrowed a bit as he thought about it. "I can't see how. It's not like you've been followed."

"We don't know that. And just because Serpenthold has fallen doesn't mean all the Redlanders have vanished."

"Yes, but it matters not, I reckon. Even if Zantherei learns of your whereabouts, Seric will never hand you over."

"It may incite a war."

"War has already come, for many seasons and many months."

That much was obvious, so she chided him for such a senseless remark. Then she said, "My presence here could stir a violence that we don't want stirred. I . . ." She faltered, fell silent.

"What, Sister? What is it you fear?"

Miriana didn't answer. She just sat there, staring at the brazier flames lapping higher and higher and bolder and brighter. Her eyes became lost in those fiery ribbons, her mind hazy with thoughts of that Redlander snake, Hiriam Thraves. All her secrets, all her dastardly deeds . . . they now belonged to him. *I had no choice, I was tortured. I had to talk.* She was quiet for so long that Vylas's attention had turned to the room attendant. He was instructing the youth on some menial domestic task, making sure it was handled in his preferred manner. Miriana watched dumbly, absently, her mind lost in her thoughts. *Is Hiriam even alive? No, he must've burned with the stronghold. He burned, didn't he?*

She lay down on the featherbed. Vylas asked in a timid voice if he should leave, but she told him to stay. He was the only one she trusted, and she told him that, too. She no longer fretted about his advances; no, ever since their reuniting he'd become a rather meek and servile man around her, even more so than when she was the empress. It was plain he wouldn't overstep his bounds again, and she was grateful for that. But she wasn't comfortable with the attendant still lingering, no matter how innocent and bashful he appeared. So, she voiced her concerns and Vylas dismissed the youth, and then he began tinkering with the incense burner on the low table. The calming scent of lavender filled the room. Miriana pulled up the coverlets, drawing the clean silk to her nose. Her eyes closed. She could sleep forever. A part of her wanted to.

When she awoke the room was eerily silent. Her eyelids struggled to come apart, and once more she thought she was still inside that lightless cell, a helpless and hapless prisoner of Raas Dragath. But then her mind cleared, and she gave a relieving sigh. It was unusually dark. At the room's center, the brazier smoldered with neglect. *What hour is it?* Her eyes swept across the room, searching vainly for Vylas. She was alone. *Where have you gone, my good brother?*

She heard a muffled creak from outside the closed door, the sound of someone's weight pressing against the floor tiles. A moment later a shadow blocked out the gap beneath the door's bottom rail. Miriana tensed. There was a muffled sound of low speech. *Vylas, is that you? That better be you.* The door began to open. Old iron hinges squealed in protest. Light from the outer corridor crept inside, too dim for daylight. Miriana called out softly to her brother. No answer.

The squealing stopped. Standing in the threshold of the doorway was a silhouette, slimmer than expected. Miriana thought it was Vylas, but the hourglass build undoubtedly belonged to a woman. For a long moment there was only silence, until at last the intruder entered the room.

Miriana could see clearly her face now—it was that cruel and jealous woman, Ravia. There was no mistaking her high cheek-bones, hooked nose, thick tufts of black hair, and red-rimmed eyes. Below the neck, Miriana caught sight of her tight outer jacket and knee-length skirt—and the sharp outline of something in her hand.

A dagger.

Miriana's heart pushed up her throat.

"I don't know what sort of cunt you are," Ravia said, "but you got in the way of my affairs. So that makes you a dead cunt."

Miriana reached out to the nearest nightstand for a vase or vessel of some kind, but the woman had crossed the room before she could find anything. "*Wait!*" Miriana shouted, a silly thing to shout, but her mind and mouth were both frantic with fear. And of course, the woman didn't wait—she raised her hands and lunged forward with the dagger. Miriana screamed, kicked up the coverlet. There was a sharp *skrrriit* of fabric tearing, and next she knew the blade was lost in the floral silk folds.

Ravia gave the coverlet a hard yank. The blade spilled free. Before she could seize the hilt, Miriana leapt on her, and now they were wrestling and scratching and pulling hair and raking skin.

Puffs of feathery eiderdown rose from the torn bedding. Ravia raked her nails across Miriana's face, and in return Miriana bit her —a hard bite, right on the breast.

When Ravia screamed, the sound was so sudden that Miriana flinched, just long enough for Ravia to grab the dagger. But before she could use it, Miriana caught her wrist, twisting and twisting until they both rolled off the bed.

Thump.

The dagger was lost once more. Ravia called her a foul name, but Miriana didn't know how to react to that, so she said nothing, and instead she focused on outworking the woman physically. *I won't let you kill me,* she thought. *I am strong, goddamn it. Strong as FUCKING silk.*

She fought and clawed and muscled her way to a top position, then she used the strength of her legs to pin Ravia's arms. *The dagger—where is the dagger?* It was nowhere to be found, but the gourd-shaped incense burner was lying on its side nearby.

It must've fallen off the low table during the scuffle. Miriana grabbed it and drove the metal base into Ravia's face, repeatedly, smashing cheeks, chin, nose, teeth.

The woman grunted, then shrieked, and after the sixth or seventh blow Miriana targeted her eyes, and after three more squelching hits, Ravia's face began to leak blood and her body began to twitch.

Miriana kept pounding away, again and again, driving the hard base into every ugly feature of her ugly face. She cried out while she did it, louder and louder until someone pulled her off. It was Vylas—and he was suddenly kneeling beside her, asking if she were all right.

Miriana was too stunned to reply. Her hands up to the elbows were painted with blood, and jagged bits of gore were dangling from the incense burner's dented bottom. When she glanced at Ravia, she saw not a woman's face but a lump of butchered beef, with blood dripping and tissue peeling and a single eye dangling from a collapsed socket. It was so horrific she had to look away.

Vylas was still talking softly to her, but Miriana heard none of it. He tried to take her in his arms, to soothe and console her—but she shoved him away. "Where did you go?" she demanded, in a voice that sounded small and distant.

Vylas's hands were still in an upraised position. He didn't seem to know what to do with them, so he began combing her short hair with his fingers, lightly, cautiously, as though she were a feral dog to be tamed. "The guards, they pulled me out," he murmured. "They said I'd been summoned . . . they insisted on escorting me out . . ." He stopped, and a regretful sigh escaped his lips. "That bitch tricked me."

Miriana tilted her head, slowly, so that her gaze lined up with Vylas's good eye. "And now that bitch is dead."

CHAPTER FORTY-FIVE

There was a lot of confusion, a lot of weeping and wailing after Chamberlain Rennerin Rothar had been stripped of his seal and thrust into a holding cell. The mournful reactions were expected—Rennerin had always been among the most likable and loyal court officials, a man of compassion and courtesy to all he met. Who could've figured him for a traitor behind closed doors?

Alarin struggled with the notion for quite some time. Perhaps the dreamstone had been wrong, perhaps it had made a mistake, or perhaps it was an underhanded scheme by its creator to falsely accuse an innocent man. After all, this was Chamberlain Rennerin, the genial and good-humored old fellow, everyone's favorite civil official. How can such a man be the perpetrator of both assassination attempts?

But it was true, and Rennerin confessed to as much. And it was a confession gained under no duress, and by no means of torture or trickery. He simply admitted to it.

The squat, boxy cell reeked of mildew and dead bugs and unwashed flesh, but it was surprisingly well lit considering its subterranean hideaway location. Rennerin sat on the sand-and-straw floor, ragged robes drawn messily to his lap, wrinkled legs and filthy bare feet exposed. His old balding head was tilted floorward, his posture devoid of the zest that once came so freely to him. "I served Lord Merio for many years," he muttered. "I loved him. But you . . . you are nothing like your brother. I *despise* you."

Alarin stared at the man through the rusted black grate, unsure of how to respond. He wasn't offended, he wasn't angry, he wasn't even disappointed. He was simply surprised. "You're an adept performer then," he said. "To keep me devoid of suspicion, to show nothing but leal duty to your master." Rennerin offered no response to that, so Alarin continued. "I've never done wrong by you. Why harbor such loathing?"

"You came here and overturned Lord Merio's world. His integrity, his influence, his loyalty to the throne—you made him question it all. Were it not for you, he'd still be alive."

"Raas Dragath killed my brother—"

"*You* killed him. You made him insecure, uncertain, rash. Lord Merio was a great man. It wasn't his time to leave this realm." His red and rheumy eyes trailed down, and his shoulders slumped like a dog habitually whipped by an especially cruel master. "I know the tales about you. How resentful you are of others, how bitter about your own infirmities. Merio was nothing like you. He was a free spirit, benevolent and sociable and passionate. You took that away from him."

Alarin thought about that. "So, you decided to base your opinion of me on falsehoods and rumors? I thought you shrewder than that."

"Don't try to turn me with your glib responses. You know the truth. When will I be executed?"

"Two days."

"By what method?"

"Public strangulation."

"I'm an old man. That is excessive."

"You tried to murder me. Twice. Such is the fate of all schemers and plotters."

He nodded sluggishly and spoke plaintively. "I acted alone in this. The White Fang Council had no part. Fanglord Byort is an innocent man." He paused, and for the first time Rennerin seemed truly afraid of his impending death. His eyes grew wide and tearful, and his mouth opened to gibber for a moment, before speaking clearly. "I beg you, my lord—incarcerate me. I bear nothing but contrition for my baseless and senseless actions. Lock me in shackles, stick me in a prison quarry, let me scrub latrine pits for the remainder of my days. I—"

"That won't work. You must understand, public execution is not a flagrancy of one's power. It is a method to exert command and enforce authority. If by executing one man the entire city will progress, then it must be done. I cannot stray from my values. Reward the small, punish the great."

Rennerin lifted a hand to scratch the thin white hair at his temple. There was a bruise on his upper cheek from when Alarin smacked him with his cane. "You are a clever man, my lord," the former chamberlain said. "You have done well to gain the power of the court and the love of the populace. You deserve all the accolades that befit a man of your status. But to me . . . and to many others, you will always be a bitter cripple."

The public square was enshrouded in uncertainty on the morning of Lord Rennerin's execution. Alarin stood on the high terrace, watching a group of handlers wheel a crude cage cart through a crowd of confused and begrudging spectators. For many, it was difficult to see their beloved chamberlain bound in chains and dressed in dingy sackcloth, and it certainly made Alarin's position a precarious one. His free hand kept a white-knuckled grip on the scrollwork balustrade, but when the man's transgressions were proclaimed and his sentencing doled out, the crowd's collective opinion began to turn. The springtide haze was thick and sticky, and the rising sun bathed the narrow, pole-like chair on the center square. Rennerin was placed upon it, a garrote was placed over his head and around his neck, and the strangulation began. The former chamberlain thrashed and struggled for several excruciating minutes before he passed from this wretched world into the next.

Farewell, my traitorous friend, Alarin thought.

When it was over, when the body was removed and the crowd was dispersed back to their dwellings and duties, Alarin exited the terrace and hobbled down the tower stairs. Szathan Mordall moved beside him, the big general taking small steps to keep from over-taking the lead. "Time to make things right," Alarin told him. Szathan only grunted at that, and the two men continued their descent in silence. Alarin's thoughts were an uncharacteristic jumble. He couldn't stop envisioning Lord Rennerin's strangulation . . . the way his plump face twisted and empurpled as his soul slowly fled from his physical form. It wasn't pleasant to see a once beloved man die in such a cruel and drawn-out manner, but Alarin had to do what was necessary for the realm.

They exited the tower and moved across a forecourt that led them to the Iris Hall. Inside, they found the White Fang coun-cilmembers seated and impatiently frowning—all except Byort. The bug-eyed man was pacing the length of the table, one hand clutching the rim of an unmarked bronze goblet. He was wearing a heavy black robe with web-like stitching along the arms, along with old leather shoes with scuffs on the toe caps. He stopped when he saw Alarin, his insectile face tightening with anger as he placed the goblet on the table.

Here we go, Alarin mused.

The limp to the dais was as lengthy as it was awkward. *Click, tap, drag. Click, tap, drag.* For most of the way, Alarin kept his head lowered, and only when he reached the foot of the dais did he make a conscious effort to greet Minister Byort. The man obviously wasn't pleased, but Alarin didn't care about that. He just wanted this to be over. "Minister Byort of the White Fang Council, my general wishes to speak." Alarin nudged Szathan, then watched as the giant man came to stand directly before Byort. He fell to a single knee, *thud,* the sound of his greave hitting the tile so loud it made Byort flinch. Szathan craned his squarish head up to look the man directly in the eye, and then . . . he apologized.

It was a sincere and sobering apology, once seemingly pulled from the deepest reaches of the general's hardened heart. It wasn't a monologue's length, but it carried a certain expressiveness that ran against Szathan's usual blunt and taciturn manner. One might even suspect that Szathan wasn't the creator of such words, but Alarin knew the big general was far brighter than others might have you believe, and certainly brighter than his ogreish features gave away.

After Szathan's powerful voice released its final, echoing word, the hall receded into an uncertain silence. Szathan remained kneeling, while Byort stood over him, a small figure before a slumped giant. Alarin wasn't sure what to expect from the bug-eyed councilman. Not only had Szathan falsely accused him of attempted murder, he'd also shamed him, dragged him off in front of his peers, and locked him in a cage kennel like a disobedient mutt. It was plain Byort wanted to shout at Szathan, to rail at him and explain in detail all the indignities and hardships he'd suffered at the hands of this rash and oversized general. But in the end, Byort did none of that; he simply gave a weary sigh, and said, "I forgive you."

And there it was, the response that both Alarin and Szathan needed to hear. The general's head rose like a leeboard on a ship, his tiny blackberry eyes widening with surprise. It was then Byort hiked up his robes and bent down to help the big man to his feet. Szathan obliged him and stood, and the two men embraced. Even though Szathan kept his shoulders slumped and his posture hunched, the size difference was so great that it appeared as father embracing child, and yet, it was a magnificent sight. The councilmen began to applaud, and this applause turned into a great clamor of cheers and hoots and whistles, so joyful and infectious that Alarin couldn't help but participate. And when Szathan turned to acknowledge him, his eyes were glassy with joy and his expression was a gap-toothed smile of gratitude. Alarin nodded to his general and friend. In his heart, he knew that a great rift had finally closed.

Later, when Alarin returned to the conservatory hall, he spent some time filing his silk missives and mandates and organizing his writing materials. When he was done, he exhaled a breath that released his concerns. *What a strange day,* he thought. *One that began in the darkness of execution, only to end in the light of forgiveness.*

Little Silas was seated on a nearby bench, an open tome under an arm, his free hand leafing through the old vellum pages. These days his reading comprehension was so proficient that a tutor no longer sat with him. He gobbled up books on his own, his eyes working fast and fluently like an omnilegent historian. *If only I could have that boy's sponge-like mind,* Alarin mused. Right now, Silas was tackling a meandering and rather prolix tome: *The Great Downward Shift,* a compendium of historical writings based on the tumultuous fourth dynasty. Alarin praised him for his literary diligence, and the boy blushed and thanked him, although he seemed rather low in spirits today, and it was no secret why. "Lord Rennerin had to die," Alarin told him. "You must understand this, Your Majesty."

The boy closed the tome and nodded with his usual bashfulness. "I understand he betrayed you, and I understand he had to be executed. But the deeper things . . . I try so hard to understand the maneuvers of imperial power. I try to understand, I do. Like this tome. I understand the individual words, but I often miss the meaning behind the full passage."

"You will understand in time. You're a boy yet, and life . . . well, it is an unstoppable juggernaut. It will hit you with events both large and small, historic and personal, consequential and not. Challenges will come from likely and unlikely opposition, and love and camaraderie may be found in the most remote places. Friends may become enemies, enemies may become friends. In this constant push and pull, this constant forward and return, you will endure a range of emotions: joy, sadness, anger, fear, excitement, shame. I don't mean to belittle you, but there is an understanding to the breadth of life that you are yet to grasp. It will come in time. Don't be afraid of it, don't cower in the shadows. Stand as tall as your stature allows, plant your feet firmly in the earth, and attack your life with intensity and passion. And whomever you choose to love, make sure you love deeply, because you can never go back, and you can never replace what is lost.

"Now I speak this to you as I would to any youth, regardless of imperial status. You have many days ahead of you, but they will pass just as they do for all mortal men and women, and if you are lucky enough to make it to advanced age, you will have a heart full of memories to look back upon. Make sure those memories are meaningful." Alarin made sure the boy understood before continuing. "Remember, one leads through strength, and one gains strength through the spirit. One day, after many nights and many years, people will come to remember you in a simplistic way, perhaps in a word or phrase, as they do for all great figures. I will always be remembered as a cripple, and not for the exploits and accomplishments of my younger years. Raas Dragath will always be remembered as a traitor, and not for his contributions to the Anir as a minister of the Hollow. And your father will always be remembered as the Savior of the Anir, never mind his questionable actions near the end of his days. Make sure you are—sorry, one moment."

A dull throb in Alarin's stump stole his focus. An instinctive hand moved down to adjust the straps of his wooden leg, but it was of little use. The discomfort was akin to someone pulling the upper limb, but since there was no more phantom pain, he didn't want to grouse about it, for fear of sounding ungrateful. *Still, I can't keep ignoring this. The prosthetic needs to be re-examined, perhaps sanded or shaved and realigned.*

Silas, ever the intuitive lad, turned and politely asked the nearest attendant to summon Master Penry. Alarin was about to raise a hand in protest but decided not to challenge the emperor's command. Instead he said, "You are too kind, Your Majesty."

The boy's posture perked up a bit. "I want to be kind. I don't want to be cruel. There is so much cruelty in the world already, so much destruction and deceit and death. I want to be kind."

"I know. And you are already kind. But you mustn't allow kindness to become weakness. That is what I meant to say before my wooden leg so rudely interrupted me. Don't let yourself be known as a timid ruler. The people will call you a pushover and a mouse. Do you understand? You're chewing your lip."

The boy stopped. "I do. I do understand."

"You must be firm in your decisions and absolute in your mindset, and you must never allow your core values and fundamental beliefs to be corrupted, nor should you ever allow your detractors and critics to slip under your skin. I've been called many things, been criticized for many faults. Some true, others not. I've been called a peg-leg, a misanthrope, and a lily-livered fool. As a man of power and standing, you must be accustomed to criticism and public censure. Lesser folk will try to deride your accomplishments and tear you down to their level. Just remember, you cannot please everyone. If anything, remember that."

"I will."

The door opened and the owlish Master Penry waddled inside. He offered a brief greeting before asking Alarin a barrage of questions to help pinpoint the discomfort. Alarin gave his most concise and plainspoken answers, and then he sat down and watched as the solemn physician undid the straps to remove the wooden leg. First, he examined the hasps and catches and straps, then he moved on to the pylon and posterior wall and quadrilateral socket, checking for signs of misalignment or warping. He worked diligently and dutifully but found nothing unusual, so he placed the leg gently on the floor and turned to inspect the stump itself.

The exposed flesh had a reddish tint today, along with the familiar musky smell of closed pores and accumulated moisture. Penry's cold fingers began to poke and press and prod, and while Alarin waited his gaze settled sidelong on Silas, who stood observant and curious. The boy's face had grown noticeably slimmer and more mature these past few months. *Perhaps he will come to inherit Demien's strong and rugged features after all,* Alarin mused. *Will he inherit his father's boldness as well?*

The physician brought out a small bronze measuring stick, and as he worked his calculations his nose scrunched, and his mouth shifted to one side. At length he raised his old head back, slow, like a turtle peering out of a pond. He asked Alarin for the specification sheet for the prosthetic leg, the one he'd drawn up during Alarin's first intake examination. Alarin had just tidied his desk, so it didn't take long to produce the document and hand it to the physician. Penry's eyes danced back and forth across the page. When he was done, he gave a firm grunt that caused Alarin to ask what was wrong.

"It's not the artificial limb," the physician said at length. He sounded a little winded, as though he'd just sprinted the length of the hall. "It's your leg."

"What about it?"

"It's . . . oh, how do I say this . . . it's *growing.*"

A sudden weight wrapped itself around Alarin's heart. "What the hell are you talking about?"

"It's growing, just as I said. Here, on the patient form, I indicated the exact length of your leg, from the anterior iliac spine to the tip of the stump with pelvis squared. But it's different from the measurement I just took."

"Maybe your measurement was off."

The physician shook his head. "I may be old, but I'm not a careless twit. The leg—something's happening to it. It's like the limb of a sea star. It's become . . . regenerative."

Alarin's head twisted and he locked eyes with Silas. Both man and youth, regent and emperor, spoke the same word at the same time: *Cloudfalls.*

CHAPTER FORTY-SIX

Ansetheral Athera was exhausted, itchy, and footsore when at last he'd found the traitor Jakken. The Vaskultan was skulking along the southern banks of the Grayling River, up and down and around jagged slabs of shale and schist, searching for a fordable point in the river. Truth be told, there was none. To the east rose a segmented arch bridge of lichened stone, but traffic was too plentiful, and the stationed soldiers were too vigilant. The white floral banners of Aster Falls made it clear this was Seric Dyre's feudatory kingdom, and no Vaskultan would find safe passage here.

Anseth assumed that Jakken would seek out another way to cross, perhaps by commandeering a ferryman's craft or disguising himself in stolen merchant togs, but the Vaskultan proved more resourceful than that. He'd spent a long moment surveying a section of the bank where the river appeared narrowest, and then he backtracked into the woods. Anseth crouched behind a nest of thorny thicket, watching the traitor chop saplings into logs, strip bare their knots and protuberances, and carry them over a shoulder for assembly near the river's edge. Once Jakken had accumulated a dozen or so, he lined them up and lashed them together using the braided cordage of plant fibers. When finished he sat near the riverside, gnawing on a trout he must've netted early that morning. He was clearly tired, and clearly vulnerable.

If there's ever a time to strike, it's now, Anseth thought. He knew the Vaskultan traitor was waiting for nightfall to cross the river and disappear among the dells of the northern Blue Wolf Hills. *Approach him from behind and cut him down. Don't dither, you must do it now. Right now.* He unsheathed his backsword, edged away from the thicket—and yet he hesitated. *Remember, this man betrayed your clan, stole your Earthstone, and tried to kill you. Why suffer this hesitancy?*

Truth was, Jakken's skills with both bow and blade worried him. If Anseth made the slightest sound moving in, Jakken could spin and shoot him down with ease. And if Anseth did get close enough but mucked up his first strike, he might have a long, grueling fight ahead of him. And he certainly didn't want that, but if he didn't take action, if he continued to mull and stall, the opportunity would be lost, and the traitor would be gone forever. Anseth knew this, and *still* he hesitated. *You've killed many and more dangerous men before. You killed Dariok, remember? He was a volatile prick, the worst of the tribe. But even Dariok didn't wrong you like Jakken had. You* must *cut him down. You must.*

Jakken was just sitting there, quiet and unmoving, as if enamored by the dusky pastel light that threaded itself through the striated clouds. He wasn't nearly as large or as strong as Dariok had been, but he was twice as quick and far more cunning. That made for a dangerous foe. *This man betrayed your clan, stole your Earthstone, and nearly killed you. Cut him down already. Do it. Just kill him. KILL HIM.*

Anseth dashed forward, light of foot and with backsword raised —but Jakken must've heard him because he turned away just as the blade screamed for his neck. *Whoosh.* Anseth's momentum drove him headlong, and suddenly he was face-down on the ground eating mud. *He tripped me.* It was a basic Vaskultan maneuver, but Anseth didn't even see it. *Damn the gods, he moves fast.*

"You should be dead," Jakken said. A curved dagger appeared in his hand, the hilt carved to resemble the spanned wings of a hawk. "I shot you, I saw you bleed. How are you not dead?"

"I'm a *revek*," Anseth said.

"That you are, but you're not getting the Earthstone. And you look like shit. I see the wilds got the best of you."

Anseth's backsword was lost somewhere in the riparian reeds, so he drew a dagger from his belt. The two men stared at each other, motionless in the muddy banks. Anseth could feel the cold muck plastered on his own face. It dripped down the length of his ratty hair, threatening to obstruct his eyesight, but the moment he lifted a hand to his brow, Jakken attacked.

The world became a storm of slashing and slicing and stabbing, with Anseth dodging and countering with unthinking fluidity. He couldn't say how long this dance went on, or how often their knives tore into leather and drew blood, but he could *sense* that time itself had ground to a halt, allowing an endless exchange of overhand cuts, backhand slashes, downward thrusts, upward drives, and straight stabs.

He can't keep this up, Anseth thought. *He can't keep this up.*

It was true. Jakken's movements were growing sloppy and slug-gish, while Anseth remained quick-footed and slick. He baited Jakken with an overextended low cut, only to whirl upwards and slice him across the forehead.

A sheet of blood poured down the traitor's face, painting a red mask. Jakken pawed at the gash, smearing blood more than swab-bing it, but if his vision were hindered, he didn't show it, and so the clash of small arms continued.

He can't keep this up. He can't keep this up. Anseth was imposing his will now, his confidence rising as Jakken's was falling, and after two more cuts the traitor fell back on his heels, nearly stumbling into a mudhole. Anseth closed the distance but nimble Jakken somehow righted himself and arced his blade in retaliation. It missed Anseth's throat by a hair, and in return he jammed his own dagger into Jakken's side, a quick in-out thrust that tore through leather and skin and what felt like ribcage bone.

The traitor squealed like a swine and began to slash wildly. Anseth seized his wrist and wrestled for control of the dagger, but Jakken was strong—stronger than expected, and when he gave Anseth's arm a forceful wrench, bolts of fiery pain shot through the shoulder.

Anseth stifled the urge to cry out, and instead used his mouth to chomp down on Jakken's fingers, prying them open. The dagger fell to the mud. Jakken disentangled himself and shoved Anseth away, then he examined his hand, frowning at the blood running down his fingers. He called Anseth a dog-fucker or something of that ilk, and then he did something quite unexpected: he spun and ran.

It was so sudden that Anseth neglected to react, and by the time he *did* give chase, the traitor had already stopped and snatched up his bow and quiver. A moment later, an arrow was nocked.

Twang.

Anseth didn't see the shot, but he heard it hiss over his head like a winged snake. Jakken tried to nock a second arrow, but Anseth was already on him.

Thump.

The traitor wasn't blessed with a tall frame, but he was as thickset and immobile as anything Anseth had ever grappled. Still, technique always triumphed over strength, and with a burst of the hips and the sweep of the leg, he lifted Jakken into the air and brought him down on the riverbank, *boom,* with Anseth landing hard on top of him.

The sound Jakken made was like the grunt of a boar—but the bastard had no quit in him. He thrust his hips and flipped Anseth over, and with a grip of the bow's end he began hammering down blows.

The first drummed against Anseth's leather vambrace, the next hit him on the side of the head. That scrambled Anseth's mind for a moment, but when the third strike missed, he managed to seize the bow, and now both men were tugging for possession.

Jakken released a hand and punched Anseth in the face. Anseth replied to that by driving his elbow into the traitor's eye. Jakken groaned and Anseth yanked the bow from his grip, but he used so much force that it slipped from his own fingers and went flying into the river.

Splash.

It was gone.

Jakken rolled just out of Anseth's reach, but neither man attempted to rise. Both lay partially sunken in the muddy banks, heaving and huffing like overworked quarrymen. Jakken's laugh was a ragged gasp. "You can fight, fucker."

"I'm a Vaskultan."

Jakken paused to spit a wad of bloody phlegm. "My earlier labors left me dog-tired. I would've beaten you fresh."

"'Would've' is as meaningless as old shit. I outwitted and outworked you."

Another ragged laugh. "So you did, Revek." He didn't speak for a long moment, just breathed long, heavy breaths. Finally, he said, "Let me go."

Anseth nearly coughed his response. "*What?*"

The traitor flung something close to where Anseth lay. "Take the damn thing." It was the Earthstone. "Now let me go. We'll never meet again."

Anseth wanted to mock the traitor for such a foolish request, yet he didn't. It was hard to explain, but after a grueling fight, the animosity between two men was often quashed—or at least staved off for a time. Anseth still despised Jakken for his actions, but he was no longer thirsty for revenge. Still, this wasn't just some petty rivalry. Jakken had undermined Anseth's rule, stolen his Earthstone, and attempted to kill him. How could such a despicable man be allowed to live?

"I meant to take your eyes," Anseth said. "You deserve it. You deserve an eternity in the Great Void."

"No Vaskultan deserves that. Just let me go, you are the undisputed chieftain. You proved it against me, just as you proved it against Dariok." He gave a weary snort. "Let me go. You'll never hear from me again. That is a promise."

"I can't do that."

"Why not? You're tired of violence. I can see it in your eyes. This isn't what you want to do. Just let me go and be done with it."

"I can't do that," Anseth said again, but when Jakken started to crawl away, Anseth didn't stop him. He wanted to, but his fighting spirit had long waned, and its replacements were soreness and ache. He simply watched as the traitor staggered to his feet, one hand clutching his bleeding side. "You hurt me good." He turned and limped toward the river's edge. Anseth continued to watch. After every step it seemed Jakken might collapse, but somehow, he made it to the raft.

Don't let him go, Anseth thought. *Don't let the traitor go.*

Jakken pushed the craft out of the shallows and crawled onto the wooden deck. He lay there for a time, sideways and panting with exertion, then, with slow and grave difficulty, he grabbed an oar and used it to prop himself to his feet. "Let me go," the Vaskultan repeated, even though Anseth still hadn't moved. Jakken used the oar to push himself farther into the river, his movements slow and strained like those of a moribund old man.

He pushed and paddled and paddled some more, and when he was a safe distance from land, he stopped and turned around. The bathing moonlight revealed his blood-painted face, which was smattered with his usual cocksure grin. "You shouldn't have let me go." His voice was an ominous call over the silent waters.

Anseth balled his fists in rage. His first impulse was to race to the water's edge and hurl his dagger at the traitor—but no, something happened. The raft must've struck something in the river, because it jerked hard, and the corded logs began to shift and shuffle and break apart.

Creak. Crack. Snap.

Jakken was thrown sideways onto the solid wood, then dumped headlong into the water. He surfaced a few moments later, arms flailing and flapping, blood trailing from his matted hair. Clumsy hands seized a drifting log, but Jakken must've been too weak or too injured because his grip didn't hold, and after a final, desperate moment of thrashing, the Vaskultan traitor was swept underwater, never to be seen again.

With that, the evening mists strolled in, obscuring the floating wreck until it became little more than a dark amorphous shroud. Anseth remained on the banks, Earthstone in hand, watching that shroud dwindle and dwindle and eventually disappear.

The gods have decided, he thought. And then he went home.

CHAPTER FORTY-SEVEN

Seric Dyre spent most of his waking hours in Miriana's private room, watching over her like a stone sentinel of the palatial hall. She'd been administered a sleep tonic that must've been a touch too strong, since it left her sprawled out on the featherbed like a day-old corpse. The scratches on her face were being treated with powdered comfrey and other mucilaginous herbs, which left her skin glistening like the sweat of an overworked drudge. There was bruising too, along the wrist and clavicle and near the pelvic area, but like the scratches they were minor. What concerned Seric more was the emotional pain and resentment that Miriana might bear. *Poor woman came to me for sanctuary, but instead she found violence and pain. Has she not suffered enough?*

Sometimes she would wake, and when she did, she'd sometimes forget where she was or what had happened to her, and once she squeezed Seric's hand before drifting back to sleep. Seric would whisper that she was safe, which seemed of little comfort, but it was all he could think to say. In truth, he pitied her. He pitied her and he loved her, and despite the facial wounds and the busted nose and bad haircut, she was still beautiful. She would *always* be beautiful. He wanted to tell her that, to kiss her lips and caress her snowy skin from the neck down to the soft spray of freckles about the shoulders. *Will I ever get to again? Will she ever forgive me for the actions of a crazed and impassioned whore?*

Ravia was dead, and he wasn't sad about it. She meant nothing to him, just as he'd oft told her, and the moment he'd learned of the assault, his thoughts were only of Miriana's safety. In fact, were Ravia still alive, he'd have her publicly flayed for her crime. Of course, he arranged no funeral. He simply had Ravia's body dumped into one of the many winding channels whose current flowed away from the city. *An unceremonious end for a contemptible woman.* A part of him hoped Miriana were awake to bear witness to it, but another part knew it wouldn't have mattered. Miriana was a willful woman; to win her forgiveness would be among the greatest of Seric's challenges.

Vylas was understanding of the situation, or at least he claimed to be. The one-eyed man spent much of his time seated on an armchair near Miriana's bed. He was there now, biting away at what little fingernails he had left, sometimes turning the finger sideways to nibble on the cuticle. He looked restless and sleepless, one eye darting back and forth like a rodent on high alert. His robes were frayed and filthy and faded, and his black halfmask was worn and missing most of its filigree design. He said little, his mouth too busy with his biting, but when Seric confessed his mistake, Vylas lowered his hand from his lips and wiped the strand of saliva that came with it. His voice was a low murmur. "We've all made mistakes with the lady."

Seric didn't know what that meant, but he decided to let it go. "I'm tripling the Zhoulish guardsmen at her door."

"Should've been done the moment she arrived, *King* Seric."

Seric didn't like his sharp tone, so he made sure his was sharper. "I tried, she refused."

"She's headstrong, you of all people know this. Should've been done anyway."

"I didn't think—" Seric stopped, lowered his eyes. *I didn't think that whore Ravia would be so jealous, or that she would be capable of such violence.* He sighed. *Unrequited passion is a poisonous fruit.* Seric turned back to Miriana, but his words were directed at Vylas. "Her wounds are minor. She will be in better spirits once the tonic wears off. She's been through a lot. We all have."

Vylas's voice was thick with disappointment. "My sister came to you; she trusted you."

"She came to me because she had nowhere else to go." He turned and glared at the smaller man. *I've had enough of your jabs.* He spoke in his most authoritative tone. "I know you facilitated the lady's arrival, so I will ignore your offensive remarks. But I suggest you give a care for how you speak to me. I thought we'd become allies since we last campaigned together in Silverleaf. Perhaps I am wrong to assume that? I need to know where your loyalties lie."

Vylas's good eye turned upon Miriana, his expression softening. "I'm loyal to her, now until my last breath." As soon as he said that, his resolve seemed to melt away, and in the end, he bowed his head in servitude. "But I'm also yours to command, my king."

Good enough, Seric thought.

For a while, the only sound was the faint droplets of rain against the latched windows, a gentle precursor to a coming storm. Thunder soon rumbled in the distance, a disconsolate sound rather than ominous. Miriana turned over in her bed and murmured something unintelligible, sounds of distress perhaps brought upon by a night terror. Vylas shook his head sadly. "She's afraid someone knows she's here. She wants to stay, but she doesn't wish to cause a war with the Hollow."

"That won't happen," Seric told him. "But if it does, I would die a thousand deaths to protect the lady but once."

· · ·

The rain had grown much heavier by the time Seric returned to his room. He could hear it against the upper roof tiles, a constant bucketing rush that was supplemented by the occasional howl of wind and peal of thunder. So distracted was he that he failed to notice his son, Veldries, standing half hidden in the shadows of a tall latticework étagère. Seric nearly leaped out of his skin.

The young man gave a quiet chuckle. "I didn't mean to startle you, Father." He was dressed in semi-formal evening wear: a bark-brown tunic, tight trousers, and shin-high otterskin boots. His shoulder-length hair was partially tied back in a knot, with the loose locks interlaced like the twigs of a bird's nest. He pushed a hand through it, a nervous action, then wiped the palm on his trousers, leaving a small sweat stain. "Forgive me, I know the hour is late."

Seric undid his belt sheath and placed Sunburst back on its wall hooks, then he moved to a dressing stand to remove his outer cloak and neckerchief. That done, he turned back to his son. "What troubles you?"

Veldries touched the apple of his own throat, as if subconsciously indicating Seric's jagged scar. "The incident with Lady Ravia . . . I'm sorry to hear of her fate."

"Don't be. It was well deserved."

He stole a furtive glance behind him, toward the entranceway. "Where are your bodyguards?"

"Off guarding someone." He unlaced and removed his boots, then spared a moment to rub his old toe injury. He didn't mean to be short with his son, but he was much too tired for inane questions, and he had a lot of turmoil in the heart concerning Miriana. An attendant came over to present a flagon of wine, but Seric told the lad he'd take it on the outdoor balcony. It was a small covered space with an openwork railing and a bamboo lounge chair, perfect to relax and view the coming storm, which Seric did.

The wine was light and bodied and semi-sweet, a suitable aperitif since he generally preferred a late supper. As he sipped his eyes drifted to the oppressive cloud cover, a crisscross of dark ripples in a midnight sky. The city below was a carpet of gray mist with rows of glistening rooftop tiles. Seric had always liked the rain; it had a certain gloom about it that he found soothing.

Veldries joined him a few moments later. "So, who are they guarding?"

"What? Oh." A hand waved noncommittally. "Just an informant. It's not important."

"Not important, yet you won't tell your own son?"

Seric waited a beat before responding. "If you mean to quarrel, you'll have to come back another time."

A bolt flashed in the sky. Thunder rolled, an angry god's prolonged growl. Veldries made an *ooooo* sound, then said, "I think that one struck the west orchard."

Seric agreed, and for a time the two quietly observed the storm. When at last the rain began to lessen, Seric looked down and gave a soft sigh. "I know I've been an absentee father since your return. My duties as a king . . . they consume me these days. But I'd like to continue your studies. Just as I learned the intricacies of battle from my father, you will learn from me."

"If you've learned so much, then why have your last two battles ended in such shameful defeat?"

Seric smiled even though the words stung. "Many believe a military leader is only as good as his last battle. That is a fool's mindset. What matters is the extent of the war, the one who remains when the dust settles and the blood dries. Listen to me, my son. Don't concern yourself with the opinions of the small. You will soon see what I can do. And you, along with everyone else in the realm, will come to admire Seric Dy—"

Booted feet stomped onto the balcony. Seric turned at once. Zirian Revil stood in the archway, his normally stoic expression replaced with a wide-eyed look of alarm. He jabbed a finger at Veldries and barked in broken Anirian: "What you *doing*?"

At first Seric had no idea what he meant. But then his eyes drifted to his son . . . and to the knife in the boy's hand.

Seric lurched from his chair like a man stung by a hornet. "*Veldries?!*"

Veldries fumbled with the knife before shoving it back into his belt sheath. "Forgive me, I . . . I . . . ."

"Speak, boy, you *what?*"

"I only meant to . . . s-sharpen my blade."

"On what whetstone?"

"I . . . I seemed to have misplaced it." The boy backpedaled a few steps, then turned—directly into the towering obstruction that was the Mad Wolf. That paled him. "F-forgive me, I am e-exhausted. I must r-retire for the evening." He bowed his head quickly to both men. "Father. Lord Zirian." With that, he sidled past the big Zhoul and withdrew.

Zirian remained in the archway, crossing his giant arms and leveling Seric with a half-lidded gaze. He spoke in the Zhoulish tongue. "General Wyath warned you of this. He told you—"

"That's enough. I know what you will say."

"Your boy meant to murder you."

"I said that's *enough*." Seric couldn't swallow the truth. *My own blessed son . . . my progeny and heir . . . would he dare commit such a heinous act? No, I don't believe it.* "This is the usurper's doing, yes, this is Zantherei whispering poisonous words into the boy's ear. And Nyvia too, that bitch. I should've strangled her when she played envoy for the tyrant."

"Arrest the boy, don't allow him to run."

"I won't do that."

"You must, he—"

"*HE'S MY SON.*" The words exploded from his mouth, shattering what remained of the pluvial ambiance. As if cowed by the outburst, the rain and thunder had all but dwindled into silence. Seric did his best to collect himself before speaking again. "If he runs I won't chase him down, and I won't issue a warrant with a sketch of his face. That said, if the boy comes to any harm, I will shove a pike up each and every perpetrator's bunghole." His hand slid up an imaginary stake. "All the way up there . . . until it comes out the mouth. Am I being clear enough for you, General?"

Zirian nodded even though his disapproval was evident, and sure enough, Veldries Dyre was gone by dawn.

Over the next four weeks Seric saw little of Miriana. His attempts at visitation were stymied by excuses of indisposition, and the few times he did see her were brief and unfulfilling. She wasn't unfriendly, just detached, and although she claimed to need more time, Seric didn't have the patience to give it to her. In truth, he ached for her intimacy. Seric had to resist once more to touch her, to hold her in his arms and to smell the sweetness of her skin. It wasn't easy, but he did it, and tonight, as he exited her private chamber, he spun and pressed his head against the closed door like a lovelorn fool. *She will come around,* he told himself. *She will come around and I will have my queen.*

The following morning reports told of an approaching rider. Seric led a small honor guard to personally greet the fellow. To his surprise and dismay, it was the same Hollow envoy that had delivered terms some months ago, the cocksure beefcake with the gaudy frock and skewbald horse.

With a self-important smile he handed Seric a silk missive, and of course this missive was from Zantherei Athera himself. Seric held it for quite some time, spinning it around his hand, feeling the crisp material between his fingers. He wanted to open it, but he couldn't, so he kept spinning it around and around until he carelessly gave himself a paper cut. After sucking the blood out of the slashed finger, he unfolded the document, gave an unenthusiastic sigh, and read:

. . .

I know you are sheltering my lovely wife. I know that you two have schemed while I'd lain poisoned and fighting for my life. I know all your secrets, and just as Raas Dragath received his punishment for treason, you will receive yours as well. Your defeat at the Shaded Plains was nothing. I will crush you and your worthless city. My blade is darkness, my army is death, and I am coming for you. - Zantherei Athera, Storm of the North, Supreme Lord of the Hollow, and Emperor of the realm, as he reigns on the fifth month, spring, year 444 of the dynasty of the Anir, year one of the Athera dynasty.

P.S. I never had faith in your boy. I knew he was a failure, just like his father.

Seric tore the missive to shreds. *Stupid warmongering fool.* His hands were trembling like autumn leaves. He unlaced his fingers to allow the paper scraps to spiral to the ground. *He knows everything about Miriana and me, or at least he presumes to. But how?* A wedge of bile rose in his throat, hot and acidic and terribly uncomfortable. *And Veldries . . . that impressionable young idiot was coaxed into taking my life. No, I won't seek revenge. I will win back his faith . . . even if I must stand at the head of my army and cut down monsters like Aldebron Pentagath myself.* Yes, there were only two truths to all this: Seric would do whatever was needed to win the boy back, just as he would do whatever was needed to protect Lady Miriana.

The envoy cleared his throat and crossed his beefy arms, an impatient frown tugging at his face. He certainly wasn't hiding his displeasure of the whole paper-shredding incident, but Seric was about to truly ruin this insufferable fool's day. He scooped up the silk scraps and stuffed them into a small leathern pouch. He then handed the pouch back to the envoy—well, more thrusting it into his chest—and barked an order to take away the man's horse. When the envoy protested, Seric had the skin of his cheeks and forehead peeled off, so the long walk back would be that much more excruciating under the late spring sun. Yes, Seric Dyre was a malicious prick, but he would do anything to make sure this goddamn realm was his.

CHAPTER FORTY-EIGHT

S zathan Mordall couldn't recall the last time he'd been dressed so well. Gray silk-stitched pantaloons (tailored specifically for a man of his leg length), a lace ruffle tunic (more like undersized tabard), and a wintry-blue outer jacket (tight-fitted and snazzy). The ensemble was completed by a double waist cincher of tiny metallic beads that matched those on his bespoke silk shoes, which were crafted by the best cordwainer around. Compliments had been thrown his way at every turn, but Szathan wasn't blind to the truth. He looked like a frost giant, a big lumbering yeti, all bright and icy-blue like the canyons of permafrost one might find in the dead of the arctic. The outfit was far better suited for a handsome and proportioned man like the late Lord Yuseth Valate, but there was no point in dwelling on that.

It had been another daylong event of feasting and reveling and honoring, but Szathan, being the hardnosed, deep-in-the-muck military type, found it all quite tedious and tiresome. His bravery in repelling the enemy siege, and for turning Gilberon Brehems back to his side, had reinforced his standing as a hero to the general populace, but unfortunately, such acclaim rarely came without extensive social obligations. He must've been asked the same two or three questions a hundred times, and he must've given the same answers a hundred times in return. As he'd often made plain, Szathan wasn't a man skilled in the art of public speeches or diplomatic graces, but so long as he did his best, the people seemed to forgive his shortcomings.

Later that evening, Silas stole him away, and in the confines of his private hall, the boy appeared slightly more confident than his usual bashful self. He was still dressed in his formal celebratory attire, a carefully chosen blend of rich blues and deep grays that made him appear as dignified as he did dapper. Right now, he was on his knees and rooting around in a large brassbound trunk, one hand rustling fabrics and clinking objects, the other upraised and motioning Szathan closer. "It's here, kept in secret."

"What's kept in secret?" Szathan asked.

The young emperor pulled out a bundle of black oilcloth. With eager fingers he unfolded a corner, then slid out a short sword with a black bejeweled hilt and a carved pommel.

It was Dreadfang.

Szathan shrank back as though punched in the sternum. "Where did you find this?"

"The first night of the festivities, it was left beside a plinth in the eastern palace wing." He placed it gingerly in his uncle's hands. The black-leathered grip felt weighty and secure, the balance firm at the base and fair at the tip. The beveled face of the blade was a flash of silvery-black steel, fullered for lightness and style, with a crossguard unmistakably curled like the horns of a Sadralen. Indeed, this was Dreadfang, the legendary short sword that belonged to the legendary hero Demien Mordall. *But what does it mean?* Szathan asked his nephew that very question.

Silas shrugged. "There's a note."

"Read it to me."

Silas cleared his throat. "'*I must profess that my words to*

Szathan Mordall were given only out of respect to the former grand commandant. The truth is, I lied. The Savior of the Anir wasn't interred with honors at a secret location.'" He paused to swallow. *"'After the battle of Wintersun, Lord Demien was taken to his child-hood village and nursed back from the edge of death. He now lives as a petty farmer in nameless obscurity. If you wish to return the realm to its former glory, you must win back your father's faith. This note has found your hand because the siege of Stormhaven has tested my faith and changed my heart. - Sabriel Soffin, Lord General of the Anir, Silver Claw of the North, and Tamer of the Western Wilds.'"*

The boy's eyes leaped from the paper and latched onto Szathan's. "I told you he was alive, I told you I told you I told you!" He was shifting his weight from one foot to the other, back and forth, back and forth, a grand smile plastered on his face.

Szathan was more shocked than pleased. *My elder brother . . . alive? Could it be true? Or is it an evil ploy to draw out and assas-sinate His Majesty?* His head suddenly felt weak and wobbly, as if his neck were no longer strong enough to support it. He rubbed his jutting brow and expelled a colossal breath, but neither did much to alleviate the stress. *What must I do? I cannot handle this alone.* "Best to have Lord Alarin examine this. Perhaps his scribes can confirm Lord Soffin's identity through comparisons in the brush writing."

The boy froze mid-motion. The smile remained sutured in place, but it became more a worrisome look. "You think . . . you think it's a trick?"

"Don't know. Like I said it's best to have Lord Alarin look at it."

"That'll take too long. You do know the location, do you not, Uncle? You do know where to find my father?"

Szathan didn't blink. "Seven Lakes." He made a sputtering sound under his breath. "Not many fond memories of that village, or of my mother for that matter." *I was the Little Beast in her eyes,* he thought.

"I want to go," Silas said.

"It's too dangerous."

"I can handle myself. You and Lord Alarin always tell me to not be so timid. You tell me to be bold. Well, this is my chance to be bold. To do something worthwhile for the good of the realm. Uncle, I need to do this. With Demien Mordall at the head of our armies, we will reunite the empire!"

"And if it's a ruse? What then, boy?" His head shifted back and forth sternly. "This isn't boldness, it's recklessness. You are an emperor. The greatest being in the realm. Your title and standing are too important to be put in harm's way."

"I'm just a figurehead, a symbol. It is Alarin Athera who rules this city."

"And he will continue to do so until you are of proper age. You must understand that."

"I do, but Demien's my father . . . I need to see him. I need him to see me as I am now. Not just as an emperor but as a boy able to speak."

Szathan softened at that, replying only after a stretch of silence had passed between them. "I'll go."

The boy's eyes widened. "You will?"

"I'll go to him, I'll talk to him, I'll bring him back."

"Truthfully?"

His eyes drifted down to Dreadfang, sharp and shiny in his hands. *I can't ignore the chance to reconnect with my elder brother, and I can't ignore the chance to return to Stormhaven with the greatest warrior this realm has ever known.* He handed the weapon back to Silas, hilt first, blade down. "If he is there, at Seven Lakes, as Lord Soffin has claimed . . . then I will do my best to win back his faith. For the sake of the—"

The thick double-doors groaned open. Szathan turned to see

Minister Byort striding inside. The slender man was dressed in his usual gloom-and-doom attire: black outer robe with long mothy sleeves, black sash with distressed stripes sewn in overlapping patterns. His eyes looked especially bug-like today, his face especially insectile, and when he approached it was with quick and calculating steps, like a creeping cockroach. Szathan kept a wary eye on the man, but his thoughts remained focused on his elder brother, and the news that he just couldn't swallow. *Demien is alive. Demien is still alive.*

Byort greeted the emperor with a bow that seemed more slimy than sincere. "Your Majesty."

The boy didn't seem to notice; he was too busy slipping Dreadfang back into the oilcloth.

Byort then turned and offered Szathan a friendly nod. "Lord General, I wish to speak with you." He made a nudging gesture. "Can you spare a moment?"

"His Majesty and I are busy. Another time perhaps."

"I promise to be brief." He turned to Silas. "May I speak with your uncle privately?"

Silas looked at Byort, then back at Szathan, then once more at Byort. His nod was soft and timid.

"Thank you, Your Majesty." Byort motioned for Szathan to follow, then he strode off to a double bay window whose edgings were carved scrollwork pilasters that rose to an upper pediment head. A pair of scrawny servants were brushing a nearby wall tapestry, some sort of floral landscape design, but they fled at the snap of Byort's fingers. The armchair Szathan chose was undersized and uncomfortable, forcing him to sit awkwardly on its cushioned edge. Byort didn't sit; he stood staring out of the window, shoulders square and firm like a hound waiting for its master to return. "You know, a lot of people ask me why I'm so fascinated with insects. It's a bit strange, I admit, but in all my years of entomological studies, I've always been intrigued by the singularity of their design. Such fierce and alien little critters, from their exoskeletons of chitin, to their many matching parts of thorax, antennae, and segmented legs, and of course their metamorphosing stages of pupae into adult. There is a lot of find fascinating, even if they are among the simplest of creatures, driven purely by instinct."

Szathan was already tiring of this technical talk. *Another man with a hundred words that mean nothing.* "Is there a point here?" He may have publicly apologized for mistreating Byort, but that didn't mean he had to like him. *You have been cleared of all fault and wrongdoing. What more do you want from me? As much as I'd like to hear you ramble, I have other matters to consider. Like my elder brother returning from the dead.*

"Ah, yes, and I am coming to that point." Byort rubbed his head and smiled that scavenging smile of his. "But wait, where was I? Oh yes. So, I've discovered that insects do have what we call nociceptors, or special signals for the detection of pain. But that doesn't mean they *feel* pain consciously, like you or I. Yes, as you can likely guess, the extent of their physiology is quite rudimentary. They are not complex enough to plan or scheme or hold critical thought, nor are they capable of harboring grudges or pursuing actions of revenge. They don't know if they've been wronged, as they do not have the capacity to understand another's motives or intentions. Simply put, they are not self-aware."

Szathan heard the words but retained little of the information. His thoughts kept pulling him back to Demien. *He is alive. Demien is alive.*

"Now humans . . . we are greedy, spiteful, prideful, vengeful, ego-driven fanatics. But how much control do we truly have over our thoughts? How much control do we have over the choices we make? Are we truly so different from these tiny creatures, or are we all just a part of this preprogrammed colony that is humanity?" The slender man began to pace back and forth, rubbing a single finger across his lower lip. "You see my point, yes? In that case, how can I fault you for decisions you made based on your primitive design? It would be unjust."

Szathan crossed his arms, making clear his impatience. All that mattered was his elder brother. *Demien is still alive, and I must go to him. I'll need a company of fifty, and a large scouting party in case it's a trap. Please, gods, let this not be a trap. I've been so lost without my brother.*

"But your actions stung me," Byort went on. "Both personally and professionally, and in ways you will never understand. For some time I didn't know how to handle it. Funny how when you are down, others tend to shove their sanctimonious advice in your face, as if they suddenly live morally pristine lives. But Lady Elisa, bless her heart, she told me that the best advice was to consider carefully the advice of all others, and then to discard it all, because the only worthwhile advice is to do what makes you happy. And then I realized . . . to truly be happy, I must be unaware. I must be like the bug." He gave a short laugh. "How strange, the similarities between the all-powerful human and the itty-bitty insect. Don't you agree?"

Yes, so strange . . . as if I truly care. There was a lull in the conversation, and Szathan turned his head to acknowledge the bug-eyed man. "Are we done?"

"Not yet. I must admit—I came to realize something. Do you wish to know what that is?"

Szathan didn't reply. *I can't believe Demien is still alive. My brother is still alive.*

Byort spoke in a cold, clipped tone. "Do you wish to know what that something is, Lord General?"

Szathan waved a noncommittal hand. "Sure, yes, do tell."

"I realized that . . . unlike those very creatures I spent all my life studying, I am not a bug, I don't want to be a bug, and I don't want to be unaware. I want to be a man who *GETS HIS REVENGE*."

Something struck Szathan; his head snapped to the side, a sudden jerk of whiplashing force. At first, he thought Byort had punched him, but when he raised a hand, he touched the cold hilt of a dagger. The blade itself was jammed into his skull. *What the . . .?* He heard Silas's concerned scream rip from somewhere across the room. Szathan felt no pain, but his whole body began to tremble, a peculiar and debilitating feeling. Somehow, he mustered the will and the strength to rise from his seat, and now he loomed like an abominable behemoth over his assailant. "You stabbed me."

Byort backed up, his hand still raised, yet his whole arm was shaking. "H-how . . . h-how are you still alive?"

Szathan replied to that by wrapping his giant hands around the man's neck and throttling him. Byort wheezed and gurgled and lashed out frantically with his fingernails, but the general didn't release his grip, only squeezed harder and harder and harder. He could feel the man's windpipe cracking under his grip.

Horrendous little sounds, like the crunching of gravel underfoot, but even still, Byort refused to die, so Szathan kept squeezing harder and harder and harder—*just goddamn die already*—until at last, the man's purple mouth fell open, his tongue lolled out like that of a panting dog, and his body went limp in Szathan's arms. He was dead.

Szathan released his hold; the strangled man collapsed to the tiled floor with an awful *thud*. Next Szathan knew, he too was lying on the floor. He didn't remember falling, but suddenly he was staring up at Silas's tearstained eyes. The poor boy was using a rag to staunch the bleeding, pausing only to sob or call for help. But Szathan knew it was of no use. He tried to tell Silas that, but the boy wasn't listening. He kept crying out: "I don't want you to die. I don't want you to die!"

Szathan told him to stop crying, told him that it would be all right, that everything would be all right. Then he felt his world slip away.

EPILOGUE

To open fully his eyes, Thayer Dal had to forcibly blink through a film of viscid black goop. The sound it made was a faint wet *squish*, and afterward, he couldn't even wipe his gummy face. He tried to, but his arms wouldn't move. *Why won't they move?*

Only when his head twisted this way and that did he see the manacles. Two rusty metal rings clamped on upraised wrists and fastened to a wrought chain that rose slackless to an overhead cross-beam. His fully bandaged arms stood outstretched like those of a crucifixion victim. *Am I a prisoner?* He didn't think so; the place seemed more like a sick chamber than a dungeon, with its heavy malodor of strange herbs and necrotic tissue. The poor lighting made it difficult to see, but around him rose tall fabric partitions like the movable screens of a theater, only much grubbier. His body was resting upon a narrow treatment table, and the oversized black shroud that covered him seemed to serve more as a winding sheet than a blanket.

How long have I been here? How long have I been bound like this? His tried to wrench his hands free, but these were chains, not twigs, and no amount of strength could break them. *I'm a trussed-up hog, roasted and forgotten on the spit.* That thought made him panic, and in this hagridden state he tried to scream, but his voice wouldn't come. It felt as if someone had stuffed a pound of ash down his throat, and with every breath he nearly gagged on the taste. That made him panic some more, and soon he was coughing and retching and spewing up globs of black spit, the sounds eerily distressing in the gloom.

"Stay calm," a man said. "And don't struggle. The chains are for your own safety."

Thayer had to crane his head to see the speaker. The owlish Physician Penry stood over him in an authoritative yet cautious manner. "That was quite a reckless move you made at the siege, Thayer Dal, but I suppose you are a reckless man by nature."

The siege. Thayer didn't remember much of that fretful day, especially after he'd swarmed the enemy like a surging fireball. There was blackness, there was death, and there was little else. *I can barely recall my own name; how am I supposed to remember the details of a battle?* Penry told him that he'd done a heroic deed, but that only made Thayer wonder why he awoke in chains. *There must be something very wrong with me,* he decided.

"You've been teetering on the brink of death for weeks," Penry went on. His voice had an unusual rasp to it, as if he'd spent all morning hollering at troublemaking children. "You are a curious case, Thayer Dal. Very curious."

Thayer was desperate to reply. *Why restrain a man who can barely move on his own?* He worked his hardest to open his mouth, and only after a great and concerted effort did his voice emerge, faint and feeble though it was. "My hands . . . why am I being restrained?"

Penry spoke solemnly, as if consoling a grieving widower. "We don't know what to do with you yet."

"What does that mean?"

His old eyes dropped to the floor. He seemed to be skirting the truth. "You . . . how do I put this . . . you've been badly burned."

"How bad?"

Penry pulled back the tattered sheet that covered the length of Thayer's body, revealing a charbroiled husk of flesh and limb, so blackened and blistered it was almost as if he had no skin left at all. Thayer gasped at the sight, and Penry promptly placed the shroud back over him

"That's fucking bad. Oh gods that's bad."

"I'm sorry, Thayer. Are you . . . smiling?"

"I know it's wrong, but I look so stylishly ghoulish. Are you going to kill me? To end my misery?"

"No. Is that what you want?"

"It must be done. When the hen ceases to lay, into the cooking pot she goes."

Penry leaned his head back, as if ending Thayer's life was the last thing on his mind. "No, we won't be doing that. We'd like to see you recover, Thayer. But that is up to the—"

"Fuck the gods. And fuck you. Just teasing. But hold on a moment." He rattled the chains that bound his arms. "What's with these? You said they're for my own safety. I look like a crispy critter, why do I need restraints?"

Penry got up and left.

Well, aren't you polite? Thayer wasn't sure if the physician had stepped out to find a privy, or if he were retiring for the day. "Thanks for your time, you old coot." He probably shouldn't have insulted him like that. *Fuck it, I'm not a man to be restrained. I'm a wild goddamn goose.* And yet, all he could do was struggle vainly with the chains, and when he grew tired of that, he stopped and stared into the gloom of the cubicle space, wondering why he'd been cursed to an ill fate by the gods. *No, you can't forsake me. I won't let you.*

An injured man moaned from somewhere across the room, and

that was followed by another's sickly cough. Thayer had been hearing these sounds since waking up, but only now did he give them mindful consideration. How many other wounded soldiers were sharing this quarantine hall? Likely a few dozen at least, but Thayer was certain that none were as charred or disfigured as he was. He assumed he'd been placed behind these partitions for special treatment, but he preferred to be put out of his misery instead. *I won't live the rest of my days like a rotten tuber.*

Master Penry returned and placed a silk-wrapped bundle on a nearby side table. The objects inside clinked and clanged, and when Penry unfolded the cloth, Thayer saw what looked like four rods of varying substances, each about a span in length, with the thickest being no thicker than a child's wrist. Penry chose one and held it up; it looked like a basic wooden dowel. "Timber," he announced, then placed the object in Thayer's upstretched hand, cautiously, like a man setting a snap trap. "Try to close your fingers around it."

Thayer must've done so, because the physician quickly retracted his own hand, no longer bearing the wooden dowel. Thayer was about to ask him what the hell he was doing, but then the object in his hand started to smoke, then crackle, then *burn*. It happened so suddenly, like a man spritzing naphtha onto embers to resurrect a fire, and just as quickly the object was gone, leaving only a trail of ashes that spiraled to the floor like autumn leaves. From his finger-tips rose thin tendrils of black smoke, but strange, there was no heat, and stranger still, there was no pain.

Penry held up the second object. "Copper." He placed the rod into Thayer's hand, same as before, and incredibly the metallic substance began to melt, a speedy drip of orange-brown liquid. The physician moved on to the next. "Cast iron." Same result. And finally: "Steel, wrought carbon." Unbelievably, the alloy melted just as the others, glowing as it oozed from Thayer's fingers like almond jelly in the midsummer sun.

The demonstration concluded, Penry folded his aged hands

together and spoke in an enunciative voice. "Everything you touch burns and melts. It seems you are a human furnace."

Thayer wasn't sure if he'd heard that right, but he didn't ask the physician to repeat himself. Instead he simply stared at his outstretched, bandaged, and manacled arms, and when at last he spoke, his voice was no louder than a hoarse whisper. "How do I stop it? How do I stop burning things?"

"We don't know. This is a kind of sorcery I've not seen before. Nor has it been recorded in the annals, or any historical texts for that matter."

More silence. What were the implications of such a condition? No longer could he touch anyone or anything . . . not even to pet a friendly dog or grip a favored blade or caress a fetching lover. *What if this is permanent? Is it a curse, or perhaps a blessing from the goddess of fire?*

"I'm sorry, General."

Thayer could feel the smile spreading on his dry, cracked lips. "I'm not."

Penry shot him a curious look, and with that, Thayer began to laugh. It came out as a weak, throaty sound at first, but there was something uplifting about it, so he kept laughing. Perhaps it was the realization that life and all its exigencies were unimportant and temporary, that death was inevitable just as birth was indisputable. No point in worrying about that which couldn't be changed. The only course was to embrace it all, and what better way to do that than to engage in a little laughter?

And so he laughed and laughed, and strangely enough, his voice became stronger and stronger after each measure, and soon it became a great whopping bellow of a laugh.

"You're quite mad," Penry muttered to him, and that only made Thayer laugh harder and more maniacal, like an imp's cackle after running off with a child's treasured toy. Louder and louder the laughter rose, louder and louder, and soon the other bedridden patients of the quarantine hall began to laugh, too. Master Penry's large owl eyes grew ever larger, but he said nothing as the wounded men and women all joined in riotous laughter around him. Then, at last, when there was a lull in the uproar, a distant man's voice shouted: "What the *fuck* are we laughing at?"

There were a few chuckles in reply, but Thayer shut his mouth and balled his fingers into a blackened fist. He spoke quietly, so quietly only Penry could hear him. "I am a demon made flesh."

CHARACTER INDEX

Character Index – Empire of Cinders

Alarin Athera, called the Thunder of the North - Imperial Advisor of the Anirian Empire. Eldest son of Lasarin Athera. Once a shrewd and powerful general, became a recluse after losing his leg at the battle of Black Gate Pass.

Aldebron Pentagath – General of the Anirian Empire. A fierce warrior.

Ansetheral (Anseth) Athera, called Revek – Second youngest son of Lasarin Athera. Captured by the Vaskultan tribe at Black Gate Pass, only to rise through their ranks and serve as commander. A small but durable and clever man.

Arden Lorian – Grand Physician of the capital city. A garrulous old man.

Balinor – King of the Zhoul people.

Briam Styrm – Warden of the capital's West Gate. Friend to Demien Mordall.

Byort Belthor – High minister of Stormhaven and member of the White Fang Council. A bookish man, fascinated by insects.

Cathia Athera – Daughter of Merio.

Cyrille Vileron, called the Vulture – Captain of the Imperial Guard. Loyal to Miriana Athera. A scarred and taciturn man.

Dariok – Son of the Vaskultan chieftain. A cruel and quick-tempered man.

Dederic – Biological father of Seric Dyre. A Zhoul.

Demien Mordall, called the Savior of the Anir – Grand Commandant of the Anirian Empire. Single-handedly saved the former emperor's son from an imperial coup. Brother to Szathan. A man of unsurpassed skill and might.

Dobbin Belthor – Father of Byort. Stormhaven's Chief of Finance and member of the White Fang Council.

Duren Lygrest – Provincial Governor of Cragspawn and Lord of Amaranth Point.

Eldrith Avelin – Brother of Lelana. A cowardly man.

Elisa – High minister of Stormhaven and member of the White Fang Council.

Emeron Mathius – Sworn brother to Ansetheral Athera and Seric Dyre. Provincial Governor of Whitecrow and Lord of Aster Falls.

Fallon, called Fusspot Fallon – High minister of Stormhaven and member of the White Fang Council.

Fenerus Soffin, called the Young Tempest – General of the Anirian Empire, nephew of Sabriel.

Gilberon Brehems, called Bearcat – Deputy Commander serving under Szathan Mordall. A burly and uncouth man.

Guriyek – General of the Serkut tribe.

Hiriam Thraves – A young general who betrayed the empire to serve Raas Dragath. An exceptional military strategist.

Ikara – A war maiden of the Vaskultan tribe.

Jakken – Subcommander of the Vaskultan tribe. A skilled but cocky bowman.

Jarreth Sorrel – Envoy serving Duren Lygrest.

Jasmina – A bawd at the Golden Zinnia.

Kaigon – General of the Vaskultan tribe, stationed in the Gray Plains.

Kalen – Alarin's personal retainer and apprentice physician. A polite and mild-mannered youth.

Keven the Unkind – Mercenary of the Jackalmen and deputy officer of the Anir. Serves under Thayer Dal.

Kirik – A young warrior and loyal bondsman to Anseth. A tough yet good-humored man.

Korval Syr – Anirian Minister of Judgment.

Lasarin Athera – Former regent of the Anirian Empire. Father of Alarin, Zantherei, Ansetheral, Nyvia, and Merio.

Lelana Avelin – A wealthy artisan of Thornberry.

Madderin Ruk – Anirian corps commander and Vaskultan translator. A charismatic man.

Merio Athera – Youngest son of Lasarin Athera. Lord of Stormhaven and ruler of the eastern province of Riverwind. A handsome and affable man.

Miriana Athera – Wife of Zantherei Athera. Lady Regent of the Anir. A former courtesan and a woman of fortitude and ambition.

Nanjen – Sijian advisor to Zantherei Athera. An eccentric man, rumored to experiment with the occult.

Nederion Perl – Officer of the Anirian army.

Nethan Dyre – Former Imperial Advisor, killed in the battle of Black Gate Pass. Adoptive father of Seric.

Nyvia Athera – Former wife of Seric Dyre. Mother of Veldries. A goodhearted woman.

Orbrey Lorian – Physician and son of Arden Lorian.

Penry – Master Physician of Stormhaven. A composed and professional man.

Perilia Valayne – Wife of Tavarin Valayne, governess of Silverleaf.

Raas Dragath, called the Red Terror – Warlord of the southern Redlands and traitor to the Anirian Empire. A ruthless man.

Rander the Ripper – Mercenary of the Jackalmen and deputy officer of the Anir. Serves under Thayer Dal.

Ravathyr Aeryn – Redlands emissary and advisor to Raas Dragath.

Ravia Ravenhair – A courtesan of Aster Falls. Tall and dark of hair.

Rennerin Roth – Chamberlain of Stormhaven. A beloved and genial old man.

Sabriel Soffin – General of the Anir. A wise and disciplined man.

Seric Dyre – A half Zhoul born out of rape. Adopted by Nethan Dyre, later educated in military strategy. A cunning and ambitious man, often self-serving.

Severak, called Bonesplitter – General of the Vaskultan tribe. A strong yet even-tempered man.

Silas Mordall – Son of Demien. A timid boy.

Sydrian Rane – Minister Steward of the Anirian Empire.

Szathan Mordall, called the Ogre – General of the Anirian Empire and Commander of the city of Thornberry. Brother of Demien. A giant of a man.

Tavarin Valayne – Provincial governor and Lord of Silverleaf. Resentful toward the Anirian Empire.

Thavian Siven – The last emperor of the realm. A boy of sixteen.

Thayer Dal, called the Wild Goose – Regiment Commander of the Anir. A brave but reckless man.

Thomen Zythara – Anirian Minister of Ceremony.

Urryk – Principal rider of the Vaskultan tribe.

Veldries Dyre – Seric and Nyvia's son.

Volduk – Chieftain of the Vaskultan tribe.

Vylas Voren – Privy Counselor of the capital and half brother of Miriana. Wears a halfmask to cover his ruined left eye.

Wyath Silth – A young military officer of the Anirian Empire. A shrewd and levelheaded man.

Xavien Vorn – General of the Anirian Empire. Serves under Lord Emeron Mathius.

Yanha'ashtu, called Yana – Miriana's personal handmaiden. A young woman from the far eastern realm of Sijia.

Yugarak – Leader of the Serkut tribe, rival to Vaskultans.

Yurin Grayheart – Mercenary of the Jackalmen and deputy officer of the Anir. Serves under Thayer Dal.

Yuseth Valate, called the Lord of Winter – General of the Anirian Empire. Serves under Lord Merio Athera.

Zantherei Athera, called the Storm of the North – Regent of the Anirian Empire, second eldest brother of the Athera clan. A stoic and uncompromising man.

Zirian Revil, called the Mad Wolf – General of the Zhoul people. A fearsome warrior.

A NOTE FROM THE AUTHOR

A Note from the Author

I'll keep this short. Thank you so much for immersing yourself in this fantasy world, and I truly hope you've enjoyed your time here. This ends book two of the Empire of Cinders series, and I would love to return and complete a third book if a readership develops for it. That said, if you enjoyed the plots and adventures between the major and minor characters, please don't hesitate to leave a positive review on Amazon or Goodreads – it would be a great help to an unknown author such as myself.

ABOUT THE AUTHOR

Despite some missteps and failures, MA Liguori has always followed his passion for writing fantasy novels. He spent many years developing his craft, and his short fiction has appeared in *Heroic Fantasy Quarterly* and *New Realm Magazine*. He lives in North Carolina with his longtime partner. Aside from working as a writer, he's also a musician, a gamer, a cat lover, a college grad, and an Autism advocate.

www.ingramcontent.com/pod-product-compliance
Lightning Source LLC
Chambersburg PA
CBHW022017050726
47499CB00004BA/1033